Praise for ANGRY BL[illegible]

"*Angry Black White Boy* gives new meaning to the term black humor. A singularly jittery blend of urban wit and southern Gothic, it's a book of buoyant rhythm and dark material. A novel of ideas above all. . . . The book covers expansive intellectual and geographical terrain, [and] its drive never falters. Mansbach gets us there by creating a tense world whose figures often are at cross-purposes. *Angry Black White Boy,* like the truest expressions of hip-hop, graffiti, and jazz, is daring and original. It stings like its hero, Macon Detornay, a self-described scorpion of race."

—*Boston Globe*

"A remarkably successful remix of the traditional race novel. Mansbach monkey-wrenches the formula of the angry black man in the white man's world and incisively cuts to the heart of the issue of race in America today. [*Angry Black White Boy*] shows us where we as a culture have come from, the distance we have traveled, and how long the road ahead remains. It is first-rate satire grounded in the absurd notion that a simple 'I'm sorry' can start to make things better. The novel will make you laugh, cringe, and read until the last page without knowing how it's going to end. It is difficult to imagine a more appropriate conclusion for the story of Macon Detornay, as the uncertainty of fiction dovetails with the uncertainty of reality."

—*San Francisco Chronicle*

"Mansbach is an able satirist of race issues . . . captures vividly the inhuman sadism inherent to racial violence."

—*New York Times Book Review*

"*Angry Black White Boy* unflinchingly delves into American racism. While Mansbach unfurls urban vernacular like a silver-tongued hip-hopper grasping a microphone, he chronicles Detornay's media-injected ascension and horrific collapse with cinematic vision."

—*Washington Post Express*

"A slash and burn novel of race relations in post hip-hop America. Sure to be dissected, reviled, misunderstood, and praised for years to come, which is exactly why you should read it now."

—*XLR8R Magazine*

"A hilarious, terrifying, and brutally honest novel about race and American identity. Satire at its finest, it should be required reading for anyone interested in the microscopically thin line between love and hate that defines race relations in America."

—*Milwaukee Journal Sentinel*

"Painfully hilarious . . . brilliant . . . leaves readers searching for answers amid the absurdity . . . not for the fainthearted."

—*Time Out New York*

"Adam Mansbach has written what will possibly become the quintessential twenty-first-century race novel, despite, or perhaps because of, the fact that the protagonist is white. A searing and dark tale of appropriated identity and racial stirring, *Angry Black White Boy* maintains a hilariously dark tone throughout."

—*Undercover* (UK)

"A bold and layered examination of race in America."

—*Minneapolis City Pages*

"Is a fresh take on race in America possible? In his breakout novel, Mansbach definitively answers: Hell yeah! A lyrical and ass-kicking romp."

—*Portland Mercury*

"An engaging, cleverly worded tale that finally gives us something more than the rhetoric-filled fluff being touted as 'hip-hop literature.' An addictively good read comes in the form of *Angry Black White Boy*—cop it."

—*Mugshot Magazine*

"Boldly confronts the issue of race while brilliantly blending hip hop, jazz, poetry, street culture, New York, mid-America, and even baseball to create a highly intense, moving, and original masterpiece." —*Straight No Chaser* (UK)

"Subversive genius . . . a ferocious punt to the backside that leaves a Timberland print on your consciousness." —*East Bay Express*

"Satirical and often funny. . . . Forget white guilt—*Angry Black White Boy* is full-on white implosion." —*Time Out Chicago*

"A novel of high-minded absurdity . . . a smart, merciless story of cultural appropriation, racial justice, and individual authenticity."
—*Creative Loafing Atlanta*

"Hard-hitting. Not since Spike Lee's *Bamboozled* has America seen as trenchant and unapologetic a satire as *Angry Black White Boy*."
—*AlterNet*

"This dude knows shit, and if you don't . . . this read will send you well on your way. It's over three hundred pages of comedy (dark), insight (powerful), and depth (deep)." —*Newcity Chicago*

"Adam Mansbach's novel is at once humorous and tragic as it delves into the complex issues of racial politics. *Angry Black White Boy* should certainly provide a unique and welcome addition to anyone's bookshelves and as such is certainly worth picking up; however, putting it down may be somewhat more problematic."
—*Grind Mode* (UK)

"A collar-grabbing satire." —*New York Metro*

"An amazing take on racial issues in the U.S. Beautifully told, the story grips you from the start . . . a race novel reworked for the hip-hop generation. It's frank, to the point, and honest, and on top of that it's one hell of a funny read, one you'll find yourself going back to over and over." —*UK Hip-Hop*

"Seamlessly accurate, biting satire. . . . By the time Macon arrives at the cataclysmic riot that is the climax of the book, we know why he's there, we can see what's coming—and, as with the best horror films, we stick around to watch as the catastrophy hits."
—*San Francisco Bay Guardian*

"Satire of the highest caliber, serious issues grounded in circumstances that at times are laugh-out-loud funny. With the same touch of humanism employed by writers such as James Baldwin and Ralph Ellison, Mansbach does for the issue of race in contemporary America what those two did for it as the Civil Rights Movement came to the forefront of American discourse."

—*Redsnap Magazine*

"*Angry Black White Boy* joins *Chapelle's Show* in filling the void [by] addressing race issues in a direct and satirical fashion. Mansbach cleverly delivers . . . with dynamic language and vivid, funny characters."

—*The Beat*

"An exercise in race consciousness that scours the clichés of white people's awareness of racial privilege."

—*San Francisco Weekly*

"An engrossing story . . . never falters in its boffo momentum. Its hilarity is studied and each fantastic flight gets a counter-punch."

—Bookslut.com

"At turns hilarious and profoundly troubling, the novel serves as a meditation on hip-hop culture and its enormous influence on the psyches of white suburban youth."

—*Dose Magazine* (Canada)

"A heady, significance-laden rumination on race relations in America."

—*Wired Magazine* (UK)

"A literary gem and an insightful lens on the never-ending conundrum surrounding white youth's fascination with black culture and black people. Mansbach explores these desires, conflicts, and contradictions with extraordinary passion, poetry, pain, self-critical awareness, humor, and complexity. *Angry Black White Boy* is a gripping story that will stay on your mind for a long time."

—Tricia Rose, author of *Black Noise: Rap Music and Black Culture in Contemporary America*

ANGRY
BLACK
WHITE
BOY

Also by Adam Mansbach

FICTION

Shackling Water

POETRY

genius b-boy cynics getting weeded in the garden of delights

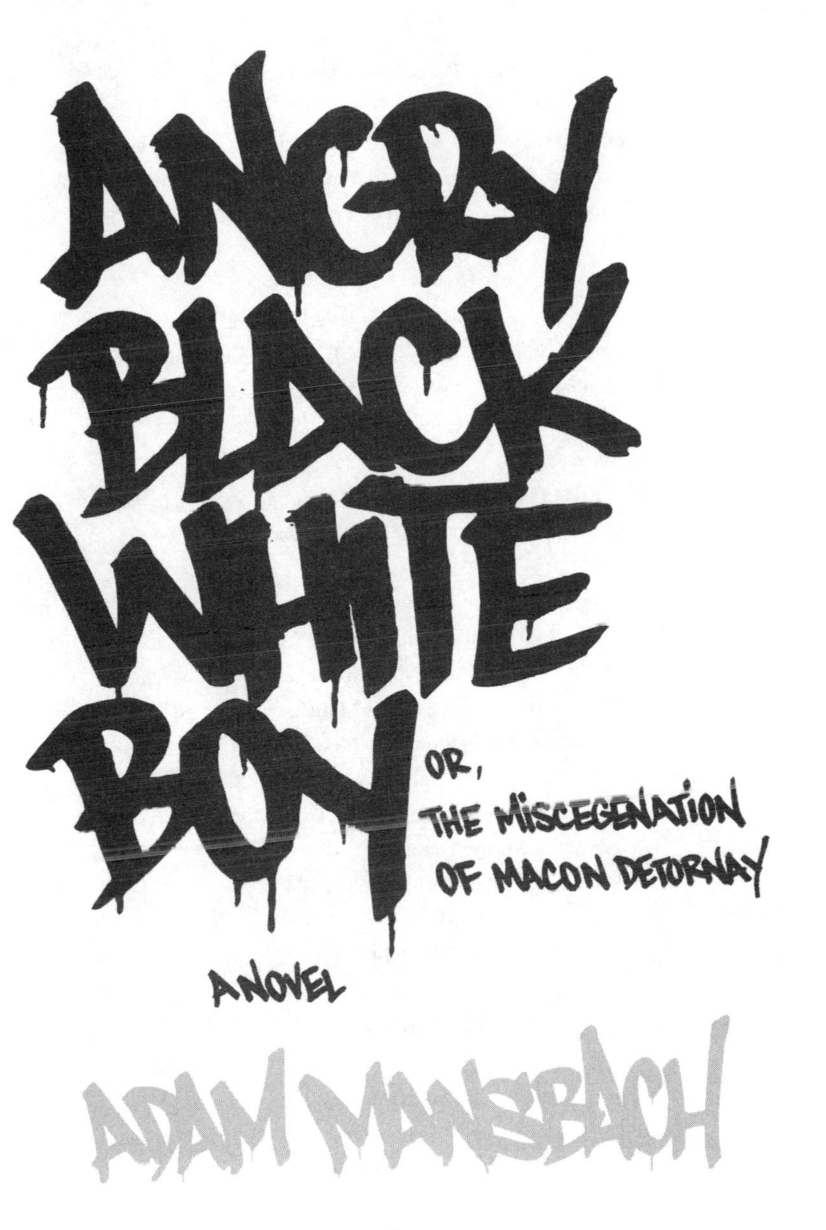

THREE RIVERS PRESS • NEW YORK

This is a work of fiction. Names, characters, places, and incidents either are the product of the author's imagination or are used fictitiously. Any resemblance to actual persons, living or dead, events, or locales is entirely coincidental.

Published in the United States by Three Rivers Press, an imprint of the Crown Publishing Group, a division of Random House, Inc., New York.
www.crownpublishing.com

Library of Congress Cataloging-in-Publication Data
Mansbach, Adam, 1976–
Angry black white boy, or, The miscegenation of Macon Detornay : a novel / Adam Mansbach.— 1st ed.
1. College students—Fiction. 2. New York (N.Y.)—Fiction.
3. Hate crimes—Fiction. 4. Robbery—Fiction. 5. Racism—Fiction.
I. Title: Angry black white boy. II. Title: Miscegenation of Macon Detornay. III. Title.
PS3613.A57A64 2004
813'.6—dc22
2004014984

ISBN 1-4000-5487-7

Printed in the United States of America

Design by Leonard Henderson

10 9 8 7 6 5 4 3

First Edition

for my grandfather, Benjamin Kaplan,

and in memory of Elvin Ray Jones

ANGRY
BLACK
WHITE
BOY

Prologue:
Letter from a Birmingham Bus

I'm here to tell the white man in the mirror the truth right to his face. I have seen the enemy and he is me. No competition, I battle myself. I'm Macon Everett Detornay, *a white nigger in the universe,* to paraphrase both LeRoi Jones—whose middle name I share, or did before he changed his—and the Aryan Nation vis-à-vis yours truly, with whom I share nothing but low melanin and politics unacceptable to mainstream America. Or so I thought.

Like Malcolm, I expect to be dead before I see these words in print. Naw, let me stop bullshitting. That's a lie. I'm broadcasting live and direct from the getaway ride as the scene of the crime fades away into the speckled past and credits roll. I'd like to send this next one out to myself, special dedication to the one I love to hate, and I wanna give a big shout-out to the universe and New York City for believing in me when I'd stopped believing in myself. This award is for the little people. I wanna thank everybody who made me as bad as I could be, who boosted me until my noggin thumped against the glass ceiling of white people's ability to give a fuck. I bled halfway to death trying to break on through and never made it, but guess what: I don't give a fuck. I did my time, and now I know what I am.

And knowing is half the battle. What is it the scorpion says to the frog as they both sink? *I told you I was a scorpion, asshole.* Except that white folks aren't drowning and black folks never agreed to give us a lift across the pond in the first place. Maybe on some spiritual Thurgood Marshall this-system-hurts-us-all level we're drowning, but most of us don't seem to have noticed. And luckily, we can afford the best in psychiatric care, antidepressants, and religion should we begin to feel the water lapping at our ankles.

So I'm a scorpion. Let me come to terms with it and get my scuttle down, cuz I done wasted years already trying to flap my nonexistent wings. Let me ease on back into the seat of privilege and lap the luxury out of some more complimentary drinks. Let me guzzle six hundred and sixty-six mind erasers and stop trying to be the exception to the rule, the face that wasn't in jailbird Malcolm's memory banks when the wise old Muslim inmate asked him if a white person had ever treated him right. Shit, if that face had existed, maybe Malcolm never would have. One good white person might have finished him before he started, and then where would we be? I'm glad it wasn't me. I couldn't live with that.

Funny how easy it all falls away, how natural that scuttle feels despite all the time and energy I've spent fighting it with spray cans and microphones and brothers in arms, not to mention the guns around which my recent battles have revolved. And all for nothing: all to realize with one hundred percent of my brain that I'm the same as everyone I've ever hated, and that it only took them ten percent to know who they were from the get-go, and they been getting shitfaced on free drinks and laughter this whole time, watching me chase my shadow.

They called me "The New Face of Hate" in *Newsweek*. *The Nation* asked, "Can America Take Macon Detornay Seriously?," with a cutesy subheadline that read, "Can Macon Detornay?" The *New York Post*, with customary good taste and restraint, screamed "Ivy League Race Traitor" and called me "the city's most controversial criminal since Bernhard Goetz." Against my better judgment, I even posed for the cover of *The Village Voice* as "The New Black Leader?" I was hoping someone would call me the white Bigger Thomas, but nobody had the nutsack even though it's an obvious comparison, what with Bigger being a chauffeur and me a cabbie. I talked a lot more shit than Bigger ever did, though. And I did what I did on purpose. And I got away.

The big question, I guess, is how I got here. Not just on this bus stirring up dust across the Bible Belt, but on this vibe. How I became who I am, or was—the poster boy for an imaginary 1950s propaganda film entitled *Nigra Madness*, the bone-chilling story of how a nice kid from the suburbs got so black and twisted, revolutionary, niggerfied, that he *renounced his race and became ONE OF THEM!*

It's an impossible question. How did *you* become who *you* are? I've scrolled back through my memory as far as it will go, looking for some embryonic moment of divergence, some split from the growth pattern of my genotype, but I can't find one. It would be nice if there was some simple answer, some creation myth—*when I was ten I watched* Eyes on the Prize *twelve hours a day for seventeen straight weeks and I been pro-black ever since*, or *I ate a special soup made from Eldridge Cleaver's boiled hypothalamus and presto change-o*, or *in a secret drum ceremony in Ghana I learned to channel the spirits of the tribal elders*, or *my daddy was a trumpet player who toured the Southern chitlin' circuit back in '63 and passed for an albino brother*—but there's not. My parents are standard-issue white liberals, just as puzzled as anybody. And like I said in damn near every one of those interviews, as far as I'm concerned, the question is not how I got this way, but how the rest of y'all didn't.

BOOK I

TRADER

I was the only player to take advantage of the grandfather clause written into the International League's new rule. All the other colored players slung their bats over their shoulders and walked on April 29, 1889, the day the commissioner announced that the motion to segregate the league had passed. Negroes under contract could serve out the remainder of the season with their teams, but the boys knew what those final months would be like, especially in the Southern cities. The grandfather clause was sarcasm, a final insult. They walked out of pride.

Out of pride, I stayed with the New York Giants. I was thirty-three years old and nobody was going to run me out of my chosen profession one second earlier than law allowed.

The man most responsible for the new rule, or at least the man claiming the most credit, was Adrian Constantine "Cap" Anson, Chicago's first baseman and manager, the greatest hitter the game had ever known. Anson had been pushing segregated play for years, some said since the day his club had lost the season to the Senators and Washington's great colored pitcher, Left Hand Baker, had fanned him in five straight at-bats.

Anson had done more for the game's popularity than any man, and when he talked people listened, even the owners. Cap Anson sandlot teams dotted the country. On billboards along every league ballpark's outfield walls, Cap Anson endorsed tooth powders and health tonics. When Anson came to town the gate receipts went up, the bleachers filled. And when he asked why niggers were allowed to play with white men and dirty up the Great American Pastime with their cheating and their coon balls, people wondered themselves.

Niggers, Anson told the owners, didn't understand a lick of strategy. They brought nigger fans into the ballparks, encouraged them to enter white neighborhoods and socialize with white folks. The excitement of the game was too much for nigger fans to handle; they got riled up and then they went out causing trouble. Athletically, niggers' big thighs and clumsiness prevented them from being good fielders. And did the league really want to risk what might happen if a nigger player lost his temper, as the race was notorious for doing, and in a fit of rage turned on a white opponent with a bat? Integrated play was a disaster waiting to happen, Anson told the owners, and the owners put it to a vote and found that they agreed. Baseball was a game of dignity and poise, a white man's game.

And thus on April 29, 1889, I was not just the only colored in a uniform, but the only colored in the entirety of Atlanta, Georgia's Robert E. Lee Stadium for the exhibition matinee between the New York Giants and Cap Anson's Chicago White Stockings. There was still a small fenced-off section of decaying bleachers marked For Coloreds Only, *but it stayed empty as the stadium filled up. Colored fans, like colored players, had walked away from the game. I wondered what they thought of me for staying. I wasn't out to be a hero, but until I looked up and saw the colored section empty, a barren, blighted patch amidst the fertile farmland, it hadn't occurred to me that folks might have thought I was selling out by staying where I wasn't wanted.*

The game began at two, so at one-thirty I took to the outfield with Red Donner, our first baseman, to warm up my arm. Red and I stood thirty feet apart and had a catch, Red tossing me slow grounders and me throwing back to Red on a line while he stood with his foot edging the imaginary first-base bag. I bent at the knees before the first roller, sprang to my toes, pivoted, threw, and watched the ball sail over Red's left shoulder, six inches from his outstretched glove.

"Say, Red, what's the matter? You lose it in the sun?"

Red gaped past me. "Behind you."

I turned. Filing into the box seats behind third base was a procession of some fifty costumed Klansmen, the white of their hoods shockingly bright in the sunlight. They moved loosely, just another day at the ballpark, glanced at their ticket stubs and found their seats and hunched with elbows on their knees and chatted.

They're going to kill me, was my first thought. I turned away, not wanting them to know I'd seen them, looked around the park and watched as fans poured in. I scanned the crowd for signs of shock, for some acknowledgment that there was a costumed militia present, but folks seemed no different than ever. How many of the uncostumed were any less willing to watch me die? Who would lift a finger, raise a voice in protest if the Klan rushed the field and a swarm of white fabric billowed up around me like a curtain in the breeze, folding me into itself until I disappeared?

I sprinted to the dugout looking straight ahead. A cheer like rifle fire rose up from behind the third-base line as I passed the delegation, passed where I would stand with my back to the enemy for nine innings, twenty-seven outs, engaged in what seemed suddenly like both an impossibly foolish, infantile game and an undertaking as serious as anything in life could ever be.

"I talked to one of them," said Buck Desota, our manager, when I hustled down the steps and into the cool refuge of the dugout's shadows. He put his arm around my shoulders and walked me toward the bat rack at the far end of the pen. "He said they're not here to cause any trouble." Buck paused, tugged at one of the round earlobes that stuck out from his big square head like handles, and looked me in the eye. "Just to celebrate the purification of baseball." He placed one foot on the dugout's bottom step, leaned on his knee, and squinted over the corrugated metal roof, down at the third-base stands. "Maybe you ought to take the day off, Fleet. I can play Eubanks today."

My eyes flickered, darted left, then set on Buck. "I'm your third baseman," I said. "You play me."

I was the third man in the batting order, and when I stepped onto the field, it seemed that every voice in the ballpark came to life. I knocked the dirt from my spikes and marched to the batter's box. The shouting was so loud I couldn't distinguish any words, but I knew they were saying nigger, coon, get out, go home. Nothing I hadn't heard before.

I called time, stepped out of the box, and rubbed my eyes with a thumb and forefinger, trying to sift through the sounds and isolate a single insult, pick out a single voice, to remind me that these were only men. Without meaning to, I turned and looked at the Klan delegation behind third. They responded to my glance with a frenzy of fist-shaking and noise, elated to be acknowledged. It was all too much. I dug in and cocked back my bat, dying to swing clean through the sea of hate.

It should have occurred to me and didn't until it was almost too late: The White Stockings were going to throw at my head. I hit the dirt as the pitch whistled past my ear and the crowd roared, keened toward me jeering, wanting blood. I stood up and dusted off, and the pitcher reared back and threw a second fastball, a body blow this time. It stung my thigh and the ump waved me toward my base. I clenched my jaw, determined not to betray any trace of pain. Held the bat a second too long before sloughing it off toward the dugout, reluctant to forfeit my only weapon, and jogged down to first, where Cap Anson was waiting.

He grinned at me around a plug of tobacco, hands on his hips. "You best to quit while you still can, boy." Anson spit a stream of juice onto my left cleat and grinned up at the fans to see if they had noticed. "You tell Buck I said to take you out 'fore things get ugly."

I didn't respond. Took a big lead, as much to get away from Anson as to get a jump on the pitch, and when it came I tore off down the basepath and slid into second in a gust of dust, spikes slashing holes in the air. The throw from the catcher was too high, and by the time the baseman put the tag on me, my leg was wrapped around the bag. It wasn't even close.

"He's out!" the umpire screamed, jerking his thumb toward heaven, and the stadium combusted. I got to my feet, read the treachery in his beady eyes, and trotted toward the dugout. Not too fast, not too slow.

I grabbed my glove from the bench and turned to find Buck

Desota close enough to smell: tobacco, rawhide, aftershave. "I know this is hard," Buck said, "but keep your head in the game, Walker. I didn't flash you no steal sign."

I slipped my hand into the cool leather glove and pounded my fist into the palm. "Sometimes a man just has to run," I said.

Chapter One

Macon Everett Detornay fisted the wheel and swung his new yellow cab downtown. Hip hop didn't raise no moon-eyed loverboys, and Macon would be dead before the thought of whittling down passion from a blunt lump to a harpoon, something you could aim at a person, would take shape inside him. All the things he loved were too big, comical to throw your arms around like carnival prize teddy bears: truth, revolution, huge nonexistent shit like that.

It was a little past rush hour now, and Macon flipped on his radio and relaxed as the venerable voice of Kool DJ Red Alert introduced an old-school set on Hot 97 FM, the station whose tagline, "Where hip hop lives," had inspired more than one underground MC to declare himself dead. As the omnipotent what's-hot-what's-not market arbiter of the late nineties, Hot 97 had played matchmaker for hip hop and psychotic materialism, advising hip hop to stop returning phone calls from former lovers like Black Power and Social Responsibility, encouraging the couple to move in together, and finally, in an exclusive Aspen ceremony attended by three hundred CEOs and only a handful of artists and project-housing thugs, to exchange diamond-flooded Rolexes and sign the merger deal in blood. When the honeymoon waned, the station placated hip hop's ornery elders, pissed and financially slighted, by paying periodic tribute to "the pioneers of the old school" with five-second announcements encouraging their audience of fourteen-year-old wannabe gangster macks to "know their history."

None of which had jack to do with Red; his drive-time show remained untainted by payola, his very employment a paean to purer days. The crossfader glided clean across the mixer and into a classic, dancing New York City's newest cabdriver straight down memory lane. "I useta roll up / this is a hold up, ain't nothin' funny / stop smilin', be still / don't nothin' move but the money," Rakim Allah intoned, smooth with the roughness, reflecting on the tax-free paper he had clocked before he "learned to earn / cause I'm Righteous": before he joined the Five Percent Nation and gained Knowledge of Self and realized that the Original Asiatic Black Man was the Maker, the Owner, the Cream of the Planet Earth, Father of Civilization and God of the Universe. Before he became part of the Five Percent of the population who overstood the Supreme Mathematics and threw off the shackles of mental slavery to become Poor Righteous Teachers.

Macon knew the Five Percenters' rules as well as any whiteboy could, first from listening to the lyrics of the Righteous and then from living at Lajuan's crib in Jamaica Plain for the last fifteen months, where black men who called themselves Gods sat around all day with eyelids quartermasted from smoking blunts and drinking ninety-nine-cent twenty-two-ounce Ballantines, talking about women who were not called Earths, as doctrine dictated, but bitches. The apartment was a degenerate sitcom: jokes and laugh tracks, heated interlocking minutes of family therapy, "Son, son, listen" interruptions, sex convo and chess games and rhymes and rhymes and beats to the rhymes and the every-occasion, rain-sleet-or-pestilence query "Who's going to the weedspot?"; long-ass conversations that flipped general to specific and then back again in an endless, fascinating, and pointless battle of verbs and philosophy, volume and religion, rhetoric and flowskills.

Macon had learned the most from Jihad, the big-entrance-making uninvited drop-in neighbor the audience loved: a Newport-smoking, monologue-spitting herbologist with matching Nikes for every rugby shirt he owned and a penchant for talking the esoteric God Body Science of the Five Percenters from one mouth corner and hustle-ego-watch-me as unfiltered as New York tap water out the other. Macon's star-vehicle spin-off, cats joked, would be a show called *Adopted Brother.* They plotted episodes in the perennial back-alley twilight that slashed in sideways from the street lamp and gave the dust something to dance in besides the glow of the forever-on TV.

Chinese takeout boxes filled the garbage can, and a ten-pound bag of white rice lived a bachelor's life in the one uncorroded cabinet. Cats would go to the store for hot sauce, barbecue sauce, ranch dressing, go to McDonald's and jack three hundred little ketchup packets, whatever you could pour on rice for flavor. Only on Sunday afternoons did they sit down and really eat, and then only because when Macon moved in he'd instituted-slash-sponsored the ritual of family dinners. They'd make turkey lasagna, Jihad and Aura grating cheese into silver mixing bowls and making Sal's Pizzeria jokes from *Do the Right Thing* and Macon sitting in Lajuan's room, where he hid to do his writing, scribbling in a notebook and listening at the same time, overhearing and folding what was overheard into his thoughts like mushrooms into an omelet.

Everything was always too much in that crib; the drinks too strong, the weed too harsh, the conversation too aggressive, the chess battles waged on the bootleg coffee table too long and reckless, the music too loud. Dudes cut each other off, spoke fast and until interrupted, acted like the dilettante scientific and social analogies they constructed were the perfect tools of proof—which somehow they often were, like "Naah, son . . . SON! Do the knowledge: Boom, it's like magnetic attraction. The gravitation doesn't work unless the shit is mutual, so 'love is blind' is Now

Cipher, God. It's like how some cats say that niggas can't be racist, you know, you know the science on that, you can't be racist unless you have the power to be racist, so boom, you can't say you in love unless you both in love; one person in love is like the sound of one hand clapping, God."

Macon switched lanes without signaling, loving the order and chaos of Manhattan driving, and made an arbitrary right turn. He'd learned his way around already, before he'd even posed for his driver's ID; it had taken him all of a week. New York was simple, a grid: choices galore, traffic laws optional. Boston, by contrast, was a lunatic maze of dead ends and one-ways, a city whose streets had evolved from cowpaths to highways with no sign of topological supervision. Macon had spent all twenty years of his life there, and even on his final day of work at the charter-car service, he'd gotten lost carting a vanful of Japanese businessmen to a suburban conference. Now exhilaration filled him and he tightened his left-handed grip on the wheel: Fuck racist-ass, provincial Boston. New York City, baby. Here at last. The center of the universe. He turned the music up, digging the unity of place and soundscape, relishing not just his understanding of each line of Rakim's verse, but the fact that he could scarcely remember a time when he hadn't known this shit.

With idle pride, Macon scrolled through some of what he knew. The Ten Percent were the bloodsuckers of the poor. They had Knowledge of Self but were not Righteous, and they preyed on the ignorance of the Eighty-Five who were Deaf, Dumb, and Blind to the truth. The Divine Alphabet allowed Gods and Earths to communicate in code; when Sadat X from Brand Nubian rhymed "the born cipher cipher master / makes me think much faster," he meant the b-o-o-m, the boom, the weed. One hundred and twenty sacred Lessons awaited mastery; Jihad had sometimes disappeared behind a plywood bedroom door to study, or claim he was studying and smoke a blunt for dolo. Elijah Muhammad's old Caucasian creation myth—the evil scientist Dr. Yacub grafts a barbaric white race from the Original Asiatic Black, a warlike people banished to the caves of cold, dark Europe but destined to rule the earth for sixty centuries—was tacitly endorsed, and white folks were called devils.

But were all white people devils? Could there be exceptions? What about that dude Paul C., who'd engineered Eric B. & Rakim's album? What about Macon, who built with the Gods morning, noon, and night, passed out alongside them on perpendicular couches with his sneakers touching theirs, high off shared wack buddha? Macon had lost sleep looking for a loophole back in 1990, when the smoovest MC on the planet was Grand Puba Maxwell, asking "Can a Devil fool a Muslim? No, not nowadays bro," and declaring, "It's time to drop the bomb and make the Devil pay the piper."

From Macon's confusion had bubbled anger. How dare black people not see him as an ally, not recognize that he was down? He retaliated by studying their history, their culture: He was a thirteen-year-old whiteboy in a Malcolm X T-shirt, alone at the first annual Boston Hip Hop Conference, heart fluttering with intimidation and delight as scowling bald-headed old schoolers pointed at his chest, demanding, "Whatchu know about that man?" Which was exactly what he'd wanted, why he'd worn it. He ran down Malcolm's life for them, watched them revise their expressions with inward elation, nodded studiously at their government assassination theories, rhymed when the chance presented itself. Tagged other graffiti writers' blackbooks and wondered what it would take to be scratched from the devil list for good.

And yet history was overwhelming, and down deep Macon knew the truth. Who but white folks, his folks, had been so brutal for so long? He'd retreated briefly into his own Judaism, *Jewish-not-white,* with its analogous history of victimization and enslavement, but he couldn't make it fit, couldn't make himself feel Jewish, didn't know what being Jewish felt like. He tossed the Star of David medallion Grandma had given him back into the dresser after a day, reflecting that race pride was a fashion trend he'd been completely iced out of. The sterling necklace's drawer mate was the red-green-and-gold *Increase the Peace* medallion Macon had bought after Three Times Dope released their single of the same name; he'd copped it from a Downtown Crossing vendor as a less fly but more plausible alternative to the Africa medallions everybody was rocking post–Jungle Brothers. Macon never even wore it in his room.

Instead he lay on his bed in his parents' house, music streaming past him low enough to go unheard in the kitchen below, and went to work constructing a rhetorical framework that would allow him to embrace the Five Percenters' truths without capitulating his soul: *White people aren't evil, but evil is white people.* There it was. Simple. Elegant. True. It bought Macon space to live in, to be special, angry, the exception, the crusader. The down whiteboy. *You my nigga, Macon. You a'ight.*

The light clicked green and Red switched up the soundtrack, segueing into "Days of Outrage, Operation Snatchback," X-Clan's song about being assaulted by cops at the Yusef Hawkins rally on the Brooklyn Bridge. Macon rolled his window down and dipped his elbow into the warm fall air, smiling. He remembered how when X-Clan's album dropped in 1990—damn, had it been eight years already?—brothers in Boston had started wearing quasi-military African pimpgear just like them: nose rings, leather ankh caps, red-black-and-green bead necklaces, knee-high boots, carved wooden staffs. Macon had just scraped together the money to buy his first set of turntables that year, some bullshit Geminis, in the hopes of becoming a DJ—hopes soon aborted by impatience, mediocre rhythm, and the fact that he was surrounded by cats who actually caught rek on the decks, who brushed him aside and onto the mic so they could do so.

Brothers would congregate at his crib after school to freestyle and make mix tapes, trooping through the kitchen en route to the basement wearing some outlandish shit and baffling the hell out of his mother. Everyone was perfectly polite—"Hello, Mrs. Detornay"—and his mother said, "Hi, guys," and smiled back, but if she had suspected before that she didn't understand her son, a legion of staff-wielding pro-black rappers marching through her kitchen and interrupting her *People* magazine perusal certainly confirmed that shit.

A hand shot up on the west side of Wall Street, and Macon swerved to the man's side. The stiff-armed gesture people used to summon taxis was only a few degrees north of the Nazi salute, Macon reflected as he hit the unlock button, and especially reminiscent when performed by somber-suited young businessmen. The vapors of entitlement that steamed from these yuppies irked him; they were so fucking sure the cab would stop for them. They'd never been snubbed in their lives, sized up and passed by because the driver thought they wouldn't pay or that they wanted to be taken somewhere ghetto. Back home, Macon had flagged cabs while Lajuan and Aura stood discreetly down the block, pretending not to be with him, approaching only when Macon had the door open. It was another way, he thought with pride, that they had cheated racism.

Two guys in their early thirties clambered into Macon's backseat. "Eighty-fifth and Fifth," commanded the one on the left, a wispy blond who didn't look up from the gold-rimmed glasses he was wiping with his necktie.

"We're already fucking late," the other one informed him. "The reservation was for six." Mr. Punctuality's dark hair was thinning on top; razor-burn flared from his neck as he pulled off his tie with a meaty left fist and undid his top button. On the night of Macon's high-school prom, when he had dropped by in his father's Camry to pick up Aura and his date, Aura's mother had told Macon to remember three things as she redid his necktie for him: Nothing is sexier than a man who wants to be wearing his suit, nothing is unsexier than a man imprisoned by his suit, and a woman can always tell the difference. These jokers, Macon thought, were prisoners for sure.

The one on the left, Mr. Eighty-fifth and Fifth, had the same rock-solid Roman nose as a guy Macon had known in high school, a senior when Macon was a freshman. Scott Cartwright was probably president of his fraternity; he'd been lacrosse captain back then. Out of the blue one day, he had stopped Macon in the hall outside the cafeteria and poked a thick finger into Macon's bird-chest.

"You think you're pretty fuckin' cool, huh, dude? Sitting at the black table, kickin' it like you're Vanilla Ice or something?"

Cartwright turned his dirty white baseball cap backward and bent into Macon's face. "People laugh at you, dude. I don't even know you, and I sit there and laugh my fuckin' ass off." Macon had stood for a moment staring back, tightroping the thread between provocation and cowardice, then asked, "Are we finished?" He'd been going for a kind of *Sir, request dismissal* tone, but Macon couldn't disguise his boredom and the words sounded insolent instead. Scott slammed him up against a locker, mad corny, like they were characters in a John Hughes movie, and Macon wanted to want to laugh, but instead his ears burned and he wanted to kill Scott Cartwright, hated himself because at that moment he cared what Scott Cartwright thought of him—felt ridiculous, ashamed. And yet Macon knew he'd courted this. He wanted his defection from whiteness and his acceptance by black people to be public, the subject of wonder and envy, anger and scorn.

Just then Omari had rounded the corner: Macon's homeboy, Cartwright's co-captain. Scott backed away, sheathed his hands in khaki pockets, watched Macon give Omari a pound and followed suit. As soon as the rapper/midfielder went on his way, Scott's finger was right back in Macon's face.

"You better watch your fuckin' attitude, bro. I don't care how tight you are with the niggers. I'll kick your fuckin' ass."

The passenger on the left, Scott's look-alike, was cursing at his cell phone. "I can't get a fucking signal on this piece of shit," he said, slapping it closed against his leg.

"Forget it, man." Punctuality rapped twice on the partition. "Hey, turn that down, will you?" Macon reduced the music to a whisper. Every passenger but one had made the same request. "I gotta hear enough of this shit as it is," Punctuality told Scott. "Two in the morning last night, these guys in their fuckin' SUVs are rattling my windows three floors up."

"What I want to know," said Scott, "is how they can afford forty-thousand-dollar cars. With custom stereos."

Punctuality laughed. "We're in the wrong business, bro."

"Seriously, dude. First thing tomorrow, I'm gonna go get an Adidas sweatsuit and find myself a nice street corner. Sell a little crack and buy myself a Lexus."

Macon tightened his grip on the steering wheel and tried to concentrate on the road. The two passengers were silent for a minute. As Macon merged onto the FDR, Scott spoke.

"So who's this girl tonight? Kim's friend?"

"Her name is Kaliyah, Kalikah, something like that."

"She hot?"

"Hope so."

"Black chick?"

"Yeah." Scott played with his phone and Macon couldn't take it: He knew them too well, better than he knew himself, knew what they were thinking and everything they'd ever thought and it was vile, all of it, smug and oblivious. The eternal fear of waking up as one of these mix-and-matchable bar-hopping assholes kept Macon clenched with vigilance, tight as a fist. Loathing frothed within him, bubbled over the sides of its containment vat, and splattered onto Macon's rational mind. It was corrosive. He jerked the wheel, hand crossing over hand. A vertebrae popped as Macon leaned into the turn; his biceps flared and he felt the tattoo there burn as if it had just been etched into his skin. A sweat-drip blotted in his armpit, horns blared past him, other drivers cursed him and their spittle flew against the insides of their windows. The cab cut right across two lanes and veered onto the shoulder of the highway. Macon mashed the brakes, and Cartwright and Punctuality careened forward, heads colliding with the scratched plastic partition, then fell back into their seats as the taxi recoiled. Macon's shirt stuck to his skin, soaked; a few seconds of adrenaline was all it took.

In the backseat, terror turned to anger just as fast. "What the fuck?" Scott roared, bracing his arms and legs against the door, the walls, the floor. "What are you, some kind of maniac?"

Macon slapped a button and the silver door locks bulleted into their sheaths. Scott clawed with his thumb and index finger, trying to pull one of the little cylinders back up. His friend watched and mimicked, laying fumbling hands on his own panel. Macon's face was as flushed as theirs were ashen, as if both their blood now flowed through his body, or he'd leaned for hours over fire. He fist-banged the glove box and the door dropped open with a squeak. Metal scraped plastic and Macon slid backward across the worn vinyl seat until the meter jabbed him in the back. With both hands clamped around it, he thrust a heavy, empty .38 caliber pistol into the small space in the partition and sighed hugely: a gust of human exhaust that filled whatever space was left in the small cabin. He could smell his air and both of theirs, all three mouths stale and disgusting, their breath meeting the gunmetal and the cab plastic and cab vinyl so that the car stank like a microphone in heavy freestyle rotation. Macon always sniffed the mic. A small perversion.

"Shut the fuck up," he said, eyes darting from one to the other, other to the one, gun barrel following his glance, mind dancing just above the moment. Control flowed up from the gun and coursed through Macon's body. He had to remind himself to keep his hands clenched as the rest of him relaxed. His toes laughed. Thighs, tingled. It was all Macon could do not to turn and sneak a peek in the rearview. He knew he looked heroic, and he knew he was invisible to them behind the mass of postings, stickers, and graffiti signatures that covered the partition. All Cartwright and Punctuality saw was a gun.

"Take out your wallets and leave them on the seat," Macon commanded, giddiness mounting as he heard his own gruff, not-to-be-fucked-with voice. He wagged the gun a centimeter, pointing. "And your phone, Cartwright." A final inspiration: "And both your neckties. Hurry. Look up and I'll shoot you in the face." Gun back-and-forth inclusive.

"Okay," Punctuality stammered, awash in more sweat than Macon had ever seen except the time he went to Celtics pre-camp with his dad and Reggie Lewis—rest in peace—was taking a reporter's question afterward and Macon, barely knowing why, reached out and touched Reggie's huge forearm, slick and glinting with warm sweat. Macon had drawn back immediately, embarrassed at the wetness, and Reggie had looked at him and smiled, and Macon had grinned back, almost crying.

Punctuality flailed, words and limbs. "Just don't hurt us," he said again and again, hand shaking as he took the necktie from his jacket pocket and, Macon noted with amusement, folded it into a neat, even swath. Scott was faring better. His tie was jumbled in his hands and he stared into his lap with great focus, as if wanting his assailant to take special note of his willingness to cooperate. The thought of making them strip naked barreled through Macon's mind, but he declined to detain it.

Two leather wallets, a flip-top StarTac cell phone, a Motorola pager, a Donna Karan tie, a Gianni Versace knockoff, and two silvery watches lay on the backseat between them.

"I didn't ask for any watches," Macon said. He buzzed down the right rear window. "Throw them out." The wristwear hit the tarmac, and Macon sealed the portal.

"All right." He turned back toward the road. "Now. Where were we going? Eighty-fifth and Fifth, was it?"

"Can-can't you drop us off right here?" Scott's voice was meek and shivery, a poverty-stricken cartoon rodent on the night before Christmas. "Please?" He threw his shoulder at the door again.

"You sure, homeboy? I wouldn't want Kim and her black friend to think you'd stood them up."

Macon's gut clenched with suppressed laughter as he wondered what they'd say to that one. A few ticks passed in silence, and then Punctuality was hyperventilating, choking on huge droughts of air, eyes bulging to the blood-veins, too frenzied for caution. "Why are you doing this to me?" he brayed as tears blazed down his face.

Scott grabbed Punctuality by the scruff of the neck and pulled him down into his lap—a blow-me motion Macon was sure he'd executed many times before.

"Shut up, dude, get a hold of yourself." Punctuality thrashed, pushed off of Scott's thigh with his hand, and sat straight, dripping tears and snot. He tried to look at Macon, but Scott yoked him again, and this time Punctuality went limp. The sobs mounted and he mumbled words between them: "What"—*sob*—"do"—*sob*—"you"—*sob choke snot sob*—"want-from-me?" *Sob sob gulp-swallow recap*. "Why me-he-hee?"

Macon considered the question for a moment, then turned to answer, his voice slicing through the slot in the partition. "Because you're an ignorant white devil asshole, and you and everybody like you deserves to be robbed every day of your life," he said. "Now get the fuck out of here. If I see you even halfway looking at my plates, I'll back up and run your stupid asses over. Move."

He hit the unlock button and they scrambled out onto the shoulder of the highway, Scott pulling Punctuality onto his feet. Macon peeled off, merged into the middle lane, and swerved so the door swung shut. He slumped low, steering with his right fist, gun wedged underneath his thigh. Shock, horror, and an absurd, spastic euphoria tussled for control of him, each one pushing the next off the podium.

By Fifty-ninth Street, euphoria had Macon's ear. *The perfect crime,* it hissed. *No photo up yet, no way those jokers saw your plates or memorized the cab ID.* He started laughing when he thought of what he'd told them. This had been the first time, Macon was certain, that those guys ever regretted the color of their skin.

Chapter Two

The elevator doors began to open and Macon broke out like a racehorse before they'd finished their slow slide; he had a hunch his roommate had arrived today. Even without a reason, though, Macon tended to walk as fast as possible. He kept pace with the sounds spinning through him, and often arrived too early for dentist appointments, lunch dates, graffiti death missions. He wound up killing time, pacing meeting places in swift, sharklike sweeps as if stillness would suffocate and sink him.

The only thing Macon was ever late for was every English class of his high-school career, and those on principle, like, *What the fuck you timid ofays gon' teach* me *about language? Who you got in your great Western Literary Canon who twiznist the King's English until it lies twitching broken-backed and screaming "I give up"? Corny greyboy Jack Kerouac and his one-sided love affair with jazz? Please. You ever heard a jazz cat holler back at him, "You got it, Jack, you understand?" James Joyce? All right, okay, J-Dub a bad mufucker, no doubt no question, but the British made the Irish niggas at home and abroad so the White Man can't have him, he's pitching for the oppressed team in today's ballgame. The real Bards of nineteen-ninety-now, the dudes slapping new words and phrases onto the language on course to surpass Willie Shak's lifetime record of 3,400 innovations, all them cats are microphone fiends and that's who the fuck I'm rollin' with, and if I pimpstrut down the hall too slow and make it late to class, so be it. I'ma still rock your dumbass midterm on freestyle chops alone and both of us know it. And when I pull the milli-mac on Willie Shak, I'll lay you three-to-five uncompromising slave odds that he'll roll over like Chuck Berry's Beethoven and scream loud enough to wake Finnegan. Let Shak battle Rakim at the Parthenon and see who moves the crowd.*

Macon's strides brushed up friction from the hallway rug; static metaphysical and otherwise followed everywhere he went like a storybook puppy, nipping at Macon's heels.

This dorm looks like my junior high, he thought, kneeling to tie his shoelace and spotting dull, earth-toned linoleum squinting through the carpet fibers. For this kind of tuition it should be all chestnut paneling and Persian rugs up in this motherfucker. Yeah, right: long forty-watt fluorescent hallways, porous yellow-painted brick, the mildewed smell of institutionality . . . Déjà vu tickled Macon's nose and he sneezed, loudly. A thin, moist spray of liberated germs joined billions of their cousins on the rug. Macon's sneezes were always dramatic events, seldom stifled by a hand or tissue, as if the First Amendment were at stake.

He reached his room, found the door ajar, and gave it a halting push. Sure enough, a dude his own height—five-eight, five-nine, neither short nor tall, an elevation undistinguished enough to inspire ardent weight lifting—turned from the window and squared broad shoulders to Macon. The blue evening, slung mellow over brownstone rooftops, outlined the follicle-fingers dangling around the cat's eyes: baby dreads too short to be tucked into the full-stuffed headband at the back of his neck. So this was Andre Walker. He was shorter and lighter than Macon had expected, and the locks were a surprise.

Macon raked a hand through his own cropped light-brown hair and meditated on the freedoms nobody but dreads had. Locks were fashion carte blanche. You could be Brooks Brothered down and get over on the contrast, or rock eccentric, idiotic shit: big butterfly-collared shirts with wide horizontal stripes, a dirty, pointless piece of string tied like a pageant sash, whatever. A dread was hip regardless, cooling nonchalant at the far end of the spectrum from where Macon huddled good-looking but not fly, forever struggling to hide the meticulousness in his cool like a bald spot, sporting the right gear and compensating for his hair by fucking with his facial growth. His sideburns flared into dramatic bell-bottoms, less stylish than aggressive—a half-successful hip hop remix of the only cross-racial revolutionary hairstyle to limp past Watergate.

Macon took a mother-may-I giant step across the threshold and Andre took two toward him on clopping Nike flip-flops and filled the space between them with his outstretched hand. Macon spoke first.

"Been wondering when you'd touch down." A double-pump handshake. "Welcome to the crib. I'm Macon Detornay."

"Andre Walker." He crossed thick mocha arms over his chest and leaned against the knotty side of a pinewood bookshelf beached in the middle of the room, evidence of his roommate's ongoing efforts to redecorate. Macon had smoked the crack of dawn on a five A.M. Bonzai Bus down from the Bean ten days ago, Columbia's first move-in day, in what had turned out to be a highly overzealous bid for first-come, first-served primacy. Living in a freshman double was going to be hard enough, he'd reasoned; if there was a nicer side or plusher mattress, he needed it. Macon had been switching beds nightly, though, and he'd developed no real preference.

"How long have you been here?" asked Andre.

"I came down for the pre-orientation camping thing. But when I got here, I realized I'd rather just have a week by myself in the city to get settled, find a job, shit like that. So I skipped it."

Andre nodded. "Yeah, me, too. I didn't come to college to learn how to wipe my ass with leaves."

Macon chuckled, mostly to cover the whirring of his brain. All summer he'd been fretting over this moment, afraid that when faced with his roommate in the physical, he'd chicken out and not say what he had promised himself he would. The full-disclosure Macon knew he owed Andre seemed so foolhardy; why drop a million pounds of cement history between the two of them before there was anything else? Macon had spent hours telling himself it would be a bridge, not a wall.

Now, at the crucial juncture, it seemed almost trivial. Macon's feet still squished in his boots, adrenaline-soaked. His jaw still hummed with the violence, wit, and ideology of what he'd done. The robbery had been a giant step into himself, into the enormous suit of warrior's armor he'd always felt it was his destiny to fill. New York was pushing him just like he'd known it would. What was history compared to destiny?

"There's something you deserve to know," Macon recited, snapping back into the moment. He interlaced his fingers, then extended his arms in a half-twist. Six knuckles popped in unison. "So here it is. First of all, I requested you as a roommate. And second, Cap Anson was my great-grandfather."

Andre's expression barely changed. "Okaaay," he allowed, trying to buy himself some time to think, realizing the limited purchasing power of the two syllables he'd chosen, and giving up. "Wow. What am I supposed to do with that?"

Resentment tinged the question. Andre had been here what, three hours, and already his roommate was heaving a musty shroud of century-old savagery over the two of them and lighting candles inside? Why can't I just do college like a normal motherfucker, he wondered, say, *What's up dude?* to my boring roommate and buy some boring books and drink some beer and meet some girls and shit?

Macon shrugged, eyes pleading for an understanding he couldn't quite pinpoint. "Honestly, man? I don't know. I found you on the Net after I read Fleet's book, and you were coming here and so was

I and it just seemed cosmically, I don't know . . . right for us to room together, so I called the housing office. The sins of the fathers and everything."

"The sins of the fathers what, dude? Shall be forgiven if the great-grandsons share a dorm room?"

Macon shook his head. "Not forgiven. I don't know, man." He was beginning to recall why the anticipation of this conversation had filled him with worry. "Something to make Cap spin in his grave, I guess."

"He's not the only one," said Andre. His mind's eye saw his own great-grandfather's caramel face turn into pale gray clay, crumple and crack, scatter in a slight wind. The headless body stood at home plate, arms swaying from shoulders. The striped cap rested for a moment in midair, hovering where Fleet's head had been, then plopped softly to the ground, raising a whiff of baseball dust. Andre wondered what it was like to grow up knowing a man like Anson was your ancestor. Had Macon's parents had a somber sitdown with their son and told him the deal, or had the recent re-publication of Fleet's book transformed a family hero into a demagogue?

"I'm sorry," said Macon. "I mean, not about Cap and Fleet—I'm not apologizing for that—I mean, I am sorry about that, but I'm apologizing for this." His laugh misfired. The adrenaline was draining away. Macon could never keep hold of an emotion for long. He'd become so good at banishing his parents' screaming indictments from his mind in the few seconds it took him to walk from the front door to the ride honking in the driveway that the process was now automatic. He poked the toe of his Timberland into a mound of plaster dandruff flaking from the bottom of the wall. He wasn't used to elucidating his motives; most people focused on the bright-burning flame of Macon's convictions, not the mass of melted-together wax from which they sprouted. "I guess the idea of living with someone I have some connection to is more appealing than life with a total stranger," he offered at last.

Andre spoke over the clatter of warning bells filling his mind. "We are total strangers, Macon." Even as he said it, Andre felt the first drop of truth melt away from the statement; there was a strange kinship between them, and he'd be lying to himself if he ignored it.

"Yeah, but we got history," said Macon.

"So what? Are you anything like Anson? Do you hate black people? Can you even hit a curveball?"

"I'm nothing like him," Macon said. "That's kind of the point of my life."

Andre swung his arms, tried to sound breezy. "Well, man, Fleet really has no bearing on my life. I haven't even read his book."

"For real? Why not? You can borrow mine."

"Chill. Ever since that joint came back in print, my mom's been on it nonstop: 'Andre, why you watching that crap on TV? Go read your great-grandfather's book.' 'Andre, stop running up my phone bill and go learn your goddamn history.' I'm getting pretty tired of that dude, to be honest."

"It's a dope book, man. Makes you realize how little anything has changed in this country."

"Is that right." He hoped he sounded rhetorical enough to disperse the speech clouds massing over Macon's head, dark and heavy and desperate to rain down transparent sheets of consciousness. Andre didn't feel like listening to his roommate relieve himself. He'd already served his time in prep school as a cardboard self-affirmation cutout. *Smile, Johnny. Put your arm around the African-American. Say cheese.* A stoic, amiable receptacle into which fake-empathetic whiteboys dumped their views, a priest who heard confessions and smoked joints with the sinners to absolve them.

Andre arced his brows into sardonic rainbows, and Macon's blue eyes darted chastened to the rug and scanned a dark, Africa-shaped stain. When he was ten, a ski instructor with whom he'd shared a chairlift had told Macon how lucky he was to have the eyes he did. "You've got those speckled irises," the guy had said, making a little circle with his finger. "Me, too. They're very rare. Women love eyes like ours."

There was more to be said about the past, the weirdness of meeting, the blood spilled between them, but Andre had no idea what. Better to back away from all that for the moment and do the getting-to-know-you shuffle until some rhythms of cohabitation had been established. Or until he could make an appointment with the housing office.

"Two grown men and they expect us to live in two hundred and sixty-six square feet all year." Andre rocked back on his heels, hands pocketed, and bobbed his head at a silver tape measure lying next to several boxes marked *Pimp Shit*. "I measured."

"Two-seventy, if you count that little-ass closet," Macon replied gratefully. He dropped onto a naked blue-and-white-striped canvas mattress and heard the metal bedframe moan beneath him. "Not that I brought much." He threw a leg over his own half-unpacked suitcase and leaned back, then wondered if the posture was too comfortable too quick, a typical cavalier-whiteboy-lounging-cuz-the-world-is-my-domain move. He flashed on the three junior-high girls he'd seen on the train yesterday, spread out slumber-party style on the dirty floor at rush hour, snapping pictures of one another with disposable cameras, oblivious to the scowl-stares and headshake censures of sardine commuters and the D train floor grime because their sense of entitlement blurred everything beyond each other. Only white kids act like this, Macon had thought. He sat up. "I took the bus down."

"No big send-off from the fam?" asked Andre, flopping stomach-first onto the other bed and propping himself up, elbows under chest, hands folded. Macon, watching him, leaned back again.

"My parents are on a two-month European cruise." Disdain rimmed Macon's voice, thought Andre, maybe embarrassment. Most likely, he assumed his roommate was poor—weren't all black folks?—and shrunk from their presumed class difference. Kids at

Princeton-Eastham Prep had always relaxed around him when they found out Andre wasn't on scholarship like the rest of the school's black population.

"I haven't lived at home in more than a year, though," Macon continued. "I took some time off after high school and moved in with my boy Lajuan."

Estranged from parents, Andre noted. He bet they were still paying their baby boy's tuition, though. *Has a black friend.* Slick how he'd slipped that in there. Unless the universe housed white-boys named Lajuan.

"You're from where?" asked Andre.

"Ten minutes outside Boston. Suburb called Newton. But don't worry. We're not gonna have any Bird-Magic, Bad Boy–Death Row coastal beef. Boston sucks." He gestured at his roommate's outfit. "Nice to see some hometown pride, though."

Andre pushed off the bed and stood up, laying an open hand against his gold-and-purple Lakers jersey. He dipped his fingers momentarily into the crinkly vinyl pocket of black Raiders track pants, then bent and pulled up his L.A. Kings socks. "I have no idea what you mean."

"Come on now." Macon grinned and hunched forward, antsy with the suspicion that he was seconds away from planting his flag in a patch of common ground. "You're talking to the only kid from the Bean who was up on L.A. hip hop before *Straight Outta Compton.* I used to get KDAY tapes from my man's cousin."

"Word?" said Andre, eyebrows disappearing into the low-leaning forest of his hair. "KDAY, huh? That's some O.G. shit." The outlines of a context into which he could fit Macon were beginning to come into focus.

"Man, I was out here talking about Mixmaster Spade and 'can't get enough of everlasting bass' and cats were looking at me like I was stone crazy," Macon recounted, pleased that he had found a pore in the conversation, however imaginary, that led to hip hop.

If only the world were as simple as it had been back in the day, when a shared investment in the still-invisible culture had granted two people a rare, automatic intimacy, laid an immediate foundation for a friendship.

They both smiled, and a moment of silence descended like a velvet stage curtain. Andre eye-checked his roommate and floated him some grudging props. Macon might be a lunatic, and his bloodlines were certainly polluted, but at least he was hip hop enough not to view black people as an alien species—even if he was the type to assume that any black kid he met was a rap head. Andre's worst roommate fear had been averted: a ten-gallon-hat-wearing good ol' boy who'd greet him with a "Howdy, pardner," crank up some Garth Brooks, and start pinning his Confederate flag up next to Andre's swap-meet African masks, explaining that he wasn't racist, just proud.

Macon used the lull in conversation to replay the robbery in his mind, and a new shudder of excitement suffused him. He felt rubbery with glee, almost flip now that he'd stumbled through the awkwardness of revealing his ancestry to Andre. "Okay," he said, "enough with all this trivial cosmic-connection shit. You blaze or what?"

Funny how green always brought black and white together, thought Andre. At least until the green was gone. "Hell yes," he said, erasing that appointment with the housing office from his mental blackboard. Macon was a pothead: Things would be all right. "And not that dirt weed fools be smoking out here, neither. Strictly the California chronic."

He darted to his luggage, pulled a large shampoo bottle from the bottom of a full-stuffed duffel bag, unscrewed the cap, and extracted a gooey sandwich bag. He wiped it clean on a Dodgers towel, wrist-flicked it across the room for inspection, and sat back down. Macon pulled the closing strip apart, and the sudden pungency of Andre's stash lit up their room like Little Amsterdam. It was insanely green, a joyous neon hue Macon had only seen in *National Geographic* photo essays about preserving the coral reefs. Tight saffron-haired buds and strong, thick stems and no seeds. No seeds?

"Hydroponic," Andre said. "Act like you know." Macon stared at the herb, overcome with the bounty of nature's blessings, and nodded respect. "Wait until you taste it, dude." An orange pack of Zigzags flashed in Andre's hand.

A few moments later, Macon had to give the credit where it was due. What now burned evenly between his unmanicured fingertips didn't even seem like the same plant as the shit he, in his Bostonian ignorance, had once called marijuana. Macon exhaled a slow plume and smoothed down his elation like a cowlick. Getting doe-eyed over ganja was for hippies with black-light posters who read fan ratings of Grateful Dead shows on the Internet, ratings that ranged from A+++++++ *(Jerry's spirit left his body and fellated me in the bleachers while his physical shell remained onstage playing "Turn On Your Love Light")* to A+ *(the band didn't show up and cops teargassed the parking lot)*. A fair number of the white kids he'd grown up with, Macon's friends from the time when friends were defined as kids whose houses were close enough to bike to, had slid Deadward. They had racks of concert bootlegs and books of tour photos just like he had crates of vinyl and a shoe box stuffed with graff flicks.

He'd hung with those kids occasionally through high school, although their entitlement and lack of chops—the rugged brain-mouth world-collaging quick wit that hip hop beat into you—bored him. Macon was a product of the same white-collar suburb they were, but while he was nuzzling up against a world clenched tight in struggle, fly as fuck, hell-bent on schooling technology in its own backyard, these laconic stoners couldn't even wrap their minds around the notion that a human being might *not* like Jerry and them. Macon had been forced to listen to the Branford

Marsalis/Dead tape—what Deadheads played people who liked black music to prove the Dead were down—in more tapestry-sheathed bedrooms than he cared to recall. Deadheads always had better cheeba than hip hoppers, though—expensive aesthete bud stored in film cases and thumb-pressed into glass bongs imbued with personalities and christened with goofy names. *Careful, dude. Oscar, like, sneaks up on you.*

Regular hip hop motherfuckers smoked like they did everything: repurposed something cheap, useless, and available to suit their needs, and turned the process into an art form along the way. They said, "Yo, kid, let's burn this branch / twist this L / blaze these trees / hit this blunt / steam this broccoli / spark this lah / smoke this shit." They split a fifty-cent Dutch Master cigar with two thumbnails, slid the cylindrical clump of cheap, stale tobacco to the pavement, dumped a brown-green stick-seed-and-shake-laced nick bag casually into the empty paper, picked out the unsmokables, twirled it up, dried it with a lighter, lit it, hit it, ashed it, passed it, and went about their business if they had some. Build and destroy.

Andre's chronic, though, knocked even Deadhead herb straight out the box, made you look at the City of Angels in a whole new light. Even made you understand their music better. This was some ol' "diamond in the back / sunroof top / diggin' the scene with a gangsta lean" shit, Macon reflected as he turned the tiny joint between two fingers, took a rich pull, and returned it to his roommate. Habit forced Macon to hit a spliff as hard as he could every time it touched his fingers; he was accustomed to smoking with three, four, five necks crowding the cipher and everybody trying to get as high as possible despite the rigorously enforced take-two-and-pass-so-the-blunt-will-last protocol.

Andre sidelonged his roommate from beneath low-slung eyelids. "Kinda name is Macon for a whiteboy, anyway?" he drawled, holding his hit in as he spoke.

Macon shrugged. Kinda whiteboy is Macon'd be a better question, he thought, one lip corner curling in a smug smile. "Macon, Georgia," he said. "Where I was allegedly conceived. Parents drove cross-country in a VW bus for their honeymoon." He shook his head. "I hate it."

"It's not so bad. If they'd gotten it on a couple hours earlier, you woulda been Buckhead."

Macon steadied his eyes, which seemed to want to roll back in his head, and rubbed a palm against his stubbled chin. "Easy for you to say. Nobody called you Bacon in grade school."

"True," said Andre. "Between all those seventies Black Power Back-to-Africa names—which I blame on drugs in the drinking water at Wattstax—and all that ghetto-fabulous eighties insanity, naming mufuckers Lexus and Guccina and Dom Pérignon and shit—black folks got kind of a dozens moratorium on names." He felt a pang of guilt for making such jokes in front of a whiteboy, and winced as if the red-black-and-green Afropick of race pride had just flown across the room and jabbed him in the ass.

Andre bent to ash the joint into a plastic garbage can, and missed the size-up glance his roommate threw at him. Macon was as attuned to signs of black acceptance as a dog was to the scraping of a can opener. Willingness to tweak the foibles of black people in front of him was a clear one; it implied that Macon was hip enough to get the joke and down enough to be unguarded around. The only thing better was when black folks started railing against the White Man in his presence, thus granting Macon transcendent status. When he felt needy or insecure, which was often, Macon resorted to initiating such discussions by ripping into his private stash of paper race tigers: Quentin Tarantino, Rudolph Giuliani, Elvis Presley. It usually got the wrecking ball rolling.

Andre inhaled sharply, pulled back his lips, and offered the joint, almost gone now, to his roommate. It was an elegant pass, thumb pressed securely to fingertip, the handoff of two experienced smokers. "Yo," said Macon, kicking his legs out as the toxicants streamed through him, thrashing like salmon, and settled in the cool underwater grotto of his stomach, "you ever seen—"

A loud knock at the door wounded their buzzes and killed the conversation.

"Hello?" Insistent, female, whiny. "It's Olivia, your R.A."

Andre leaped to his feet and flicked the roach toward the open window. It hit the top ledge, showering sparks down the pane, and whipped out into the wind.

"Shit." He reached for a can of Right Guard and sprayed a loud, wide arc around the room. Macon, dazed by the whirlwind his roommate had become, grabbed his own deodorant, realized it was a roll-on, and felt stupid.

"One second," called Andre, wading through the knee-high detritus that had somehow managed to accumulate in just three hours. "Wonderful," he muttered, "not even here a day and already I'ma be the stereotypical fire-up-the-spliff natty-dreadlock-inna-Babylon Rastaman-vibration nigga and shit."

He yanked open the door and a short, mousy-haired girl stared up at him through fingerprint-smudged glasses. She looked like she wanted to come inside, but Andre blocked the entrance with his body. A lecture on Knowing Your Rights given by some haggard ex–Black Panther at a weekend retreat his mother had sent him on because she worried he wasn't black enough came back to Andre: *A cop can only come inside your house if you give him permission.* The knowledge was intended to prevent the pigs from fucking with young revolutionary brothers, but he had only used it when the Santa Monica PD busted up the keg parties his football teammates threw when their parents were out of town.

The girl crossed one slippered ankle over the other and pursed her downturned mouth to speak.

"Hi!" Andre said before she could, pursuing a policy of jaunty innocence. He grinned, orthodontized teeth gleaming, and extended his hand, forearm swollen from a summer of weight lifting; Andre hoped she'd notice but she didn't. Beyond offering his body for perusal, he never quite knew how to flirt. "Andre Walker. Wow, I—Those are really cool sweatpants." Behind him, the sizzle of aerosol indicated that Macon was freshening the air with an entire semester's worth of Right Guard.

The Resident Adviser looked him over with authoritarian disdain and Andre's arm fell to his side. "First floor meeting's in ten minutes," she said, then paused and frowned. "What's that smell?"

"We can't make it," Macon squawked, lunging to his roommate's side and dropping a buddy-pal hand on Andre's shoulder. "We've scheduled on-line appointments with Career Counseling."

She cast a doubtful squint at them, then reeled it in. "See me tonight to find out what you missed," she relented. "And don't let me smell that smell coming from your room again." She padded off with nary a farewell.

Andre closed the door. "Where the fuck did you come up with that?"

Macon pointed to a blue booklet lying broken-spined on his desk. "*Columbia Guide to Living*. An invaluable resource."

"Well, it's definitely time to be out. I'm supposed to meet my man Nique downtown. You wanna roll?"

"Sure. I was gonna hit this poetry slam at the Nuyorican later, anyway. Who's Nique?"

"My boy from high school. He's a junior at NYU. Completely nuts. You'll like him."

Andre yanked open a dresser drawer and plucked a folded red shirt. "Soon as I decided I was coming to New York, I went down to Blood In Blood Out on La Brea and scooped hella red gear." He shucked the Lakers jersey and pulled on the polo. "I'm so sick of wearing neutral colors I could shoot somebody in the face. Preferably some mark ass set trippin' buster ass fool."

Andre opened the door and he and Macon phased into public post-smoke mode, flipping up their cool like trench-coat collars. "Listen . . ." Andre said. He stopped talking as they passed the

TV lounge housed in an alcove between their room and the elevator, already full of lame kids killing the eight minutes before the floor meeting by soaking flaccidly in talk shows, then resumed as they reached the elevator bank.

". . . don't mention this Cap Anson shit to anybody else, okay? Especially not Nique."

"I wasn't planning on it," said Macon, caught off-guard. "But why not?"

"Because it's fucking weird, dude. I hope you don't need me to tell you that." He's already checked it off his list, Andre thought. A little weed, some hip hop, he thinks it's all good. "Plus, I don't wanna be known as the guy who's rooming with his—" Andre broke off. "His whatever."

"Fair enough," said Macon quietly. He jabbed at the down button for the second time. "You ever heard that story," he asked after a moment, "about these Bloods who bailed into a gay S&M club in L.A. by mistake, rocking red flags?"

"Nah," said Andre. They stepped into the lift. "Do tell."

"Apparently, in that scene you rock flags to show what you're into—yellow means piss on me, white lace means submissive, whatever. A red flag means beat my ass, make me bleed. So cats beat their asses silly. Supposedly."

"Sounds like bullshit to me," said Andre.

Macon nodded. "Yeah, you're probably right." The doors closed.

Chapter Three

Peep game, Macon ordered the world, pushing the front door so hard it one-eighty slammed against the dorm's facade. By the time it slow-swept backward, clicked and froze at a welcoming seventy degrees, he and Andre were in the wind, weak sunshine on their cheeks and the building's long five o'clock shadow behind them like getaway music.

"Campus or the streets?" asked Andre, posing what Macon took at first to be a philosophical conundrum, with whom you rollin' when the comedown come down, edumacated shot-caller big-baller types or the untalented nine-tenths with unknockable hustles, unprintable résumés? But naw, fool, the question is which route to walk.

Not that streets versus campus connoted the old, traditional, good-natured, spite-filled townies-against-college-boys fair fight regardless. Columbia owned every damn thing in sight. Why be a mere institution of higher learning when you could also be Harlem's number-one slumlord, second-largest landowner in money-makin' Manhattan after the Catholic Church? Andre hadn't toured the campus yet, so they ignored the street exit and strolled down College Walk.

A domed building with the air of a state capitol, protected by a row of pillars, sat atop a long sprawl of shallow stone steps: Columbia's gleaming white administrative black box. The steps sloped down for days, giving the building a distant, unapproachable aura, as if to say *the road to knowledge is long, laborious, and gradual,* or *each one you climb represents a grand you owe us for your education, sucker.* The steps bottomed into an open plaza, flanked by giant granite fountains. Outreach to the heavily encroached-upon community took its best-financed form on these few hundred square feet: biannual free concerts featuring mainstream bohemian rap acts and second-string alternative-rock bands, overseen by tripled security but open to neighborhood residents if they somehow managed to find out about them. Milking the college cash cow by rote, the performers usually kicked lackluster forty-minute sets in fulfillment of their contracts and bounced, forty thousand dollars richer and muttering about lame college audiences. The only exception had been when the Events Committee unwittingly booked the Boot Camp Clik, a camouflage-rocking bevy of lyrical gunclappers from Brooklyn. Macon had caught the concert as a high-school junior on the requisite college-road-trip-with-the-parents. It had influenced his choice of school as much as anything.

Half of Bucktown had journeyed uptown for the concert, and a sixteenth had made it past the rapidly retripled security in time to see the spot get blown. Grimy, reconstructed drums had boom-clacked through the rarefied air, gotten even non-heads nodding, and the next thing Macon knew, Boot Camp's five-foot microphone don Buckshot was rocking his verse from atop an eight-foot vibrating speaker: *How the fuck did money climb up there and how come I ain't see it?* Macon had snapped a flick of Buckshot's cornrowed head sandwiched between the engraved names of Plato and Sophocles, etched into the stone above the columns on Butler Library across the plaza.

After Plato and Sophocles came Herodotus, Aristotle, and three or four more Western Thought All-Stars. As Macon had found out that weekend, Columbia shepherded all incoming students through two years of comprehensive Western literature and philosophy courses, the cornerstone of the famed Core Curriculum despite being taught largely by underqualified and overtired grad students while the actual professors labored over their forthcoming books in the well-heeled privacy of Riverside Drive faculty apartments. The courses, intended to allow young scholars to drop cocktail party references to Adam Smith's economic theory and jest fraternally about Aristophanes' sex comedies, bonded the university community by ensuring that all Columbia graduates forgot the same things.

Andre and Macon turned left onto a cobbled pathway and headed toward the high black iron gates that announced the street entrances and allowed Columbia to shut out interlopers and imprison residents in times of trouble, i.e., the student uprisings of the 1960s and more recently the ethnic studies protests of 1996. The University, as the administration was called, exercised a subtle yet totalitarian control over its population, low-key enough to convince naive students that threatening to sit in Hamilton Hall until they were allowed to study the contributions of people of color to American life might catalyze a conversation with the administration. Instead, the stunt prompted a call to the police, a series of arrests and unfavorable editorials, a tacit backpedaling compromise to drop the charges and develop a research committee, and finally the quiet dissolution of said committee once the attentions of the media had waned and the angriest students had left for the summer, graduated, or found girlfriends.

Andre and Macon passed through the gates and into Morningside Heights, a neighborhood semantically divorced from Harlem, rechristened to convince jumpy suburban parents that their children didn't live in the Capital of Black America and would be as safe at college as they had been at their prep schools. It was a virtual bubble of safety, except for the occasional date-rapist football player. Even the bums, thought Andre as he and Macon descended into the cleanest subway station in Manhattan, seemed handpicked for their effusiveness.

They stepped off the train at West Fourth Street and crossed Washington Square Park, New York University's no-campus-having answer to Columbia's pristine, sequestered lawns. Students, locals, and outtatowners shared twilight space on the green wooden benches and around the central fountain. Backpacks nudged briefcases, and fresh-cut grass mingled airborne with pretzels and cigarettes. Rastafarians in red-green-and-gold tams leaned together over one chess table, gesturing at the wooden pieces with long fingers. A crew of high schoolers held down another, sneaker treads gripping the smooth marble as they chewed brown-bagged soda straws and girl-watched. Mutts and pedigrees sniffed each other's asses with studious democracy inside the fenced dog run; the owners greeted each other's dogs with enthusiasm and each other with indifference.

"So what kind of job did you find?" Andre asked.

Macon watched a yellow cab tear past the park, swerving to avoid pedestrians, and bang an illegal right turn as the traffic light clicked red. The driver conducted a symphony of angry horns with his middle finger as he caromed out of sight.

"I drive one of those," Macon said with pride.

"Word? You must overhear some interesting shit. People probably assume you don't speak English."

"You'd think so, but so far it's been pretty boring. Lot of single fares." Macon fingered the wad of bills clogging his pocket and wondered what he was going to do with the money, nearly two hundred bucks. He considered buying Andre dinner, then worried his roommate would think he was trying to pay reparations.

"Huh," mused Andre. "You didn't want to wait and get a campus job?"

"I'm not work-study eligible. My grandfather put away dough for my education back in the day, so no student loans. I'm still broke on the day-to-day tip, though."

"Parents won't help you out?" asked Andre, wondering whether to take Macon's stark financial portrait with a grain of salt or an entire pillar. Those suede Tims his roommate was rocking looked about a week out of the box.

"I won't let them." Self-reliance had been Macon's economic policy since leaving home, and like communism it worked well in theory. In practice, he had shame-facedly accepted cash infusions twice so far: once just after bouncing to Lajuan's crib, so he'd have weed throw-down scratch—the definition of a good houseguest in Macon's circle being a cat who sponsored blunt sessions—and again only two weeks ago, when he'd wanted new gear for school. Macon soothed himself with the knowledge that Cuba had been surviving on handouts for damn near forty years now.

They made their way across the park, movements tracked by more than two thousand hidden security cameras installed by the City of New York for an amount of money that, had it been distributed amongst the ten to twenty drug dealers the cameras were intended to monitor, would have allowed all of them to retire in comfort.

It seemed to Andre that a different homeless cat approached them every few feet to request assistance, as if the park were sectioned into tiny, invisible fiefdoms. He brushed past each supplicant without bothering to slow his pace or eye-flicker an apology. Macon, meanwhile, threw on the brakes at every timid "Excuse me." Three times, Andre realized he was walking alone and doubled back to gather up his roommate, only to find Macon listening with botanically enhanced patience to whatever involved plea or bogus medical history the guy was running down. Macon's sidewalk manner was impeccable: constant eye contact, sympathetic head-nodding. He let the vagrants run through their whole spiels and make their requests before letting them know he had no money and wishing them well. Their eyes hardened with disappointment, but each one left Macon with a "God bless you," to which Macon responded, "You, too," smiled a good-bye, and walked on secure in his compassion for his fellow man.

"It's not like this in L.A.," Andre explained as they exited the park, feeling like a callous asshole.

"Car culture," Macon replied absently. He was busy trying to balance an internal triple-beam scale laid heavy with luck, greed, and pragmatism, calculating how much loot was clockable if he robbed motherfuckers for an entire shift.

Andre nodded. "Yeah. L.A.'s not too big on chance interaction. Or humanity. But we've got Shaq and Kobe."

He double-checked the directions he'd scribbled on the back of a matchbook. They turned left and walked past hot-dog and hot-nut vendors, a sidewalk bookstand, knots of students sucking cancer sticks beneath the purple flags rippling from NYU's main library. Nique's high-rise was on the corner. Andre called his boy from the dorm's cramped lobby, and seconds after he'd replaced the courtesy phone, a lanky, dark-skinned dude barreled down the side staircase, holding on to the rail bars like parallel beams and swinging himself down four steps at a time. He cleared the last set, landed clean on burgundy-and-black suede Pumas, pushed his metal-framed sunglasses up onto his forehead, and gangled an arm around Andre's back as the two exchanged the standard shoulder-bang embrace.

"Wassup, fool," Nique exclaimed, reverting to Left Coast slangisms in the presence of a Westside homey. He pulled away without unclasping Andre's hand and ended the shake in a finger snap, gold bracelet sliding halfway up his arm as he recoiled from the motion.

"You *know,*" bayed Andre, voice plummeting two octaves on the final syllable. It was an expression seldom heard so far east; Macon knew from listening to old Mack 10 records that it was roughly equivalent to *I'm chillin'* or, in the parlance of those old school enough to get away with sounding corny, *livin' large.* "This my roommate," said Andre, tapping him on the chest with the back of his hand, "Macon." Their eyes met, and each one wondered whether Andre would appendix an endorsement. "He's cool," Andre finished at last.

"Whaddup, dude. Dominique Lavar." Intelligence lit his long, smooth face powerfully from within as he offered Macon a thumb-topped fist and they exchanged a one-potato-two-potato pound. "Come on upstairs, y'all. The kid finally scored a single this year." He tossed a head nod at the brother working security, and the man tossed one back, withdrew the sign-in sheet and pen he'd slid toward Macon, and gestured *Go ahead.* Andre smiled to himself: Leave it to Nique to get cool with the guard right off the muscle, thus deading the minor hassle of visitor sign-ins.

"Good lookin' out, Felix," Nique said over his shoulder. "California love," he explained to Andre. "Homeboy's from Inglewood." He took the steps two at a time and pounded open the stairwell door.

Nique's room was immaculate and tiny, smelled of clean bed linen. A portable refrigerator doubled as a nightstand for a low-slung bed that almost touched three walls. There was space for a desk, but Nique worked on the fly and so he'd marooned the extra furniture in the hall. "I haven't finished freaking the place yet," he apologized, leaving Macon to wonder what further freaking could be done. Every inch of wall space was covered; there were movie posters for *Coffy, Truck Turner,* and *She's Gotta Have It,* and a reproduction of the famous photograph of Tommie Smith and John Carlos at the '68 Olympics with heads bowed and Black Power fists held high. Tupac Shakur gangster-squatted against the floor, shirtless, tattooed, and defiant, both hands twisted into W's, and above Nique's bed was framed a blurry black-and-white freeze-frame of a scene Macon had never forgotten: six of L.A.'s Finest, so murky that they might be figments of imagination, swinging billy clubs with pickax motions as if the huddled mass of Rodney King might be a craggy slab of granite or an arid patch of land.

"Nice picture."

Nique turned and scowled. "Nice? Either you got a real limited vocabulary or a serious problem. Ain't nothing nice about the shit."

Macon shook his head. "No, I mean, of course not. I— What I meant was . . ." He gave up on speaking and pushed the left sleeve of his T-shirt to his shoulder. Tattooed on Macon's biceps in small green characters was *4-29-92*. It was the day the verdict had been handed down, the day Los Angeles had burned. Andre and Dominique peered in to read it, then looked up at Macon.

"A Jewish kid with numbers tattooed on his arm," said Andre blankly, taking the beer Nique passed him. "Now I've seen it all."

Macon lifted one mouth corner in a half-smile that looked more like a twitch. "That's exactly what my mom said." The numbers glistened slightly on his skin, bathed in the soft light of Nique's halogen. "She started going off about the Holocaust. I was like, 'Please. Nobody in this family has been inside a temple in three generations. How am I supposed to be Jewish enough to know better?' " Macon broke off, accepted a bottle from Nique, and plugged his mouth with it, swigging until he trusted himself not to speak.

I'm not Jewish, Andre thought, and I know better.

Nique looked from Andre to Macon and then back to Andre. He ran a hand over his smooth-shaved head. "Who is this dude, Dre?" he asked with cinematic incredulity and perfect comic timing, the results of an upbringing replete with four movie channels and unlimited TV privileges. "Mufucker got a Rodney King tattoo? Shit, I thought I was black."

Macon walked over to the photo-still and stared at it. The night in question firecrackered through his mind. Without turning from the wall, he spoke. "It was an important day."

"For niggas in L.A., no doubt," said Nique. "But you gonna have to enlighten me as to why it was so crucial for a whiteboy from . . ."

"Massachusetts," Macon said.

"Right."

Macon shrugged. "Things changed."

"Ain't shit change, man."

"Things changed for me."

Nique looked at Andre. "Is he always like this?"

"I've known him for two hours, Nique." A good old-fashioned race man, Andre thought suddenly. He smiled at the notion of his roommate decked out in Black Panther garb, and decided that living with this cat might prove to be the most exhausting task he'd ever undertaken.

"Fine," said Nique. "We'll play twenty questions. How did shit change for you?"

"I stopped believing in justice even a little bit. Any faith I had left in the system, or in white people, pretty much evaporated when I noticed that no one around me gave a fuck."

Nique rested his chin on his thumb, drummed long fingers against his temple, and nodded. "Interesting." Macon hoped it was enough. He didn't intend to tell the story, no matter how hard Nique pressed him.

Andre tabled his empty bottle with a thud. He still drank to pacify an invisible throng of jocks chanting *Chug, chug*. "All right," he said. "Enough. I been trying not to ask, dude, but I gotta. What's up with all this 'white people' shit? You like an undercover brother or something?"

Nique rocked forward in anticipation, and Macon bounced his sonar off them, scanning for hostility. He was glad to find a trace. Black people's friendship meant nothing unless they were suspicious of whites.

"Not at all," he said plainly. "I don't even have one of those grew-up-in-the-hood stories to justify myself." I'm so real I don't need one, read Macon's intended subtext, Nique thought. The wigger goes poststructuralist. Could be his next term paper.

Below the subtext ran another meaning, one that Andre grasped immediately: I can have dough and still be down. Against his will, Dre sympathized; he was touched with a similar angst. Being black and middle class sometimes felt like a contradiction in terms, and only one of the two could be disguised. He'd had his comfort thrown in his face, *punk Oreo cookie motherfucker,* enough to know how to pretend, guiltily, that he was lower-bracketed.

Nique quick-plucked the cigarette from his mouth. "So you just don't like white people," he said, hand blooming into gesture, elbow resting on his knee. Nique was made of angles, from the planar jut of his neck to the wide, cagey V of his smile. Macon's stomach did a little fear-excitement flip-kick. *Now we're getting somewhere.*

"I don't like whiteness. And as a white person looking for some heroes, it's lonely out here. The museum's empty. Look at me, for instance. Sure, I might have missed a couple ferries back to Honkytown, but so what? They run every hour. I can sunbathe on the island of Blackness all summer. But when the seasons change, will I hunker down and spend the winter in my vacation spot?"

"Dunno, nigga, will you?"

Macon smiled, pleased with the mockery. "Everybody thinks they will," he said, chest swelling with furtive superhero pride. "But there's no way to tell who's down, really, until we hit the crucial moment." His hand twitched, remembering the feel of the gun, and Macon's brain secreted an obedient montage of authenticating moments: late-night graffiti missions with Aura, the two of them smearing fame across the belly of the ghetto, and dinners presided over by regal black matriarchs, the mothers of his closest friends—Macon so black he used more hot sauce on his food than anybody, so much that little sisters with antenna-looking braids peered over the table at his plate wide-eyed.

Macon kept such snapshots on instant recall; they occupied a larger percentage of his memory than of his life. Their opposites, the times Macon had felt awkward and abandoned by blacks and whites alike, the awful moments he'd let *nigger* glide unchecked from his white friends' mouths instead of punching them in the face—moments when vigilance had been too much of a hassle to disrupt the party for—were stored where Macon didn't have to see them.

Nique slow-rolled the tip of his cigarette against the lip of a glass ashtray liberated from a restaurant. "Ah, yes." He smirked. "The crucial moment. When rivers of blood gush through the streets and Uncle Tom's ghost pulls white folks' hearts out of their chests to balance them against a feather."

Macon exhaled short and shallow through his nose, approximating a laugh. "No racial apocalypse needed. Individuals face individual moments of reckoning. And most bitch out."

"How 'bout John Brown, Harpers Ferry?" suggested Andre.

Nique rolled his eyes. "Leave it to Dre to pull a heroic white man out his ass."

Macon sat forward and cracked his knuckles. "You know why John Brown tried to free those slaves? His old lady left him for a slave owner. The whole thing was a crazy, ill-conceived act of revenge. Fuck John Brown."

Nique rocked in his chair and clapped his hands. "Oh, man," he said, clutching Macon's shoulder as if he was about to present him with a trophy. " 'Fuck John Brown.' I love it. So you're it, huh, dog? The downest whiteboy in history."

"I didn't say that," Macon protested, declining to counter with a name.

Andre's eyes were narrow. "I never heard that shit about John Brown."

"They don't teach it in school."

"True." Nique nodded with quasi-comic vigor. "True indeed. Feeding the black man nothing but his-story, tricknowledgy, and sinformation. Locking him away in the library, where the white man buries the lies." He elbowed Andre in the ribs and Andre knocked his arm away, not in the mood.

"And charging him an arm and a leg for it," Macon added, trying to lane-merge with Nique's flow, play deacon to his pastor.

Nique took the cue. "Yes indeed. Causing the black man to fall deeper and deeper into financial bondage until he is forced, despite his fancy degree, to return to the ghetto from whence he came and sell poison to innocent black babies, just like whitey planned. Because the only B.A. worth a damn in this world, brothers and sisters, is your Black Ass."

"Amen," said Andre dully. "Can I get another beer, Minister Farrakhan?"

Nique opened the mini-fridge with his foot. "Help yourself."

"Much obliged." Dre popped the cap with his lighter.

"Don't mention it. So listen. For real, though: You kids wanna make some cash?" Nique crossed his legs, downshifting into a Nino Brown impression that had, over time, grown almost indistinguishable from his actual personality. "Come work for me. I'm makin' moves this year."

"That's my middle name," said Macon. An old joke. "Macon Moves."

The abrupt crackle of Nique's laughter tickled him. "This motherfucker is all right, Dre," Nique said, then turned appraisingly toward Macon. "Might be able to do business, Moves. Don't worry. I'm an equal-opportunity employer. No Crow Jim laws here."

"What is it, exactly, that you do, Nique?"

"Give you a hint, dude. I'm a young black entrepreneur from the ghetto who can't rhyme or run ball. What does a lifetime of media saturation tell you I do?"

"Sell drugs?"

"Give the man a prize."

Andre crossed his arms and snorted. "Nique's been talking this high-roller street pharmacist shit since he was selling fools oregano nick bags in high school. He ain't got no game."

Nique splayed a hand in Andre's grill. "Whatever. That was then, son. Your boy is on some shit now. Besides, I had clientele even when I was slinging oregano. Don't hate. Congratulate. Anyway."

He lowered his voice. "Over the summer I landed this gig manning a tollbooth on the highway out in Queens. Now, you may ask yourself, 'What does a big pimpin' motherfucker like Dominique want working a tollbooth like an asshole?' " He paused rhetorically, winked garishly, resumed. "Unsupervised hand-to-hand transactions, baby. Feel me?"

A molasses grin spread over Macon's face. "You're pumping from a tollbooth?"

"Drive-through service, baby. You hit me on the cell and I tell you which terminal I'm at. No fuss, no muss. Gone in thirty seconds."

Andre shook his head. "I gotta give it to you this time," he conceded. "That shit's kinda brilliant."

Nique beamed. "I know." He turned to Macon. "It's getting so I need occasional assistance of a clerical slash product-managerial nature. If you're interested, perhaps we can schedule an interview."

Macon couldn't tell if Nique was serious or fucking with him. Not that it much mattered. "I don't think I have the curriculum vitae you're looking for," he said.

Yesterday the gig would have grouted a wide chink in Macon's self-image, satisfied the slice of him that needed to be linked to illegality somehow. Outlaw was an occupation, not a mind state; you couldn't claim it if you didn't hustle, and you couldn't be denied it if you did. Players might like you if you weren't one of them, but they wouldn't respect you unless you lived by wits and broke the law. In Boston, graffiti had been Macon's entrée: an unprofitable crime, a gray area at best, but it still carried some cachet. He didn't have the time, skills, or energy to paint in New York, though. World-class writers from organized crews dominated the few piecing spots, simple street bombing was thankless and dangerous, the community of writers was secretive, political, and caustic, and the vandal squad was no joke.

Just who these hustlers were that Macon sought to impress was another story: a pantheon he'd downloaded from books and movies and his past who traveled with him still, whose approval kept him honest, gritty, and real despite their being largely imaginary. Mental saloon doors swung open and Macon sauntered past Priest from *Superfly* and Goldie from *The Mack* to bum a smoke off Butch Cassidy and sweep a waiting beer from the bartop. Never mind that Macon had hardly held a burner before last week—only the one time when the drug dealers who hung on Aura's block got so drunk outside the liquor store that they'd started brazenly comparing pieces, passing them around and chatting about weight and range with the enthusiasm of longtime ruddy-faced sportsmen. In the dark thieves' den of Macon's mind, he'd always been a major mover. Pimps he'd crossed the street to walk past, drug dealers he'd lingered outside stores in Boston to observe—sipping soda with one leg cocked back against the wall and one knee jutting forward until his empty can and pointless loitering had embarrassed Macon into moving on—looked up from their billiards games to nod hello. Macon raised his bottle in solidarity.

"Honest answer, Mr. Moves." Nique's hand swept toward him and Macon braved a familiar instant of panic before he caught it in a satisfyingly well-executed pound. Botched handshakes made him feel lastingly lame, the flustered white dude stumbling through the Negro Greeting Ritual. He checked his watch: 9:10. Time to get in the wind if he was gonna make the show.

What you need to do is go someplace quiet, sit down, and think this robbery shit through, Macon's brain chastised. But he wasn't the type to break plans, even with himself, and he liked to do his thinking in stolen snatches of time: between songs, during conversations and commercials, while asleep. Besides, Macon had been waiting years to peep the Nuyorican, to be able to say he'd rocked the mic at America's most famous poetry spot. He drained his brew, said his good-byes, and stepped.

"Well," said Nique, lifting his bottle to salute the door Macon had just closed behind him, "at least your boy there's trying. More than you can say for most of them."

Andre shook his head. “Heroes. It’s always about heroes.”

“Shit,” said Nique. “My new hero is this motherfucker they got on the news tonight. You seen this shit?”

Andre shook his head. “Nah.”

Nique waggled a finger. “This is why I love our people. Only niggas do some shit like this. My man’s a cabbie, right? And for whatever reason, he just flips. He’s put up with enough bullshit from white folks or whatever, and he just flips and robs these two yuppies at gunpoint. Dumps them on the FDR and skates. Channel Nine said he ‘unleashed a racial tirade’ while he jacked them.”

“Macon drives a cab,” said Andre.

“Word? Maybe he knows this guy. Course, the only description they have is that the dude is black. Narrows it down to like ten thousand cats. Then again, knowing Macon, they’re probably drinking buddies.”

Andre jowled one cheek. “Please. Macon barely knows himself. Two words for you, Nique. Harley Koon.”

Chapter Four

Dennis Lavar flicked his wrist and banished the live coverage of Rodney King's desperate can't-we-all-get-along news conference from his modest living room. He turned from the television slowly, ran his palm over the close-cropped bristles of his beard and the meat of his lips, and then dropped it to his side and let the gold-link bracelet slide and settle. For hours now, he'd been imagining he heard the riot rounding the corner of their quiet Compton block.

"I know you think I'm being hard on you, Dominique, but it's for your own good. Nothing but trouble out there."

Nique threw a leg across the leather sofa and settled himself for the lecture. He'd grown up on Pop's politics like home cooking, ransacked his father's bookshelves as a way to understand the old man and discovered Stokely Carmichael and H. Rap Brown—found the entire movement wedged between the cinder-block bookends of his father's workroom. He'd studied up and watched his father watch him, proud of his father's pride. It was just the two of them, and Nique understood how much his father had at stake in raising his son.

They went through Pop's records on Sundays, Dominique DJing and Dennis sitting on the floor, back up against the couch, fingers interlaced behind his head, legs spread under the coffee table, telling Nique what songs to play and where to find each slab of vinyl. Dennis had been collecting albums for thirty years, and there were easily a thousand lined up in cream-colored milk crates along the base of the living-room wall, ordered according to a system only Dennis understood—really just randomness Nique's pops had memorized.

Dominique learned all the words, began to feel the dusty testaments belonged as much to him and his time as to his father and the past. They were streaked with power, these sonic artifacts; they came alive as soon as stylus hissed against vinyl: James Brown popcorn-strutting through the new new heavy jungle funk, chopping down whatever vegetation swayed before him with a *hah!* soul brother number-one machete: *I'm Black and I'm proud. Give it up or turn it loose. I don't want nothing from nobody. Open up the door, I'll get it myself.* The Last Poets standing on the runways of Babylon with flare guns to the skies to lure the revolution into landing: *black people, what y'all gonna do when you wake up and find that you're dead, with maggots and roaches eating the pus out of your prostituted minds and white deathly hands massaging your hearts with red-hot branding irons? Speak not of revolution unless you are willing to eat rats to survive.* Albert Ayler clawing at the speakers, bleating and screeching, witches and devils swirling from his sweating horn bell and that white-heat beard streak shooting from his chin to lower lip like a bolt of lightning, electrifying the jacket photo.

Dennis fisted his hands and propped them on his hips. "I remember the last time folks here tried this, Nique, in '65. I watched black folks burn down their own neighborhoods, smash windows and grab TV sets out the white man's stores and act like they were winning somehow. Brothers carrying stereos back to houses that are charcoal when they get there."

Dennis dropped his pose and went back to pacing the living room, glancing in turns at his son and out the window. "Here we are almost thirty years later, doing the same shit again. That makes me madder than the verdict. I knew those fools would get off, video or not. A black man versus six white cops? Please. I'm old enough to remember Emmett Till. Thought maybe folks would know better than to loot their own neighborhoods this time around, though."

"Nobody's touching anything black-owned, Pop. Just the white stores and the Korean ones."

Dennis stopped pacing and screwed his eyes at Dominique. He never raised his voice; he never had to. Nique was a handful to everyone else, teachers and coaches and the like, but a stare from Dennis cut right through him. Andre and every other friend of Nique's who'd spent time at the house thought Dennis should win Father of the Year.

"Those stores are still in our part of town, Nique. You destroy them, how are folks supposed to eat next week? This is a party to you kids." He swept his palm across the neighborhood. "We had a movement going. Cats were reading, organizing. We were talking revolution."

"And where did all that talking and reading and organizing get you, Pop?" Nique stabbed his chin at the window. "Like you said. Shit is still the same."

"The hell it is." Dennis sat down so his leg touched Nique's. "I got a son in one of the best preparatory schools in Los Angeles. Couple years you'll be in college. You're gonna have access, Dominique. That's revolutionary."

"Huey woulda called it selling out."

Dennis stood and faced the window, folding his hands behind his back. "And where is Huey now?" he asked softly.

"Not on the curriculum at Princeton-Eastham Prep, that's for damn sure."

"But he's on yours. And if you can get what you need from P-E and still keep your priorities in order, that's a revolutionary move. Not running around screaming 'Rodney King' until somebody zaps you with a tazer. This war isn't gonna be fought in the streets,

Nique. Revolutionary thrills without revolutionary skills will get you killed."

It was a line that had been floating around the community for forty years, and Nique felt as histrionic hearing it as Dennis did saying it. Nique shot his father a look far from acquiescence, a shade short of defiance. Only in the past few months had he dared turn such eyes on his pops. It was a development that was not lost on Dennis.

He rejoined his son on the couch, sitting farther away this time. "I spoke to Andre's mother on the phone," he said. "After school tomorrow, you'll go home with him. I'd rather have you there than here until things cool down."

Dominique scowled. "I'm not allowed to come home?"

"Not through a war zone, no. This time tomorrow they'll have called in troops."

"And what about you?"

"I'm gonna work from home tomorrow."

"Can't I just stay home from school?"

"No."

Nique stood up, walked to his room, and slammed the door. He lay on his bed, imagined the mood tomorrow at school, and shuddered in distaste. The skylights built into the ceilings of the forty-million-dollar main campus building allowed plenty of sunlight to filter in, but they blocked rage. The riots would be just another current-events quiz to his classmates. They'd slouch placidly in their seats and it would be business as usual. He and Dre would try to sit by themselves in the cafeteria, hunched over their trays, and as soon as they began to talk, some goofy white kid, one of their friends, would plop down next to them and start flapping his gums about the Lakers game or some chick he wanted to bone.

Nique didn't think he could handle the burden of acting like everything was cool tomorrow. He didn't remember Emmett Till like Pop did; this was the sharpest slap justice had taken in his lifetime. He wanted to cry and lash out, but most of all he couldn't stand to be alone, to sit at his desk or in the living room with Pop, watching the violence on TV in grim, hot silence. He wished he could sleep for a week, wake up and stretch like a cat in the sun and have all this over with. And yet he never wanted to forget this feeling of impotent, sad, restless fury.

Nique turned onto his back, hid his face in his elbow crook, and let imagination place him in the middle of it all, inside the rage and release of the burning streets. Behind closed eyes he saw brotherhood surging, an army of black men roaring up and down the streets and him among them, one with every other newborn soldier, toppling cop cars and pumping fists in a synchronized instinctive dance clipped from a music video. He opened his eyes and sighed until his lungs were empty, feeling he was missing the defining moment of his generation, the call to arms, the fire.

Nique stood up and flipped through his music collection, looking for a tape to listen to. His father scorned hip hop, but rap's aural-ideological DNA helixed through Dennis's record crates. His music was the raw material hip hop had diced and recycled, twisted and reformatted, thrown on a conveyor belt and squeezed through compressors, samplers, and sequencers. The black sounds of the seventies had been fattened for slaughter, intimidated and distorted, chopped and untuned and unkeyed and unpitched, stripped like an abandoned car and rebuilt like a cyborg. Rappers raped music of its musicality, threw a few cents' retribution and a deadpan nod of respect to its parents and then saddled up, riding the unholy metalwork contraption toward the apocalypse as it bucked and snorted fire underneath them. *This shit ain't even music;* the argument was dead to Dominique.

"Who gives a fuck if it's music?" he responded, turning up the volume.

"They're just stealing other people's shit."

"Yeah, yeah, welcome to America. Just listen to the lyrics."

Generation gap in full effect. Dennis grudgingly admitted that rap had potential, but he remained disdainful, found no inspiration in the lyrics of Ice Cube or KRS-One. "Irresponsible bullshit rhetoric," came the pronouncement. "These guys are entertainers pretending to be leaders."

Nique put on his headphones, cushy foam-and-leather joints that sealed him off from any other sound, and reflected that Cube had predicted what was going on outside his window at this very moment: the City of Angels up in flames again, cops versus niggers round infinity just under way beneath the whirring propeller blades and laser searchlights of the ghetto bird, and the odds set at four billion to one in favor of the boys in blue.

"Pop got me thinking last night," he told Dre the next morning as they sat in homeroom, perched on the radiator by the window. From behind her desk, Ms. Gardner gave them the same scorn-and-pity look she did every morning. How sad, her face said, that they insisted on hiding behind those sullen, put-upon demeanors, refusing to acknowledge their good fortune at being at an institution of this caliber, wasting this wonderful opportunity. As always, they ignored her.

Nique leaned closer, pulling his knee up to his chest and brushing invisible dust from his high black Chuck Taylors. "He was saying how black folks riot stupid, burning our own neighborhoods and shit. How we gotta point our guns at something besides our brothers." A hard, crafty glint danced in his eyes. "You know what would happen if every gangbanger in L.A. stopped trippin' off of colors and united to take on the cops?"

"Yes," said Dre, "and so do you. L.A.P.D. would roll down Crenshaw Boulevard crushing lowriders with tanks and blasting anybody dumb enough to be outside past the new seven P.M. curfew. In two weeks every black and Latino male under twenty-five would be dead except the thirty-five percent of us already in jail, who they'd probably wax too, just for good measure. And then Daryl Gates would run for governor." Dre hadn't smiled once all morning, nor unballed his fists. Last night he'd sat in front of the

TV for more than seven hours, watching riot footage and the King tape until sleep glazed his eyes and he collapsed. His mother, for once, had stayed out of the way.

"Don't get grandiose," he told Nique tersely, "and don't let the fire fool you. This is no time for revolution."

"How 'bout retribution?" Nique leaned even closer. "We should beat Harley down this afternoon."

Andre swiveled so he could look at Nique dead on. "Are you nuts? Harley's one of the only cool kids in here. What did he do?"

"Not him. His father."

"Harley fucking hates his dad, Nique, probably more than we do."

"That's not the point. His dad hurt one of ours, now we hurt one of his. Rodney King didn't do anything either, and look what happened to him. The only way black folks are ever gonna come up is if we stop worrying so damn much about which cracker is guilty and fight fire with fire."

"Rodney King was speeding and blowing lines on the freeway, Nique. Harley is sitting in his homeroom, probably listening to 'Fuck Tha Police' on his Walkman."

Dominique stood up, apoplectic with rage, and threw his lanky arms in Andre's face.

"So fucking what? Whose side are you on, anyway? Shit, I'm the one that's gonna lose his scholarship. You're actually paying to go here."

Dre let the insults slide off him and tried to hold Nique to the point. "Harley's our boy."

"All the more reason we should beat his ass. You gotta put personal shit aside for the sake of the cause."

"Yeah, brilliant. Goebbels's 'One Jew' theory remixed for niggers in the nineties."

"Goddamn right. Until we get cold-blooded like them motherfuckers, black folks will keep on losing every time."

"Or, put another way, 'niggers should start acting more like Nazis.' "

Dominique flung an imaginary cigarette to the floor in frustration. "Stop being an asshole. That's not what I'm saying and you know it. Weren't you paying attention when I made you watch *Apocalypse Now*? You got to be willing to cut people's arms off and throw them in a pile if that's what it takes. You got to be willing to eat rats to survive."

"Dominique, what the fuck are you talking about? Why do we have to eat rats? Isn't the food in the cafeteria bad enough?"

Nique dropped his hands and stalked off, then stopped and spun dramatically in the doorframe. Heads popped up all around the room, sensing the imminence of drama. Ms. Gardner bookmarked her copy of *Pride and Prejudice* and tapped her manicured nails nervously against her desk, wondering whether to tell Dominique to sit back down.

"You know what, Dre? You don't want to do shit, fine. I'm too mad for business as usual. I don't care if I do the right thing or the wrong thing. I just want to see some fucking blood—his, mine, whatever. I'll be in the parking lot." He slammed the door behind him.

Ms. Gardner sighed with resignation and returned to her reading. Jeremy Gold approached Dre, wiping blond shags from his face with a hemp-braceleted hand. "Dude, why's Dom so worked up?" he asked.

Dre stared back blankly. The eternal token-brother-at-a-prep-school question bobbed at him again: whether to explain, whether to educate, whether to even bother with these kids. Not for another year, when he would begin smoking pot in earnest, would Andre find even a toehold's worth of common ground with the three hundred Jeremy Golds who comprised Princeton-Eastham's student population.

"Stock market," he said, and followed Dominique.

Halfway down the hall, he decided against catching up; better to leave Nique alone and let him come to his senses. Instead, Andre headed toward Harley's homeroom, only to find him crumpled before his locker, face buried in his hands.

"Hey." Harley glanced up and Dre winced; tear tracks ran from eyes that looked like they hadn't rested in days.

"S'up, Dre," he mumbled, letting his head fall again. "I can't believe they let the fuckers off." He shudder-sighed and swiped his wrist beneath his nose. "Got any drugs?"

"Sorry."

"I mean, the fucking tape . . . It's right there on the fucking tape." A fresh drop dribbled down the worn runway of Harley's cheek. He clenched his fist, then let it go limp. "My dad and the rest of them are having a fucking victory barbecue tonight. I mean . . ."

Andre crouched beside Harley, shoulder to shoulder, and tried to sound calm, comforting. "I know, Harley, I know. There's nothing we can do. Listen, I came to warn you. Dominique is on some kind of crazy eye-for-an-eye trip, which will probably pass in half an hour, but for now he wants to kick your ass to teach your pops a lesson, so you'd better steer clear. Don't take it personal. He's in the parking lot."

Harley's mouth grew hard. He sprang to his feet and headed toward his car with heavy, swift steps. Andre followed, a pace behind, remembering the ride he, Nique, and Harley had taken to Fatburger last month when Harley got his license and gym class was canceled, Harley telling them how his dad had gotten the car for next to nothing at a police auction.

What kind of crappy drug dealer drives a Nissan Sentra? Nique had asked, his mouth crammed full of french fries.

When they reached the parking lot, Nique was pissing flamboyantly on Harley's ride. A wide arc of urine glistened in the sunlight, spattering loudly on the metal hood.

"Hey!" shouted Harley. Nique looked up, tucked away his dick, and swaggered toward the cop's son, glaring.

"I been waiting for you," he said, hooking thumbs into belt loops and standing his ground, legs locked shoulders' width apart. He glanced left and right as if expecting tumbleweeds to blow past.

"Dre says you want to kick my ass," responded Harley, squinting rather than glaring. He sounded more inquisitive than angry. "So, uh, here I am. Beat the shit out of me."

"What?" said Dre.

"Please," said Harley. "It would make me feel a whole fucking lot better. Come on, Nique. Teach my father a lesson. Just, ah, watch the face."

Nique walked toward him. "You ain't gotta ask me twice," he said, arm in motion even before he finished speaking, "and fuck the face." He clocked Harley in the nose and knocked him back a pace. Nique was skinny, but he hit hard and he moved fast.

"Come on, Dre," he shouted, landing a body blow that bent Harley in pain, "get some."

Dre shifted his weight from foot to foot, wrinkled his brow, and shook his head.

Nique threw three more body blows, bouncing on his toes like a boxer, then dropped his hands to his knees and bent, panting. He saw Harley struggling to stand straight, and the realization that his adversary thought the fight was over spurred Nique back to action. He wiped his brow on his forearm, straightened, and pushed Harley with both hands, flicking them out from his chest as if he were passing a basketball. Harley stumbled, off-balance, and Nique kicked his legs out from under him, knocked Harley to the ground and brought his foot down on the kid's arched back again and again. Harley flattened and then curled, knees tucked against his stomach, arms shielding his head.

"Okay," he wheezed, voice muffled by his hands and thick with bloody saliva. "Stop. Please. That's enough."

"The hell it is," Nique said, kicking him again. He was trying to wedge his foot in between Harley's knees, catch him in the chest or throat. "No time-outs left, bitch." He kicked again and stepped back. Hearing Harley speak had calmed him down a bit, thought Dre. He hoped Nique would yell for a while, tire himself out.

"The nerve of this fuckin' cracker," said Nique, glaring at Dre as he gestured to the crumpled body lying between them. He bent at the waist to shout in Harley's ear, like a drill sergeant demanding push-ups. "This ain't no fuckin' confessional!" He reared his leg again and Dre winced at the flat slap of rubber against flesh. Harley groaned and wrenched. "That guilt kinda fades when motherfuckers are beating your punk ass, huh?"

"Okay, Nique, he's had enough," said Dre abruptly. Halfheartedly, he locked his arms around Nique from behind and pulled him a few paces away. Nique twisted backward, looking at him with wild eyes.

"You crazy, nigga? I'm just getting started. You hear me, Harley? Why don't you try to get up like your boy Rodney? Try and make it to your car."

"Nique, homeroom's almost over. Somebody's gonna come out here."

"Do I look like I give a fuck? Come on, Dre, kick him. You'll feel better." Nique wriggled out of Dre's arms, kicked Harley again and stood defiant, hands crossed over his heaving chest. "We're not leaving here until you kick him."

"Hell no."

"Come on. How do you know you won't like it till you try? Go for the face."

Dre looked around. "If I kick him, we can go?"

"Deal."

Dre swallowed, feeling sick, and kicked Harley in the back, harder than he'd planned to. Much harder. Disgust fought back against the surge of power rising in him and disgust lost quickly. Against his will, Dre understood what Nique had meant: If you blurred your eyes to things like friendship, troublesome notions of allegiance, you could find the coldness to do anything. He could pound all his rage into this body, this receptacle, and never see it. Dre unloaded again and a clipped yelp escaped the boy. It jolted Dre back to his senses and he stopped short, foot drawn back in midair. He looked down and it was Harley on the ground again, squirming in pain. Dre dropped his leg and felt his stomach bubble with nausea. He raised his hand to his forehead and touched the same warm sweat that covered him after football practice, a reminder of how hard he'd worked. A rivulet trickled past his ear, and Dre thought he'd vomit. Relief that he was back inside himself tangled with horror at the proof lying before him that he'd been out of control.

Nique looked at him and smiled; Dre refused to meet his eyes. They stood in silence and never heard Mr. Rossini, school lacrosse coach and disciplinarian, swagger over on his parking lot patrol.

"Hey! Walker, Lavar! What are you two doing out of homeroom? The bell doesn't ring for another—" He shuffled sideways through a row of cars and saw Harley lying twisted and blood-streaked on the ground.

"Holy shit!" Rossini yelled, red-faced. He pointed at Harley with the lacrosse stick he always carried. "What the hell is this? What happened?"

Neither Andre nor Dominique had any words. They stood mute, guilty as hell, and finally it was Harley who spoke. He pulled himself up, leaned against his piss-soaked car, and said, "Coach Rossini, this . . . this isn't what it looks like. I fell and hit my head, and Dre and Nique were just helping me up."

Rossini didn't buy it. "You fell and hit your head on what?" he said, staring down the parties he held responsible.

"On my car, I guess. I don't remember."

Rossini grabbed Nique's arm and shook it at Harley. "Why's Lavar covered in blood? You're telling me he didn't hit you? Don't be afraid, son. Tell the truth."

"They . . ." Harley coughed and clutched his stomach. "They didn't do anything. They were just trying to help."

Rossini looked from Harley to Dominique to Andre, his tiny Mesozoic brain thumping along as fast as it could go. "You two come with me," he said, pointing meaty fingers at Nique and Dre. "And you, you'd better get yourself to Health Services before you ruin that nice shirt."

Chapter Five

The world-renowned Nuyorican Poets' Cafe was an inconspicuous little joint on East Third; from the street there was nothing to see but a bald man with neck rolls plugging a doorway with his ass. Macon walked past twice before he realized he'd found it. He paid the five-spot cover and stepped into a long, narrow room pungent with Egyptian Musk, Official Fragrance of the Underground.

Legions of backpack rap kids milled around him like hot atoms, and Macon eye-checked them with a chilled blend of amusement and scorn. The scene spawned such generic denizens these days. Jansports and cargo pants were everywhere, set off with overstated polos, rugbies, and sweatshirts blaring the logos of hip hop designers. Hip hop designers: The phrase echoed oxymoronic in his head. The fact that the world courted hip hoppers these days, tailored fashion and advertising to seduce and reflect them, was still a mindfuck. You could buy your jeans cut baggy at the Gap now, instead of buying a pair six sizes too big and cinching the waist with some crazy industrial-strength belt. The days of appropriation and self-modification were over: Just hit Macy's and grab your b-boy outfit off the rack, slide through Rock & Soul and cop a set of turntables—or, God forbid, CD players—engineered for beat-matching and back-spinning. No need to refit your spray cans with oven-cleaner nozzles anymore; just jaunt over to your local graffiti boutique and pick up a ten-pack of fatcaps.

Macon cut his derision short, realizing how hackneyed the goddamned-kids-today flow sounded in his head. He was no older than these knucklehead new-jacks, but they were of a generation he despised—for their presumption and their ease, the way they'd sauntered into hip hop like it was their parents' living room and thrown their legs up on the coffee table. Hip hop hadn't extorted them for any dues in return for the right to claim it as their own; it had been too busy to make them cover their eyes and count to a hundred and then find the jam session unfolding behind the unmarked door. These kids were hip hop's third generation. Not the pioneers who'd conceived it in an orgy of sacred doubled drumbreaks and presided over its birth in the asphalt schoolyards of the Bronx. Nor the inheritors who'd nurtured the culture through adolescence, studying its brief history compulsively and feeding it bolder sounds, bigger ideas. This was the desultory multitude who'd never known a world in which hip hop didn't dangle from every corner street lamp.

When Macon had started listening—ten years ago, and a good four or five before most of these kids, he guessed as he watched them strut by in their headphones and Kangols *(I'm so real I'ma wear my Walkman even in the club, son, just in case the DJ plays some bullshit)* at a ratio of three males to every female—information had been precious, limited. New York radio tapes, Red Alert on KISS-FM and Special K and Teddy Ted on WBLS, were dubbed and redubbed, passed from hand to hand, brawled over if lost. Macon had trained himself to wake up five minutes before two A.M. on Sundays to tape Boston's only radio show; he couldn't set an alarm or his parents would hear. He'd sneak downstairs and sit in front of their living-room stereo, yoga posing before some ten-watt city lighthouse of a station, ear to the speaker, volume knob at one. Even at such tiny volume, the subsonic ripples strained his parents' unfit speakers and nudged the dial into Spanish feminista talk shows. When Macon memorized the tape, *dime el problema con su esposo mi hermana* cut through breakbeat breathing space inside a static sheath, becoming una parte de la rhyme scheme for all time. Now those cassettes were a reminder that the music was a sliver once, a tiny shard of drum and hard-speak coded into shortwave binary and squatting at the low-rent end of the FM dial, at 90.3 and 89.1, significant degrees below normal body temperature. Those who listened then were arctic nomads, becoming friends for life when they converged on frozen roads to trade supplies.

How, Macon wondered as he cut a path toward the small stage at the back of the club, had the backpack rap set gotten so self-righteous so quickly? These kids were as dogmatic as the bitterest old-school has-beens, oozing with keep-it-realness and wistful reminiscences of a misimagined past in which hip hop hadn't been shackled to capitalism. The backpackers scorned commercial success and radio airplay—*corrupting the culture, yo*—but spent all their money on niche-marketed hip hop accoutrements, from breakdance videos to old-school Pumas. They ordered water at the bar, not for fear of being carded or out of a desire to stay sharp-witted for the freestyle ciphers to come, but because their giddily professed pennilessness nudged them closer to the underground rappers they admired—rappers who for the most part would have traded all the adolescent-male dick-riding for a major-label advance check and used the money to move out of the projects.

This was hip hop's whitest generation yet, the growth factor exponential—to the point where a white presence onstage or a white audience majority came as no surprise—and yet they never seemed to wonder what their proper place was, whether they were lounging at tables marked *Reserved*. Why should they? They were keeping it real. That was their only responsibility, not figuring out what real was, what it was, or for whom they were keeping it. They were masters of affect, strangers to cause—conspirators in a huge, fragile, hypnotic agreement of which Macon refused to believe he was a part: *Okay, easy . . . nobody call anybody out . . . shhh . . . buy each other's records . . . nod your head like this . . . good . . . the important thing to remember is that none of us is full of shit. . . .* He had only himself to blame for hip hop's gentrification, Macon reflected. If people like him hadn't fallen in love with the neighborhood and put down roots, these clowns never would have found the courage to move in and ruin it.

Macon scowled, a touch of claustrophobia tickling his neck as he pretended to scan the room for a friend. Fly women speckled the crowd, and he found a spot along the back wall, posted up and smoldered his eyes at them, hoping in vain to catch some rhythm in return. Macon consoled himself by imagining how his lot would change once he'd busted his poem; hours too late to sign up for the slam, he'd settled for the open mic to follow.

The DJ killed the beat and the hum of the room softened as the host took to the stage to start the show. The eight competing gladiators prepped themselves for battle in the front row, and the diminutive peroxide blonde standing to Macon's left, apparently assuming all back-wall players to be as cynical as she, curled her cocktail to her chest and began a low-spoken commentary. The first competitor, a statuesque black woman, strode to the mic and Macon's neighbor leaned back and crossed her ankles. "I've seen her before," she murmured, turning her lip ring with her tongue in a way that Macon found repulsive and yet sexy. "This oughta be just great."

"Staring into you as we move together as one," the poet intoned, low and throaty, shutting her long-lashed lids and making a slinky, obscure gesture with her copper-bangled right arm as she drew out *one,* "pulsating with a single heartbeat as you come to life inside me . . ."

"Pussy poem," hissed the blonde. "Chick stands up, talks about getting fucked, audience gets hard and eats it up. What bullshit."

Macon smiled. "You a poet?"

She flicked her eyes at him. "No." They clapped politely as the pussy poem climaxed to huge crowd noise and a serious-looking bald-headed brother in boots, baggy blue jeans, and a tight black T-shirt trooped onstage.

"Black Power poet," said the girl. "Wanna bet he'll make a 'Revolution will not be televised' reference?"

"You must come here a lot."

"Just enough to remind myself why it sucks."

"And why's that?"

Without looking away from the stage, she gestured broadly, implicating the entire room. "They're performers, not poets. Nobody deals with language. It's about getting high scores from audience judges who wouldn't know e. e. cummings from B. B. King." Or CeCe Winans, thought Macon, his mind off and running along the random track she had prescribed. Or Dee Dee Bridgewater. He loved this kind of game. G. G. Allin. A. A. Milne. J. J. Johnson. LL Cool J. KK Rockwell. ZZ Top.

The poet, as predicted, was making emphatic use of such phrases as "no justice, just us," and "each one, teach one." Macon groaned, then squinted at the silver lining.

"This probably woulda been the bomb in, like, 1973."

"I'm sure," she responded, "considering he stole the rhyme scheme from the Watts Prophets."

A fat, bearded white guy was up next. "Category three," the blonde narrated. "The self-deprecating poem. Vaguely titillating, incredibly embarrassing, actually a cry for help. Poet looks for sympathy and courage points."

"If you could get paid for jerking off," opened the poet, rubbing one palm viciously against the other in what might have been either showmanship or an unconscious tic, "I'd be a millionaire. I am a master of masturbation, a sultan of self-abuse. If there were Onanism Olympics . . ."

"Three for three," Macon congratulated her, offering his hand. She took it, pumped once, and held it for a few seconds before recrossing her arms.

"I can't take much more of this," she hissed.

"Come on now, you gotta wait till I go on. I want to know which category I fit into." Macon's literary confidence, firm already, was engorging with each reading.

"You sure you want to know?"

"Positive. I'm lead-off on the open mic. What if I buy you a drink to ease the pain?"

"I'll take a Cuervo with a beer back. Thanks."

The Black Power poet, after vanquishing the pussy poet, went on to dispatch a Mohawked punk-rock poet who paced the club while screaming about the day he found his father with a shotgun in his mouth and his brains on the floor. In the finals, however, he was trumped by a woman whose "iron spears of oppression" poem, recited on her knees with eyes closed and hands clasped to her chest, managed to address both the violence of slavery and the politics of sucking dick. It cost Macon two more tequila shots to keep his homegirl around, but it was a small price to pay to have an ally in the house. He'd downed three rum-and-Cokes himself just to keep pace, and by the time the MC introduced him, mangling his last name, it was something of an effort for Macon to navigate the thinning crowd with his usual élan.

"Okay, uh, I'm Macon Detornay and this joint is called 'Mouth to Mouth Resuscitation,' " he said, unfolding the quartered pages from his back pocket. "I wrote it last year, when I was visiting a friend of mine at USC. Sorry I haven't memorized it. Next time, I promise. Okay:

shirtless in the first real day of LA heat
i can see poverty curling back
the edges of the campus
like burning newspaper
LA & fire wedged together forever for me in my mind
good cop bad cop shock drop bad cop
no rupture in the revolution of the loop
of the song

rap is on the microphone:

can't we all just get a bong?

trade you my africa medallion
for the name of your weed spot

no audobon assassins
memphis snipers
or government conspiracies needed

hip hop was born
with a silver nine in its mouth
already cocked & just waiting
for hammer time

my man lajuan is down with single gun theory
claims that same dallas bullet
just been ricocheting around
for like 35 years now

flew thru saigon & the south bronx
moving like the old cartoon singalong dot

bounced thru south africa on a world tour
pit stops from bosnia to watts

caught scott la rock & kids on every block

hit john lennon bounced right off ronald reagan

struck the jackpot when it caught hip hop

but like that retarded kid on tv said

life goes on

meanwhile
i'm tryna deal with a down syndrome of my own

when i reminisce
it's video clips
as baby pics

i feel like
bigger thomas's mother or some shit

it never fails

when they map
rap's family tree
invariably between staggerlee & leroi
some defender of the realm
like me
will invoke richard wright

as if that proves something

i mean hell
try getting my parents
to take responsibility for
some of the shit i've pulled lately

how you gonna be twentysomething years old &
let your great-granddaddy
fight your battles anyway?

looking for inspiration i

slide down the family tree
til i reach the last poets

umar bin hassan
afro aflame
chucking chinese throwing stars
thru white people's spines

a stance later modified

see he ain't talkin bout me
he means um

alright I might be a white devil but

i'm beginning to hate with love and love with hate

i'm down right
i can relate
watch me
cruisin stick n movin showin & provin

manchild in the promised band

hopin he's groovin

if i were a jazz musician
i'd be wishin for an invite to sit in
legs wrapped round my horn case like a barbershop pole

but i'm not
this hip hop
act like you know

so i stay
strapped
with a symbolic list
of anti-colonialist accomplishments
for when somebody ask

who dis
potential brutus
judas iscariot

driving in place &
pumpin mix tapes to demonstrate
the unity of the proletariat

starting to sound like jesse at the convention in 88

my forefathers came here on slaveships
his forefathers came on immigrant ships
but whatever the original ships
we're all in the same boat now

boom shocka lock
hip hop is not plymouth rock

any more than america's the great melting pot

i could recite
a battleworn litany
of moments & events   gasps of death

from the sugarhill gang's
grandmaster caz
grand larceny creative

the borrowed notebook that made rap famous

to the train buff
graff's chemical death bath
somebody said you could actually hear the colors shrieking
as they melted into welfare cutbacks

and all the way up to sprite ads

but nunadat is where it's at

suffice to say the other day

the faded ghost of hip hop's past
      tiptoed to my side & grabbed my wrist

            arms out   pressed us sideways
            fingertips to tips

we did the wave
    b-boy vulcan mindmeld
    b-boy energy ripples twist into infinity

    but then i always been the type to get sentimental
    over shit that might've never existed

so i can't say for sure
if all this means
    that hip hop's not as raw
    or that i ain't twelve no more

then again   check out some of these cats who are

leave it to a music that saturation mined
the backlog annals of recorded history
lookin for the perfect beat

to double back & diagnose itself
with advanced acute nostalgia
for its own barely vanished youth

you'd think hip hoppers
would be natural historians   correct
but only for eight digital seconds at a time

Macon refolded the paper slowly, drawing out his face time, and nodded humbly at the floor as the audience accorded him a smattering of applause. He looked up to realize that the room had half-drained during his reading, but he told himself it was to be expected; folks only came for the slam. The sliver of Macon that had expected to be mobbed by newborn fans was disillusioned, as usual, and as usual his ego swooped gracefully to the rescue, catching his self-image on the first bounce. Fuck all that theatrical bullshit, he thought as he returned to his spot against the wall, I hit motherfuckers with some content and if they're not ready for it, then fuck them. This place is wack, anyhow. Another ten years, hip hop'll be like jazz: The only black folks in the club'll be onstage.

"So what's the verdict?" Macon asked, hoping he sounded like he didn't care. The blonde smiled at him, and Macon chose to interpret the sight of her gleaming upper teeth, the front two endearingly crooked, with a liberal dose of self-aggrandizement.

"Not bad at all." He tried not to hear pity in her voice.

"Yeah? It was okay?"

"I'm willing to go with okay. Now stop fishing for compliments. That's not my style." Her style—it was a loophole, and Macon squeezed himself through it: *It isn't that my poem wasn't dope, it's that she doesn't want to say so.* Macon scoped her when she looked away and told himself she was playing it cool because she liked him, but he didn't believe it. New York loomed large and menacing, and for a moment Macon felt inconsequential, mortal, a yellow leaf spiral-flitting to the ground only to be taken up by the current of rainwater in the gutter and whisked down the street and gone. The suburbanity of the image disturbed him.

The blonde stuck out her hand. "I'm Logan." A roving stage light lit up her aquamarine eyes and they pinned Macon like a butterfly. He went limp with strange embarrassment, as if she'd caught him doing something nasty, glimpsed some hidden lameness. Macon felt awkward in his clothes—hot, itchy, smelly—and wondered if the backpackers' uniforms shielded them from some pernicious radiation to which he wasn't hip.

"Macon. This is my first time reading in New York." It sounded like an apology. "I'm from Boston."

"Really?" She cocked her head. "Where'd you go to high school?"

"Newton South?"

Logan frowned. "That's not Boston. That's the suburbs. Birthplace of the Fig Newton."

Macon's heart punctuated her line with a rim shot; he felt himself begin to perspire and wanted to bolt then and there, before Logan called him out further, unearthed something horrible in him. You need to chill, he told himself, brushing back his hair as an excuse to squeegee the sweat from his forehead. She wouldn't be talking to you if she didn't like your poem.

"Got me," he admitted, going for rueful. Fuck did rueful sound like? He'd never tried rueful before. "I just say Boston because most people have never heard of Newton. I wasn't trying to front."

"Yeah, sure," Logan teased. "I'm from Cambridge," she explained. "I went to Rindge and Latin."

"Really?" It meant he could name-drop Beantown graffiti artists, place himself inside a tradition of bad-man neon hand-skills, earn her respect that way. "I went bombing with a lot of Cambridge cats. Maybe you know my boy—"

Logan cut him off. "Probably," she said. "Listen, I'll tell you what. Let's skip the name game and just bond over candlepin bowling. You know there's no such thing in this city?"

"That's horrible," said Macon, affecting a look of playful dismay. He was pretty sure he nailed it, and fought the urge to raise his arms like a gymnast after dismount. He'd been bowling maybe three times in his life, all at grade-school birthday parties. What a weird thing to bring up, he thought. Maybe she didn't like my poem because she's deranged.

The lights swaddling Logan chose that moment to swing elsewhere, and she and Macon were cast into shadows. "It is," she said. "New York might have everything else over the Bean, but it'll never be home to me until somebody builds some candlepin lanes."

"You might like big-ball bowling," Macon said, sidestepping double-entendre landmines. "Maybe we could go sometime." Logan smiled and flipped her tongue ring. Her eyes pulsed at him in the dark.

"I doubt it," she said. "But call me if you ever read again."

I'm a pimp, Macon told himself as he walked out the front a quarter clock-flip later, Logan's number scribbled across the back of his poem and vague, out-of-focus sex-with-Logan movies playing in his mind. Forgotten were his tepid reception, his disappointment with the club, the strange panic that had bubbled up under the heat of Logan's stare. Macon jogged to the subway station like a home-run hitter circling the bases, caught the R to Times Square, transferred to the 2 Express, and felt like a bona fide New Yorker until the train passed Ninety-sixth Street and began traveling east, a subway quirk that left him no choice but to exit not at 116th and Broadway, under the protective eyes of the fake Roman statues adorning Columbia's main entrance, but across the park at 116th and Lenox, a sketchy neighborhood at two in the morning even if you knew your way around.

Chapter Six

Shortest distance between two points is a straight line, Macon reminded himself, trudging resolutely toward the park that separated Columbia from Harlem. Besides, people always exaggerate these things. Can't be afraid to walk in your own city. That's the first step toward self-segregation.

Broken glass crunched underneath his boots and Macon snapped into Indian hunter mode, super-alert and darting his head whenever a twig cracked, gauging the ramifications of each rat scurrying across his path and making the appropriate spiritual recalibrations. He was testing himself, granting danger the opportunity to meet him without actually inviting it. He wanted to emerge unscathed and be able to say, *People are tripping. The park is fine at night.* And then he'd never set foot there after dark again.

Macon followed the left-leaning pathway to the top of the first hill. A notty-bearded black dude staggered into view around the next bend, waving a goose-down jacket as he approached Macon. Neither of them spoke in words. The cat mumbled something garbled and garrulous, jacket draped over his arm as if he were a wine steward and the filthy fucking thing a lace napkin, and Macon replied by putting sound into his exhalation, making a noise like *nuhh* as he walked by. "Not even the season for that shit," he muttered, wiping sweat from his forehead and shaking it from his hand onto the pavement. Macon turned his head sideways, checking out his shadow underneath the streetlights and the scant moon, hoping to see a Classic American Profile. Instead, his face was stretched flat against the ground, pale and distorted.

He made another turn, emboldened by the success with which he'd navigated past the crackhead, glanced up and saw the huge frame of a man in front of him, outlined against the moonlight.

"Yo." A deep voice, bouncing off the trees. "Ayo. C'mere a second. You." A tall, thick brother in a black skull cap walked into the light, massive arms dangling loosely from his shoulders. Macon froze. "C'mere," the man said. "I ain't gonna hurt you." He turned and hollered back behind him. "I found somebody. Let's do it." The distant response sounded like hand slaps. "I said come here," the man demanded again, flaring the nostrils of his wide nose. Macon gangled toward him.

"Follow me." The brother ambled off the road, into the darkness, and Macon did as he was told, scared witless, too afraid to run. He saw nothing but the man's broad back in front of him, gliding boldly through the underbrush. Sticks broke underneath the man's feet with a violence that made Macon's heart beat even faster. He didn't turn around to look at Macon once, as if the thought that his captive might turn and run had never crossed his mind. Or as if the man were hoping he would make a move.

Clammy sweat pasted Macon's clothing to his skin, but he didn't dare to lift his shirt and let his skin breathe. Any suspicious motion might provoke his captor to whirl around and slap him to the ground.

The man stepped into a clearing and the noise of his footsteps abated. He crossed his arms and hulked, immobile. The woods were still save for the shallow sounds of Macon's breath. Suddenly a flashlight blazed, and Macon realized he was surrounded by six large black men, all standing or copping cholo-squats, all dressed in black from skullies to boots.

"Welcome to the People's Cooperative Guerrilla Theatre," boomed the sentry who had snared him, thrusting a paperback at

Macon, "an aggressive, community-based literacy program headquartered here in Morningside Park. We recruit randomly and don't take no for an answer. Tonight's reading is of Henrik Ibsen's classic *A Doll House.* We would be honored to have you play the role of Nora. Are you familiar with the play?"

"Uh, no, no I'm not," stammered Macon. He blinked, befuddled, and almost wet his pants in relief. "And actually, I'm kind of tired. It's two-thirty in the morning. Why do you perform so late? And in the woods?"

A squatting man sprang to his feet and rushed at Macon. "Arms up," he barked. Macon jumped back, then obeyed. The man bent and snaked a tape measure around Macon's waist. "Size ten, size ten," he muttered, and remerged with the shadows.

"There isn't a whole lot of support in the community," explained the sentry. "Not since we expanded our focus beyond African-American playwrights. It's hard enough getting black folks to come see theater to begin with, but do you know what it's like trying to convince the Frederick Douglass Playhouse to let you do *The Importance of Being Earnest* or *Rosencrantz and Guildenstern Are Dead*?"

"I can imagine," said Macon. "But what's wrong with African-American playwrights? I think—"

"We ain't a monochromatic people!" shouted the sentry. "I got a lotta colors in my closet, you understand? Black man got a right to wear pink when he damn well pleases. Got a right to wear turquoise and chartreuse and motherfucking polka dots if we want to. I ain't just a raisin in the sun. I'm a tomato in the rain forest."

"A cantaloupe in the desert!" someone bellowed.

"A dandelion in a fine sea mist!"

"I understand." Macon nodded. Bereft of other options, he decided to be the best damn Nora the People's Cooperative Guerrilla Theatre had ever seen.

"Which only makes the work we do more vital," resumed the

sentry with an air of satisfaction. "Costume!" He clapped twice. "Chop-chop."

The man with the tape measure returned, a long floral-print dress laid across his arms. "This oughta fit just great," he whispered. Macon stared at him, eyes wide, then at the sentry.

"Over your clothes is fine," the sentry said, to Macon's continued relief. "Now let's get started. Act One, Scene One. A small townhouse in the center of Oslo . . ." Macon stepped into the dress. The sentry zipped him up.

Chapter Seven

"What happened to you?" asked Andre over his shoulder, straightening the piles of folded T-shirts in his dresser drawer. "You get laid or something?"

"Waylaid." Macon rubbed his eyes. He'd taken his final bow at four in the morning, accepted a bouquet of black lillies from the People's Cooperative Guerrilla Theatre, and stumbled home to nightmares.

"How was the Nuyorican?"

"Pretty wack. How was freshman orientation this morning?"

"Very educational."

"How so?"

"I learned there are a lot of stupid motherfuckers here."

"Anything else?"

"Let's see . . ." He tapped two fingers to his upper lip, then raised them in recollection. "Apparently, somebody in Housing decided to play a joke and make the fifth floor of John Jay the All Dave Floor. Most of the Daves are pretty pissed. What else . . ."

Macon looked down at the bedsheets twisted around his frame. He was a violent sleeper. "When do classes start, anyway?"

"Today, fool. They assigned us academic advisers; you're supposed to meet with them before you register."

Macon threw off the covers, swung his legs onto the floor, and rifled through the untouched information packet on his desk. "Dr.

Enzo Palermo-Wang, professor of biology. I'm sure he knows a shitload about which English classes I should take."

"Mine taught grad-level Farsi, dude. She didn't even know we had a poli-sci department. Skip it." Andre closed the last drawer and sat down.

"It's not like we have that many choices, anyway," said Macon. "Gotta take Lit Hum, Art Hum, Music Hum."

"Put Deez Nuts in Your Mouth and Hum."

"Cute." Macon flipped through his coursebook. "Here we go: Seminar in Black Fiction: Weldon Johnson to Baraka. Hell yeah. Professor A. Jenson. Ever heard of him?"

"Her. She published a book called *Why I Feel Like Bigger Thomas and Look Like Mary Dalton: Black Power and White Feminism.* I read part of it in high school."

"First class is at six. Interested?"

"Nah. I'ma chill, hit Intro to Black Studies at quarter to five, then try and holler at this Barnard chick I met last night. I love the fact that we've got this huge reservoir of women right across the street."

"They're supposed to be chickenheads, though."

"Exactly, dude, exactly. You ain't checking nothing out before six?"

"Gotta work."

An hour later Macon was behind the wheel, unshowered, unshaven, and unsure. Duct tape covered every ID number in the cab, just in case. He steered aimlessly, meandering through Midtown and ignoring white passengers for their own good. The urge to rob them was too strong, and so for the first hour of his shift, Macon only picked up one fare: an old Asian woman whom he shuttled across Central Park to East Ninetieth without incident. There was a delicious pleasure in restraining himself, driving past these suits and knowing he could pick up and pick off any one of them; they'd stand shaking and dispossessed wherever he chose to leave them, with Macon's castigations burning in their ears and their sense of privilege wrenched loose. How long would he hold out before he chose one? Who knew. He would make an art of it, let his instincts turn the wheel while his mind wandered.

A little mood music, perhaps. He turned on Hot 97 but they were playing R&B and he flicked off the radio, disgusted, stewed for a moment and remembered he was in New York and turned it back on and pressed scan. The numbers gyrated across the dial and Macon passed through foreign regions: rock and jazz and Spanish music, more jazz and then, finally, at the tip of the dial, a whimsical college DJ, bless his heart, was rhythm-scratching a bass drop over the "Ain't No Future in Your Frontin" instrumental, a funky, forgotten, painfully obvious blending of two classic breakbeats which had yielded MC Breed's only hit and put his hometown of Flint, Michigan, on the map for a hot second. Macon nodded with bump-and-grind nostalgia, waiting for the DJ to stop teasing and drop whatever it was he kept hinting at with his limber left hand.

And here it came. Oh, shit. "The Nigga You Love to Hate." When word had trickled through Boston that Ice Cube had hooked up with the Bomb Squad, Public Enemy's production team, for his solo record, the cross-coastal handshake had been an alliance of such magnitude, a got-your-back move of such potency, that it had filled Macon with surging uplift. It was a moment on par with Luke Skywalker's *Return of the Jedi* back-flip-off-the-plank-catch-the-light-saber-from-R2-and-start-fucking-fools-up, or that chapter at the end of every Hardy Boys book when just as things are looking hopeless, their pops and two of his buddies bust down the door and double up their fists.

And then the song was in full cacophonous rollick and it was April 29, 1992, again, and all Macon wanted to do was scream *Rodney King!* and kill every white person he saw, starting with his town and ending with himself. Macon walked out of his house that night and didn't make it four blocks to the train stop. As he juked through the sleepy streets of suburbia, every quiet house was an affront. Lamps glowed pleasantly behind windows. Living rooms flickered with television, the white noise of laugh tracks fizzing from open windows. Kids did algebra homework upstairs and Macon sat on the clean, grassy curb, three thousand geographic and racial and economic miles from ground zero and in no danger at all, and cried for the first time in years. He wanted to see some fucking flames, to make some if he had to. He peered into anonymous windows and ripped at blades of grass like a three-year-old and felt the violence race around inside him.

What were they all watching in there? Macon's mind composed a montage, quick-cuts from the greatest hits of U.S. entertainment: Amos 'n' Andy blackface crooning, Ali roaring over Liston, Louis Armstrong knee-deep in soap bubbles, wearing a leopard-skin toga in some 1930s b-flick with his trumpet in his hand, the good Dr. Heathcliff Huxtable surrounded by his loving brood of bougie laughing children. Courthouse cameras capturing the wholesome grins and hearty handshakes of Emmett Till's acquitted killers, fire hoses knocking folks across the block as Brooklyn turns to Birmingham in Spike Lee's *Do the Right Thing,* Abernathy freeze-frame pointing at the skyline as King slumps dead onto the terrace floor, stage lights glinting off the highlights in Chuck Berry's processed hairdo as he duckwalks down into forever, George Wallace all bad teeth and rigid fingers in the doorway of a Southern college, Big Jay McNeely blowing high notes on his back on the bar-top as frantic Marlboro-sleeved whiteboys pump their fists. And finally the gruesome dance of billy clubs, boots, and tazers across the prostrate, foggy form of Rodney King, a recital Macon had memorized.

Outside, under the visible infinity of sky, was no place to be when you felt the world collapsing. Better to go somewhere with a ceiling, so you could pretend that elsewhere might be different. But this was the same sky they had in Los Angeles, and Macon felt like this moment, this hollowness, would stretch forever. Life could never untwist. He'd still be weeping, quietly, years from now as he took out the trash and fed the dog and checked his kids' homework.

He sucked down a deep, shuddery breath and wiped his nose against his wrist and stood up, knowing he wasn't going downtown to meet Lajuan and bomb the outside of the warehouse in industrial Braintree they'd been scoping. He wondered how long Lajuan would wait before going home or hitting the spot by himself, and then it struck Macon that he wasn't there at all. Why would he be? Lajuan was somewhere thinking fucked-up thoughts too, on his rooftop or the corner where the men stood, outside Giant Liquors.

Part of Macon wanted to be there, the only whiteboy milling angrily about and pounding fists against mailboxes, trying to figure out how riots started, plotting what to loot. Part of him always wanted to be there, but tonight it was a different part. Tonight Macon wanted to be Whiteness Itself, not to blend in but to tear his shirt off and blind them with the paleness of his skin and let them claw it from him, make his contribution to the struggle by providing whiteness for the stomping. The part of him that wanted it was weak, though, too weak to act. And what it truly wanted, Macon knew now, was absolution, not abuse. To make its sacrificial gesture and be turned down, told Not All White People Are Like That.

He walked the rest of the way to the T stop just to do something. The first train that pulled in was going outbound, deeper into the suburbs, but Macon didn't care. He hunkered on the lurid orange seat with elbows on his knees, and at the next stop three white cops got on the train and stood together in the middle of the car: bulky, fleshy, uncomfortably stuffed into their uniforms. Avoiding people's eyes, then giving them the once-over when they looked the other way. As eager to pick a fight as any high-school bully.

Macon clenched his jaw until his cheeks rippled, and stared

bloody murder at the sides of their heads: an imaginary act of courage. The way their meat hooks rested atop their service revolvers was grotesque. They felt good about being hated, it was clear; had learned to regard the hatred with contempt and the people who hated them as criminals, potential if not actual.

Macon got off at the next stop. The station was the fulcrum of a small commercial district; next to the tracks lay a parking lot and across the street were stores: a post office, a barbershop, a deli. Everything closed promptly at six. You couldn't get a bite to eat around here after dark, thanks to blue laws intended to preserve the burb's Quaint Village Charm.

For once Macon was thankful for the soulless, leafy quiet, so different from the crosscurrents of music and conversation that made him feel so recklessly alive when he hung on Aura's treeless block. His all-black painting coveralls hung damp and baggy; he felt small and weak, malnourished, empty. It only took a few minutes to go from thinking the crying would never end to knowing he'd never cry again. Sadness dried and hardened, tightened on his face like sweat. Froze into salt and anger. Evaporated, turned to pain, then rained again.

Waiting for the first new drops, Macon swiveled his head and saw a cop car squatting empty and alone in the parking lot, a regular cruiser just like the one Lajuan had been thrown up against last week. They'd stopped and searched him for no reason in front of the bodega on his block, twisted his arm behind his back so hard he'd thought it broken: a white and black duo who drove off covering their badges. The old men playing Beat the Champion timed chess across the street had looked over from their folding chairs, their eyes level with Lajuan's as he lay facedown on the cop car, but they only met his stare for a moment. They were embarrassed to look too long, Lajuan told Macon the next day. Been playing chess on that same block since the days of Joe Louis and couldn't do a thing but look away.

Macon tried to remember what he'd seen first, sitting there at the train stop: the trash can or the newspaper bin. The moment when he took the lighter and the spray paint from his pocket was the one he'd never forgotten. Sometimes he and Aura practiced piecing in nasty, vermin-filled alleys, the better to be ignored in, and Aura had figured out that not even rats are stupid enough to keep fucking with you once you demonstrate the ability to shoot fire, so Macon always carried the ingredients for a flamethrower when he went painting at night.

The trash can was solid metal, rusted on the inside from wet garbage. They'd already replaced them in the city with the grated kind—harder to start a fire in—but out here in the burbs they hadn't bothered. The can was next to a recycling bin piled high with *Boston Globes,* artifacts from the commuter ritual of throwing out the day's news at journey's end to preserve the work/home dichotomy. Each late-edition paper was folded past the front-page flames consuming black Los Angeles and open to the sports section. The Red Sox win again!

Newspaper burned too quickly, so Macon stepped out of his coveralls and threw them in the can, too, figuring they'd catch for sure because of all the aerosol fumes with which they were saturated. In Nikes, boxers, and his threadbare *Welcome to the Terrordome* T-shirt, he lifted the trash can sideways to his chest and found it lighter than expected, carried it over and threw it clean through the windshield of the cop car. The glass collapsed around it with a beauty that reminded Macon of the way a wave will sometimes break, furling over itself and smacking the sand with a perfect circular sound. Even the shards, the tiny bitlets, glittered in the moonlight like a whole shitload of diamonds.

The trash can rolled to a quiet stop on the front seat, half its contents spilling out, and even though he should have been concerned about the crash and acted quick, Macon was cool. There wasn't another soul in the world right then, just Macon and the ghosts of a thousand cops, a million handcuffed kids, smoke drifting east across the continent. He stood for a good five minutes, staring at what he had done, not quite crying but breathing in big soblike gasps, before he clambered up the car's hood like a little kid, as if this crippled monster were his jungle gym, flicked his lighter and aimed a blast of Krylon flat silver and brought the flames dancing in his head into the world.

The coveralls flared up immediately. Macon made sure everything was burning good and strong, that the fuzzy cop floor mats themselves were thoroughly aflame, before he rolled down off the hood and ran across the parking lot and waited underneath a streetlight.

If what he'd heard was true, it wouldn't take long for the fire to reach the gas line and spread to the fuel tank, and then *kaboom.* Lajuan had this uncle they called Revolutionary Stan, because all he talked about was When the Revolution Comes. His hobby was explosives. He wore army fatigues with a Black Panther Party button on the heart, and Macon liked him as soon as they met because Stan lifted his nappy, balding head up from the fridge and said, "Lajuan, get this whiteboy outta my kitchen before I tan your hide." Every time Macon saw him after that he made sure to have something with him he knew Stan would like, a book like *Soul on Ice* or *Seize the Time* and once a Gil Scott-Heron tape, and soon Stan thought Macon was ridiculous and later they got cool. That was something most white folks didn't get: "Fuck white people" was almost always a statement made of mesh, nothing absolute or personal. It was caution, logic, history. Not all snakes are poisonous, but only a crazy man runs around hugging every snake he sees until he finds a good one.

Revolutionary Stan might not have had a job or a girlfriend, but he knew a few things about destroying cars. Orange started flaring out from underneath the body, quick flashes of flame, and then all of a moment the whole thing just blew and automotive shrapnel was twirling through the sky and rattling down onto the pavement and the smell of burning tires wafted past him. In thirty seconds the whole char-black thing was nothing but an arcane sculpture, almost unrecognizable. Macon walked over, close enough to hear it sizzle, and rubbed soot from the wreckage underneath his eyelids like warpaint.

He sat down in his underwear on the cold asphalt, brought his knees up underneath his chin, rocked back and forth, and watched the rubble smolder itself down to practically nothing. He didn't so much feel better as less alone, as if the ashes stinging his cheeks and watering his eyes connected him to something. He'd unlocked a secret weapon in the cosmic game of Rock, Paper, Scissors: Lawbook beats textbook, but matchbook beats them all. His former identity had been erased, like superheroes' when they fall into vats of toxic waste and leave their mild-mannered ways behind, shouldering the mantle of power, unwanted though it may be.

"The Nigga You Love to Hate" ended, and Macon brought his taxi to a halt on Greenwich Avenue and allowed a middle-aged white man, casually dressed, to lumber into the backseat. Why this guy? Macon wondered, staring through the rearview as the man seat-belted himself in, palmed his chin, and stared placidly out the window. What's he done?

"One Sixteenth and Broadway, Columbia University, please."

Macon turned the music off and drove. He knows why, thought Macon. It doesn't matter if I do. He knows.

Mr. Cavanaugh. That's who he looked like. Something about the guy's thin, flinty lips. Mr. Cavanaugh from the Brookline art store, who'd gotten jacked for hundreds of dollars' worth of spray cans all because of his own mistrust, so many spray cans that he'd finally locked the aerosol section behind glass. Month after month, Lajuan and Aura had sauntered up and down the narrow aisles being black, hands pocketed, and while Mr. Cavanaugh followed surreptitious and suspicious, Macon crammed his knapsack full of fatcaps, cans of Krylon, Magnum 44s, felt-tipped markers for their blackbooks, even Rustoleum when it was still around, and slipped out the door while Mr. Cavanaugh was still trailing his decoys.

Or Mr. Andrews, Aura's guidance counselor at Newton South, where Aura and a few dozen other black kids got bused to integrate the system and escape the crumbling Boston schools. Same bulging Adam's apple, making him look as if he were perpetually lurching forward. Andrews had scheduled weekly meetings with Aura freshman year, taken a special interest in his studies, social life, and family. The meetings Aura hadn't skipped he'd filled with fabricated drama, and Andrews had hunched toward him, wide-eyed, eager to digest the latest installment in the cramped, drug-infested welfare nightmare that Aura alleged was his life. By mid-October, Andrews had called in Aura's mother to congratulate her on her son, taking her hand as he professed his sorrow at the violent ends met by her sons Raekwon (a promising basketball player gunned down over a Twix bar), Yusefalitis (his chitlins poisoned by a rival crack czar), and Shaka Yoohoo (a child preacher, also gunned down over a Twix bar). Aura had been grounded for a month behind that shit.

When Andrews took him out for breakfast near semester's end, presented Aura with a copy of *I Know Why the Caged Bird Sings* and told him that he was the subject of a paper Andrews had just had accepted by the *American Journal of Secondary Education* called "Teaching the Unteachable: Inroads to the Inner City," Aura had demanded half the publication fee. Andrews had explained that that wouldn't be ethical; he made a modest donation to the United Negro College Fund in Aura's name instead.

Macon turned left at Ninety-sixth Street, passed Riverside Drive, and pulled over on an isolated stretch of road along the water. "Excuse me," the man in the backseat ventured. Before he could further pursue his inquiry, an arm snaked through the small gap in the plastic and a gun was in his face. The man threw his hands up on instinct, staring transfixed into the round black hole from which death flew.

"Leave your wallet on the seat and walk, motherfucker," Macon growled, ducking behind the partition. He could hardly see the cat. "Look back, I'll bust a cap in your flabby white ass." It occurred to him that this guy probably had no idea what that meant. But context ought to make it fairly clear.

"You people are a fucking plague on this planet," Macon couldn't resist adding as the man clambered—sweaty, weak, pathetic—for his wallet, mouth going jowly as he bobbed for breath. The epidemic flavorlessness of white men, their arthritis of the soul, sickened Macon; that oblivious lack of style was at the root, even, of his frustration with himself.

"Hurry up," he prompted. "Get the fuck outta here." The victim scurried. It wasn't as exciting as it had been the first time; the rush was quieter but in its place was cold new confidence, a steely professionalism that gratified Macon almost as much. He wheeled the cab around and drove downtown. The shift had just begun.

Chapter Eight

Intro to Black Studies, Room 415 Hamilton Hall, 4:45 P.M., Associate Professor of American Studies Umamu Shaheed Alam presiding: three hundred plus two dime-sacks of esteemed chocolate-brown scholarship poured into an expertly tailored girth-streamlining double-breasted olive suit, accented with Armani eyewear and compromised by rubber-soled load-bearing loafers.

In the front row of the cavernous slant-seated lecture hall, Andre slouched next to a light-skinned honey in a headwrap. She'd smiled back at him, then unsnapped a leatherbound notepad and crossed her legs, pen poised, preparing to look busy instead of sideways until class started. The hall was full when Professor Alam entered, swinging his legs around his belly in an overweight pimp-shuffle. He strode directly to the podium and tapped the mic twice with a sausage forefinger, silencing the room.

"Good, ah, afternoon to you all." He held up a shiny red-black-and-green hardback and gave a practiced smile. "I'm sure some of you have read my book, *Black to the Future. The New Yorker* called it a 'much-needed guide to gangsta culture and black youth.' If not, don't worry, it's on the syllabus. You'll find it under my former name, Boyd Randow, which I changed two years ago. Umamu Shaheed Alam means 'esteemed prince and wise leader.' "

Andre clicked his pen and opened his ratty notebook, the same one he'd used all through senior year at Princeton-Eastham Prep.

He'd never been one of those back-to-school buy-new-supplies kids. A notebook was a notebook; you used it till you filled it. *Why is it,* he scribbled, *that fools always change their names to some impossibly grandiose shit? How come you never meet a cat whose junk means 'midlevel bureaucrat' or 'lecherous drunken retard'?*

"My book," Alam was saying, "has met with considerable success. I've been very lucky. I was a poor young brother growing up, from the streets of Miami. Put myself through school. My mama was a factory worker all her life. Daddy drove a city bus until he left. Now, I drive a Range Rover." He reached into his pocket and held up a shiny set of keys, dangling from a gold pendant reading *USA*. "I've been interviewed in *Vibe* and *Essence,*" Alam continued, "and I'm in negotiations with BET for my own show, *The Rap on Rap*. And even though I'm a tenured professor now, I'm still true to the game. Ya heard? I still love my Black Queens." He stopped and scanned the room, presumably for black queens. "As I argue in my book," he went on, "the young African-American brothers and sisters who are making these songs need to be supported and celebrated, not silenced."

Alam took a step back from the lectern. What's he waiting for? Andre wondered. Applause? The professor pushed his spectacles up the bridge of his perspiring nose, eye-surfed the class, and paused momentarily on the swells of Andre's neighbor's chest. She crossed her arms and he resumed his lecture. "You see," Alam explained, "a lot of my colleagues in the academy don't understand that rappers are some of our most talented actors and storytellers. That's why a brother like myself has got to get 'em in the ring and do a l'il boxing!" He stepped out from behind the podium and began rocking back and forth, from his heels to the balls of his feet, hands up around his shoulders, class rings flashing from both hands. " 'Murder was the case that they gave me,' " he recited, transposing the languid lyrics into an enthusiastic, preacherly refrain. " 'I can't die, my boo's about to have my baby.' " Alam looked around the room, trying to gauge how his shit was going over. Students seemed to be avoiding his eyes. "Snoop Doggy Dogg," he enthused, "Dogg Pound Gangsta for life!"

"I consider myself the Academic Gangsta," he went on, stepping back behind the podium. "Gangsta meaning Goal-Achieving Nigga Gonna Stay True Always. Nigga meaning Never-Ignorant Go-Getting Asiatic. I'ma continue to defend rap, brothers and sisters, no matter how the words of an educated black man, a best-selling author, might intimidate rap's critics."

"Everything about it?" The question, high-pitched and incredulous, came from the distant rear. Andre spun in his seat, grinning in recognition. Here we go.

"Pardon me?" asked Alam, his tone making it clear that what he meant was *shut the fuck up*.

"I said, you wanna defend everything about hip hop? What about the violence? What about the misogyny?"

Alam squinted, but the recessed lights shaded his interlocutor's face. He was debating a mystery man.

"As I argue in my book," Alam said, hefting it again, "rappers are postmodern actors interrogating the dislocation of organic sensibilities. We don't demand responsibility or predicate realism from the characters Arnold Schwarzenegger plays, so why should we insist that rappers conform to some notion of authenticity? So what if they claim to be real—that's what actors do. Why can't we just enjoy the fiction?"

Go 'head, Macon, slay this joker, thought Andre, and he turned, together with his classmates, toward the anticipated comeback.

"It's easy to celebrate hip hop if you call it fiction, Professor. But if it's fiction, nobody has to answer for anything—not rappers or the people responsible for the problems rap addresses. If it's fiction, we're just crying wolf."

"If it's fiction, it's art!" Alam boomed into the podium mic, remembering that superior technology was at his disposal. "Rap's critics are trying to dilute art with politics and denigrate the form."

Macon tried to interrupt, but he couldn't compete with the sound system and Alam knew it: rode roughshod over him and ignored the raised hands sprouting all around the room.

"As I argue in my book," Alam continued, crossing his arms over his chest, "rap is here to stay, and it is what it is." The hands began to waver, flutter, droop, and drop as students realized the moment had been contained, the space reclaimed. Andre kept his up, dying to ask, "How much respect can you have for something you refuse to criticize?" and "You call that an argument?" and wondering why the academic discourse on hip hop always boiled down to uninformed attacks versus overzealous defenses, both sides dipping from the binary debate in new Range Rovers.

Macon, livid at being silenced, leapt from his seat and disappeared through a rear exit, the door exclamation-point slamming behind him. A brown shopping bag containing twenty-two wallets, nineteen neckties, and more than four thousand dollars in cash pendulated from his clenched fist.

Chapter Nine

Macon flicked a switch and the off-duty sign lit up atop the cab. He was only driving as a way to think; the four grand he'd clocked yesterday was quit-while-you're-ahead dough, and Macon intended to cruise through one final shift, park his cab at the garage, turn in his keys with nary a word of explanation, and stroll away without pushing New York City's limits any further.

Fuck a culture, Professor Alam, he thought, jaw flexing to match his forearm on the wheel as he dipped and bobbed through the streets. Hip hop's a superpower worn incognito by cats like me, who move with the venom of every rhyme ever spit, cleave courses with the cold-fusion speed-of-sound precision of every turntable cut scratch slice transform and crossfade, and think with the dexterity of every theatric unsolved b-boy battle tactic, from showstop uprock down to linoleum headspins and impossible whirling-dervish cardboard axis chiropractics. I chew on gnarled roots, rock grimy sweatpants hoodies and boots, throw cold steel in motherfuckers' unsuspecting faces and skate away unseen, muttering knockout punchlines in cartoon-bubble frozen breath. Then I dip into a phone booth and emerge jiggified, in tailored clothes with refined flows, my beard trimmed down to elegance, gesturing Shakespearian and quoting Machiavelli in a tone that makes the Western canon bawl.

So what if hip hop turned out not to be the Revolution like we hoped? So what if all my one-time idols are withered and ridiculous and KRS-One never learned to move objects with his mind and Chuck D's black CNN is more like a satellite dish now, with two hundred channels of wack movies, cartoons, and home-shopping networks? It still made me the motherfucker that I am. He remembered what Lajuan had said the day he lopped off his shouder-length locks, buzzed his dome with the two-blade, and stuffed fistfuls of hair ropes in Dutch Master cigar boxes, as if they might come in handy in the future, in case he had to rappel his way up the castle tower to bone Rapunzel: "I don't need 'em anymore," he'd said, shrugging, scissors in hand, when Macon, mortified, entreated him to reconsider. "They're growing on the inside now."

Macon flicked his eyes at the rearview like a celebrity checking for paparazzi, then watched a clutter of pedestrians transverse the crosswalk before him. His gaze returned to the mirror and now he was an outlaw twisting backward on his horse, money sack in one hand, six-gun in the other, grinning at the distant cloud of dust that was the posse in cold pursuit.

The Fifty-ninth Street Bridge loomed on his left and Macon decided to visit Nique at his tollbooth and bum some weed: Why not? Kid Untouchable in full effect, full grown into the moves he'd rehearsed long and lean in his bedroom mirror and stashed inside some inside pocket of himself as he stepped catlike through a glossy suburbia that wasn't ready for them.

Every stereotype had rubbed off on Macon; every handshake and shoulder-bang embrace had darkened him imperceptibly, and he'd welcomed the transfer of every myth: coolness, danger, sexual superiority. And reaped the benefits, played both sides against the middle on some *Fistful of Dollars* shit. As the closest thing to black that was still safe, he'd even scooped the occasional white girl looking for a cross-cultural experience but too timid to actually fuck a brother. He'd flipped hip hop attitudes in places where they'd gone unrecognized, aced high school just on the strength of intellectual aggression, the ability to cut and paste ideas with the democratic, genre-crossing dexterity of an old-school party DJ. He'd cloaked his swagger as he snuck through the sepia city, so that unknown brothers would not mistake it as ill-considered.

A hip hop motherfucker carried hip hop everywhere he went, thought Macon, knew when to hold it on his shoulders and when to hide it in his heart. He flashed on a memory of coming home to find his father planted in the center of Macon's bedroom, clocking the walls as if it were a museum, hands thrust deep into the pockets of his khaki Dockers with the braided brown belt, 360 degrees of *Wordup!* magazine foldout poses boxing him in and Alan Detornay thinking, What? Who are these niggers? Who are these cultural bellwethers? Who is my son?

Your son is hip hop, Dad. Hip hop oozes from the way he half-closes one eye, like Big Daddy Kane did in those foldouts, when he's propped up on an elbow looking at his lover. It's hip hop that makes him hyperaware of personal movement in a way that enhances his cool rather than ruining it, hip hop that wrote up the tattered, stale, ghettonomics-of-crack black-people-don't-own-no-boats conversation he had a thousand times at Aura's crib last summer. Hip hop is the interplay between beautify and destroy when cats discuss bombing the city's subway trains. Hip hop is not talking to your parents, but talking over their records. Hip hop means trying to knock your idols out the box, hearing a rumor that your favorite MC's new record is wack and not even buying it to find out if it's true, you fickle motherfucker. Hip hop moves so fast that new jams are outdated by the time the last snare snaps, but hip hop recycles everything, so it all evens out. Hip hop finishes your sentences for you because you talk too goddamn slow, and rolls its eyes at any and all attempts to define, explain, categorize, or even celebrate it. Hip hop knows what it is and who it's in and has no problem with leaving all that shit unspoken, but secretly it wishes somebody would hit the nail right on the head and so it half-listens to everybody's overwrought, emotional, esoteric, poetic, theoretic bullshit and is always disappointed.

Macon turned on the radio and "King of Rock" backspun the planet: 1985, the year Run-DMC broke MTV's color line, busting through the doors of the Rock 'n' Roll Museum in black bowlers and Adidas jumpsuits, fat gold-braided ropes swinging like pendulums to footfall rhythms. Kings not of rap but rock, as in we laying claim to your suddenly quite institutional and honkified decaying Woodstock rebel music; we some young, savvy motherfuckers hip enough to understand that if we throw guitar wails over the neck-snap drums, then rock 'n' roll and thus Springsteen-age America will pay some mind and Jann Whatshisname and the burnout torchholders down at *Rolling Stone* will fall for it and canonize us with paternalistic goodwill, meaning we blow up and sell six million albums without changing out of our jailhouse-laceless kicks or ungrabbing our nuts. Never mind that when you think rock, it's Mick Jagger and Neil Young, and Hendrix for affirmative action, black but hippied out and fronting white bands, too extraterrestrial to be black militant, and for us rock is Big Mama Thorton, Chuck, Fats, and other motherfuckers who got beat-jacked by Elvis and Pat Boone, and that rock to us is nothing but a gimmick, the muscle-bound guitar riffs of uncredited studio musicians, just something else to fuck with.

And when hip hop finished sucking on rock's power chords and moved on stronger, and Run, D, and Jay gave Aerosmith the soul-shake kiss-off and banked the proceeds, only then did Jann Whatshisname and the rest of America's gray-ponytailed rock critics abandon their visions of black rap youth and young white rockers partying together, their desperate horny dreams of rock 'n' roll rubbing rap supersperm into its crackly skin, absorbing it until the music moved again. The black bastards used us, they snarled, and went back to hating rap and *It's not music* and *The culture of appropriation* and et cetera. Until the Beastie Boys emerged a year later, Run-DMC magically transformed into a trio of degenerate white brats through their mutual fairy godmother Rick Rubin's gun-toting Blimpie-sandwich-eating fuck-you dirty cracker sleight of hand, a great white hope and a reason for rock critics to use words like *irreverent, fresh,* and *clever* where *thieving, irresponsible,* and *droning* once sufficed.

Macon had hated the Beastie Boys, or the B Boys, as ignorant suburbanites called them, not realizing that b-boy stands for beat boy or break boy and DJ Kool Herc made up the term to give some shine to the cats who waited until the hottest part of the record to flex ill kung fu capoeira snapneck acrobatics on the dance floor back when he used to throw parties in the parks of the Bronx, plugging his sound system into jimmied-open lamp posts and thus jacking postindustrial post–Cross Bronx Expressway post-budget-crisis New York City for a little bit of get-back in the form of pure energy, Marshall McLuhan eat your heart out. Years before Jimmy Carter stepped out of his limo just long enough to shake a dismayed, bucktoothed face across the charred blocks, cats were creating culture from spare parts in the tradition of lemonade when life rains ghetto citrus and soul food from unfit pig scraps.

Macon hated the Beastie Boys for bringing hip hop to kids who'd never heard of b-boying or Kool Herc or park jams, and who didn't bother to find out; for flipping the game around so that instead of having to do extra work to be down, whiteboys could be dilettantes in hip hop, self-conscious clowns whose very presence was a joke that deprecated the culture even as it pretended to deprecate itself. The Beastie Boys made the white kids in his neighborhood think it was okay to start rapping, and the black kids who got bused into his junior high from Boston decide white rappers were automatically wack. They made white people ridiculous, tore down everything Macon had begun building, slashed his whole fantasy of being the only cracker cool enough to be up in this hip hop shit. He didn't want any white role models, especially not three whiny-voiced, non-lyrical motherfuckers who dressed like bums and wasted dope beats and went triple platinum on some raunchy frat-boy mass-appeal shit. Yeah, okay, so they were Buddhists now. Too late. The damage had been done.

Macon was a few blocks from the bridge ramp, gas-brake-honking to the last echoes of "King of Rock" and remembering how many times he'd listened to its sequel at full volume in his room, manually censoring the songs by turning down the sound on DMC's two curses. Thin walls in the Detornay household, no privacy. His mother didn't have to read his journal; you could hear a telephone conversation damn near anyplace in the house. She shoulda gone back to work way sooner than she did, he thought. The bane of Macon's mother's generation of middle-class white women was the fact that they'd redirected all that well-nurtured, hard-won ambition toward their families instead of using it to fuel their own lives, thus driving their children fucking insane. Of course, Macon conceded, the angry-kid equivalent to Virginia Woolf's five annual Benjamins and a room of one's own had been knowing that no matter how long he spent over on the wrong side of the tracks, fighting the good fight and hating the hypocrisy of the system in which his entire community was so entrenched, when he came home teary-eyed and stoned or scarlet with outrage an hour past his curfew, there would still be leftover chicken in the fridge to sate his revolutionary hunger.

A tall white woman, twenty-five maybe, was bouncing on the balls of her feet, hand raised to Macon's cab. A desperate look dampened her face, and Macon swerved instinctively to the rescue.

"Thank God," she exhaled, leaning back into the seat, hands tucked beneath her thighs. "I thought I'd never find a white cab-driver."

Macon's body stiffened. "What?"

"I'm not taking any chances with that maniac on the loose." Her eyebrows arched at his silence. "You haven't heard? It's all over the news. He's some kind of black militant wacko or something." The woman shook her head. "I'm not a prejudiced person. But this guy . . . he robs white people and the cops can't find him. Nobody knows what he looks like." She shuddered. "I don't want to get raped."

"Better safe than sorry," Macon heard himself respond. His brain was foaming, overflowing like an ill-poured draft. He'd done it: found some kind of worm hole in the white psyche, some uncharted reflex, and here he stood, divorced from his own color by the violence and conviction of his actions. Those fools hadn't seen white knuckles gripping that gun. They couldn't. Their brains weren't wired to link whiteness to the words Macon had hurled at them, the fear he'd made them feel. It had to be a nigger. Macon was invisible. Shock fluttered his stomach.

"This city," his fare said, shaking her head.

"Mmm." Did the world merely call traitors to whiteness black? What was the turning point, the secret password, the moment when you were no longer recognized, the instant when your picture faded from the ferry pass and you had to stay on the island of Blackness forever or swim back on your own? How many of Macon's victims had taken part in shaping this description of him? Had the first two or three declared him black and the others merely cosigned the police sketch? If the later ones had known about this enraged, dusky criminal—an image of the nonexistent man took shape in Macon's mind, a blue-black Rastus with granite-hard veined forearms and a clenched mouth and stark pearl teeth and eye-whites, crazed deadly eyes—wouldn't they have looked him over as this woman had, affirmed that he was safe before they strapped on their seat belts?

It had all happened too fast, perhaps. A flurry of robberies quicker than media saturation, faster than the leap from the back of the Metro section to page one. Hell, he didn't watch the news himself, and he was the motherfucker on it. There were eight million people on this small, cramped island, and even the biggest news never reached some ears. Those were the ears that ended up on juries.

Macon massaged sudden fatigue from his eyes with a thumb knuckle and finger, and thought about all the black cabdrivers who had to be starving behind this shit, all the white people shaking their heads and adding another twig of anecdotal evidence to their bonfires. Cap Anson slid into second base, spikes high, laughing his ass off and spraying a stream of dirt in Macon's face, then stood and smiled and extended a hand to his progeny. We're wearing the same uniform now, Macon thought, appalled.

He pulled to the curb and the woman handed him the fare, along with a generous tip. He watched her swift calves and imagined the clunk of her heels until she disappeared into a doormanned building. Macon's brain flopped like a dying fish on the floor of a rowboat and he banged a U-turn and headed back toward the highway, Queens-bound. Ten minutes later he was parked at Nique's window, holding up traffic.

"Damn, Moves. You look like death eating a sandwich, dog." Commuters honked and Nique craned his torso out of the tollbooth, checking to see if any of the cars belonged to drug customers. They did not, and he ignored them.

Macon slumped forward, forehead resting on the wheel, rubbing his temples with two fingers to the dome. "I feel like a bullshit-ass Raskolnikov," he said in the slow, textured tone reserved for times when he felt wickedly removed, smoother and older and hipper than his interlocutor or else half-dead. The voice hinted at a Southern drawl; Nique suspected Macon had cribbed it from some PBS jazz documentary.

"Just comparing your life to classic literature doesn't make your life classic literature," Nique informed him. "Fuck happened?"

Macon steeled Nique with a confidential stare, exhaled elaborately, then changed his mind and shrugged and parried. "White people are really losing their minds over this cab thing, huh?"

"Man, they love it. They're having a field day. You been listening to the radio? They did a whole hour on it earlier. Interviewed all these outraged white people talking about hate crimes and 'We entrust these people with our lives,' playing the victim role like they been practicing for years and shit. Then they talked to a couple of black folks who were like, 'Hey, cabs are finally stopping for us 'cause everybody white's afraid to take 'em.' "

"Huh." Macon mulled that over and warmed into a grin.

"This is my favorite," said Nique. "There's this group that's boycotting the cab companies until they find the criminal, right? And dude, they organized a fuckin' carpool for crackers to get to work. It's like the Montgomery bus boycott on acid. I love this shit." He laughed. "You must be in high demand out here, huh? White cabbie in this city right now? You the man."

"Not me," said Macon, shifting into drive. "I can't even get arrested in this town." He peeled off, whipped back to Manhattan as fast as he could and trolled the streets, face flushed red, desperate to make things right before he considered the consequences and lost his nerve.

It didn't take long to find a fare. "Boy, am I glad to see you," chortled the square-headed meatbag businessman, tucking the folds of his raincoat around himself and smiling as if he'd just told an inside joke. Blue suit, white shirt, red tie. Fucking presidential. Macon grunted, drove half a block, slammed the gearshift into park and hit the locks and spun. It was the middle of the day, middle of the avenue, middle of Midtown, the light green up ahead. Cars swerved and honked around him, and Macon thrust his head into the space in the partition and eyeballed his startled customer. The future drained away like water spiraling out of a bathtub, and Macon watched it disappear. Prison flashed through his mind, cinematic: a lengthy sentence, weight-room brawls, gradual wisdom, comradely strolls around the yard with Morgan Freeman. None of it mattered; no fate-specter was going to spook Macon. Life was only now, this single instant and the necessity of shouldering the weight.

"What color am I?" he demanded.

The man shrunk back against the seat, maximizing what space lay between them.

"Look at me. What color am I?"

"Y-you're white," he stammered.

Macon opened the glove compartment, grabbed the gun, and poked the first inch of the barrel through the partition. He rested his chin on the hammer.

"Now what color am I?"

The man blanched.

"It's not a trick question!" Macon screamed. "Take a good look. What fucking color am I?"

"White." The syllable leaked from him, a weak gust of terror.

"Jesus. Thank you. I thought I was going insane here. Now give me your wallet and that lovely tie, asshole, and get the fuck out of my cab." He gestured with the gun. "Hurry. Before you forget what I look like."

BOOK II

TRAITOR

I pounded my fist into my glove as Anson stepped into the box for his leadoff at-bat. The crowd chanted his name, and he tipped his cap with practiced grace. Arty Sullivan, our rookie pitcher, fingered the rosin bag and patted down the pitcher's mound with his toe, trying to compose himself. It was only his second start of the season, and here was the game's most feared hitter and the ugliest crowd he'd ever seen. I crouched into a fielder's stance, bouncing on my toes, grateful that with Anson at the plate, the crowd seemed to have forgotten me.

"Ban the nigger!" came the cry from behind third. I flinched, almost turned, and clenched my fist atop my knee. "Ban the nigger!" It spread through the stands, bouncing like an echo from third base to the bleachers and the seats behind the plate. Anson swung at the first pitch and hit a line drive foul down the first-base line, hard enough to energize the crowd and rattle Arty even more. Where was the kid's head at? He was ignoring an unwritten rule of baseball. I walked from third to hold a conference at the mound.

"They throw at my head and you give him something to hit? Whose side are you on? You knock him on his ass right now, you understand?"

The next pitch was down the middle and Anson poked it through the infield for a single. Sullivan refused to meet my furious stare. Cap lingered at the bag, replenishing his chaw and chatting with Red Donner. Chatting! I surveyed the baseball diamond and realized with a pang of fear that these men wearing my uniform were not on my team. How could Donner exchange first baseman/base runner pleasantries with this man, the darling of the Klan? How could Sullivan refuse to retaliate on my behalf?

With this new clarity of vision came clarity of hearing; the jumble of noise began to shake and settle, and I realized I'd been foolish in wishing to pull voices from the din. I could hear them now, each one, and it was worse. Folks were having a good old time in here today.

"Time's up, nigger!"

"Swing that bat like you gon' swing from a tree!"

"This game ain't for your kind, Fleet Walker!"

"No slave labor in the infield!"

"We'll be waitin' for you, Moses!"

"Ban the nigger!"

The Stockings' two-hitter bounced into a double play. Sullivan walked the third batter and whiffed the cleanup man and I tucked my mitt under my arm and my head into my chest and jogged back to the dugout. I tried to look unruffled, to move neither too fast nor too slow. Eight more innings of this. Three more at-bats, at least. Then what? A team bus ride? Another game tomorrow?

I walked to the far corner of the dugout and hunkered down alone. There were seven hitters ahead of me but I grabbed my bat anyway, held it between my legs and rested my chin on the flat bottom of the handle. Red followed me and sat down by my side.

"I know you saw me talking to Anson, Fleet," he said, leaning in. "I told him he's a chickenshit son of a bitch, and that if he was half the man you are, he'd spend less time complaining to the owners and more worrying about why he can't hit a lick off colored pitchers."

I looked at Red and forced a smile. "Thanks."

"I also told him that if they try to bean you again, I'll slice him to ribbons. Be the only ballplayer ever slid into first base."

It wasn't until the fourth inning that I returned to the plate. I came up with a man on first and one out. The pitcher looked over at Anson; Cap nodded his head and I knew to duck before the pitch even left the hurler's hand. I moved too soon, though, crouched into a ball and gave the fellow an easy target. The pitch caught me in the arm. It wasn't thrown very hard; the pitcher had to sacrifice some speed because he changed the placement of the ball so late in his delivery.

I stood, triumphant: That didn't even hurt, you bastard. *Dusted myself off, saluted the pitcher with two fingers to my cap, and listened to the crowd go apoplectic with rage.*

Anson was waiting for me. "You better get used to this," he said. "Every pitcher in this league gon' throw at your head, boy. I noticed your man Sullivan ain't been too quick to throw back, neither, has he? Why you s'pose that is, Mr. Moses Fleetwood Walker?"

"Maybe he's better than that," I said.

Cap threw back his head and laughed. The fans followed suit, as if they were in on the joke, and for a moment the entire stadium went rancid with the sound. At the plate, Joe Wagner took a second called strike. Anson shook his head and opened his eyes wide, affecting rueful bemusement. "Maybe he's better'n that. Yep, that's prob'ly it, all right. Good thing you don't take it personal. You know, Fleet, I'm not just havin' Hoss knock you down to make a fool of you. I wanted to get you to first so's me and you could have a chance to talk. I don't understand you, Fleet. Every other nigger in the league knows he's not wanted and he leaves. You mean to tell me you're even stupid for a nigger?"

I adjusted my cap and got into a base runner's stance: knees bent, arms outstretched, poised on the balls of my feet. "Maybe you're afraid to pitch to me," I said without taking my eyes off the field.

"I'm not the one who should be scared," Anson replied.

Wagner dribbled a grounder back to the mound and Hoss threw to third and put out the lead runner. I got a good jump and beat the relay to second standing. "We'll talk later," Anson called.

"Don't listen to him," said the second baseman. He stood close behind the bag to hold me, prevent me from taking too much of a lead. "Don't listen to any of them. Just hang in there." I turned and stared at him. Hoss threw strike two down the middle. "I'm from Queens," the kid went on. "I used to cut school to watch you fellows take batting practice, shag flies, anything. This is my first year up from semi-pro, and you know what?" He glanced around and almost winced. "I don't want to be a ballplayer no more."

"Well, I do," I said. "Too bad you and I can't change places."

The inning ended with a fly-out to right field, and the game continued scoreless into the bottom of the eighth inning. I had handled only two balls the entire game, fielding each one cleanly and throwing my man out to thunderous tumult. Heaven forbid I made an error. Their heads might have exploded. In the seventh, Hoss had brushed me back twice before finally hitting me in the shin, the most painful ball so far. I'd been thrown out at second on the next play, a lazy broken-bat roller to third that I would have beaten if I wasn't hobbling. Anson had been quiet at first base. "You look like you've got a lot on your mind, Moses," was all he'd said. "I'ma be quiet so's you can try to think."

Hoss Rawlings was the Stockings' first batter in the eighth. Desota called for time and walked out to the mound, beckoning the infield in to conference. "You listen to me, Sullivan," he said. "This son of a bitch has hit Walker three times now. If you won't throw back, I'll call in someone who will, you got that?" Sullivan nodded into his glove; I gazed off into the stands, grateful but embarrassed. Whatever happened, I knew I'd never speak to Sullivan again.

The pitch was tight and inside, a fastball, and Hoss twisted to avoid it and got plunked on the elbow of his pitching arm. He fell to the ground and that was it for him. Anson sent in a pinch runner, some overzealous rookie who took a long lead and got picked off on the second pitch. The next batter grounded out to short, and then it was the top of the ninth and I was at the plate.

The new pitcher was Randy Garrett. He'd been a Giant for two seasons. He and I had never spoken much, but we'd gotten along fine. Garrett was a quiet guy, a farm boy still adjusting to life on the road, but not stupid, not a rube. He knew enough to shut up, to listen to the vets and try to learn the game instead of running around whooping and hollering with excitement like a lot of these hayseed kids did when they got out on the road.

I watched him throw a final warmup and stepped in. Garrett nodded once. Was he responding to the catcher's sign or greeting me? What sign would he need if he was under orders to go for the head? I tightened my grip on the bat, optimistic enough to expect the first real pitch of the day. It came in low and outside, far from a strike but not a brushback, either. Anson called time and ran to the mound. Garrett towered over his manager, rubbing the ball between his hands and furrowing his brow. He glanced up at me, looked down at Anson, nodded, slipped his hand back in his glove, and dropped his gangly arms. Anson barked some curt last order and marched back to first base.

I steeled myself, ready for whatever might come down the pike. It was a fastball on the outside corner, and I thanked God in heaven and walloped the hell out of it. The crack of bat to ball hushed the crowd; the stadium watched in silence as the white blur soared past the outstretched glove of the leaping shortstop, still on the rise. The centerfielder turned his back to the plate and sprinted to the wall, but there was nothing he could do. The ball cleared the fence, dropped into the empty section of bleachers marked For Coloreds Only, *and rattled around under the seats, loud against the stunned silence of several thousand fans.*

Chapter One

Macon walked into the Malcolm X Lounge fifteen minutes late, wild-haired and imagining slavering consequence-monsters lurking behind every corner; he had summoned them and now he waited. Forty deep, the Black Student Union held its breath for a split second, heads swinging away from the podium, over the open bags of chips and pretzels and the two-liter Coke bottles scattered on the huge mahogany tabletop like primitive settlements. Eyes abandoned the Dorito-laden plates nestled in the laps of couch dwellers and resting by floor sitters' knees to check out the pink-skinned whiteboy lingering by the door, glistening with who-knew-what—exhaustion, embarrassment, fear? They waited a moment, expecting him to mumble an apology—*Whoops, sorry, wrong room*—and duck his ass into the hall. Instead, Macon's eyes lit up and he beelined it to the refreshment table, poured himself a Sprite, and chugged it. "That's the dude was fucking with Professor Alam," somebody whispered.

Amy Green pursed her lips and squeezed the sides of the pressboard podium with both hands. Like everything else in the recently reappointed and redecorated former Richard Wagner Lounge, it was secondhand and battered. After years of organizational homelessness, the BSU had persuaded Columbia to give them a space by threatening to send letters to black alumni that began *Dear Brother/Sister, How ghetto is Columbia's Black Student Union?*

When we want to meet, we gotta check the weather forecast. The Malcolm X Lounge was a converted music-practice room, stripped of its piano but not its soundproofing. A papier-mâché Malcolm with a papier-mâché shotgun had guarded the window in the BSU's first year of occupancy, but the university objected to the depiction of a weapon and so some comedian had switched the shotgun for a mop. The selection of a new prop was now a yearly BSU tradition; Malcolm had held a farmer's hoe, a three-foot bong, a dented saxophone.

Now he stood empty-handed and Amy glanced from him to Macon, who was guzzling a second soda, and wished X still had his gat. This distraction was not on her mimeographed meeting agenda, and there were two things you didn't fuck with Amy Green on. You didn't challenge her assertion that her glossy mane was natural, not a weave, and you didn't slow up her tightly run meetings with bullshit. Amy was the BSU's returning president and the auteur of Booty Madness II, a dance in the student center that had attracted more than three hundred brothers and sisters from schools throughout the five boroughs and featured an open bar, the renown DJ Bubble Lex on the ones and twos, and a special midnight performance of "It Takes Two" by Rob Base and DJ E-Z Rock, whom Amy had talked into playing for free as a way to rejuvenate their careers and perhaps bag some college chicks. You didn't want to get on her bad side.

Andre was cooling a few feet away with two other dudes from Carman eleven, and Macon joined them and gave his roommate a pound. Andre accepted it reluctantly, figuring that if Macon could ignore the who's-the-whiteboy? glances bouncing off him from around the room, then he could handle being the dude the whiteboy knew. He had always been the dude the whiteboys knew; at least in this room the whiteboy was the minority. But Macon liked it that way. Whiteboy wins again.

"Our next order of business," Amy clarioned, back in command, "is to decide what speakers we want for Black History Month and how much of the budget we're willing to spend." She lifted a sheet of paper and tucked a ribbon of hair behind her ear. "Suggestions so far are Henry Louis Gates . . ."

"Boring," muttered Macon, too loud to be accidentally too loud. His jaw hummed with expectation, his head swam with martyrdom, his stomach churned with terror. Andre's shoulders tensed, and instinct told him to put some physical space between himself and his roommate before Macon hit the red.

Amy double-pumped dramatic eyelashes she swore were God-given, then fixed Macon with a hair-trigger stare: the first time in the organization's history she'd ever encouraged the population to take its eyes off her. Macon, indifferent to the second round of looks, plucked a Dorito from Andre's plate, devoured it loudly, and smeared powdered cheese onto his jeans. He was blacker than each and every last one of these bourgeois motherfuckers.

". . . Angela Davis . . ."

"Irrelevant," said Macon, not quite under his breath.

". . . Pam Grier, Chuck D, Toni Morrison . . ."

"Sagging, finished, Oprahfied."

Andre handed him the plate and edged away. Amy pinned her list against the podium with five hard fingertips and pointed her fresh manicure at Macon.

"You have a suggestion, brother?" she asked, jutting her chin at him on *brother* in case he didn't get the message.

"I do." His Adam's apple bobbed like a buoy, and he wiped the back of his hand across his mouth. "I don't want to intrude, though. If y'all want me to leave, I will." The humble request for an invitation was always a respect-getter, a perfect way to carve out space for himself where none existed. Not that it mattered.

Murmurs spread across the room, and Macon found himself remembering a play his class had done in grade school and how when it came time for the background-chatter scene, where all the villagers turn to one another and begin gossiping in hushed, excited tones, Mrs. Davis had told half the cast to repeat *watermelon* and the other half *Columbus,* and that was the secret. Macon darted his eyes around the room, lip reading, ignoring looks both curious and hostile, convinced that folks were manufacturing a fake Columbus-watermelon murmur, that all this was a game, that their agenda sheets were scripts outlining some elaborate plot against him.

"Go 'head, man, say what you got to say," some dude shouted from the floor. Macon snapped back.

"My suggestion," he said, balancing his plate on the arm of a couch so he could gesture more expansively, "would be not to hire a speaker at all. Put the money toward something that would actually benefit the community. Buy a gun and kill a cop, for instance."

The scattered laughter gave Macon a boost he didn't need and barely wanted. Who cared what these kids thought of him? Macon was on the front lines, way the fuck up in the mix, and they were hibernating in their dorm rooms. Holding meetings. Please.

"There's too much going on out here to be worrying about some bullshit Black History shortest-month-of-the-year gig," he went on. "You know what Rosa Parks would tell you if you hired her to speak? You know what Frederick Douglass or Fred Hampton or Ida Wells would say?" Andre raised a quiet eyebrow and matched it with a lip corner, amused and disgusted at the prospect of hearing what words of wisdom Frederick Douglass might utter through the worldly portal of Macon's mouth.

"They'd tell you to get ready for battle, because you're inside the belly of the beast right now," Macon revealed. "They'd ask if you were ready to die for the cause. Whether you were learning to speak truth to power and how you planned on preventing yourselves from being co-opted by the system you're becoming more a part of every day you're here."

He cut himself off, electric with energy but wanting to keep it short and sweet. At the podium, Amy stood silent, charm-school erect, maintaining regality, scanning her equally hushed subjects. A low, approving buzz, it seemed to Macon, was snaking through the crowd. Watermelon! Columbus!

Finally, a hand rose, and Amy recognized the next speaker, a lanky cat in warmup pants who sat wedged against the back radiator.

"Yes. Charles."

"How 'bout Tyra Banks?"

Before any debate on Tyra's merits as Black History Month speaker could ensue, before Macon's speech could be castigated, lauded, or further ignored, before Amy Green could suggest the formation of an event-planning subcommittee or anybody could remember to ask what was up with ethnic studies, Officers Dick Downing and Ray McGrath of the New York Police Department strolled into the room and asked if a Macon Detornay was present and then if Mr. Detornay could step into the hallway please.

"Yes?" said Macon once they were outside. He felt the eyes of the BSU on him from behind the door. "Can I help you?"

"Mr. Detornay, you are under arrest. You have the right to remain silent. Please place your hands behind your back."

"No, really," said Macon, obeying and feeling cold steel encircle his wrists and clamp shut. It felt more or less as he'd imagined. "I swear, I was invited to the meeting."

They ushered him out of the building and across the campus, past the stares of hundreds of his colleagues. Fleetingly, Macon hoped he'd pass a tour group of prospective students and their parents so he could bare his teeth and snarl something about the wonders of the Columbia experience at them, but no such luck. He felt neither surprised nor worried, but oddly numb. This seemed somehow more silly than threatening, an overwhelmingly incongruous result of what he'd done. The sheen of invincibility with which the robberies had coated Macon didn't peel away so easily; even as he marched past his dorm in shackles, he couldn't manage to rouse panic.

Instead, Macon occupied himself by emulating the stoic annoyance he'd admired on the telegenic mugs of apprehended gangsters: arrest as routine inconvenience, minor hassle. Macon had never been inside a cell and he had no idea what to expect, but he soothed himself by running down his privilege profile: white, collegiate, middle-class. It was poor, black, publicly defended cats who went to jail, did time, rejoined society disenfranchised, couldn't find work, went back, kept prisons growing faster than any other industry in America, kept America's incarceration rate the highest in the world.

The cops stuffed Macon, not ungently, into the backseat of a squad car parked on 114th Street. As they were pulling out, Andre ran up to the window. Roommate loyalty had kicked in about fifty seconds after Macon's departure.

"Where you taking him?" he asked.

"Twenny-sixth precinct." Andre straightened and watched the car go, tapping his fist to his heart, and Macon twisted and stared back. Carman Hall shrunk behind him, higher and higher stories visible in the rear window-frame until the whole squat monster fit. As they turned uptown on Amsterdam and the school disappeared, an icicle of fear shanked Macon: short, shallow jabs to the chest and arms, the neck. It wasn't fear of the future. Not yet. Just the present.

"Detornay," mused Officer Downing from the passenger seat. "Whatchu suppose that is, Ray? French?"

"Sounds like it could be either French or possibly Italian, depending how it's spelled." The ride was smooth. Perfect shocks, superior alignment.

"Sure doesn't sound like any African-American name I've ever heard though. Huh, Ray?"

"No, sir, it does not particularly."

Downing slid open the partition separating front seat from back and threw his beefy freckled arms over the wall so he was leaning right in Macon's face. He held his nightstick in his hand. "You sure had us fooled, buddy," he said. McGrath made another left and they crawled west down 126th Street, through an auto-body district abandoned for the night. A small, cold bead of sweat rolled down the inside of Macon's arm, sickeningly slow. A melted icicle.

Downing broke into a smile. "You look nervous, buddy," he said, swinging the club loosely by its strap. "Relax." He raised his voice to address his partner. "I think Mr. Detornay here's seen too many cop shows, Ray."

McGrath steered the car down the deserted street at six miles an hour, one finger on the wheel. "He's waiting for you to hit him, Dick. That's how us pigs are known to treat young radicals. Right, Macon?" McGrath chuckled. "You might disappoint him if you don't take a poke. Bruise the kid's self-esteem."

Downing smiled, as if to say *never mind my partner.* "Can I ask you a question?"

Macon clenched his jaw. Fuck this cat-and-mouse shit, he thought, watching the gray street slide by. Let's cut to the chase.

"I'm not saying shit—"

"—without my lawyer," both officers chimed in. Downing conducted the three-man chorus with his billy club.

"Sure, Macon, I understand that. I was just hoping you could shed some light on, you know, some of the issues of the day. Seeing as how you sympathize so strongly with the African-American community and all."

Macon waited for the punchline, the bait-and-switch, the bad-cop rejoinder. But Downing just stared at him, clear-eyed and waiting. There was a shade of the familiar in the cop's demeanor, and Macon's sense of recognition only scared him more. He rifled urgently through his mind, desperate to identify Downing's tone in time to guess where it was going and dodge the blow to come. The nightstick dangled inches from Macon's chest, swaying like a pendulum. McGrath wheeled the car into a broad U-turn and crept back up the block slower than ever.

"What can I do for you?" asked Macon warily.

Downing chewed his lower lip for a moment. "I'm in Harlem every day," he said. "And it seems to me that there's a lot of anger there. The black—the African-American community is just very . . . angry. Would you say that's right, Macon?"

So. Downing was *that* guy: the interested observer, the fellow spy. How many of them had sidled up to Macon over the years, at parties he'd attended with his parents, eager to swap and hoping to learn? The dirty little secret they shared with him served as sufficent introduction: mutual fascination with the coloreds. It was pure plantation instinct, wrapped in a cloak of earnest anthropological befuddlement: a desire to monitor the levels of rage out in the slave shacks, cock back the rifles at the first sign of trouble.

"Why don't you ask them?" Macon answered, trying to keep any hint of attitude out of his voice.

The left side of Downing's face twitched and settled. "Yeah, right," he said.

" 'Five-oh, nigga, run,' " McGrath mimicked, cupping a hand to his mouth.

"Exactly," said Downing. "That's all we get. So I'm asking you, Macon. You're a real nigga, right? You get mad love in the hood."

"You'd better," added McGrath, "because white folks might have a bone or two to pick with you, son. Robbing them and calling them the devil and all."

"Look, Macon." Downing lowered his head and eyed Macon over his own brow. "Here's the thing. I'm really not a racist guy. But if you'd seen what I've seen on this job, you might come to the conclusion that African-Americans—not all of them, mind you, but a hell of a lot—are permanently fucked as a species because they're too stupid and self-destructive to stop killing each other and get their shit together, know what I mean? And I don't want to believe that, Macon. I'd rather find some way to blame the white man myself, but for the life of me I just can't figure out how. So I'm hoping maybe you can help me out here." McGrath chortled into his palm, and Downing smiled despite himself. "Cut it out, Ray. I'm serious."

"Fuck you," spit Macon, seething. He tried to ball his fists, but the handcuffs cut even deeper into his hands when he clenched them.

Downing cocked his head sideways. "Now, why would you say that, Macon? I don't understand. And I'm quite understanding. Aren't I quite understanding, Ray?"

"He's quite understanding, kid. We have to complete a lot of sensitivity training."

"I'm trying to have a nice, friendly conversation with you, and you tell me to fuck myself. That Ivy League school's gone to your head, man."

"Like I told you, Dick." McGrath lifted his hat and scratched viciously at the crown of his scalp. A dusting of dandruff fecundated the shoulders of his uniform. "He's gonna feel unworthy if you don't give him a couple trophies to remember us by. You know, martyrdom and all that."

Downing sighed and reached back to fumble with his utility belt. "I suppose you're right," he said, Macing Macon in the face.

Macon howled, jerked blindly, tried to rub his eyes against the vinyl seatback. Snot bubbled from his nose; it felt as if he were crying hot sauce. Downing yanked him upright and jabbed Macon in the gut with the nightstick, acupressure-precise. Macon gasped, struggled to draw air into his lungs, tried in vain to twist away. There was nowhere to go.

Downing leaned back, red-faced with the effort of beating him. "There. I hope that'll do, Macon, because quite frankly I'm exhausted, and it's about all I can manage." He palmed his chin and watched Macon thrash, eyes shut to fight the fire of the Mace.

"I'll bet you're from the suburbs, aren't you?" Downing asked. He sheathed his nightstick and turned to gaze out his passenger-side window.

Chapter Two

Macon sat alone in a cement holding cell, rubbing his eyes and trying not to move as his stomach ripened with bruises. The unlidded toilet radiated a shit smell that infected most of the room, and the gray bunk bed marooned in the least pungent corner mocked him with its faint evocations of summer camp coziness and late-night secret-sharing. He'd stood dripping tears while McGrath and Downing filed an arrest report claiming Macon had sustained minor injuries due to a nasty spill on the way from the cop car to the precinct, then been escorted down a pair of long corridors and installed here.

Four hours and one cheese sandwich later, Macon had seen no one, had nothing explained to him, knew nothing of his fate but what he'd learned from the semi-mobile clot of muscle tissue squatting in the cell next door. Silk was a bald-headed white dude who spoke with the gruff, throaty voice of a professional wrestler. "I been here eight days, gettin' skinny. I'll give you five cigarettes for that sandwich." Macon declined the smokes, but hit him off with half out of the goodness of his heart. Silk rammed the morsel into his gullet and, before falling into tugboat slumber, told Macon he could expect the chance to post bail tomorrow. Macon's bank account housed less than two hundred dollars, and he'd known nobody in New York longer than three days; maybe Columbia would let him take his midterms from the slammer this semester.

There was no one in the Bean to call either, Macon admitted to himself, not for dough or even moral support. Self-pity was wrapping itself around him now, a thin shawl, and Macon forced himself to think about Lajuan and Aura and the trivial financial drama that had estranged him from his boys. How, he wondered, had the couple hundred bucks they owed him in past-due phone bills come to matter so much?

Because, he answered himself, you can't let yourself get punked. All three of them knew Macon had access to money in ways they didn't, though they'd never once discussed it. The phone debt wasn't killing him. He should have told them to forget it, but they'd hardly apologized for jamming him up, never even given him ten bucks to show good faith, never seemed to fear that he'd step to them and demand it. Soon Macon's resentment mounted—not just over the money, but the position they'd forced him into from the moment he'd put the account in his name. Macon didn't want to play landlord, sniping at his boys for loot he knew they didn't have. But the longer the debt went unresolved, the more Macon felt like he was paying for their friendship. He didn't know what to do, so he just stopped hanging out.

Lajuan and Aura treated him the same as always, and that made it worse. Macon hated them for revealing his kindness as weakness, hated himself for sitting and scowling at everything they bought, smoked, drank, and ate with what should have been his money. He felt petty and glaringly white, and his last month at the crib had been as sour as the milk in the refrigerator. Finally, the night before Macon left, Lajuan had given him the gun as payment: an attempt to hand Macon back some of his manhood. They'd parted with a pound, as had Macon and Aura, but there was coldness there. They wouldn't call him, Macon thought. Not even if they saw his face on the news.

A long scream sounded and Macon walked to the barred door to see what was going on. Six guards labored toward him, dragging a struggling black man by his hands and feet. They stopped directly before Macon's cell and he backed away, taking refuge on the lower bunk as the man twisted and flailed, trying to free himself.

"Turn me loose," he shouted again and again. "Turn me loose." The guards heaved him inside, locked the door, and strode away. The prisoner lay on the ground for a moment, panting, then scrambled to his feet and grabbed hold of the bars.

"Give me back my papers," he screamed, with such force that his entire body shook. "You won't get away with this."

"Say, man," said Macon, venturing cautiously over. The cat turned and stared at him with eyes so crazed and bloodshot Macon jumped. "You all right?"

"No, I'm not all right," the man raved, returning his attention to the long-gone guards. "I'll report you to the president, you hear?" he shouted down the hall. "You want to destroy my evidence, but you can't cover up your crimes! I'll publish them to the whole world!"

"Make them take him outta your cell, kid," advised Silk from next door. "He'll kill ya. He went nuts from studying too much. Claims he'd gotten to the bottom of why black folks are treated so bad and he was gonna write a book and tell the president and have things changed, see? He says his professor had him locked up. They found him in his underwear in the lobby of some dot-com building down in Times Square, trying to get an appointment with the president."

The lunatic turned and grabbed Macon's hand. "You've got to help me," he said. "You've got to call this number and tell them where I am." He produced a crumpled page from his pocket and closed Macon's fist around it. The man's palms were slimed with sweat, and Macon jerked his hand back, looking the prisoner over with a blend of sympathy and fear. "They'll know what to do," the man insisted. "They'll contact the president and tell him of my research. Promise me you'll call." He leaned in close and Macon saw white spittle clouding the corners of his mouth. "I know who really killed Tupac and Biggie Smalls," he hissed, eyes bulging. "And Albert Van Horn and Geronimo Pratt and Len Bias." He turned and threw himself once more against the bars. "You'll never get away with this," he screamed into the hall. "I know why you put me here!"

A group of white-jacketed men strode quickly toward the cell, wheeling a stretcher. They unlocked the door and grabbed the yelling man, laced him in a straitjacket, threw him on the stretcher, and carted him away. Macon sat back on the bunk and unballed his fist. The phone number was written on, of all things, a page torn from *Native Son.* The jagged sheet was smeared with dried blood, almost translucent with sweat. A single fragment was underlined faintly in yellow marker: *but Bigger, if I say you got the right to hate me then that ought to make things a little different, oughtn't it?* Macon read it again and again.

"No," he said aloud. "That doesn't change shit." He twisted on the narrow mattress, exhausted but restless, wishing he had enough information to draw the fear up from his stomach, where it lay dormant, or else to banish it outright. But he felt numb. Whatever happened happened. Macon tried to think forward to the pleasure he would derive from beginning sentences "When I was in jail . . ." It soothed him for a moment. He found a modicum of comfort lying on his side, hands pillowed underneath his head and shirt draped over his eyes to block the dull, humming fluorescence of the hall lights, and drifted to sleep cursing and blessing the timing that had placed his parents six thousand miles away, floating in the middle of the ocean, in his hour of need.

Macon dreamed that he was watching television in their living room, feet on the ottoman, remote control in hand. He flipped to *Beverly Hills 90210,* the show that had been his dirty little secret at fourteen, and watched as Luke Perry strutted through a crowded nightclub, made his way to the pool table, pouted, sank a bank shot. Luke turned to the bar to pick up a waiting beer, and when he swiveled back the club had become an Old West whorehouse. Hookers in frilly pink lingerie and garters lounged on wicker furniture, smoking cigarillos from delicate glass holders. The camera panned right, seeking the source of the raucous music, and revealed Thelonious Monk sitting at the house piano, dressed in a Nike track suit and a porkpie hat and banging out the head to Mingus's "All the Things You Could Be by Now If Sigmund Freud's Wife Was Your Mother."

Luke sifted his lips, scanning the hookers. "Kel," he said softly, "Kel, how could you do this to me?" He pulled a pair of John Woo silver handguns from his waist and cocked them back, but before he could waste a single lady of leisure, the saloon-style doors swung open and Ol' Dirty Bastard sauntered in, a sheriff's badge glinting on his ruffled pirate shirt and a pink bobbed wig tilted atop his sloppily cornrowed head. He walked straight up to Luke, thumbs hooked in his belt loops, and stuck his gold-front laced grill two and a half inches from the actor's chiseled mug.

"We got a muthafuckin' problem here, nigguh?" he asked, word-slurring, clearly angel-dusted. He swigged the dregs from a forty of St. Ides, flared his nose, and exhaled malt liquor fumes like a degenerate dragon. Luke blinked and turned away.

"Yuh see, deez hoes mah hoes," Ol' Dirty drawled, flinging the empty bottle behind him with a reckless backhand motion. Monk caught it without looking up and set it atop the piano, deftly quoting "Shame on a Nigga" as he did so. "So if you wanna blast my hoes, you gonna hafta pay the Ol' Dirt Dawg, you unnerstan'? Cuz I'll dunk yo' ass in the moonshine and shit on yuh grave, mah nukka." He sniffed elaborately, poked a finger into Luke's chest, and gestured behind him with a wandering eye. "Thatcho ride parked out front, God?"

Luke tried to look past him, concern for his cherry-red Mustang convertible glinting in his soft, romantic-yet-rebellious eyes. He nodded, forehead wrinkling adorably.

"Well, not anymore, big homey, cuz my cousin-in-law Generic Assassin out there stealin' that mufucker right now." Ol' Dirty lifted his face to the sky and laughed his ass off. Monk caught on, and soon everybody in the joint was howling. "Drinks for all mah niggas and mah niggarettes," Ol' Dirty shouted, pounding the bar. A wheeled robot bartender chirped in acquiescence. "And where the weed at? Somebody roll me a blunt up in this muthafucka! This yo' sheriff talkin', God, don't make me buck my nine! It's about to get all kindsa ugly!"

Inexplicably, Macon flipped the channel. He landed on an old *Seinfeld*. "I don't know where Kramer went," said Jerry, throwing up his hands and trying to hold back his ever-lurking look-at-me-I'm-acting smirk. George Costanza and Elaine Bennis lounged on Jerry's couch and love seat, reading magazines, not listening. Elaine held an apple. Jerry minced across the kitchen in his white sneakers. "He just disappeared, and I think they've rented his apartment to somebody else."

Just then, the front door flew open and Ol' Dirty Bastard made a frenetic, sliding entrance, dressed in a bowling shirt and slacks, hair blown out in an electro-Afro and adorned with random pink bows. The studio audience went wild. He headed straight for Jerry's refrigerator, removed a bottle of Cristal, and took a long, loud swig. "Uh, excuse me," Jerry brayed, annoyed, "but who are you?" Elaine crinkled her nose; George lifted his head from the magazine, brow furrowed behind his glasses.

Ol' Dirty wiped his mouth against his sleeve, spread his arms, and stared down at Jerry. "I'm your new neighbor, nigguh. Fuck you think, God?" He noticed Elaine and threw a head nod her way. "What up, shorty," he said. "I see you holdin' it down over there, girl. I'm sayin', how you like to take a l'il ride with Big Baby Jesus? I plant seeds in fertile soil to popuh-late the earth, na'mean?

God made Dirt, so this Dirt won't hurt. Wu-Tang killa bees on a swarm, Jerry." He poked his head into the fridge, crammed a carrot in his mouth, then straightened and pointed his chin at George. "Who this bitch-ass nigga, Jerry?"

George stood up, waddled over, and extended an obsequious hand. "George Costanza," he said, smiling up at the rapper. "I really, really like what you've done with your hair." He framed Ol' Dirty's head between his hands as if he were a movie director. "Sort of a *Mod Squad* meets Betty Boop thing."

"Man, shut the fuck up before I smack fire out cho' ass," said Ol' Dirty, slapping George's hand away and strutting past him to join Elaine on the sofa.

"I'm sorry," said Jerry, a shit-eating smile on his face, "I don't believe I caught your name."

"I'm the Osiris out this motherfucker, Jerry." He threw an arm around Elaine, who touched her hand to her throat, blinked, and smiled politely. Jerry's buzzer sounded and he walked over to answer it.

"Yeah?" he said, crossing his ankles and rolling his eyes.

"Yo, it's the God, God," a voice responded.

"Come on up," Ol' Dirty yelled over his shoulder, leaning in to nibble Elaine's ear. She giggled coquettishly and slid her hand up his thigh. A moment later, Jerry opened the door and fifty Wu-Tang crimeys bailed in, each one giving Jerry a pound and saying, "Peace, God," as he entered.

"Peace, God," Jerry responded. "Make yourselves at home. No Wallabees on the coffee table, though, dogs." His eyes jumped with panic, as if his brain had relinquished control of his mouth and he was shocked to hear what he was saying. "I've got forties and Hennessy in the fridge, and we're about to make a weed run, ya heard?"

Macon turned the channel and eased back as the camera panned a quiet brownstone block and the *Cosby Show* theme played. But inside the familiar Huxtable household, things were amiss. The stately living room was filled with screaming children—shitty-diapered infants wailing, swaggering toddlers opening mahogany desk drawers and flinging the contents behind them, teenagers in bubble-goose jackets and work boots ciphering in front of Claire Huxtable's mantel-mounted Romare Bearden painting, a tuxedoed six-year-old with a propane lighter working to ignite the moldings, three bead-braided junior-high-school girls playing double Dutch in the foyer with a pair of live snakes as jump ropes. A massive drumbeat boomed from the stereo speakers and the vibrations knocked jazz records from the shelves onto the floor, where a pair of eight-year-olds in Rick James jumpsuits were flinging them at the chandelier. Ol' Dirty Bastard lay supine on the couch, boots up on the hand-carved coffee table. Muddy footprints tracked his path from the front door.

"The God got thirteen beautiful mothafuckin' black babies," he drawled, patting one on the head as she crawled by clutching a throwing star. "Ten baby mamas, three platinum records, fourteen gun charges, six drug cases, two gunshot wounds, and no dough. But yo, I'm loungin', God. Up in the plush crib, like whaaaaat?" He picked a framed photo of the Huxtable clan up off the floor and stared at it, slack-eyed. "Damn, Denise an' Vanessa some fine-ass bitches." He flung it behind him, and the glass shattered against the wall. "Shiii, y'all coulda stayed," he mumbled, crossing his arms and closing his eyes. "We coulda hadda party."

Macon woke up, stiff and disoriented, to the metal-on-metal scrape of his cell door opening.

"Detornay," a hatchet-faced guard said. "Let's go. You made bail."

"No shit," muttered Macon, swinging his legs to the floor and knuckling the crust out of his eyes. He followed the guard down the hall, buttoning his shirt as he walked.

"Paperwork's all taken care of," said the desk officer. "Sign here." Macon signed.

He walked out of the station and into a different life. Megawatt flashbulbs exploded, leaving shooting-star trails singed on Macon's eyes; he blinked through them and saw an antic stroboscopic collage of heavy grated chrome news station microphones and numbers, a lysergic-demetholated *Sesame Street* pastiche, *today's show was brought to you by the numbers,* five four seven two one dip-wave-diving at him, connected by gyrating pink, black, green, and flesh-colored reporters' arms. Huge white gleaming television mouths and cigarette-stained print media teeth, enormous boom mics hanging in the air like evil bumblebees, and all of it drowned in poreless cacophony, no register of human voice depth unfilled: shrieking soprano alto baritone questions, tenor bass questions, undifferentiated voices clenching and unclenching. Macon stood, baffled, and let it wash over and into and around him, and the clock ticked two, three, four, five times, and even as he realized that they'd never stop, never hush even if he stood silent like an invalid for minutes, he began to understand words, focus on shrill individual sentences. The frequency of the flashbulbs slowed.

"Macon!" clamored sixty vying voices.

"Will you comment on the charges, Macon?"

"Did you know they thought you were black?"

"How does it feel to be the most notorious New Yorker since Bernhard Goetz, Macon?"

"Are white people evil, Macon?"

"Why did you pretend to be black?"

"Who paid your bail, Macon?"

A ripple through the throng caught his eye. Boom mics swayed, reporters pitched forward on high heels and reached out their talons to clamp on to someone or something for support. The ripple amplified and the cluster ruptured down the middle and Andre pushed his way through like a defensive linesman, crouching low, with Nique behind him. Macon watched, entranced. When Andre broke into the clear and opened his arms, Macon half-expected to be quarterback-sacked.

Instead, Andre wrapped him in a bear hug. "Yo, man!" he said, mouth to ear. "You all right?"

"Don't answer anything these fools ask," said Nique, his arms around them both. "Leave everything to me."

Nique turned to the media and threw up his hands like Richard Nixon. "Ladies and gentlemen of the press, if any," he said, and Macon looked up, shocked at the silence. "Please allow me to present Mr. Macon Detornay, a young man whose stunning honesty, intelligence, and courage in addressing the question of race in these United States make him one of our most valuable new thinkers."

He rotated slowly as he spoke, letting the three hundred degrees of cameras, microphones, and recorders immortalize his every goddamn word just like they should. "At this time," Nique went on, "Macon cannot answer any questions pertaining to his legal situation." Andre watched the smooth curve of Nique's dome and surged with confidence and glee, thinking of all the public relations courses his boy had aced. "Any inappropriate questions," Nique continued, raising a finger in warning, "and we're out of here."

Macon grabbed him by the shoulder and spun Nique around. "What the hell are you doing?" he whispered fiercely.

"I knew it was you, dude." Nique grinned, clasping Macon back. "I fucking knew it."

"Maybe you didn't hear me." The hum of reportage was cresting again. "I asked you what the hell you were doing."

"You're full-blown, dog," Nique responded. "Front page of the *Post* today—'Visible Man,' with a picture. Lead story on local TV last night, and the networks mentioned you, too. Motherfuckers want to kill you and elect you mayor. You're the New Radicalism. You're what happens when white people listen to hip hop, according to KRS-One on the *Times* op-ed page. Mad kids are loving you on some revolutionary Robin Hood shit. You talk, the fuckin' country listens. So talk, goddammit. And don't worry about prison. I've got everything worked out."

Macon wanted to believe it, so he did. "KRS said that?" he asked, heart quickening at the mention of his one-time idol.

"Uh-huh." Nique wrapped an arm around Macon's back and pushed him toward the spotlight. Another frenzy of lights and questions ended when Macon opened his mouth. He felt fate hanging strange and heavy in the air, as if he'd been barreling toward this moment his entire life without quite knowing it. He turned toward the array of microphones and took a deep breath, savoring the focused silence.

"I want to talk about white people."

Behind him, Nique smiled and clenched his fist. A killer opening. Macon was good. The possibilities were endless.

"Like you?" shouted a reporter, eliciting light laughter. Nique menaced the dude with a finger and he cowered.

Macon nodded, astounded at his own serenity. The stress headache, the grime of jail, were gone. He gazed calmly into the throng, thought, Yes, this makes perfect sense, and felt his heart thump an amen. Yes. I will talk and they will listen. Ready or not, motherfuckers, here I come.

He nodded again. "Right. Like me. I want to talk about white people because if I expose them for what they are, maybe they'll change. Or at least change the way they act. Seems like embarrassment's the only thing that works. Black folks are just lucky they happened to be sitting at Southern lunch counters at the same time that Third World liberation and the Cold War forced a change in U.S. domestic policy so we didn't look like slave masters compared to the Russians, and capitalism could win a few more territories on the Dark Continent." He noticed a reporter scribbling frantically, and realized he was talking two-point-two kilometers a minute.

Macon paused to let those unfortunate enough to be without recording technology catch halfway up. He's loving this, thought Andre from the sidelines, with equal parts elation and resentment. All Macon's faults were virtues in this setting. The crippling self-awareness. The insecurity. The dueling desires to offend and please.

As soon as he stopped talking, there was another ruckus of questions and waving hands. Macon ignored it, stood for a moment lost in thought, and then continued at his leisure.

"The funny thing is, though, who am I exposing white people to? It ain't news to black folks that whites are still racist. I guess I'm exposing white people to themselves. We've gotten so good at pretending we're not racist that we've started to believe it. We act like racism got dealt with back in the sixties, and treat anybody who dares to bring it up today like they're wearing Day-Glo bell-bottoms or something. We teach our kids the doctrine of color blindness, tell them not to notice race. Which is impossible in a society as racially stratified as ours, so all they really learn is not to talk about it. To ignore it and deny it like their parents."

Macon stopped and cracked his knuckles, and the press went ballistic again. Nique stepped in front of the throng: "Hands, people, hands!" They complied and Nique scanned the knot like a kid at recess deciding who to draft onto his kickball team. He grinned and called on the reporter with the biggest breasts. "Yolanda Prince, Channel Four Action News."

She flashed a smile at him and Nique winked, blew her a kiss, and slid back into freeze-frame. "Macon," said Yolanda, "how does a white kid from an affluent suburb end up with such disdain for white people?"

Macon laughed indulgently, impressing himself with the gesture's generosity. "You just answered your own question. Where I'm from is so insulated and complacent that I think the real question is why more people don't freak out and get like me. And you know what? I think plenty of white people do know deep down that they're part of an evil system, and they learn not to think about it, because it would disrupt their lives. We're very short on courage."

Yolanda wasn't satisfied. "But you personally," she pressed. "What makes you—"

Macon nodded and cut her off. "Right, right. The puzzle piece you're looking for is hip hop. That's what led me not only to make friends with black people, but to hang out in black communities. Most white people, even if they have black friends, never expose themselves to any situation that will make them feel uncomfortable or like the minority. Me, I feel uncomfortable if I'm not the minority. I even get suspicious when I see other white folks poking around black culture."

Andre ground his teeth until his jaw flared. Well, bully for you, he thought.

Next to him, Nique smirked: Trap-laying motherfucker. Float them a whiff of paradox and watch them salivate.

"But Macon, isn't that hypocritical?" shouted Dale Kinsley of the WB 11 *News at Ten.*

"Of course," said Macon easily, catching the question like a rubber ball he'd just bounced off a building. "You'll find I'm highly hypocritical. Part of me believes we're all the same, and part of me believes in every racist fairy tale I've ever heard, even the ones that contradict the other ones. I'll look at a black kid standing on a street corner and part of me will decide that he's probably some undiscovered, disadvantaged genius, and want to step in and help him turn his life around like in one of those dumb-ass oh-thank-you-mister-white-man movies. And at the same time, another part of me will look at him and see a menace, a drug dealer, somebody who probably hates me, and want to cross the street to get away from him. And part of me knows that my fear is really guilt, because there are X number of reasons why he's standing on that street corner and I'm not, and I feel like he has the right to hate me for reaping the rewards of a system that excludes him—even more so since I'm aware of it. And another part rejects all that and gets self-righteous about the whole thing, like 'It's his fault, he's where he deserves to be.' Even though for all I know the guy's just waiting for his grandmother to begin with.

"Meanwhile, another part of me is busy blaming you guys, the media, for feeding me so many images of black people as violent criminals that I can't shake them all. Then there's the part that wants more than anything in the world for that kid to nod hello, because that would validate me, make me feel for a minute like I'm not white, not different from him, not responsible for his oppression, or like I'm cool enough to get this murderous gangster thug's respect.

"And meanwhile, another part is busy reassuring me that I am cool, reminding me of all my black friends, and resenting this kid for treating me like just another white dude, not realizing how down with black people I really am. And right next to that is the part that remembers how I once watched a crew of white kids jump a black kid after a pickup basketball game and bust his face open and piss on him and call him every kind of nigger, and I did nothing, didn't say one word. I didn't even call an ambulance. So don't expect anything coherent to come out of my mouth. I'm struggling with this. I do know one thing, though: I'm finished being quiet."

Macon paused and the throng tightened their grips around the necks of their microphones and waited. His burst of honesty had turned the professionally aggressive newspeople docile. Those who'd covered traffic accidents felt a familiar, wincing sense of fascination. Macon was hauling out the bodies, his own the bloodiest of all. The reporters didn't know if they were watching a clever zealot, whose wide-eyed veneer disguised incredible instincts for emotional manipulation, or the unwitting self-annihilation of a mentally deranged kid.

"All I know," Macon went on, making his voice low and serious, "is that even the most concerned white people have always been able to back away from race—and alter their perceptions in amazing ways when the truth is too ugly or complicated." Nique poked him sharply in the back, signaling that Macon was wandering too close to self-incrimination, and Macon took the hint and redirected. "We've got to handcuff white people to race and not let them loose no matter how much they scream," he concluded. "Treat them like they were kicking heroin."

Hands shot up and Nique selected a fly, straight-haired blonde, despite her AM news station's obscurity.

"What would you tell other white kids like yourself, Macon? Will hip hop do for them what it did for you?"

Macon blushed at the hint of flattery embedded in the question. "Probably not," he said. "There's a lot more to it than that. There are millions of white kids listening to hip hop already—more white kids than black kids, actually—and I doubt it's changing their fundamental ideas about race. Plenty of white kids have their little hip hop phase, and they don't all turn conscious any more than all Pink Floyd fans become acidheads. Hip hop's not some magical elixir, it's just a doorway. And nowadays, it probably reinforces more stereotypes than it breaks."

He paused, and wagged a finger at the nearest camera. "All you white kids out there who like hip hop," he said, "keep in mind that hip hop doesn't need you—I mean us. Maybe you should leave it alone. No, wait, keep listening to it but don't try to rap. No, all right, buy it but don't listen to it. No, okay, you can do whatever you want, just be respectful and realize that you're not who it's for—well, at this point, maybe you are who it's for, but you didn't create it and your people are exploiting it like they have every other . . ." Macon trailed off, snarled in his thoughts. "See, that's the problem," he said. "You're only gonna put me on the news for thirty seconds, right? I'm supposed to distill everything into a sound bite, and I'm no good at that. This stuff is too complex; we need to be talking about it morning, noon, and night. I'm down for that, if anybody wants to join me."

Nique tapped him on the shoulder and Macon leaned back and listened as he whispered something. Macon smiled, straightened. "Okay," he said. "Here's a sound bite. White people aren't evil, but evil is white people. Coming soon to a T-shirt near you."

"Cut!" said Nique, stepping in front of Macon and waving his lanky arms like an air-traffic controller. "That's a wrap, folks. Nothing more today. Go home, file your stories, have a drink. Have ten. We'll be in touch." He and Andre ushered Macon into a waiting cab and took off.

"Why'd you do that?" Macon protested as they turned the corner. "I was just getting warmed up."

"Wave," Andre suggested, buzzing the window down.

Macon waved.

Chapter Three

"You were great," raved Nique, stalking 1107 Carman, cigarette in hand. Andre had granted him full smoking privileges on the hunch that the R.A. wasn't going to be fucking with them anymore. "Honest, articulate but not too polished. Disarming, provocative, quirky. A natural." Nique sped his pace and began cutting figure eights around the two desk chairs. "This is gonna be some shit," he said for the hundredth time.

Andre perched on the radiator by the window, watching the street, a mug of instant cocoa in hand. "They're still out there," came the update, *they* meaning the hundred-plus protesters flooding 114th Street, a bloodthirsty and bizarre non-coalition waving signs that ranged from A WHITE RACIST IS STILL A RACIST to VIGILANTES DESERVE VIGILANTE JUSTICE to SELLOUT DIE. A fistful of reporters covered the zealotry and a six-pack of cops kept the demonstrators lazily in check. Columbia security massed in front of Carman, a loose phalanx. Andre shook his head. "In the pouring rain, too. Not good."

"Are you kidding?" Nique scowled. "The more the better. We're getting ricochet publicity off them. Shit, Moves, I'm gonna make you a star."

Macon lay facedown on his bed and didn't answer. Adrenaline had powered him through the impromptu press conference and now he was twitching through withdrawal, on the brink of passing programs that sound good to me, and if we hustle, we can do them all. You can talk to the newspapers tonight and we'll stall the magazines until the buzz builds even higher. We freak it right, we'll get some covers."

"Whoa," said Macon, waving his hand as if he were shooing a fly. "Whoa, whoa. Hold up. I should be worrying about getting my ass a lawyer and staying out of jail." He glanced toward the window and winced. "Not to mention alive."

"Listen," said Nique. "Why do you think those wackjobs outside are so mad? Everybody knows you're guilty as sin, but the case against you is flimsy as a hooker's panties, and everybody knows that, too. All the victims would have to reverse their statements about you being a brother, for one thing, which would make them look ridiculous. That just leaves the one guy as a witness, and he can't even say if the gun, which they don't even have, was real. It's assault and petty robbery, dude. For all they know you could be a copycat criminal, and the original cat is still on the loose. A decent lawyer will get you off with a suspended sentence, at worst. And if you get famous enough, Moves, we can hire one of the best, Cochran or somebody. So let's get you famous, motherfucker."

"It's true," Andre agreed, in his most soothing tone. "They really don't have shit, Macon. And the best way to cover your ass is to become a celebrity. You know that." As if on cue, he and Nique turned up their palms and raised their eyebrows.

Macon dropped his thrumming head into his hand. He didn't want to let on, but he felt tremendously reassured. "How much was my bail?" he asked.

"Twenty-five grand."

"What?" Macon sprang to his feet, and a sharp pain shot through his head. He sank back down onto the bed. "Where the hell did you guys get that kind of dough?"

"You had four," said Andre. "I had six. My mother spotted me the rest. She owes me big. She's an entertainment lawyer and I out—a brink from which he would have gladly plummeted had Nique and Andre not been plotting his hostile takeover of the media and then the world between incoming phone calls.

Radio, TV, newspapers, Web sites, magazines—everybody wanted the well-spoken white criminal race traitor. Andre had adopted the role of press secretary, dutifully cataloging the whos, whats, and wheres in felt-tipped pen on the side of a huge, still-packed cardboard moving box marked *Pimp Shit III: This time it's personal.* Macon had declared a moratorium on decision-making of all kinds until he could get some rest, and so dozens of invitations and interview requests were going unanswered, much to Nique's dismay. He had taken to calling Macon "The Franchise," and to slapping the back of one hand into the palm of the other as he spoke to convey the urgency of his words, even if all he was saying was "We need a pizza."

Nique's patience with his star was running low. "Yo, Moves," he said again. Macon propped himself up on his elbows and rubbed his eyes, resigning himself to the fruitlessness of trying to sleep in this madhouse. He could hear the protesters like they were in the next room, or at least he imagined he could.

"What, Nique, what?"

"You wanna answer the door? Opportunity is knocking."

"He shoulda called before he came."

Andre laughed. "Come on, man," he said. "I saw you up there, having the time of your life. Ain't no way I'm buying this reluctant-hero prima donna shit now, so you might as well sit up and get your game face on." He paused. "I'll roll a joint, if that will help."

Macon turned onto his back, clasped his hands behind his head, and sighed. "I wouldn't stop you. All right. Hit me."

Nique did a quick lateral slide into a chair next to the bed, then stood, flipped it backward with a flick of his wrist, and straddled the seat. Andre rotated the notated side of the *Pimp Shit* box toward Macon, and Nique brandished a pen. "Okay. I say we hit radio tomorrow morning and TV in the afternoon. There's three out—a brink from which he would have gladly plummeted had Nique and Andre not been plotting his hostile takeover of the media and then the world between incoming phone calls.

Radio, TV, newspapers, Web sites, magazines—everybody wanted the well-spoken white criminal race traitor. Andre had adopted the role of press secretary, dutifully cataloging the whos, whats, and wheres in felt-tipped pen on the side of a huge, still-packed cardboard moving box marked *Pimp Shit III: This time it's personal.* Macon had declared a moratorium on decision-making of all kinds until he could get some rest, and so dozens of invitations and interview requests were going unanswered, much to Nique's dismay. He had taken to calling Macon "The Franchise," and to slapping the back of one hand into the palm of the other as he spoke to convey the urgency of his words, even if all he was saying was "We need a pizza."

Nique's patience with his star was running low. "Yo, Moves," he said again. Macon propped himself up on his elbows and rubbed his eyes, resigning himself to the fruitlessness of trying to sleep in this madhouse. He could hear the protesters like they were in the next room, or at least he imagined he could.

"What, Nique, what?"

"You wanna answer the door? Opportunity is knocking."

"He shoulda called before he came."

Andre laughed. "Come on, man," he said. "I saw you up there, having the time of your life. Ain't no way I'm buying this reluctant-hero prima donna shit now, so you might as well sit up and get your game face on." He paused. "I'll roll a joint, if that will help."

Macon turned onto his back, clasped his hands behind his head, and sighed. "I wouldn't stop you. All right. Hit me."

Nique did a quick lateral slide into a chair next to the bed, then stood, flipped it backward with a flick of his wrist, and straddled the seat. Andre rotated the notated side of the *Pimp Shit* box toward Macon, and Nique brandished a pen. "Okay. I say we hit radio tomorrow morning and TV in the afternoon. There's three brought her the biggest client of her career last spring. This fool named Hank Barrows who used to wash my car. He just sold Fox this sitcom about a Black Muslim leader whose distant cousin dies and leaves him custody of three white kids. *Li'l Devils,* it's called." He paused. "Plus I told Moms about you and Cap Anson. That really affected her, somehow."

"Andre, I mean . . . Thanks, but . . ." He tried to size his roommate up. "I've known you four days. Why would you . . ." He sighed. "What do you guys want from me?"

"I've decided to believe in you until you give me reason not to," said Andre, rifling through dresser drawers in search of his stash. A deliberate attempt to stay busy as he spoke, it seemed to Macon. "Somebody's gotta light a fire under white people's asses. Every time a brother does it, somebody up and kills him, so it might as well be you."

Macon rose, walked over, and extended his hand. "I appreciate that, Dre," he said softly. "I promise I won't let you down."

Andre stopped what he was doing long enough to give Macon a rushed pound, then resumed the hunt. "Listen to this fool," he said over his shoulder. "Sounding like a politician already."

"He damn well better," Nique said. "A chance like this doesn't come along every day. For any of us. We gotta make moves here and now. Pun intended. That twenty-five is an investment, Moves. A year from now, I'ma be selling stock in your ass."

"Twenty-five grand." Macon shook his head. "If I was black and robbing black folks, it'd be twenty-five bucks." He stopped and mused. "Then again, if I was black and I'd robbed all those crackers, it'd be like—"

"Be like your ass was still in jail," said Nique.

Macon stood. "I gotta get some air."

"Try Connecticut."

"I'm going uptown to my man Drum One's pad," Macon decided. "Don't book anything yet. I need to think this through."

"Drum One TDK?" asked Andre, looking up.

"How many Drum Ones you know?"

"Wow. He's like the grandpa of graffiti. What's he like?"

"Weird. Call you up and run his jibs for three hours about some twenty-year-old beef he has with some writer you never heard of over who was king of the 1 train in 1978. You don't say five words the whole time—matter fact, you put the phone down, go make a sandwich, and come back just in time to hear him say, 'Yo, you know what I like about you, man? You listen. Stay up.' Then you don't hear from him for six months."

"Well," said Andre, "he can do whatever he wants. How'd you meet him?"

"We've never really met. He used to publish a graff mag and I sent him some flicks of my shit. Actually," Macon confided, failing to keep the pride out of his voice, "judging from the amount of time I've spent listening to him talk about 'the white man,' I'm pretty sure he thinks I'm a brother, too."

"Not if he reads the paper," said Nique.

"Well, he only knows me as Easel. That was my tag."

"Why Easel?"

"Good letters for bombing. Plus, whatever you write Easel on becomes one."

"Nice," said Andre. The bag of herb was in his hand now. He dropped a bud onto his desk, hunched low, and began breaking it apart. "But just to bring it back to reality like Soul II Soul—"

"Or Intelligent Hoodlum," interjected Nique.

"Who just sampled the Soul II Soul song."

"Who just sampled the drums Marley Marl gave Biz for 'Pickin' Boogers.' "

"Who sampled them from some funk record we don't know about regardless," finished Andre, impatient. "Point being, you can't just mosey on downstairs and hop the train, dude. There's a mob calling for your blood outside."

"Hey, I bet there's already Macon Detornay Web sites up," said

Nique. He reached over and pressed a button, and Andre's laptop whirred to life.

"Can anybody in this room focus on anything?" asked Andre. He turned to Macon. "I think you should stay here."

"Suggestion duly noted and rejected. What good is you bailing me out if I'm a prisoner in my room?"

"Well, at least be careful. Here, wear my lid as a disguise." Andre tossed a wide-brimmed fisherman's hat across the room.

"Take my Rineharts," Nique offered. Macon put the glasses on. The room swam green.

"I'm not even gonna look in the mirror," he said, "because I know this looks ridiculous."

"We should come with you," Nique said dully, hands moving over the keyboard like manic spiders.

"Nah," said Macon. "I wanna be alone for a minute."

Nique shrugged and his eyes widened. "Damn, five hundred and sixty-three matches. Ain't that some shit."

Macon hucklebucked eleven flights rather than risk one elevator stare. His footfalls echoed in the cement quiet, and the cement sounds of jail resurfaced for a second. I'm not going back there, Macon told himself, chest cavity tremoring with the sudden applicability of such a hackneyed line. He flipped his jacket collar up and hunched into it, pulled the hat low and thanked God he had the sunglasses, a filter for the world. He remembered a sci-fi book he'd read dog-eared as a kid. A monster in it was so stupid that it wouldn't eat you if you closed your eyes, believing that if you couldn't see it, it couldn't see you.

The tug of Macon's desire to walk among the protesters frightened him as he stalked through the lobby and banged a military-sharp left turn onto campus, away from the crowd, refusing himself even an over-the-shoulder glance. He longed to glide unseen through the throng's ranks and scream with them—to smell their colognes, their breath, the wet wool of their sweaters, anything. Instead he hurried over to Broadway and hailed a cab, arm outstretched at a hitchhiker's angle. The rain splattered against his hat, fat drops amplified by the soaked cloth and sounding solid, like BBs. He slid across the taxi backseat, the fake leather cracked and patched with duct tape, glanced at the driver's ID and told himself he was above dwelling on the irony of now-I'm-riding-in-a-cab.

Drum lived up in Washington Heights, fifty blocks north. Macon leaned back and sighed. His chest felt tight and his head still throbbed with metronome consistency, engorging with pain and draining slowly. He stared at the sheets of rain sloshing over the cab windows and studied the unmatched tempos of the windshield wipers compressing the water down into small moisture-hills, the way the left wiper slashed in and then retreated as the right advanced. When he was little, Macon had always imagined that the wipers were boxing, knocking each other down. The timing was cyclical, and without thinking, Macon counted the number of times the wipers moved between their closest synchronicity and their most dissonant point. Every sixteenth wipe, it turned out, the tips almost kissed. Then they grew apart until they were so distant they were close again.

Macon overtipped the driver, sprinted into Drum's foyer, and pressed his buzzer. No answer. He rang again and sat down on the windowsill, out of ideas. It hadn't occurred to him that Drum might not be home. The cat was pushing fifty, and as far as Macon knew he only stepped out of the lab to put in appearances at graff events, gallery openings and film screenings and whatnot, sign blackbooks for starstruck new-jacks a third his age. Like many old-school writers, Drum was on some paranoid conspiracy shit, refusing to have his picture taken without shielding his face behind a gas mask, sunglasses, or a camouflage army jacket. Periodically, he disappeared overseas, departing abruptly and making veiled, ominous references to "shit" being "hot." There was no point in trying to figure him out, Macon thought; Drum was as indecipherable as the wild styles for which he was famous: twisted, polymorphous letter-forms spiraling through white space, glinting fluorescent, illegal as all hell.

While some of his contemporaries, the first generation of New York writers, graffiti's inventors, had pursued art world acceptance and made the transition from trains to canvases, Drum had stayed underground. Permission walls were not a part of his agenda; artistic terrorism was. To him, *graffiti T-shirt* and *legal piece* were oxymorons. Most of the guys who'd gone legit, Drum was quick to point out, had been pimped and dismissed by the fickle art community, treated as ghetto curiosities, and pushed off the cutting edge as suddenly as they'd defined it.

A few writers were still selling canvases, but that shit looked static, dead. Trains moved; that was the genius of graffiti: words flying through the city, jags of color shrieking every which way, the motion of the pieces locked in violent competition or beautiful harmony with the motion of the trains. It had been a city-sponsored, rotating exhibition seen by five million New Yorkers a day, ridiculously competitive and growing ever more involved until only the secret community of writers could read the names sprayed in interlocking, tangled angles and raging, moving color.

Macon loved knowing the codes; he had studied graff history assiduously from afar, read everything he could get his hands on before he'd ever boosted a spray can. His adrenal glands splayed open as the older heads on the subway station benches handed down the folklore: stories of how writers had taken over New York City, juiced by the prospect of outlaw fame and the double impulse to decorate and decimate a place that had pushed people who looked like them to the margins of existence. Middle-class straphangers commuting in from Jersey and Long Island had been horrified by the secret conversations taking place on public property, the thought that insane black/Latino vandals were beating the city, hiding and striking like ninjas, Zorro to their corrupt Spanish colonizing force, mastering the subterrain and sneaking in and out of train yards and eluding cops and dogs and deadly electrified third rails to rock their shit.

The politicians found it a convenient code. The Mayor's Office declared a War on Graffiti, which sounded nicer than a War on Young People of Color, and beefed up yard security. The city removed perfectly functional trains from the tracks until they could be cleaned, and encouraged the good citizens of the five boroughs to rat out writers and reclaim their neighborhoods and transit lines. They forced captured writers to destroy their own work, jailed and fined them, tried to demoralize them by repainting whole subway lines at once, erasing thousands of pieces.

All of it backfired. Writers met and networked while cleaning cars, formed new alliances and traded information. The clean trains solved the dilemma of artistic overcrowding, and ushered in a golden age as masters competed to cover the new spaces with burners. It took New York City almost twenty years to win the war—from the early seventies to 1988, when the deadly chemical buff finally eradicated all train art with pure robotic precision. And even then, it was a Pyhrric victory, because graffiti had gone worldwide and cats in Copenhagen and Berlin and Johannesburg, not to mention in every town and hamlet of the United Snakes, had picked up on the vibe, studied the New York masters, and started painting burners of their own. Graffiti proved to be the element of hip hop culture that translated best; kids across the globe could understand graff's twin cultural pillars of resistance and self-representation. Even on the home front, it was hip hop's most integrated art form, the only one with a tradition of white innovators: Billy 167 and Smith and Sane and Zephyr.

Hall of Famers like Drum and Blade and Phase 2 and T Kid 170 and Lee and Seen got superstar welcomes from writers worldwide, showed up and vitalized the local scenes. In New York, fresh generations of artists hit up handball courts and walls, and later freight trains, and stubborn, nostalgic old-schoolers kept right on hitting subway cars, knowing full well that their work would never leave the yards and would only be seen by other writers, ghosts, and transit cops. It was sad and elegant and noble, Macon thought, reminded him in some vague way of elephants marching to the graveyard. The dignity and genius of graffiti always made him shiver if he thought about it long enough. The fact that plenty of rank-and-file black and brown people—their neighborhoods doubly bombed by aerosol and urban decay—had hated graff as much as the mayor did only made Macon feel more special, for understanding what they'd failed to.

He stared at Drum's doorbell and wondered what came next. He could wait, but for all Macon knew, Drum was out rocking a mural in Senegal, or informing a breathless delegation of Australian graff nerds that he, and not Kid Panama, had been the first to paint the flying eyeball character.

Street bombing, Macon mused, clouds drifting through his mind. The medium is the message. . . . Clouds massing, growing darker. Take it to the people. Flash. Thunderclap. Brainstorm.

He flipped open Nique's cell phone and called home. Andre picked up and Macon told him to get the word out: Nueva York's favorite alleged criminal slash race theorist slash now-and-again poet will be giving a free public reading tonight on some ol' grassroots rock-the-boulevard shit.

"He will?" asked Andre.

"Old school, baby. Can y'all find me a soapbox?"

"I don't think soap comes in boxes anymore, dude. What about snipers?"

"They don't come in boxes, either." Macon heard Nique shouting in the background, then a muffled argument. Then Nique was on the phone.

"I'm feeling you, Moves. Some underground messiah shit. We'll hook it up so only the media and the truly down will be there. I'll do some real selective publicity, hold it to like a hundred heads.

NYU, Columbia, a couple little hip hop activist chat rooms . . . Hell yeah. Have cats standing in the pouring rain to hear you. Where you want to do this?"

"One Two Fifth and Lenox, right where Malcolm used to preach."

"Perfect."

Chapter Four

Macon sidled through the early-bird crowd, hat pushed low and *got to wear your sunglasses so you can feel cool.* But he didn't. An hour earlier he'd had to corral himself against the bulletproof impulse to walk amongst his teeming enemies, and now weaving through a crowd gathered on his behalf scared Macon numb. He clenched his teeth and prayed for a few more minutes' anonymity, a chance to gather up his cool before they clamored at him. Eyes downcast and slicing left-right-left as he navigated the umbrellas, Macon recognized his homeboys by their footwear and grabbed Nique's elbow from behind.

Nique whirled with caffeine reflexes, then smiled. "Damn, Big Time, look at you. Incognegro like a mug." Macon glanced around, dreading the recognition that might come at any clock-tick. A hundred people? Shiiit. Three times that were huddled underneath umbrellas, rain bouncing syncopated on black, white, and blue vinyl. The whole northern side of the block was crammed solid with folks; the occasional unaffiliated pedestrian had to cross the street just to get by. Television trucks bookended the crowd, parked against either curb. Stage lights threw heavy beams across the area and baked the masses in their raingear. Visibility was fifteen feet, and a strange hush hung weighty; Macon had the bizarre realization that this was the quietest he'd ever seen three hundred folks outside a place of worship or a movie house. Anticipation simmered and mumbled, but the stage lights and the rain, the heat and wetness, had wilted conversation down to nearly nothing.

Andre's massive black umbrella domed the three of them in privacy. "This is fifteen phone calls and two chat-room postings," Nique confided with glee. He pushed his sweatshirt sleeves to his elbows, and Macon watched the steam rise from his skin.

Andre rolled his eyes. "Of course, Yolanda Prince was first. She's Dominique's new girlfriend."

"Yolanda's a hell of a reporter," said Nique, flicking a sidelong glance at a cluster of NYU girls smoking cigarettes, "with her fine ass." Macon followed Nique's gaze, then snapped his head away as he made inadvertent contact with a white girl in a baby-blue jacket, neck open to reveal a gold name-chain that matched her hoop earrings, each one the circumference of a coffee cup. Her eyes jumped and she whispered to her friends.

"I haven't even told you the best part," Nique began, then stopped and jabbed his chin as if to say, *Look behind you.* The Franchise turned to find the baby-blue girl poised to tap him on the shoulder. Before he could speak, she leaned forward and pecked his cheek, leaving a dark red imprint on Macon's face and blotting the lipstick left on her own grill down to a matte. She rested one hand on her jutting hip and gestured with the other, sending several bangles clattering up her arm.

"I been, like, watching you on the news, man," she said, pointing a three-inch fingernail at him. A Latina inflection tinged her words and bent her *L*s. "And my family is like, 'Who is this asshole?' but I feel you. For real. I told all my girls, 'You need to listen to what he's saying because he's telling the truth.' " Macon squeezed her hand, half-listening, and wondered if she'd set off a ripple, broken the seal; was a line forming? The combination of his distaste at the thought of interacting with his fans and the false intimacy of the hand squeeze—where had that shit come from?—made Macon feel like a hack politician.

"I appreciate that," was the best he could do, weak and low-spoken. He knew it wasn't what he should have said, who he should have been, by the slight dulling of homegirl's eyes. The refracted failure slapped him in the face and Macon's spine straightened; his mind perked into new alertness. The shittiness of missing like that, failing to connect, overrode Macon's reticence and *boom*: He had his game face on.

The girl was doing her best fadeaway. "I'm gonna let you do your thing," she said, twisting to look over her shoulder and locate her crew. "I just wanted to say hello."

She gave his hand a little good-bye squeeze, and Macon responded with a hold-on-a-second tug and said, "Hey." She looked up, surprised, and found his eyes sizzling; a smile like sunrise blazed across his face, and she grinned back. She loves me again, Macon found himself thinking, delighted. I'm such an idiot, he rhapsodized. "Listen, thanks for coming," was his benediction. She beamed at him and slipped away, demure and happy. Macon slid back beneath the safety of the umbrella, reinvigorated.

"Question," he said to Andre.

"Shoot."

"Why is it that white b-boys try to act black and white b-girls try to act Puerto Rican?"

Before Andre could posit a theory, a stocky white kid in a matched-set PNB Nation sweatshirt and baseball cap muscled up into the cipher out of nowhere. "Yo, son," he said, voice straining to function in the octave at which he had submerged it, and gave enthusiastic pounds all round, ignoring the who-is-this-fool brow-beats they threw him in return. He hunched in close, as if he were outlining a play, and out of habit Macon, Andre, and Nique pricked up their ears and bowed their heads, eyes trained solemnly on the circle of pavement between their eight shoes as they waited for the jewels of wisdom to drop from the dude's goatee-encircled mouth.

"You keeping it mad real, na'mean?" His face was taut with earnestness. "Yo, people wanna hate, you know what I'm sayin', but you just gotta keep ya head up, na'mean? No justice, no peace. Power to the people. You don't vote, you don't count. No more Chernobyls. Tawana told the truth. Free Mumia. Free the Chicago Seven. Save the whales. It'll be a great day when our schools have all the money they need and the Air Force has to hold a bake sale to buy a bomber. Rock the vote. Chevrolet: We build excitement. One love, dog." He tapped his chest with an open palm, then hit Macon's with the back of his hand. "I got your back, dog. Stay up. Harambe. Peace and blessings. I'm out."

"A'ight," said Nique, bobbing his head. The kid bobbed back, gave Nique a forceful, finger-snap-release pound, and stood nodding in rhythm at the ground, showing no signs of being out. Nique decided to ignore him, and turned to Macon.

"So anyway," he said.

"Hi, Andre!" called Amy Green. They turned to face a Columbia BSU squad rolling twenty deep. Ms. Green stood beneath a two-handled Kinte-striped umbrella held for her by a pair of twin freshman two-guards. She air-kissed Andre three times, left-right-left, squeezing his shoulders with her palms to hold him in place so she could properly execute the Continental maneuver. "Thanks so much for the invite." She grinned at Macon and offered her hand. "And you," she said.

Macon waited for her to finish her sentence, then realized she was being fabulous. "Did you tell Macon what we talked about?" she asked Andre, fluttering thick eyelashes over wide Japanimation eyes until Macon swore he could feel a light breeze on his cheeks.

Flustered, Andre looked at the BSU troops massed behind her. "It's like this," he said to Macon.

"Well, I'm here now," snapped Amy, charm-school finish falling to the pavement like a chrysalis. "I can tell him myself." She cocked her head toward Macon and the smile reappeared. Andre retreated half a pace and wondered what it was about Amy that made him want to impale himself for failing her.

"Columbia is auditing us," she said. "They know you got arrested at our meeting, and they think you gave the BSU the money from the—"

Nique, in the middle of a new conversation but standing back-to-back with Macon and monitoring this one, turned his head and interjected. "Alleged money."

"Alleged money," repeated Amy. "From the alleged robberies. So now they're looking into our financial records, which means they're going to find out that we're insolvent because nobody came to Karen's stupid Come As Your Favorite Broadway Character dance last spring. We need money, Macon. And as I was telling your roommate"—she ushered him back into grace with a smile, and Andre bounded to her side and backed her with a steady head nod, feeling like a Pip—"it would really help us out if you'd be our Black History Month speaker. You're a major draw."

Macon's grin felt huge even to him. "I'd love to," he said.

"Wonderful." She nodded to her umbrella bearers, and lifted a thumb-and-pinkie telephone to her ear. "I'll give you a bell."

The Tourettic, high-end jerking of synthesized horn stabs, whistles, and sirens cut short further political pleasantries, and three-hundred-plus heads whirled to see a neon-green-streaked van pull to the curb, quivering with earthquake bass.

"They're here," Nique enthused, turning to throw an arm around The Franchise. Macon scowled at him, refusing to shape the obvious question into words. "I been trying to tell you, dude. *Rebel Yells* is doing a segment on you. International exposure." He smiled with self-satisfaction and presented a fist for Macon to boom. "Who's your boy, Moves?"

"Are you kidding me? The MTV show that interviews pretty-boy actors about nuclear proliferation and then acts like mufuckers are radicals? That tails junkie rockers and pretends their tantrums are political?"

"They do some real shit, too. Your boy KRS been on there."

"It was him, Reese Witherspoon, and Iman talking about organic farming, Nique."

"Well, they're here for the Macon Detornay Show today, so get ready to freak some shit. I'll introduce you."

The van door slid open and the music blared out in concentric circles, pushing back the crowd. A fortyish technician wearing a Pantera T-shirt poked his shaggy head out and took quick stock of the audience, then disappeared inside. The techno cut off, and the boho boom-bip of A Tribe Called Quest's second album, awash in mellow horn loops, silky live bass lines, and abstract poetics, replaced it at a lower decibel. A good choice, Macon had to admit. It was a perennial progressive favorite, an album white college kids bumped in their dorm rooms, feeling hip, included, unthreatened, and hard-rocks acknowledged as a classic, a beat fiend's uncut fix. Musical crossover without compromise, something neophytes and old-schoolers alike could dig. An album that, when it dropped in '91, made even novice listeners self-righteous and indignant about the other directions the music was taking. My First Album and This Is What Hip Hop Should Be wrapped into one.

Eight young women, outfitted for spring break in Miami, bounced from a second vehicle. They surrounded the music van and squealed with wholesome sexy delight, shaking ass and tits to the music, whipping manes of hair back and forth over their shoulders and smiling invitations to the hoodied-down default-position-surly *I don't wanna see no dancin' / I'm sick of that shit / Listen to the hit* nine-decca stalwart b-folks, who looked at them and then each other and then patted their breast pockets on this-shit's-too-bugged bluntquests.

So that's where girls like that come from, thought Andre. Crates of beverages appeared along the dancing girl circle's perimeter, and the crowd edged forward suspiciously to squint at the proffered refreshments. Andre craned his neck to read the flowing script airbrushed on the van's side: *When a Rebel Gets Thirsty, a Rebel Yells Fruitopia.*

"A toast," Nique said, returning from the front with three bottles of Revolutionary Raspberry Iced Tea and distributing them to his cohorts. "To The Franchise. The baddest whiteboy going. Personally, I still think you're full of shit, but hell, go 'head and keep proving me wrong. Let's take it to the stage." He bent the bottle skyward and gulped the sugary contents until his Adam's apple piston-pumped.

"I'll drink to that," said Andre quickly, hoping his roommate would let it go and knowing there was no way.

"Full of shit how?" Macon inquired.

"In all the usual fake-martyr, last-ferry-to-the-mainland ways. Don't take it as a dis, though, dog. It's more of a disclaimer."

Macon pursed his lips so hard they whitened. "Fair enough." For all his rhetoric, he tired easily of black people's skepticism; by now, he expected to be off the hook. "Maybe I am. But here's to showing and proving." Andre exhaled relief.

Macon took a nip of iced tea and felt it dribble down his throat, dissolving patience. "All right," he said, "let's do this thing."

"They've got some kind of soundstage by the vans, it looks like," Andre observed, standing on tiptoe. A wolf pack of dudes had formed around the dancers, hands pocketed and backpack zipper-strings swaying.

"Fuck a soundstage," said Macon. "This is my show, not theirs. People can turn around, shut up, and listen."

Nique shrugged. "Keep it rugged, I guess." He took a deep breath and cupped his hands into a makeshift bullhorn. "Ladies and gentlemen," he bellowed, "children of all ages." A few dudes half-turned to look at him, without unplanting their feet. "Turn off the fucking music!" Nique yelled, and moments later it faded out. The dancers retreated to their van, donned sweatshirts, and left the doors open to listen. The crowd reshuffled to face Nique, who dropped his hands and paced a little figure eight as he spoke, marking off some territory. Macon, sensing that he'd have to make an entrance of some kind, receded back into the fringes and stood with Andre, the umbrella low enough to shield his face. The rain had eased into a drizzle.

"I'm about to bring on Macon Detornay," Nique hollered, drawing claps, whoo-hoos, and whistles from the crowd. He swung his arms, long-striding, bright-voiced. "And I know y'all want to see my man. Right?" The backpacked masses validated the assumption with more noise. A lifetime of viewership had versed them in the tropes of hype-man theatricality; like every audience everywhere, they knew what was expected of them.

"We got some ground rules for y'all first, though," continued Nique, scanning the crowd on tiptoe when he hit the far curves of his eight. "Cuz this a poetry reading, yunno? It ain't a press conference, a rally, or none of that shit. There'll be a time for all those things, too, but we out here tonight to check out my man's artistic side, and we out here on the street because this is all about the people, you know what I'm sayin', coming together and grabbing ourselves some public space instead of paying to be up in some wack-ass club." He paused, and the crowd took its cue and clapped.

"We glad to have the media here, but if y'all disrupt the proceedings, you'll be asked to leave. It's been a crazy week for Macon, so after he reads he's gonna break out. You won't have a chance to talk to him. We don't mean to be rude, but shit is just a little hectic right now, as I'm sure you can imagine. We appreciate everybody coming out tonight, braving the elements and whatnot, and I hope y'all will stick around afterward and maybe some other poets or rappers or whatever from the audience can do a little something, too. Turn this into an open-mic type thing. Y'all feel me?"

The audience nodded, offered up low-toned *a'ights*. A vibrational low point, to be sure, thought Andre, but Nique knew re-hyping them was as easy as "So y'all wanna hear Macon?"

"Yeah!"

"One more time: Are y'all ready for Macon Detornay?"

"Yeah!"

Macon stepped forward to center stage, into the warm spotlights of the TV trucks, and peeped the mass of clapping human beings gathered in the wetness to hear him. He stared into the crowd as if it were a jungle, and the moment accelerated straight toward him, rushed at Macon like a tiger leaping from the dense lush greenery and pounced. It knocked him over: the dick-hardening realization that all this was real. People were listening. There were other kids like him out there—right here—skating along the edges of whiteness as disgusted as he was, looking for a leader, a mouthpiece, someone to tell them what to do and validate their angst before it turned sour or misfired or faded. There was enough energy compressed into the sidewalk of this city block alone to set shit thoroughly aflame.

For the first time, Macon thought about the legions of white people out there who, if they weren't as committed as he was, were at least highly suggestible. Perhaps even open-minded enough to learn to be self-critical—and it would be cake to make people feel good about being self-critical, venturing far enough outside themselves to analyze and bat around the forces that made them think the way they did. Until they saw where it was going, anyway.

White liberals did it all the time for kicks: It was an out-of-body experience, an alibi. They reentered themselves warm with the pleasure of self-castigation and went back to whatever they were doing, probably ripping the skin off somebody's baby daughter. But what if he pulled these kids in and then pulled the plug, caught them in a whirlpool? All that half-conscious, timid whitekid energy beaming down, all those scattershot rays in search of focus and *Macon Everett Detornay, magnifying glass.* Or *Macon Everett Detornay, mirror,* flashing that energy back toward the heavens, melting its source like plastic soldiers and remolding them somehow. Wiggers of the world, unite.

This was getting too goddamn abstract. Macon Everett Detornay, standing on a rainy Harlem block lost in thought with a court date looming and the unharnessed energy of all those white kids shining on nothing but him. He took a mental note: Don't fuck up and become the toy soldier yourself.

"This joint is called 'It's Your World Tour,' " he said. "Because it's kind of all over the place. I wrote it awhile back, when I was still living in Boston. It's about, I dunno, a lot of important shit . . . why we're all so fucked up, I guess. I don't really know what else to say about it. Last time I read, like half the audience walked out on me, so I hope you guys are a little more receptive." He got the laugh and began, hoping the crowd wouldn't notice how much the pages were shaking in his hand.

peep the dj as counter-revolutionary
starting one by stopping one

backspinning beginnings
cutting space time continuums

cut & paste   drum & bass   peep the dj dropping one

falling to his knees
in the garden of delights
transplanting funk perennials
to bigger flowerpots

pre moistened
with the mississippi goddamn water wrung
from lunchcounter revolutionaries'
soaking clothes

pop's vinyl crackles thru the den
phil ochs folksingin   i ain't marchin any more

that's word

just sit right here and do my thing

destruction has two opposites   preservation & creation

plus the ambiguity & dislocation
of the postmodern moment & my left shoulder
prevent me from holding signs aloft

voice too hoarse from rhyming into broken mics to sing along

we shall over   sle-e-eep

i used to get politically ill back in high school
make aura drive me to one of those
hundred deep encounter group weekend retreats
& wait outside   engine running

white kids united against racism or
liberal activists for peace love unity & havin fun   some shit

i come in   kung fu paper doors down
with an urn of malcolm x's ashes balanced on my head
& start schoolin the masses like a
sub with a one week
curriculum jump on his classes

y'all pretentious no experience
nonsense talkin guilty conscience
nonslickniks & hippychicks
can't & won't do shit
need to sit down & read this this & this

that was me

tell the white man in the mirror
the truth right to his face
then split

sometimes girls followed me outside

guess i was black enough for them   revolution is a bitch

so amidst our talk of change i'd pitch
pennies at the tattered waxpaper cups
of those from whom i'd cribbed my strut

i sure do sympathize bruh man it must be tough

to shuck an honest buck
when yo performance space invaded
by the puma tracks
of doo doo wack
backpack rap cats
who just don't give a fuck

makin clique tracks up 6th ave
with plastic fat beats bags
& killer crossover vocab

at least i pledged an oath
they pledgin hip hop like a frat

so now i trail behind
strapped with a notepad
pretendin to be

the caucazoid shaharazad ali
revising the white man's guide
to understanding white rappers
& their sublimated racial pride

everytime a cracker
drops a twelve inch single
these jokers go into

great white hope
conniption fits yo this the new shit

jack they johnsons
until they bust all over
the heavyweight tradition

& wipe up the viscous liquid mess
with misappropriated quotes

yo rakim said
it ain't where you're from it's where you're at

race privilege where ya at?

is the caucus mountains in the hoooooouuusse? ho-oooo!

mufuckers so self-righteous
they wanna talk about the racism
that makes black people
think whiteboys can't rhyme

but the new shit
is the same ol shit
you shitheads

understanding culture from the essence of the root of the tree
and not just from the leaves falling to the ground

as drum one said
before he skipped the continent himself

i gotta be invisible for a minute
he told me on the phone
& by the same time next week
was gone

imagine that   this is a cat who made
high profile invisibility an artform

cleaving thru parties on the diggy low
in camo suits and shades
pretendin not to know
that he's a legend
with styles & names
trapped beneath the paintjobs
of a zillion trains

i tried to catch him in bologna
but all i saw was
two drum walls
each one bout ten feet wide
& ten feet tall

clearly visible
from the passing eurorail

that's what i'm talkin bout
canvas the neighborhood

each one
a swooshing graceful
hydra snake of steaming color
interlocking   triple jointed
& seeming to spin slower & faster
perpetual & self-sufficient
a maze of motion
the perfect power source professor
if only he would tell us how it works

pinks moving into blues & green
exotic shades of sunrise flesh & plasma
radiating in n out themselves a
miscegeny swirl of statement & magenta
bubbling & bulging
with the struggle of containing itself
along preposterous smooth curves &
ginsu racing edges

i wish i'd been with him when he
perfected graff
but i was tied up in
mrs joseph's kindergarten art class

making those drawings
where you rub a craypa
vibrancy of color mishmash

over the whole page
& cover it with black

then paperclip scrape
a little bit back off & bam
you got an art project

thin raised welts of color all that's left
enough to get
a kid like me
diznizzy with regret

depressed by those pathetic silhouettes
& wishin just once mrs joseph

would let me leave my shit
unbuffed uncuffed & scuffed

lucky for me i wrote with my left
& thus kept
a smudged n smeary copy
of all my work on hand

so maybe long before i boosted a spray can
or picked up a pen to chisel myself
into the piece of work i am

i was filling in the
overlapping panel of this
human venn diagram
connecting culture to belief & who we are to what we be

makes sense to me but see
you gotta understand
i come from a fam steeped
generations deep
in contradiction

not even my ancestors could enter a temple
without clenching their fists

against the bullshit that was religion
but everybody always felt culturally jewish

i couldn't even say that much until

my homegirl
told me about golems

these mythic kabbalistic
jewish mystic

anti-pogrom
secret weapons

unbeatable warrior giants
inscribed with the hebrew word for truth
& made of clay

that come alive

entered by whatever
spirit you summon when you pray

& fuck up
all your enemies
like a supernatural bruce willis

when they're finished
you erase the alef
turning truth to death
& they die

i was like damn
i never knew us jews

had some shit like that on our side
hell i'm down   just show me where to sign

that's the type of ally
might make me overlook my
early religious education at the
so you think you might be jewish
sunday school and grill

where the aged
mr israel kaufman
taught us kids
about the jewish exodus

from roxbury in the fifties

him his wife n family
split like the red sea
& benny goodman swingstepped to suburbia
when the neighborhood went technicolor
like an old charlton heston movie

& now he sits as if
on mt sinai & kicks

lesson plans

about how blacks are shiftless & lazy
except satch sanders from the old celtics

to a preadolescent audience which
inhales without filtering for content

shoving things into their minds at 12 years
as they shoved things into their mouths at 12 months

i had to get out of town man
i was on the verge
of giving up

spent nineteen summers undercover   playin i spy
pretendin white was my disguise
& drinkin brewskis with the guys

came to realize
these cats don't even bother
to synthesize alibis

because they've never thought
about their crimes

it always takes me a little while
to readjust my eyes
& remember
how white people act so blind

unaffected & dyslexic
interested not obsessive

they don't even think about it

not that i'm claiming for a second
some kind of transcendental
whiteboy living with the brothers
exemptive double consciousness
honorary blackness or
complex composite status

quite the opposite
i'm more indebted
to the white skin privilege
of waking up

& not having to think
about this shit
than i'd care to admit

not to mention
the debt i rack up
when i submit

this poem to
i dunno know the new yorker
& they publish it

They were silent until Macon bowed: deep from the waist, an overgesture. Only when he finished did he realize it had stopped raining; the umbrellas had been folded, tucked under arms and shoved in bags. And then a new rainstorm began, a monsoon of applause. Macon stood and let it drench him, mingle with the exhilaration dancing on his skin and rivulet over his shoulders. He smiled, feeling suddenly like *Macon Everett Detornay, lightning rod.* All the energy he'd sensed crackling a few minutes before was coursing through him now, making him strong. This is gonna work, he found himself thinking. We're gonna harness all of this and change the world. He knew the notion was vague, meaningless in its uncut form, but he felt hope's champagne-colored tingle nonetheless. I'll look back at this moment as a glimpse of destiny, he decided, refusing to be embarrassed by the notion's melodrama.

For a moment, the thought that he was about to be assassinated, cut down where he stood in sudden gun spray from the front row, flashed through Macon's mind. He shrugged it off. None of his premonitions ever came true. It was enough, though, to convince him to wave thank you and retreat from the hallowed circle hollowed for him, to make the exit Nique had advised: Head for the sunset with applause still jangling your ears, Moves.

Andre and Nique flanked him and the cadre hustled unmolested through the pliant, cheering crowd. An MTV cameraman duck-walked beside them, filming Macon's getaway; the Franchise grinned into the camera, glowing, waved good-bye as he and his team outpaced the guy and made a clean escape.

"I can't believe how smoothly that went," Andre said a block later, spinning to look back at the still-knotted crowd. Laughter rippled through it; someone else must have taken the stage.

"Hey, Macon. Did I miss the show?" Logan was walking toward them down the quiet street, swinging the strap of her knit purse in wide arcs. A pink tank top exposed her lean shoulders; Macon studied the tattooed snake curled around her upper arm with interest. She gave him a quick hug and a kiss on the cheek, then turned to his friends. "How'd he do?"

"I'm sorry," said Macon, off-balance again in her presence. "Andre, Nique, this is Logan. We met the other night, at the Nuyorican."

"Back when he was nobody," said Logan, smirking. She punched Macon in the arm. "You were supposed to call and tell me when you were reading again, man. I had to hear about it from my girl."

Macon snapped his fingers. "Oh shit," he said. "That reminds me. Nique, gimme your phone." He rummaged through his pockets until he found the page ripped from the screaming inmate's copy of *Native Son,* and dialed the number scribbled on it. "This might solve all our problems," he told them as the phone rang. A man picked up the line, and Macon's face clouded with confusion.

He covered the mouthpiece with his hand and flared his nostrils. "What the hell is Justin's?"

"Puff Daddy's restaurant," said Logan. "Why?"

"Lemme get a table for four in half an hour," Macon said into the phone.

Chapter Five

Justin's was all unseen light sources and supple curves, heaps of cream and ice-blue laced with dashes of mahogany and gold, as if whoever had designed the spot was begging for a movie to be shot there but only had the budget for music video opulence and had cribbed his sense of luxury from MTV regardless. It was a cavernous, multi-leveled room on Twenty-first Street, flashy on a nascently hip block, soul food for the new-money black bourgeoisie and their attendant wannabes. Anita Baker crooned on the sound system, barely audible, as R&B-looking slicksters in suits and band-collared shirts leaned over appetizers toward impeccably made-up women. Jewelry and teeth flashed. Almost every table was full. It was the kind of place at which Andre would have liked to feel at home, but didn't.

"The Puffster's restaurant, huh?" Nique muttered as the hostess showed them to their seats. "What do they do, mix together scraps of food more talented chefs cooked in the eighties?"

Andre deaded the small talk as soon as the barbecued salmon, fried chicken, collard greens, and cornbread hit the table. Logan had lost cool points by ordering the smothered swine chops, but they let it slide without comment. Her affinity for filthy and treacherous animals, pigs and serpents, was less noteworthy to Nique and Andre than the fact that Macon had apparently taken a liking to a girl with little titties and virtually no ass.

I would have thought he'd like black women, Andre mused, running a visual inventory on Logan from across the table. She wasn't pretty, per se, but something about her made your eyes happy. A revelation tickled him: Macon likes white chicks on some transgressive shit. Like he's a brother. As if he's crossing some line.

Had Andre broached the subject of racial preference, Macon would have shrugged and said he dug all women. The dregs of New England Puritanism swirling through his upbringing kept him embarrassed about things like pornography, so Macon would not have mentioned the role a certain well-worn videotape had played in the formation of his sexual politics.

Macon had owned one fucktape in his life, and he'd stolen it from Jihad; he'd never buy one. It was called *Black Anal:* one low-resolution clip after the next of hugely endowed brothers dicking down sisters, spreading their asses with brutal indifference. Macon had watched it plenty, since it was the only show in town, and slivers of silver intimidation had rubbed off the tape and lodged in Macon's brain, frustrating his logical mind. Here was the metaphorical big black dick made flesh, the rudder steering the ship of white America's frenzy and fear and fascination, everything Macon didn't want to believe, tried not to believe, but did—did, and benefited from. Just being down with the brothers gave him a bigger dick by association, swelled his masculinity like it did that of every kid thugging it up in front of his bedroom mirror, rhyming along to a rap song. That was where most of those kids' relationships to blackness began and ended: It was an ideal against which to measure your pubescent self, a Staggerlee costume to try on, arms swimming in the sleeves for a shameful minute, an ironic hour, a strutting day, then push as far back in the closet as it would go.

Macon had considered acquiring a white porno just to promote image equality, so he wouldn't be objectifying black people in isolation. The sexual voyeurism of porn didn't faze him, but as he lay on his bed, cock in one hand and VCR remote in the other, it became increasingly difficult for Macon not to think about the fact that the masters had liked to watch the slaves go at it, too, from time to time. Not to mention the sport they'd made of rape; it had been America's national pastime back then. Macon shuddered and turned away from the TV, unwilling to even contemplate the implications of all that. He could convince himself that black dudes' acceptance of him might be legit, but not black women's. If a sister wanted to take him to bed, it didn't mean he'd passed a test, it meant she'd flunked one. As much as he would have liked to feel otherwise—and as much as some black women seemed to appreciate him—that was the only way Macon could make himself see it. How might the world change, he wondered, if science could somehow prove to the satisfaction of every white man that all races were hung equal? Or was that after the fact, besides the point? He remembered hearing that the Nazis thought the Jews had horsecocks, too.

Eventually, Macon had said fuck it, and thrown *Black Anal* away. It wasn't even his fetish, he reminded himself one final time, staring across his bedroom at the garbage can in which he'd buried it. He couldn't be held responsible for any of this. It was Jihad's goddamn tape.

Logan's presence at the table had sent Nique, too, into a mental tailspin; he smoothed his sweatshirt, eased back into his velvet chair, and theorized about the wisdom of having Macon seen in public with a female companion, and furthermore with a white female companion, and on top of that a weird, tattooed, punk-rock-looking white female companion. Not that a sister would send quite the right message, either, Nique supposed. A left-out-of-the-conversation minority member might add an interesting dimension . . . a Filipina honeydip, perhaps? Nique was on the verge of concluding that women were too problematic, emblematically speaking, to deal with at all at this point in Macon's career when Andre chopped the heels of both his hands against the table, as if showing them how long a fish he'd caught, and hunkered down to business.

"All right, kids," he said. "I'm not sure why we're here, or how we're gonna pay for twenty-five-dollar-a-plate soul food, or why some dude Macon met in lockdown is our new *Zagat Guide,* but I'm okay with that. What I'm not okay with is the fact that we have twelve hours' worth of interviews requested tomorrow, ten minutes to confirm, and an interviewee who's still stalling about what he wants to do. Not to mention what he's gonna say. You care to address any of this, Mr. Franchise, or would you like to hear a few compelling arguments from Nique and myself concerning why you've got to do the shit?" He sliced a piece of salmon and added a daub of mashed potato to the fork. Andre ate like he was painting.

Macon wiped barbecue sauce from his mouth, refolded his napkin, and looked around. "I asked for hot sauce like ten minutes ago," he complained. "How I'm supposed to eat this mac and cheese without no hot sauce? Man, Puffy is slipping. Frank White must be spinning in his grave." His dinner companions stared at him. Nique went so far as to begin drumming his fingers on the tabletop.

"Sorry," said Macon. "Sorry. Okay. No, you don't have to convince me of anything. I want to do it all. Being in front of that crowd tonight made me realize I've got to run with the ball."

"The end zone," Andre prodded, "being where, exactly?"

"That I'm not sure yet. I tend to, you know, think on my toes."

"Only on your toes?"

Macon ignored him. "It's just a question of going in there, answering whatever they ask me, and coming up with some kind of brilliant plan on the fly." He shoveled a heaping pile of greens into his mouth and crossed his arms over his chair.

Andre took an agitated pull of sweet tea. "That's so Zen it makes me want to smack you in the mouth. This isn't a grade-school book report, dude. People are gunning for your ass. Don't you think we should brainstorm a little?"

Macon shrugged. "If you really want to help me," he said, "figure out how to make white kids think I'm cool enough to listen to when I tell them to do shit they don't wanna do. How do we make feeling stupid and vulnerable sound cool?"

Andre rested his elbows on the table and brushed cornbread crumbs from his fingers. "Sounds like you've already got a plan." Hope and suspicion mingled in his tone.

"Not really. I just know I've gotta put some pressure on white people. Challenge them."

"That's good," said Logan. She slid her knife and fork to one side of the plate, and gestured at Macon with a gnawed-clean swine bone. "The best defense is a good offense. And believe me, you're gonna need one—do you know what people are saying about you? In the mainstream media, I mean. Sure, the backpack crowd is gonna like you, but have you read the *Wall Street Journal* today?"

Six eyes stared at her. "You read the *Journal*?" asked Nique.

"I have to. I'm a financial consultant. Pricewaterhouse-Coopers."

"Get the fuck outta here."

"Hey, I got sixty grand in student loans to pay off before I can go open a pottery studio in Vermont or some hippy-dippy shit like that. I cover the tattoos with a suit, gel my hair down, and tell companies how to spend their money. Except I don't tell them to stop wasting it on financial consultants. It sucks, but you gotta do what you gotta. I try to steal as many office supplies as possible. Anyway, the point is that the press is covering you like you're a dangerous lunatic, not some great new thinker. Even the folks who like you think you're nuts. You've got to change that."

Andre nodded through Logan's last few sentences, and when she finished he reached over and patted the back of her hand, as if they were an old married couple. "I couldn't agree more, Moves. You've gotta hit them with some history. Some scholarship. Quote DuBois and shit. You know."

"Start an organization," Logan suggested, sweeping her crumbs into a little pile and then mashing them into the table with the heel of her hand. "The second people hear *association* or *foundation,* they start taking you more seriously."

"The space you want to occupy," Nique chimed in, "is Black Media Radical. As long as there's TV there's gotta be one. Malcolm was the first, and the best. Farrakhan doesn't want the job anymore. Khalid Muhammad's too extreme, Jesse's too mainstream, Reverend Al's too ghetto. You've gotta be part demagogue so they can use you to scare white folks, but still come off as credible enough for whites to assume you speak for all black people. There's never been a white one, obviously." He moved a bite of yams from fork to mouth with casual precision, wagged an I-ain't-finished forefinger at Macon, and parked the food in his left cheek so he could speak.

"But that's a Crow Jim law I'm willing to topple." Nique glanced at the waiter and tapped his empty Jack-and-ginger glass. "Right now, I think airing white folks' dirty laundry and scaring them shitless is the most important thing." He pointed a sharp pinky at Logan and downed the final drizzle of his drink. "I like the organization thing. Makes it seem more real."

"How about something with 'Evil is white people'?" suggested Andre, wanting to say something. It was important to provide Nique with speed bumps when he started to rev up. Otherwise he'd hit the red and you'd be plastered flat against the passenger seat until he ran out of gas. "That's our sound bite, right?"

Nique grimaced. "Too out, dude, too crazy. If we stick with it, we'll alienate the world."

Macon looked at Logan's hand, resting flat against the table, and noticed her long, slim fingers and perfect ovaline nails. Then he thought about Vermont and pottery wheels and Logan in little terry-cloth shorts, legs smeared with blue-gray clay, nipples poking through a cotton undershirt as she threw pots late at night.

"The Race Traitor Project," he announced, with an air of finality.

Nique's lips pooched in evaluation and he looked like the catfish he'd just devoured. "Not bad." He nodded. "Catchy but scary. Forces reporters to ask you what it means, so there's a built-in launching pad."

Macon turned to Logan. "You want to be the CEO?"

"Hey," said Nique. "Hold on a minute there."

"I think it's gotta be an all-white organization," explained Macon. "So I can talk about how white people need to get their own house in order, police each other, stop burdening black folks, shit like that."

"We should get advisory titles, at least," persisted Nique. "Right, Dre?"

"Man, I don't give a fuck."

"I wanna be Minister of Information."

Macon threw up his hands. "Fine."

"And Andre can be Chief of Staff."

"Whatever."

"All right," said Nique, "now that that's settled, I'll get on the horn and book your ass." He pulled his cell phone like a pistol and yanked the antenna with flair. "So start working on a plan."

"Trust me," said Macon. "At least as far as you can throw me."

The waiter laid a round of peach cobblers on the table, vanilla ice cream dolloped on top. "Compliments of the gentleman in the corner." He leaned in close. "Give those crackers hell, Macon," he whispered, then straightened. "No offense."

Macon smiled. "None taken." In the corner, waving, fork in hand, sat Professor Umamu Shaheed Alam.

Macon waved back. "Ballsy fucker. I guess I should go over, huh?"

Dre raised his glass to Alam in tribute, then glanced at Macon and found him clocking the professor with cagey, narrowed eyes. "I'll come," he volunteered. "Might as well lock down my easy A."

They sauntered over and Alam wrung both their hands without standing. Unwedging his belly from behind the table, which was covered with so many dishes that the tablecloth was practically invisible, looked like a procedure of almost surgical complexity. "I'd like you both to meet my fiancée, Anna-Lena," he said, indicating the young Swede seated beside him, blond bob shimmering in the soft light. "I was just today telling my colleague Professor Jenson," Alam said, cheeks blubbering up into a smile, "how fortunate I am to have discovered you, Macon—not so far in advance of the world, I'll admit, but nonetheless. I'm looking forward to more discussions like the one we had in class the other day—an account of which, incidentally, I've just sold to *Transition.*" He took Anna-Lena's hand and winked at Macon. "Two brothas like Alam and Detornay, it sells itself."

Macon opened his mouth and Dre spoke first, preempting hellfire. "We've really got to get back to our friends," he said, familiar Princeton-Eastham diplomatic instincts kicking in. "Thanks again for the desserts. It's nice to see you."

"Give me a call," Alam said, reaching up to pat Macon on the forearm as Andre edged The Franchise away. "We'll talk persona commodification. I'll introduce you to my agent."

"All right, then." Andre half-bowed, nodding nice-to-meet-you at Anna-Lena. "Enjoy your meal."

"I always do." Alam smiled, brandishing his silverware.

Macon sat down hard, glad Andre had ushered him away but ready to vent: *The nerve of that goddamned twelve-sandwich-eating pimp. Shove your peach cobbler and your "discovery" up your fat ass, you—*

"Moves," said Andre. "Moves!"

Irritated: "What?"

"A little grace, huh? So what, he makes five pennies off your dollar? Shake it off. He's harmless."

Macon winced and gave a Stevie Wonder head swoop in defiant disagreement. "See, it's not even that," he said, "it's—"

"Dude!" It was Logan. He stopped to look at her.

"Your cobbler's getting cold."

Macon shut his mouth, and picked his fork up like a scalpel.

Chapter Six

"Ready, champ?" asked Nique, rubbing his boy's shoulders from behind at seven-thirty A.M. in the dimly lit corridor-cum-waiting-room of WAKM-FM, the city's premiere talk-radio station.

"Ready, Coach," said Macon, throwing a left jab and a wicked head fake at the water cooler. It bubbled in fear. Andre and Logan, cutting school and work, sat half-asleep on the dusty leather couch, Dre's head on Logan's shoulder. Macon had consented to a lengthy crash course in interview skills, and until the break of day the team had tradeoff-peppered him with questions and advice to illustrate what Nique called the Basic Presidential Principles. Macon had learned the Reaganesque technique of responding to hard-nosed inquiries with tangential homespun anecdotes instead of facts, the Nixonian gambit of talking shit while simultaneously claiming high moral ground as a non-shit-talker, myriad Clintonian methods of sidestepping a repeated and reworded question, and the general tactics involved in subverting the agenda of any interviewer and saying what you damn well pleased regardless of circumstance or status.

"Knock 'em dead, Moves," Andre mumbled, fetal posture tightening. His foot disappeared into a couch crevice. "Like Rappin' Ron said, go out there and win one for the nigger."

The Franchise rolled his eyes. "That's terrible." The cue light turned green, and Macon opened the studio door, blinking through a blast of stale air. Joe Francis beckoned him into a chair and handed him a set of headphones, then leaned over a hanging mic, pushed his nebbish glasses up his nose, and launched into his introduction.

The host had gotten his start as a reporter on the local TV news, and switched over to radio twenty years ago, when he'd begun to lose his hair. He was on the air from five to ten A.M. six days a week, and one look at his work environment slashed any illusions Macon might have harbored concerning the glamour of radio. A half-eaten cheesecake, two empty packs of Camels, several foam coffee cups, and half a dozen White Castle bags littered the table behind Francis. Even if they hadn't, Macon would have surmised such a diet; the man had the look of an astronaut who'd been in orbit, alone, for far too long. He shaved only when his beard began to itch, showered only when he started to offend himself. On the air, he was a mild-mannered liberal, but Francis's off-air communication—with the ponytailed engineer in the glass-walled control room across the hall, the squat producer sitting next to him, the haggard receptionist who'd showed Macon inside—consisted entirely of caustic bickering. He and his staff had clearly spent hundreds of squalid, climate-controlled hours learning how to best annoy one another.

Francis's politics were still sharp, though, even if nothing else was. Nique had booked the appearance as a test run, a chance to tighten Macon's game before moving to the high-stakes world of television.

"And now," Francis was saying, "*The Joe Francis Show* is proud to bring you the first live, on-air interview with Mr. Macon Detornay, here to discuss his new organization. . . ." He consulted his clipboard and pronounced the name with a touch of disdain: "The Race Traitor Project." Francis swiveled his worn chair a few degrees and looked at his guest for the first time. "Welcome, Macon," he said, passing off a moment of gastrointestinal distress as a smile. "Thanks for being here today."

"No problem." Macon popped three left-hand knuckles in rapid succession. Francis waved at him to stop, and Macon flinched, mouthed an apology, and clasped his hands in his lap.

"Let's begin with the events that made you famous, Macon. Without asking you to comment on the charges per se, I'd like—"

"Afraid I can't go near that with a ten-foot pole, Joe. What I will address, though, is the sense of entitlement with which white people grow up, and which they hold on to for their entire lives. I don't advocate violence, Joe, but white people, especially white people with money, need to consider how they got where they are. We owe a great moral debt, and we should be giving back. Before the people we exploited decide the time has come to take back."

Francis glanced outside and wished he hadn't. His waiting room was a ruckus of cheerleading. Andre interrupted his back-and-forth hall-sweep just long enough to bang fists with Nique at Macon's cut-off technique; Logan stood on the couch thrusting imaginary pompoms at the sky. The Franchise watched the host watch them and smiled.

"Is that what you would consider someone who robbed white people to be doing, Macon? Taking back?"

His entourage froze and scowled, but Macon seemed unfazed. "In theory, Joe? It would depend. Who is this person? What does he or she do with the money? I hope, as we all do, that no one else will have to resort to crime. But crime has been the modus operandi of the powerful since the beginning in this country—since Europeans stole people from Africa to work land swindled from Native Americans. Those are the ground rules America set, and the disenfranchised have no option but to play along. I want to say this to white people out there who might be thinking of committing crimes, Joe: Please, make them white-on-white. Maybe if we rob each other for a while, it will give everybody else a chance to get back in the game."

Joe Francis hunched over his mic and smacked his chops once, silently. "I don't know if I'm supposed to take that seriously or not, Macon." Nique, pacing too now, grinned as he crossed Andre's path, loose-gaited and elated. He'd had a hunch this dude would be a faithful straight man.

"You know what, Joe? Neither do I. Maybe I said it just to shock people. I'm shocked every day of my life, and I want everybody else to be as well. I want to whip people up into a frenzy, until there's nowhere for them to run and they have to confront themselves. My job is to make whiteness visible. I want white people to look at me, Joe, this crazy kid who won't shut up about race, and realize, maybe for the first time, that hey, whiteness is an identity. See, white people don't really see themselves as white, they see themselves as normal. You ever heard a white person describe someone as white? 'What's Ed look like?' 'Oh, he's about six-two, white guy, mustache.' Never. But if it's a person of another race, they'll mention it every time. First thing, usually. 'John? Black guy, three feet tall, with a big prehensile tail and an extra arm growing out of his back.'

"Whiteness is off the radar, Joe. There's no analysis of what it means to be white, historically and socially and psychologically. The only people who put forth any kind of argument at all are the total psychopaths, the super-racists. And, of course, what whiteness means to them is mostly just that you hate everybody else and, you know, keep the white race pure. Come to think of it, historically speaking maybe that definition's not so far off. And before you even ask me, Joe, I'm gonna go ahead and answer your next question—"

Andre and Nique were standing inches from the window now, bugging out as if Macon were a racehorse in the stretch run. "Oh shit," said Nique, punching his cohort in the arm just to do something. " 'Before you even ask, I'ma answer your next question.' That's the shit, son, that's the shit." Andre nodded vigorously and rubbed his arm, although it hadn't registered that he'd been hit.

Logan jumped off the couch and did a shaky row of cartwheels, down the hall and back, then leapt into Andre's arms and struck a grand-finale pose. Joe Francis tried hard to ignore them.

"—by explaining that no, I don't think everything is white folks' fault. I'm talking about them because they're my responsibility. When I talk about white people, I'm talking about myself."

Francis saw an opening and lunged. "That's interesting, Macon, because many people seem to consider you the blackest white person they've ever seen."

Nique smiled. "He thinks that's a curveball," he said, wrapping an arm around the panting, dismounted Logan. "He doesn't know this motherfucker graduated Persona Commodification 101."

"Well, thank you, Joe. I take that as a compliment, because I consider whiteness an affliction. That's what the Race Traitor Project is all about: encouraging people to take the first step of recognizing the privilege and the historical legacy that whiteness represents."

"And, I would presume, becoming 'traitors' to whiteness."

"It's not an easy thing to do, Joe. White people can fall off the wagon at any time. Even John Brown, the legendary abolitionist killed in the raid at Harpers Ferry, didn't really die for the cause. He was acting out of vengeance, trying to liberate slaves owned by his ex-wife's lover."

Joe Francis rubbed a thumb against his chin and cut his eyes, and for a hot second Macon panicked: He'd taken it too far and Joe was going to slay him on his bullshit answer, call Macon's ass out. The world would realize just how little he had studied and stab him fatally through the holes in his scholarship—learn Macon was no statistical quick-draw and face him down with reams of data, machine guns full of bone-dry ammunition, take the game to a theoretic realm where he couldn't compete on just the logic of everything he'd ever seen, the anecdotal snapshots of an unjust world. They'd cut his Achilles' heel to ribbons and box up all the things he'd stirred in people, red-stamp INVALID, DISCREDITED across it, and drop Macon unceremoniously, screaming, off the undisrupted spinning planet, two giant Godfingers squeezing his head like an eyedropper.

But no. Joe Francis played All Media to Macon's prevaricating Reagan. "Fascinating," he said. "I did not know that. We've only got a few minutes left before we bring on our next guest, illiterate high-school basketball star and alleged cocaine dealer Chip Vanderworth, so let's let our listeners in on the conversation, shall we? The phone lines are open. Are you there, caller?"

"Yeah, hi, Joe. Listen, I wanna know what this guy's even doing on your show. Are we gonna provide a forum for every wackjob to tell us what's wrong with the country?"

"You care to respond to that, Macon?"

"Not really, Joe."

"Fair enough. Next caller?"

"Morning, Joe. Listen, Macon: I'm a fifty-seven-year-old Jewish man, and I've been a civil rights worker all my adult life. I was on the Freedom Ride in Mississippi, and I saw white and black people die side by side trying to change those laws. How dare you belittle the advances we made and the courage it took to make them? Where do you get off with these ludicrous generalizations? That's the kind of thinking we fought against, son. I beg you to stop saying these outrageous things. You're doing more harm than you know."

Macon palmed his chin, struck dumb by the man's reasonable tone. His first impulse was to wonder how he could attack it. He knew he had to overcome this uninformed, hip hop desire to dis every well-meaning voice, clown every hero of the past. He couldn't allow his outrage and his need to be unique to paint the entire history of white engagement in the struggle as bullshit. He had to learn to recognize his allies, to build coalitions without feeling that it compromised him.

Joe Francis tried to catch his guest's eye and couldn't. "Macon?" he prompted. Dead air was the enemy. A fart was better than silence.

"First of all, sir," Macon began, deliberately, "I have nothing but respect for you and what you've done. I'm not trying to belittle your accomplishments, but you changed laws, not hearts. What now? The schools are integrated, but black people get worse educations even when they're sitting side by side with whites. The lunch counters and buses are equal: great, but so what? I hate to say it, but those victories just make it easier for white people to act like racism is a problem that got solved back in the sixties. We're running out of things to point at, branches to cut down, and the bottom line is that white folks still are not invested."

Macon felt himself slipping into just the kind of alienating rant he wanted to avoid. "I am speaking in generalizations," he conceded. "Maybe what I'm saying doesn't apply to you at all. Then again, who knows? Plenty of people believe in civil rights, or even affirmative action, and then have a heart attack when their daughter starts dating a black guy." Macon broke off, flustered by his own hostility.

"I guess what I wonder," he resumed, "is where people with your kind of courage—and there aren't many—should direct it today. It's easy to fight Bull Connor, because he's siccing German shepherds on people. But what do we do about your next-door neighbor, who only says the n-word in his mind? And who just so happens to be a loan officer at the neighborhood bank, and president of the local P.T.A.?"

Macon glanced into the hall and saw Andre, Nique, and Logan standing quietly, their faces set. He imagined the caller—a great guy, probably, an ally—switching off his radio disgusted, and he felt the guy's disgust, felt like a young punk.

No time to dwell on it; Joe Francis punched in the next caller. "Yo, whaddup, cuz. This is Crazy Chris from the Cheshire, Connecticut, Rollin' Crips, and I wanna give hella love to my dog Macon. It's about time fools recognized that us crackas be bangin', too. We catch bodies, cuz, we put in work. It ain't just niggas that be gangstas. That's some racist shit. Keep bangin', cuz. I'm out." The line went dead.

Macon pointed a finger at the switchboard. "That guy may be an idiot," he said, back on firm footing, "but there's potential there. The so-called 'wigger'—which is a term I'm not really down with, actually, since it's generally used by white people to insult other white people by likening them to blacks—if his energy is harnessed, he can change the face of race in America. It might be for the wrong reasons, but he cares about black culture. Maybe he just feels entitled to claim it like everything else, but he does step outside himself in the pursuit. He wants to connect. We can work with that. One love, Crazy Chris, you jackass."

Chip Vanderworth's arrival truncated the discussion. Joe Francis ushered in the gangly All-City point guard like an old army buddy, segueing like mad. He couldn't wait to see the last of Macon's obnoxious ass, ratings be damned.

A network car picked Macon, Andre, Nique, and Logan up on the deserted early-morning street outside WAKM and shuttled them across town to another unassuming industrial-gray building on an undistinguished block. This was the home of *Rise and Shine New York*, a saccharine TV variety hour hosted by a fawning blonde named Kim Sheffield who interlaced cooking segments with celebrity chitchat. Why they wanted flyboy raceman asshole Macon Detornay was anybody's guess, and probably some wire-service-combing intern's fuckup, but it was high-profile and a welcome breather after Joe Francis and before the afternoon's political roundtable.

The show, set in a faux living room before a studio audience, began with toothy grins, pressed-cheek introductions, and a tightly edited clip from last night's edition of *Rebel Yells*. Macon felt underdressed and sweaty in his track suit and Nikes, and wished he hadn't let Andre and Nique convince him that only schmucks dressed up for TV. Why was he taking fashion advice from a couple of Los Angelenos, anyway? People out there rocked shorts, socks, and flip-flops. Together. Actually left their homes like that.

"Fabulous," gushed Kim when the clip ended, leaning over her own crossed legs to touch her new friend's knee. "So we can expect more of this in your book?"

"Uh, yeah, I guess," said Macon, sipping lukewarm tap water from the *Rise and Shine New York* mug on the coffee table before him. "If I ever get around to writing it." Logan made a rounded hand motion from the front row, as if shooing poisonous fumes away from her nostrils. *Effuse,* she mouthed. Macon raked back his hair with an exaggerated overhand arm sweep, flexing his biceps and smiling as he did so. It seemed like something the kid from *Dawson's Creek* might do. He wondered if Kim Sheffield had the foggiest notion who he was.

"Who are some of your favorite writers?" she asked, the question unnaturally sexy between her pouted lips. Macon couldn't believe how much makeup they slathered her with. Not that he wasn't covered in foundation himself. He felt like a powdered doughnut.

"Gunnar Kaufman, Raven Quickskill, and Daniel Vivaldo Moore," he said. Kim nodded as if enraptured, and glanced past him at the next cue card. Nowhere she could go from there.

"I notice your studio audience seems to be all white today," Macon bantered, taking advantage of the pause. "Why do you suppose that is?"

Andre steepled his fingers, pressed them to his lips, and leaned forward. This should be good.

"I'm sorry?" Kim smiled and batted her eyelashes, pretending to have missed it.

"What is this show about, anyway?" asked Macon, gripping the arms of his chair and pivoting to look over each shoulder as if in search of the answer. He tightened his left cheek until an adorable dimple, dormant since his sixth birthday, appeared. "I mean, it's pretty much about nothing, right? It's more a way to distract people."

"Distract them from what?" Jovial noncomprehension glossed Kim's face. She thinks he's setting up a joke, Andre realized, exuberance mounting.

Macon took a final glance around and thought, Fuck it. Something about this set, this woman, the notion of millions of suburban housewives studying him from their couches, was too much. He had to bust this shit wide open.

Macon let flirtation edge his voice. "You know what the cop who arrested me said, Kim?" Nique and Andre exchanged nervous looks. "I'll tell you, Kim. He said, 'Niggers are lazy, stupid, and violent.' I wonder what your audience thinks of that, Kim. I bet they wouldn't say 'nigger,' would they?"

"N-no, of course they wouldn't," said Kim, a frown folding her lipstick in ways the sponsoring brand would never have approved. "It's a terrible word." She looked offstage, for her producer, but he was nowhere to be found.

"Oh, come on, Kim." Macon caught her eye and took a stab at a disarming smile. "I think it sometimes, don't you? Haven't you ever found yourself thinking, Why are niggers always so loud at movie theaters? Or, I'm standing on this elevator with three niggers? Even though you don't mean to? Even though you like black people?"

Oh shit, thought Andre. Kim Sheffield was nodding with Macon's every word, her legs wrapped tight around each other, her facial furrows deepening each second.

"How do you feel when you catch yourself?" pressed Macon gently. "Do you think it makes you racist?"

Andre looked down and saw that he was clutching his arm rests so hard his fingers ached. Macon's just a little too happy to have an excuse to use that word, he thought.

Kim opened her mouth and said nothing. She leaned forward and grabbed ahold of Macon's arm. "Yes," she whispered desperately, nodding fast, nails digging into her guest's skin. He wanted to pull away, but didn't. "I, I . . . sometimes I do." She pressed her palm to her breastbone, blinked, and gulped back tears. Macon offered her his water and she took it gratefully in both hands.

That was all the forces behind *Rise and Shine New York* were willing to sit still for. The cameras spun out toward the audience and Kim Sheffield rose and strode swiftly off the set, chin to her chest, heels clicking across the parquet floor. Her producer ushered her into his arms, lit her a cigarette, and walked her out into the wings. With burly efficiency, two security guards informed Macon, still seated, that his segment was finished, and escorted him to the greenroom.

Andre and Nique were huddled by the food table, smoking a joint, when he arrived. Logan sat on a leather love seat, a silver tray of bagels resting on her lap. She chucked one after another at the garbage can across the room, scoring with seventy percent accuracy.

Macon poured himself a cup of coffee, snatched the joint from Nique, took a quick pull, and drowned it in a pitcher of fresh-squeezed orange juice before anyone could protest.

"Y'all motherfuckers are supposed to be prepping me. How the fuck you gon' be blunted and shit?"

"How the fuck you gon' ask Kim Sheffield if she thinks 'nigger,' nigga?" Nique retorted, gravel-voiced, still holding in his hit. "I should smack you in the grill." A weed-induced tear rolled down his cheek and he flared his nostrils, exhaled through them, and turned on Macon. "You think her little breakdown makes you look good out there? You think people are gonna book you on their shows if they're afraid you'll pull that kind of junk?" He tapped his forehead with his finger. "Play smart, Moves. Don't get ejected. You were scheduled for five more minutes."

Andre fished the joint out of the juice and ate it. "Moving right along," he said, "*Pedantic Perspectives* is up next. A weekly roundtable on current events. Nationally syndicated. Excellent ratings, for what it is. They try to mix it up: conservatives, liberals, random crusading celebrities"—he put a hand on Macon's shoulder—"and the occasional miscellaneous loon. The moderator's a pundit by the name of Eric Lyle, a real bastard. He writes a column called 'Shut Up and Listen, You Idiot' for the *New York Post.*"

"I've read that," said Logan. "He's the guy who said we should draft homeless people into the army and use them as missiles."

"Right. And yesterday he blamed school busing for creating what he termed 'a generation of Macon Detornays.' He says making blacks go to white schools disrupts the fabric of both communities and results in 'confused values.' "

"He's got a point," said Macon, bouncing on the balls of his feet.

"His solution is to give niggers standardized intelligence tests at age five, educate the top scorers at state-run all-black boarding schools, and teach the rest of us to repair refrigerators and air conditioners. He calls it the Talented Ten Thousandth Plan."

Macon gulped his coffee and stretched a calf on the table as if he were a ballerina, squashing a plate of assorted Danish beneath his sneaker. "Lovely. Who the guests be?"

"Glad you asked." Andre unfurled a finger for each name. "Conservative-as-hell black congressional hopeful and ex–New York Giants nose tackle Marcell A. 'Jackfruit' Preston. Grassroots Harlem organizer and owner of three Dream Weavers hair salons Alan Umfufu McDowell—not a fan of yours, by the way, called you 'an unwelcome loudmouthed interloper in the fate of the black community' in the *Amsterdam News.*" Dre dropped his chin and stared daggers at Macon. "I wouldn't drop any n-bombs in front of him if I were you." When no response was forthcoming, he continued. “And finally, Professor Andrea ‘I Want Some Black Dick’ Jenson, noted scholar and author, Columbia English professor, and one of your more outspoken supporters to date.”

Logan tossed her last bagel. “I still haven’t heard a plan,” she said as it thunked against the inside wall of the trash can. “I hope you’re building up to it.”

“Relax,” suggested Macon, pouring himself a refill. “Everything’s under control.”

Chapter Seven

"Maybe I should start speaking with a Southern Baptist accent," Macon mused, sitting backstage as a makeup man repainted him. "You know, like MLK or Cornel West. Those cats can be ordering some super-sized fries and it still comes off like the most spiritual, profound shit ever said."

"Maybe you shouldn't," said Nique, squeezing kiwis from the fruit tray in pregame boredom. All these greenrooms were identical, down to the food. He shook an underripe banana at The Franchise. "Don't forget, we want cats to be completely perplexed that anybody ever thought you were black. So keep it nasal, homey."

"We'll be watching on the monitor," said Logan. "Good luck." She kissed him on the top of the head, prompting Andre and Nique to do the same. Macon followed a production assistant into a muted burgundy-and-oak studio and took his place around a shin-high coffee table. The other guests were already seated. Squat Jackfruit Preston, clean-cut in a two-button navy suit and FBI shoes, stared down at his folded hands. Lanky Alan Umfufu McDowell rocked a black-and-yellow dashiki and chatted with Professor Jenson, who was seated next to Macon. She was an elegant, birdlike woman in her forties, tall, thin, and draped in pink silk. A short plume of black hair spiked from her head.

"Hello, Macon," she stage-whispered. "Pleasure to finally meet. Do you know Alan?"

"Hi." They shook hands. Macon turned to Preston and repeated the ritual, unsure whether he should be fraternizing with the enemy.

Eric Lyle entered last: a tall man with a perfectly trimmed beard who dyed his graying hair a ludicrous jet-black and thought nobody out in televisionland could tell. An easy, limber gait brought Lyle to his center seat, just higher than the other chairs. He folded himself into it, crossed his legs regally, and made a show of examining his cuticles while he waited for his presence to silence his guests.

It took only a moment, but Lyle waited another before looking up. He swept his slate-gray eyes across each of their faces without pausing on any one, then set his gaze on the camera and ran his hands over his hair without touching it.

"Welcome." He nodded left and right, eyes still trained on the lens, and smiled—at the resonance of his own voice, it seemed to Macon. "So good to see you all. I can tell this is going to be a fantastic show."

"On in five, Mr. Lyle," a techie shouted. Macon cracked his knuckles. Jenson flashed him a sympathetic smile. "Nervous?" she whispered. Macon didn't answer. The question made him feel like a kid, reminded him he was the panel's amateur. He gave her a twitch of a smile, so as not to offend his only ally with rudeness.

Lyle pulled his shirt cuffs more prominently from his suit coat. "No biting, eye gouging, or kicking," he joked by rote.

"Three . . ."

He licked his pinkies, smoothed his eyebrows, and dropped his fists onto the arm rests like a pair of gavels. "And remember, it's my fucking house."

"One."

"Welcome to *Pedantic Perspectives*. I'm your host, Eric Lyle, and today's topic is that most persistent of American conundrums, race relations. Joining us, as always, are four experts in the field—

including one, Macon Detornay, whose recent exploits have drawn national attention and regalvanized discussion of the issue. Welcome, Macon. We'll begin with you. What do you see as the biggest obstacle in improving the state of race relations in America?"

"White people," said Macon. He sat back and crossed his legs.

"I couldn't agree more," Professor Jenson blurted, fastest racehorse out of the gate. "Until more white people commit to opening channels of dialogue—"

"Forget channels of dialogue," interrupted Macon. "That lets them off the hook too easy. How can you even start talking without a basic acknowledgment of culpability?"

Jackfruit Preston threw his bulky ex-athlete's frame forward and pushed his overlarge glasses against his forehead. "The last thing we need to do at this point is worry about assigning blame, Eric," he said, holding his palms a foot apart as if clutching an invisible football. "Our duty as a nation is to move beyond the problems of the past and embrace the principles of equality on which this country was founded."

Macon burst out laughing. "That's funny for so many reasons," he said. "You think the black community should just forgive and forget and look ahead? Ahead to what? All those great token jobs? Getting shot by cops, talked past in school, turned down by banks, and thrown in jail? Ahead to leadership that tells them to pull themselves up by their bootstraps, learn to fit into white society, and laugh at racist jokes around the water cooler?"

Alan Umfufu McDowell thrust a splayed hand into Macon's line of vision. "And what makes a twenty-year-old whiteboy such an expert on the black community?" he demanded. "What we need is to be left alone by outside agitators like you and bourgeois politicians like Brother Preston and allowed to build our own economic and political power bases."

Macon turned and smirked at him. His discomfort had melted away under the heat of good old-fashioned open antagonism. This was just like sitting on the couch at Lajuan's crib—and none of these fools was anywhere near as hard to interrupt as Jihad. "Economic and political power bases, huh?" he asked. "You think white people are gonna stand for that? Not in a million years. We'll be in there slanging St. Ides and gentrifying blocks before you can say 'Each one, teach one.' Unfortunately, the fact is that y'all can't rebuild the black community unless white people decide to let you do it."

Lyle, sensing that Alan was seconds away from leaping across the coffee table, stepped into the fray. "So you contest that the burden rests solely on white people, Macon?"

"The word *burden* shouldn't even be used in the same sentence as 'white people,' Eric. The burden is being treated like a criminal when you walk down the street, getting convicted twice as often as whites in courts of law and incarcerated twice as long for the same crimes. And you know what? Even if white people do decide to get down with some dialogue, the burden will still be on black people to try to explain what's wrong."

"The days of white people apologizing for their sins are over," said McDowell ominously.

"Thank you," said Preston, smoothing his yellow club tie.

"When did they start?" asked Jenson. "Malcolm said whites should be walking up to every black person they pass on the street and asking for forgiveness, but it's never happened."

"It's not a bad idea," mused Macon. "It won't change anything, but it might be good for white folks to humble themselves like that." He stroked his chin and *boom.* "What the hell," he decided. "Let's do it. On behalf of the Race Traitor Project and in the name of El-Hajj Malik El-Shabazz, I hereby declare this Friday to be the first annual Day of Apology in the City of New York. I want white folks to meditate on what it is they're apologizing for and then to follow Brother Malcolm's advice and walk right up to black folks on the street and say they're sorry. Don't expect forgiveness; the point is to acknowledge how fucked up—whoops, sorry—how messed up things are and to take a little bit of personal responsibility. How's that?"

"That's the most foolish thing I've ever heard," sputtered Jackfruit Preston, sweating through his suit. "Black people need to take responsibility for their own lives. This is more preposterous than welfare and affirmative action rolled into one."

Alan Umfufu shook his head and stared at Macon. "An idea like this makes a mockery of the problems facing the black community," he seethed. "What's next, Take a Nigger to Lunch Day?"

"What's wrong with white people acknowledging the roles they've played in oppression?" asked Jenson. Macon wanted to kiss her.

Eric Lyle was outraged. "I take umbrage at the suggestion that moral, law-abiding white citizens have anything to apologize for," he thundered.

"The death threats they're going to send me for saying they do," said Macon, "will prove it."

"Annnnnd cut," came the voice from on high.

"Great segment!" said Lyle, clapping McDowell on the back with one hand and Preston with the other.

Alan Umfufu stood up, straightened his dashiki, and pointed a hostile right index finger at Macon. "You've got some nerve," he said. "If I have to spend my weekend fending off guilty white people hell bent on apologizing to all of Harlem, I'm going to be really annoyed."

"Relax. Maybe white chicks will start sporting weaves and double your business."

"Fuck you. I hope whatever blue-eyed soul brothers you send uptown catch a serious ass-whipping."

Macon's face lit up. "Wow, yeah," he said to McDowell's back as the activist stormed out. "I didn't even think of that. That would be fantastic, wouldn't it?"

Chapter Eight

The Black Like Me rally in Washington Square Park was Dominique's idea. He envisioned it as high theater of the absurd, a Million Wigger March where white folks could show up after a hard day of apologizing to Negroes and renouncing their whiteness to eat bean pies, have their hair cornrowed, and absorb abuse from a lineup of venomous speakers.

"Maybe we can get Khalid Muhammad," he fantasized. "You think he'd speak to an all-white group?"

After *Pedantic Perspectives,* things had gotten hectic, to the point where Macon longed for the relative calm of forty-eight hours ago, when going outside had been as simple as walking past a teeming clot of protesters, head tucked to his chest and with a two-man escort. Those salad days were gone now. Macon hadn't left the dorm at all. Andre tried to go to class once, fought his way through the reporters, and didn't have the energy to do it again. Logan, still a media cipher, ran errands for all of them. She hadn't been to work all week. Nique had gone in only once, and his loyal, neglected customers had created a highly suspicious traffic jam.

The Race Traitor Project's press release, detailing the objectives of the Day of Apology and the time and location of the Black Like Me rally to follow, had been reprinted in newspapers across the map, with fanfare and op-ed like a motherfucker. A surprising number of papers had also printed the mail-order offer that accompanied the statement: Write care of Dominique Lavar to order your official Day of Apology T-shirts, quality 100 percent cotton garments available in a variety of colors and designs, available for a limited time for only $16.95 plus shipping and handling.

The media, geeked off Macon Mania, of which they were both cause and tool, ran with the ball, and Nique pimpstrutted with I-told-you-so bravado through the sound bites, anguished screams, and weed-smoke billows of Control Room 1107, a tiny brain trust enclave, mountain hideaway, refuge, and dungeon—TV brain screens dense with snow and everybody poised/exhausted, horrified, bemused, up for the downstroke, senses dulled but overloading as the shit flew by: Macon Detornay's Day of Apology; the racial apocalypse is now upon us; whiteboys lead the charge into the inkwell; Amos and Andy show up at the local hospital requesting surgery, seems they like coon stage paint better than their birth mugs; *this is madness/this madness is madness;* throngs of screaming *Fuck No* protesters and fans both local and imported clash all up and down Columbia's frat row, nearest point of entry to the freshman dorm where any minute now, thought Macon, any time, one of those Never Apologize crackers down outside my window might lay hands on some Columbia ID and shuffle past the front desk, ride up here and mosey down the hall and blast me.

A thousand *I'm Listening* letters, e-mails, phone calls, sixty for every *Nigger Lover Die,* whiteboys and whitegirls sneaking arsonist looks all around them, *this is wrong, just wrong, my parents friends life wrong,* many interested, cautious, curious, sad, pissed off, skeptical black folks wondering, glancing up and down the fresh-pressed length of this potential/disaster, *mufucker apologize to me I'll wring his neck—Please, fool, you'll take whatever these white folks dish out like always—finally some progress*—in the news today the news today the news today:::colossal joke? inside the mind of Dominique Lavar, Macon Detornay's spokesman and some say the spinmaster behind the the thethethe—tired feeling always behind Macon's eyes, even five minutes post–morning piss, everybody always crashing to sleep instead of drifting, passing out with their shoes on in sudden narcoleptic snatches. One time Andre started snoring with a half-eaten pizza slice in his hand, conked out for three hours like that. Fleet Walker's book seemed glued to Macon's hand at all times now; he read and reread and sometimes insisted on speaking whole sections aloud to Andre, who quietly despised listening but had started picking up the book himself when Macon put it down. Sometimes one or the other of them would devolve mid-convo into grunts of agreement, and then the other, or Nique, or Logan, would notice that the book was open:

We mulattos have felt the push and pull of white and blackness like perhaps no other race—if a race is in fact what we are. Throughout my life, I have glimpsed opportunity and oppression as though I had two sets of eyes, or as though I were in the practice of opening first my left and then my right and then my left, watching the world bounce back and forth between the two perspectives, never quite synthesizing or settling: African, American, African, American. The insertion of a hyphen between the two, as favored by some of the newer Negro leaders, serves only to render a fellow cross-eyed.

A general fallacy among white Americans is the tendency to assume mulattos to be the result of miscegenation. The truth is that many families, including my own, have been that way for generations: half-and-halfs marry half-and-halfs and thus a caste is born. But the belief is at the crux of the dilemma we mulattos face. We are walking proof of something white and black people alike would rather pretend does not occur, proof of either violence or intimacy between the races. Our existence is the punch line to a dirty joke.

Many whites likewise indulge in a belief that the only education afforded blacks during Reconstruction was to be had in one-room schoolhouses—just as they think that in slave times the only way we learned to read was if Miss Anne took a liking to a lucky young house nigger and taught him at her knee. That, too, is hogwash. There were more black senators and congressmen during Reconstruction than there are today. More black businesses, too, and better ones. My father, a freeman born in Ohio, was a doctor throughout my youth. My brother Weldy became one in his later years as well. He went to school and earned a degree in homeopathy, in point of fact.

I myself graduated from Oberlin College, the first integrated institution of higher learning in the nation, almost fifty years ago now, as a member of the Class of 1882. Passed up law school to play baseball. Or, as my father was fond of saying, "chose a boy's folly over a man's life." He still came to cheer me on, though.

I wish I could recall more of what went through my mind when I was in the public eye, what I did with all the rage my dignity and refinement forced back deep inside me—so deep that it began to corrode, disintegrate me a little at a time. By the end of my playing days, I hated myself and the two races swimming together in my bloodstream. I longed to slice open my veins and watch the double fountain spray from my upturned wrist, white blood spurting right and black blood geysering left toward Africa, their years of fighting inside me finally done.

How do you react when you pick up the newspaper after game day—year in and year out, mind you—and read, "The brunette catcher Walker carried himself like a perfect gentleman," when some reporter's attempt at liberalism is to dutifully report the startling news that the nigger didn't rip anyone's arms off today, didn't revert to his savage ancestral ways and eat the umpire or beat on homeplate with his mighty member while chanting voodoo curses—but there's always tomorrow? Are you grateful when they compliment your comportment, laud your game-winning hit, or is every word another brushstroke in the coon painting, evidence either for the prosecution or the defense, and it doesn't matter which because what's on trial is your humanity and that's bad enough?

Perhaps it was too much for me to handle. I've got a few firsts to my name besides first black major leaguer that might lead you to think so. First nigger in Ohio to kill a white man and go free—the victim an Irish laborer who assaulted me on my way home from a tavern two years after the end of my playing days and soon discovered that I was not so foolish as to walk through this white world without a knife. I pled self-defense and righteously so, although my own celebrity and the team of white Oberlin law professors who assembled to take up their old student's cause was what truly carried the day.

First black man—among the first, leastways—to grow so sick and frustrated with this country and the hopelessness of being black and being white and being black and white that, when I was fifty years of age—the first thirty-five of them spent integrating what is now known as the Great American Pastime, and which has now long been entirely segregated—I said to hell with this damn nation, with its absurd notions of living side by side, former slave and former master, hate glinting back and forth across the rhododendron bushes. Let's evacuate the Negroes en masse, by force if necessary, and return to Africa.

I wrote a tract to that effect, entitled "Our Home Colony," which remains quietly on file at the Library of Congress, and almost nowhere else—its general failure to galvanize a response a blessing in disguise, because if there was anything I hated more than white prejudice at that time, it was black people. The century had just turned, and I had been forced out of baseball and begun to drink and to despair. In myself, blacks, whites, mulattos—you name it, I'd lost faith in it. If it was inside me, I didn't want it.

A man can only compromise for so long before he forgets he's compromising at all, before some part of him feels he deserves the treatment he's receiving or blames something close by for it. If black people could only act more like me, I often thought, then I would not have to suffer guilt by association. Toe the line long enough and the world beyond the line blurs. A man learns to hate above all else whatever is close enough to lash out at, becomes conditioned to attack only that for which he will be rewarded.

Self-hatred, of course, was no cause for embarrassment. Open any black magazine and you could read your fill of advertisements for skin-bleaching products guaranteed to make you white. Visit your local university and you could hear any number of black scholars and lecturers lamenting the American Negro as the lowest, basest son of Africa. I thank God that I no longer count myself among their ranks.

"It is contrary to everything in the nature of man and almost criminal to attempt to harmonize these two diverse peoples while living under the same government," I wrote whilst in the grip of that madness. "The Negro has no ideals of his own; nor can he have. Everything that pertains to his own ethnic type he despises, and this is done in most cases unconsciously."

The strange wisdom of these words becomes clear to me now, for even as I wrote such things—and it was mulattos for whom I saved my harshest words, writing that "It is impossible to make a hybrid race of men. What is to prevent this progeny from being worse than animal? Such creatures are more dangerous to society than wild beasts, for these last can easily be hunted and shot, while the former go on procreating their lecherous kind without hindrance"—I never truly included myself. I condemned the American Negro and the future of race in America with vigor and venom, called for the wholesale return of blacks to Africa and authorized the use of force if it proved necessary, but never for a moment did I intend to leave the country. Perhaps I realized, even then, that I would only have been running from myself. I've dashed from clusters of reporters and mobs of white folks, raced against low throws on a line from right field to home plate and after trains gathering speed outside Atlanta, run for my life and for my livelihood, and nothing is so exhausting as trying to sprint past your shadow.

I've often reflected that perhaps the small taste of equality I had as a student was what made the world outside seem all the more oppressive. Never in my life have I been able to forget that I was black, but at Oberlin I came the closest. Today, the entire campus has fallen victim to de facto segregation, but during my time there I ate and studied alongside white people and felt more or less the same as everybody else—and often better, because I could hit a baseball farther.

I left school nurturing the naive notion that while I was on the baseball field all else would be forgotten. Politics and hatred might surround the idea of my participation, I told myself, but once I crossed the foul line chalked in the brilliant green grass, I would enter a sanctuary, a place of peace governed only by sportsmanship. When I stepped up to the plate to take my three swings at immortality, the same as any player got, those crowds would be forced to see a man.

But when I joined the International League, the world reasserted itself with a vengeance, and I was once again a lonely black man playing a white game in which the rules kept changing. I learned two things my first day on the job: As long as I played I'd be risking danger and humiliation, and as long as I played I'd be guaranteed the spotlight. I didn't realize until the following morning, when I picked up the newspaper, that as long as I played I'd also be the foil for a public discussion of race. From that day on, my name never appeared in the newspaper without some epithet before it, benign or malignant—I was the colored Walker, the coon Walker, the brunette or dusky or Spanish or mulatto or nigger Walker. A traveling symbol of blackness whose performance would, for a few hours, condemn or confirm the dogmas of white racism.

In truth, it would confirm them regardless of what I did. Should I comport myself badly, it would be taken up as proof of blacks' inferiority, our flawed and primitive physiologies, as confirmation of the U.S. Sanitary Commission's 1865 report stating that mulattos were "of inferior vitality" to blacks and whites alike.

I still remember the excitement with which the Darwinists awaited the census figures of 1880; they were convinced that the black population would be shown to have dwindled because Negroes couldn't survive freedom. Scores of fans, likewise, were certain that I would collapse, mid-season, due to exhaustion. If I did well, on the other hand, my successes were attributed to enormous, animalistic strength; surely, my gentleman's demeanor cloaked a jungle beast, and it was a good thing my muscles were distracted with baseball because otherwise I was certain to lunge at the nearest white woman.

I suppose we should be thankful that even as America pretends to advance—as it allows young men like Louis Armstrong and Booker T. Washington to flourish, men who might never have had such chances had they been born when I was—we are still provided with regular displays of brutal, crystalline honesty. We should be glad, on some level, for the gruesome spectacle of lynchings. Whatever scant morality we retain cries for the killer to stand over his kill without averting his eyes, to glory or sorrow openly in the blood on his hands.

Alas, such images no longer hold any power over me now, in my old age. Instead, when I begin to soften toward America, when I find my sense of outrage fading, I think not of the lynch mobs I have seen, or even of the one from which I myself once managed to escape. More real to me, somehow, and more horrible, is the simple memory of the 1904 World's Fair held in St. Louis, Missouri, which I attended with my wife and children.

Perhaps you can recall the exhibit; it has been forgotten now, but at the time it was quite famous. In St. Louis—where, incidentally, I played my first professional game, on an empty stomach because service was refused me at my team's hotel—African Pygmies were imported and displayed like animals. Dropped into so-called reproductions of their "primitive" habitats, made to sit before shacks and behind fences and stage mud fights to demonstrate what life back home on the Dark Continent was like.

In the name of science, the "savages" were used to justify the white man's every prejudice. The fair even sponsored an Anthropology Day, on which the "specimens" were forced to compete in wholly unknown sports. Nothing—not even an 0-for-8 doubleheader from the brunette Walker—reinforces the doctrine of Negro athletic inferiority like the sight of a fifty-year-old sprinter hobbling around a track, or an African "champion" who has never before thrown a shot put making comic attempts to learn the technique before an audience of hooting fairgoers munching on snacks. Fairgoers both black and white, I might add.

The Pygmies were such a success at the World's Fair that one of them, Ota Benga, went on display in the New York City Zoo when the exhibition in St. Louis closed. To no one's great surprise, he took his own life in a matter of months. I wonder what the first visitor who passed his cage and saw the Pygmy's lacerated body thought. Zookeeper, oh zookeeper? Is that animal supposed to be bleeding like that?

Chapter Nine

By Thursday, Macon had been cover boy fifteen times over. When they plugged it in, the phone rang off the hook: redneck death threats, thirteen-year-old punk-rock chicks asking for The Franchise's hand in marriage, reporters and more reporters. The media had found a new darling, one to whom they had almost total access any time of day or night, and they were eager to convey Macon's views on things he'd never even thought about. Nique and Andre had developed the habit of spewing whatever bullshit came to mind when they fielded such calls, as a way to blow off steam. So many disembodied voices clamored for answers, and dutifully scribbled down whatever they were given, that it hardly seemed to matter.

"Mr. Detornay's views on forestry conservation? Brother Macon feels that the felling of redwoods is a metaphor for the felling of young black brothers. Black male sexuality is metaphorically castrated as white men chop down these mighty dusky-colored trees."

"The Middle East? Brother Macon laments the monies lavished on unstable foreign governments while people barely survive in the ghettos of this country and Rick James languishes in jail. The U.S. has been an unwanted world policeman far too long. Let these people work it out themselves, shit."

"Extraterrestrials? Fool, Macon Detornay is down with aliens.

How you think them Nubian motherfuckers built the pyramids while white folks were still gnawing on pterodactyl wings? The black man, in his glory, been visited by alien races who passed the wisdom of the cosmos to the elders of Ancient Egypt. Knowledge that."

"Interracial relationships? Let's put it this way: Back in the day, the most threatening thing a black man could have wasn't a gun, or an education, it was a white woman. Scared white folks so much they'd lynch him on the spot. Nowadays, what's the one thing that makes a black man a thousand times less intimidating? A white woman on his arm. So yes, interracial marriage may eventually dismantle racism by producing millions of mixed babies, but not until it's provided just the kind of symbolic black emasculation that America so yearns for in the first place."

Organizations checked in around the clock to pledge their allegiance, register their dismay, and confess their confusion. Matzel Toffee Candyworks, a Lower East Side confectionery run by three Jewish brothers, was the first business to declare its support, offering to distribute free sweets at the rally. The proprietors had grown up watching the Last Poets perform in Harlem, and the lyric "they have stuck lollipops up the asses of our leaders to pacify their Black Power farts" had inspired them to get into the candy game.

Many of the businesses Logan approached for Day of Apology sponsorship wanted nothing to do with the rally, so the CEO curved her sales pitches accordingly. Domino's Pizza, notorious right-wingers, had been happy to commit three hundred pies once Logan explained that she was throwing an all-white rally for racial solidarity.

Most of the major rap record labels, realizing that thousands of white people willing to troll the streets apologizing to blacks represented their dream demographic, had offered free performances and sound systems for the event. Andre, as chief of staff, had booked only the two groups that seemed the most threatening: the Ann Petry Dish, a soul-singing, rhyme-slinging trio from Queens, and the Spooks Who Sit by the Door, a Chicago-based collective of MCs whose self-produced debut, *COINTELPROBLACK*, spoke passionately about decapitating and skull-fucking FBI agents, schoolteachers, and anybody who didn't celebrate when Orenthal J. Simpson was declared not guilty.

Macon had invited the People's Revolutionary Guerrilla Theatre to perform any scene they felt appropriate, and for some reason clear only to themselves they had decided on the marriage of Agamemnon and Clytemnestra from Euripides' obscure play *Strange But True Greek Wedding Night Follies*. Nique had tried to impress upon them the importance of performing something relevant, and suggested a scene from *Dutchman*, but they replied that they refused to be pigeonholed and Macon advised his Minister of Information to drop it.

Busloads of supporters, including the entire active Killer Crip population of Topeka, Kansas, and a Macon Detornay Fan Club comprising a dozen teenybopper girls from Dallas, were expected to descend on the city in what was rapidly becoming a major tourist event. *Newsweek*'s incendiary "The New Face of Hate" piece had reported on a small but worrisome delegation of bigots from North Dakota, interviewed as they loaded pickup trucks with jerky, beer, and shotguns for the trip to New York, where they planned to "not apologize to no niggers for nothing." *Teen Steam Magazine*'s answer piece, "The New Face of Hot," had launched a few buses itself; Macon's robust upper lip and dreamy eyes were winning him support among people who couldn't have cared less what came out of his mouth.

To stave off cabin fever, Team Detornay ran daily wind sprints in the hallway, testing the weight and breathability of the free gear arriving steadily from hip hop clothing companies hoping Macon would rock their shit in public and double their sales in the suburbs, where legions of whiteboys had finally found coolness personified in someone who looked like them.

"I think I'd feel more comfortable with a bulletproof vest,"

Macon announced, returning to the room after a visit to the TV lounge. He crossed the threshold just in time to see Logan and Andre jump away from each other like two suddenly charged batteries and pretend they hadn't been kissing; Andre turned and hunched over his computer, while Logan busied herself with a copy of *High Times* that Nique had left behind. Okaaay, thought Macon. Sure, why the hell not. I'll play along. Whatever.

He walked through the space between them and picked up an envelope from the stack of hate mail piled atop the dresser. He'd taken to defusing such letters by reading them aloud, bumpkin twang and all—*Whah doan yeew come ahwn down heayur an' say them thangs, boy*—and to correcting their grammar with a red teacher's pen. It didn't help much. He flopped onto the bed, threw his legs up against the wall, and stared at the dangling laces of his Timberlands, feeling vaguely surprised and dimly wounded. Logan sat Indian-style on the floor, just outside his line of sight, and flipped listlessly through her magazine.

"Vests are illegal," Andre replied in a deliberate monotone, some thirty seconds after Macon's comment. "A ton of rappers have caught cases for wearing them."

"The logic being what? That it's illegal not to die if someone shoots you in the chest?"

Andre shrugged and went back to drawing up the rally schedule on his computer. "Are we gonna let Professor Jenson speak or not?"

"Sure. She's the only academic who hasn't reduced me to a sociological aberration. Put her early, though. She's beside the point with all that gender stuff."

Logan cut her eyes at Macon, saw that he'd said it just to irritate her, and turned back to her reading.

"Upski and Danny Hoch confirmed, but Khalid Muhammad and Leonard Jefferies still won't return our calls. Who else can we get to really abuse motherfuckers?"

Macon swung his legs around and sat up, restless. "I figure if shove comes to push, we can call the Black Hebrews." He wondered if he was hungry, and tried to remember how many hours had passed since the last time they'd ordered in. Pizza boxes, Chinese takeout cartons, Styrofoam roti containers, grease-soaked Indian food paper bags, and plastic sushi casings had littered the room until half an hour ago, when Andre had decided he couldn't take the sleaze any longer, dumped everything into a giant cardboard moving box, *Pimp Shit IV: The Wrath of Dolomite,* and left it in the hallway to fester. His latest hobby was baiting the R.A., knowing she'd sooner knock on a wasps' nest than their door.

"Them cats who be preaching on cable access? The Twelve Lost Tribes of Israel and shit?"

"Yeah," said Macon. "They're the only group around who'll just straight-up call whites 'devils' to their faces. I've seen people try to argue on the street and they'll be like, 'Shut up, cave bitch.' "

Andre weighed the suggestion for a moment, then side-nodded in disapproval. "Culpability is one thing; getting a whole crowd of white folks to stand around and listen to some fool in a turban read Bible passages that prove they're going to hell is quite another. We don't want a riot on our hands."

Macon stood up, stretched, rubbed his eyes, and then collapsed into a beanbag. The past few days had been like a fucked-up, never-ending game of musical chairs, with more seats than players. "No comment," he said, yawning. As Friday approached, Macon had to fight the growing urge to do nothing, to let the Day of Apology float past him and be whatever it was destined to be: hand-holding and kumbayah, fire and brimstone, whatever. He felt helpless to shape it, clueless about what it should look like, and increasingly glib about the whole matter. He wished someone would slap him out of these bouts of rubbery apathy.

Andre rustled a copy of *The New York Times.* "According to the latest poll, sixty-five percent of blacks like the idea all right in theory. But it's mostly church folks who answer these things. In reality, I'm guessing black people will find the whole shit mildly to incredibly annoying, paternalistic, insincere, and offensive. But there's so many x-factors. What are crackers gonna say? 'I'm sorry for the crimes my people have committed'? 'Sorry I'm racist'? 'Sorry about slavery, segregation, church burnings, glass ceilings, Jim Crow, and stealing rock 'n' roll'? What?"

Macon sighed, switched to a desk chair, and tipped back on two legs. "I have no idea."

Andre dropped his arms and the pretense that he was working and looked straight at Macon. "What do you want them to say, dude?"

"Anything. Just as long as they acknowledge something."

"For all we know, folks might get on some personal confession shit. 'Sorry I called this guy a nigger in a bar fight.' 'Sorry I vote Republican and don't give a shit about hiring practices.' Some ol' feel-good, confess-and-be-forgiven, love-your-fucked-up-inner-honky shit."

"Mmm," said Macon, vacant. His hand twitched, wanting Fleet's book. "I guess we'll have to wait and see."

Logan threw her magazine aside. "That isn't good enough. You think when they asked Oppenheimer what the bomb was gonna do, he was like, 'I guess we'll have to wait and see'?"

"He knew the ingredients," retorted Macon, leaning forward to stare at her. "We don't know shit. And there's no need to gang up on me," he added.

Great, thought Andre, shutdown mode. Neither he nor Logan quite knew how to push Macon past it, or what would happen if they tried. Silently, they agreed to let The Franchise slide, and wished that Nique was there.

Macon sprung to his feet, climbed onto the bed, then walked over to the radiator and scaled that, too, stood atop it with his head brushing the ceiling. "You know what we need around here?" he asked. "One of those Magical Negroes, like in the movies. You know, the black person who's some kind of mystical guide or font of down-home soulfulness or whatever for the white man? I want one of those. Can't you be the Magical Negro, dude?"

"I can be the Smack the Taste Out Your Mouth Negro, if you like. Get down from there. Go take another walk or something. You're driving me crazy."

"That's how you talk to the—what did they call me on *MTV News* tonight? That's how you talk to the Rap Generation's Answer to Robin Hood?"

Andre palmed his head, isolated a lock, and began twisting it to tightness with both hands. "I'ma say this one more time," he told Macon. "If you keep quoting your own press, I'm finding a new roommate." He snorted. "Robin Hood. What a crock of shit. That money went straight from their pockets to yours."

Macon stepped down to the bed and began trampolining. The box springs heaved a tired warning. It went unheeded. "Suddenly you have a problem with that?" he asked as he bounced.

Andre shook his head without looking up, still engaged in follicle maintenance. "Not at all. What I have a problem with is the suggestion that a middle-class white dude stealing from other middle-class white dudes is somehow redistributing the wealth."

"I would argue," said Macon, stepping back onto the floor, "that the act of robbing those fuckers was, in itself, a revolutionary move."

"I'm sure you would," said Andre. "And I'm sure that if we hadn't blown the cake on bail, you would have used it to start a free breakfast program for underprivileged kids in Harlem, too."

"Why are you tripping? All I said was—"

"All right," said Logan, "all right. Enough already. We've been cooped up in here for way too long, we're tense, we're out of weed, we smell bad, and we need to chill. If we're gonna talk about something, how about Macon's opening speech, or transportation to the rally?"

"At least robbing people takes some balls," said Macon. "What did you ever do, Dre?"

"Yeah," said Andre, "you're right, Macon—you're a real hero. I wish I was so brave. Maybe then I wouldn't bother to think about the consequences of my actions, either. I could leave that to my underlings to handle."

"Look, I never asked for anything from you, okay? If you're tired, jealous, fed up, whatever—fine. I understand. Just bounce. Don't act like I'm forcing you."

Andre threw a hand at the window. "Bounce? There's thousands of people coming here tomorrow, Macon. I can't just—"

"What? You can't just what?"

Andre threw his head back in exasperation. "Aren't you worried?"

"I'm scared shitless!" Macon spread his arms. "What do you suggest we do? Huh? Call it off?"

"There's nothing we can do." It was Logan. They both looked down at her. "And yelling at each other won't help."

Andre pointed at his roommate. "I want you to acknowledge that this is some irresponsible shit, Macon."

"What good will that do?" He flicked his hand into the air and let it fall back to his side. "Okay. It's some irresponsible shit. Happy?"

Andre shook his head slowly, blinked long. A sharp snort of fake laughter escaped him. "You're a dick, dude. You know that?"

"I've been told."

"You've been told. Great." Andre rubbed his temples with his fingertips, bent at the waist, and winced as several vertebrae popped. "I'm fuckin' exhausted," he announced. "I'm going to bed." He glanced down at Logan. "You staying?"

She stared at him, then tossed her magazine aside and stood. "Um, no. As inviting as that sounds. I should go home." She slung her bag over her shoulder and strode to the door. "See you tomorrow."

They watched her go in silence. Andre shuffled to his dresser, opened a drawer, and removed his toiletry kit.

"Hey, Dre. Listen." Andre turned to find his roommate standing with his fist extended, offering a pound. "It's just the stress. I'm sorry, man."

Andre looked him up and down. "Save it for tomorrow," he said, and walked into the bathroom.

Chapter Ten

The Day of Apology jumped off partly cloudy, with predicted highs at sixty-five, and Macon woke up to a bowl of Frosted Flakes and the worst headache of his life. He and Andre sat slurping sugar-tinted milk in silent solidarity, bleary-eyed and apprehensive, limbs weighty, every gesture taking on an air of ceremony. Neither one was yet ready to look outside. They'd been up for fifteen minutes when Nique burst in, beaded with sweat and already halfway through his daily pack of cigarettes at nine A.M.

"It's cracker Halloween out there," he said, going straight to the window. Chests pressed to the glass, Andre and Macon peered down and saw the stretch of pavement between Broadway and Amsterdam street-fair dense with rippling humanity. Macon's heart fluttered with nervous excitement: Here it was. He imagined flinging open the window and addressing them from here. *My loyal subjects . . .*

"Whoa, whoa." Nique's voice was unnaturally high-pitched, and Macon abandoned the reverie in time to see his Minister of Information crank open the window and stick his head out.

"What the fuck is this?" Nique screamed, with so much force that the tendons in his neck strained. "What are you doing?"

A long line of blue-uniformed Columbia security guards had materialized out of nowhere, and they were marching up the middle of the block, splitting the crowd before them.

"They're driving the cattle," said Andre in disbelief, and sure enough the crowd was cleaving, shuffling toward the ends of the block as the guards flushed them out with gentle pressure: *Sorry, but you're breaking fire code, people, you can't be here, move it along now, folks, you can't stay here, come on, let's go,* ignoring the moos and lows of protest and disappointment. In less than a minute, the block was nearly empty. Only a tight central cluster of people remained, penned in by more security men.

"Why do they get to stay?" wondered Macon, squinting at the knot. "What's so special about them?"

Nique was livid. "Columbia's not getting away with this shit," he vowed. "Come on, let's get down there before they try to pull anything else." The three of them hustled down the grime-caked stairs and surfaced on 114th Street, now cordoned off by rows of security at Broadway and Amsterdam, no coming or going. A cheer went up and the crowd of remaining white folks—fifty? seventy-five?—began chanting Macon's name.

The cluster was mottled with kente cloth suits, dashikis and kufis, Afro wigs and scattered signs reading I'M SORRY and BLACK POWER.

"Where the fuck these people from?" asked Andre. "Andromeda?"

"Close," said Nique. "A little place between California and New York that I like to call America."

An adolescent kid in blackface squirmed his way through the bodies and ran up to Macon, grinning through white greasepaint lips. The Franchise gaped—*What have I done?*—wondered if he was looking into some kind of metaphysical fun-house mirror, *this motherfucker me, this how I look, this who I am,* pictured his ethos echoing through space only to be decoded wrong, misconstrued and acted on, flags stabbing up the ground in Macon's name, *am I the captain on the ship of fools?* Before he could stop himself, Macon popped the kid in the nose, leaving skid marks on his paint job. The crowd gave a collective gasp. Tears sprouted from the kid's eyes and he looked up at Macon through the wetness, hurt and confused.

"What's the matter with you? Go clean yourself up this instant."

"Yes, sir," he choked, and scurried out of sight. He wasn't more than twelve or thirteen, Macon realized: a child who'd come to the Big City all the way from West Bubblefuck, cajoled some parent into letting him take a bus or maybe snuck away, imagination stirred and heart aching, inspired and perplexed by Macon and all this justice talk. And so he fucks up, okay, he doesn't really understand, nobody around him knows any better, nobody's there to say, *Wipe that shit off, boy, that ain't right to be wearing,* but the kid wants to be down and so he gets off the bus and finds the man himself, the guy they came to see, and he runs up expecting to be loved, embraced, he who made this daring journey, and instead the hero of the whole thing, the guy who lit up his TV and mind and got him on the bus, for whom he skipped school and convinced or defied Mom, the guy socks him in the nose like it's nothing.

"Hey, come back," Macon called, immediately sorry. "I didn't mean to do that." But the kid was gone.

"Speech! Speech!" clamored the crowd, forgiving him—ecstatic that they had been selected from amongst thousands to share this moment with Macon. New York City subway maps stuck out from their back pockets like tail feathers. Red circles marked the South Bronx, Harlem, Flatbush. Cameras and binoculars were slung around their necks; fanny packs rode the crests of their asses. Behind them, set up on the stoop of a frat house, a gaggle of TV cameras poised to capture Macon's starter-pistol speech. Reporters mingled with the crowd, asking folks how far they'd traveled to be here today, complicit in the fiction that this horde was the entire crowd.

Macon folded his arms over his chest and stood stock-still, composing himself to speak. He wanted to set things off with a bang, but Columbia's sabotage and the garish assemblage before him had sapped his motivational juices. The hush swelled up, electric, and Macon grimaced, swallowed, and opened his mouth.

"What's with the costumes?" he asked weakly.

The crowd turned to one another, concerned: *He doesn't like our outfits?*

"We wanted to dress black," shouted a large, Southern-voiced woman. "Those people just have so much spirit."

"You're not black," Macon informed her. The murmuring increased; Macon sensed the potential for total demoralization and quickly shifted gears, not wanting them to trudge back to the buses. Time to snatch victory from the jaws of ignorance.

"Look, just be yourselves," he said, walking over to a tall blond man wearing a red-black-and-green liberation jumpsuit, removing his leather Africa cap and handing it to him. "The whole idea is to recognize who you are and take responsibility. It's not time to start embracing our inner blackness yet, y'all. Right now it's about atonement. You don't have cultural permission to dress like this, you understand?"

Unease rippled through the crowd. "Are they gonna beat us up?" a panicked male voice shouted from the back. Nique and Andre slapped their foreheads with Olympic-quality synchronization.

"No," said Macon. "No one's gonna beat you up. Not that you don't deserve it." They smiled. Bunch of fucking masochists, thought Andre.

"Look, you're here because you recognize the injustice inherent to the system, right?"

They stood silent.

"Right?" Macon repeated.

"Right," they called back, catching on.

"You're here to take a tiny first step in the marathon toward change," Macon told them, starting to get into it. A King Jr. "I Have a Dream" freeze-frame stirred him, and Macon lifted his voice on some resonant vibrato baritone shit. ". . . to say, 'I understand' "—drawing out the *I* all preacherly and hitting *stand* hard, then grace-note pausing midsentence and soaring back up— " 'that mah whiteness . . . is o-ppressive.' You are here . . . to plant your feet and commit . . . to work . . . toward dialogue."

"Where can we buy our T-shirts?"

"Will you sign my T-shirt?"

"Are there any sweatshirts?"

"Forget the fucking T-shirts!" Macon screamed. Andre stepped forward and touched him lightly on the forearm, rebalancing the charismatic leader with a tiny show of confidence. Macon turned and met his eyes, nodded gratefully, and inhaled deep. "This isn't a party," he said, trading righteous dignity for tired grade-schoolteacher sternness. "It's not a sight-seeing trip or a group tour. Do not run around trying to set the record for most apologies, people. Do not ask anyone to pose for pictures. Just split up, go about your daily business, and speak to the people you happen to come across."

"What about mule-attos?" twanged a scruffy front-row yokel in a dreadlock wig. "Do they count, too, or jes' one hunnerd percent Nigroes?"

"How do we tell the difference?"

"Don't we get a box lunch?"

"What are we supposed to say when we see 'em?"

"If I already got my T-shirt on, am I supposed to take it off?"

Macon's face turned red. He gritted his teeth, glanced at Nique with a look that said, *I'm about to start choking motherfuckers,* opened his mouth to respond, and found he had no words. He stood mute for a moment, the crowd blinking studiously at him like, *Yes, jolly good questions all. What shall we do about the mule-attos and the lunches and the dialogue, old boy?* Then Macon turned on his heel, stalked up the block, and disappeared into the dorm. The herd stood stupefied, pawing the ground and wondering what had happened.

"Okay," said Andre, stepping in to save the day. "You can practice on me."

"We're sorry!" boomed the crowd.

Andre nodded his head and shot a searing glance at Nique: *Go after him, yo.* Nique stayed put.

"Thank you," Andre told the horde. "I appreciate that." They beamed at him and one another; this wasn't so hard.

"What are you sorry for?" he asked, stalling. Their faces dropped.

"Are they gonna ask us that?" The fat woman in kente cloth looked worried.

Andre shrugged. "They might." The murmurs, rimmed with terror, grew. "Don't you know what you're sorry for?"

"We're sorry for them?" someone asked hopefully, sounding like a third-grader jerked out of a daydream by a teacher's question.

Andre stared at them. "Anyone else?"

Nique had heard enough. He strode to the front of the crowd and paced back and forth, swinging his arms. "Imagine you're walking home late at night and you see me coming down a dark alley right toward you," he shouted like a drill sergeant. "What's the first thought that crosses your scared honky minds? Apologize for that." A few people nodded slowly—*Oh, I get it*—and sprouted little smiles. Nique scowled and kept pacing. The knot of people tightened. "Imagine I work at your job and I get the promotion you're after," he bellowed. "What's the first thing you think? Apologize for that. Imagine I ring your doorbell to take your daughter to the fucking junior prom. You get the picture?"

"Yeah!" they screamed, confused, agreeable, invigorated.

"You're a bunch of racist-ass hillbillies. Right?"

"Right!"

"Black people have been putting up with your paternalistic bullshit for too long. Right?"

"Right!"

"Are you sorry?"

"Yes!"

"Say it!"

"We're sorry!"

"The fuck you are. You crackers don't get it and you never will. Even for white people you're pathetic. Say it!" He threw his fist in the air.

"We don't get it and we never will! Even for white people we're pathetic!" Seventy-five fists punctured the sky.

"Now get out there and make your little insignificant bullshit gesture you don't even understand, and maybe you'll learn something! Go!"

The crowd dispersed, afraid to stay: a shattering kaleidoscope of African prints and glinting electronics. They pulled out maps and meandered up and down Broadway in groups of three and four, averting their eyes as they passed Nique. A middle-aged woman, tall and conservatively dressed, was the only person to approach him.

"That was brilliant," she gushed. "I'm a communications professor at a small college in Iowa, and I thought that was just wonderful. You really got those people thinking." She paused and swallowed, smiled shyly. "I might as well start here." She straightened her long skirt, then raised her head and looked Nique squarely in the eye. "I want you to know, from the bottom of my heart, that I truly am sorry. Racism is something we grow up with—Lord knows I did—but I'm doing my best not to pass it on to my children." When Nique said nothing, she kept talking. "I'm deeply thankful for this opportunity to express my sorrow and recommit myself to trying," she finished.

Andre gave her a smile. She returned it gratefully.

Nique darted his eyes away, then back to hers. "If you're so sorry, gimme your watch."

The woman blinked. "I-I'm sorry. What?"

"You're so sorry, gimme your watch."

"Give you my watch?" she repeated. Her face creased, and she wrapped her right hand around her left wrist.

Nique sucked his teeth. "Thought so," he said, and walked away. "Come on, Andre," he called over his shoulder, "let's go find the fucking Franchise."

Andre backed away from the woman, who remained rooted to her spot, perplexed. "Thank you," he soothed her. "Really. Never mind my friend. His father was a Panther." He sprinted after Nique, and the two of them walked swiftly and wordlessly through the Carman lobby and stood stoic, sweating, in the elevator, imagining the thousands of outtatown white folks roaming the five boroughs like escaped zoo animals this very second.

They found Macon naked from the waist up, leaning his palms against the bathroom wall as if waiting to be frisked. He tapped his head against the tiling every two seconds, like a blind man's stick against the pavement: hard enough to hurt, but not much.

"What"—bang—"the"—bang—"fuck," said Macon, before they could scream at him. He looked up. "What the fuck?"

"What the fuck you expect?" countered Nique. "A bunch of erudite, die-for-the-cause radicals? Of course not. A few sincere cats and boatloads of retards is what we were bound to get, specially selected or not."

"Which is okay," said Andre quickly. "Maybe having black people tell them to go fuck themselves will be a good experience."

"Or, more likely, they'll get back on the buses like, 'Fuck those niggers,' " said Nique. "Which at least is honest."

"Malcolm never said what black people's response should be when white folks started apologizing," Macon said in a small voice.

Nique slapped his hand against the wall in frustration. "That's because it was a rhetorical statement, Moves. Don't you dare try to pretend you didn't know that."

"This is gonna be a disaster, isn't it?" asked Macon, stomach sinking as he acknowledged what he'd always kind of known.

"Hell yeah. Question is how we're gonna spin it."

"You think they'll even show up for the rally?"

"To kick your ass, if nothing else," said Nique. "When black folks start rebuffing their ever-so-sincere attempts to shoulder the burden, crackers gonna want some get-back."

"You know," said Andre, bright-voiced, "that crew was the worst of the worst. Maybe productive exchanges are taking place in office buildings and on stoops throughout the city."

"You think?"

Andre shrugged. "Not really. But it's possible."

"Only one way to find out," said Nique. "Let's hit the streets. And if you run away again, Moves, I'ma put my foot so far up your ass the water in my knee will quench your thirst. You're the goddamn captain, you hear me? Your job is to go down with the ship."

Chapter Eleven

In front of his campaign headquarters in Midtown, Marcell A. "Jackfruit" Preston was busy assuaging white people's guilt and courting their votes. He stood beneath a large red-white-and-blue banner that, between twin smiling photographs of himself sporting a tuxedo and a New York Giants cap, read HARD WORK, NOT APOLOGIES. Flanked by two young women handing out CONGRESSMAN JACKFRUIT campaign buttons, the candidate pressed the flesh with a long line of white people eager to hear his message.

"Good morning to you, sir," he said, shaking hands with a pair of business-suited whiteboys on their way to work. "You haven't done anything wrong, have you? Look like a couple of hardworking, responsible young men to me. Vote Jackfruit for Congress: I believe in hard work, not apologies."

Twenty flights up from where Jackfruit stood, in the corporate offices of Roderick, Stern and Sons, Attorneys at Law, senior partner Jeffery Roderick buzzed his secretary. "Doris, send in Mr. Dayton, would you?"

A minute later, first-year trial attorney Robert Dayton entered the office, wiping the fatigue of another night's work out of his eyes. He'd been with the firm only five months, since graduating law school. He was busting his ass to make good, and trying to ignore the feeling that his job was more or less to be paraded into court when the firm thought a black lawyer might appeal to the jury.

"Sit down, Bob," said Jeffery, "this won't take long." Roderick put one foot up on his desk and pressed his fingertips together thoughtfully. "Bob, I want to know . . . do I—do we—do I owe you some sort of an apology? Are we . . ." The senior partner trailed off, collapsed his brow, and made a vague inquisitive gesture by separating and re-pressing his fingertips.

Dayton gulped, feeling his Adam's apple bulge against the knot of his Brooks Brothers tie. "No, sir," he said, shaking his head. "No, sir."

"Ah," said Roderick, removing his foot from the desk and affecting a grim, leathery smile. "Good. Well then. Thank you, Bob. We really must get together for a drink one of these days. You're doing fine work, Bob, fine work. Thank you."

Dayton nodded, smiled, and left his boss's office. He walked down the hall to the washroom, locked the door, checked to make sure all the stalls were empty, and punched his fist through the mirror that hung over the sink. Shattered glass filled the white porcelain basin and blood spread slowly over his hand. He was careful not to let any of it drip onto his tailored navy suit.

A few blocks farther south, three skinny black fourteen-year-olds stalked through Bryant Park, confronting the low-level corporate-mailroom types who ate their deli-takeout lunches off their laps along the park's perimeter. The boys halted before an effete white man in his mid-twenties and stood with their legs spread shoulders' width apart and their hands on their hips. The man continued to eat his tuna sandwich until one of the three plucked the Walkman earplug from the man's left ear. He looked up at them, frozen in surprise and apprehension, as the tinny strains of Madonna's "Material Girl" escaped the tiny speaker.

"You got something to say to us?" the boy asked, twirling the wire between his thumb and forefinger.

"Huh?"

"Don't you want to apologize and shit?"

"For what? What did I do?"

"Man, ain't you watch the news? Macon Detornay and shit? You s'posed to apologize for oppressing my black ass. Whussup?"

"Um, sorry, I guess," the man said, tucking his hair behind his ear and crinkling his nose at his tormentors.

"Thank you. You gonna eat that pickle? I demand that pickle as reparations. Whussup?"

"Go ahead." He raised his hands to his shoulders, leaving the food unprotected in his lap. The boy snatched the pickle and crunched it loudly.

"Word. Now sit here and consider your crimes. Peace." The three walked off in silence. Ten feet from the site of the pickle-jacking, their solemnity exploded into raucous, back-slapping laughter. They scanned the park for another victim, arguing over who got to go next.

In a downtown office building, Gloria, who was white, was chatting with her best friend, Cynthia, who was black, between cubicles. "This whole Day of Apology thing is pretty stupid, isn't it?" said Gloria, filing a stack of memos by subject. "I mean, we're best friends. Our kids play every weekend, we eat lunch together every day. We're practically the same person."

Cynthia shuffled a sheaf of papers until they were neat, then stapled them into a packet. "My grandfather's brother was lynched," she said quietly, without looking up from her chore. "My great-uncle Jeremiah. For smiling at a white lady. Has anyone in your family ever been lynched?"

"No. But nobody in my family's ever lynched somebody, either."

"Has anybody in your family ever stopped a lynching?"

Gloria put down her pen and cocked her head. "Are you mad at me?" she asked.

Cynthia stiffened. "Why should I be mad at you?" She spoke through pursed lips, as if hoping Gloria would know the answer.

Gloria put her hand on her best friend's arm. "Do you want me to apologize, honey?"

Cynthia was on the verge of tears. "I don't know," she said, lip trembling. "I don't want you to, but I don't want you not to, either." She smiled and her raised cheeks forced the tears hanging in the corners of her eyes to fall. "I feel so silly," she whispered. "I'm sorry."

Gloria stood up and hugged her. "It's okay, baby." She rubbed Cynthia's back. "It's okay."

On a desolate street corner in Brownsville, Brooklyn, a ghetto so remote you had to take both a bus and a train to get in or out, a dozen white apologists from Colorado were about to shed blood for the cause. They had wandered out of the bus station, glancing left and right at the boarded-up tenements and dingy storefronts, the bodegas and the lone Chinese takeout joint, shrinking from pedestrians pushing baby strollers and junk-piled shopping carts alike, and made it exactly a block and a half before running into trouble.

"What the fuck you want?" asked Teri "Street Sweeper" Framboise, chairwoman of the newly christened Neighborhood Welcoming Committee, poking a length of hollow metal pipe into the narrow chest of an ex-hippie junior-high-school teacher from Boulder who was attempting to shepherd his social studies class through what was shaping up to be the worst field trip ever.

It had seemed so brilliant back in Colorado—sort of a nineties twist on the way he and his acidhead Merry Pranksters–inspired pals had handed flowers to the riot cops and Black Power demonstrators at Berkeley in 1968. Scale the walls of misunderstanding in hiking boots of love, man. Walk right up to those hostile, snarling Negroes and kiss them on the cheek, make them smile, smoke a joint together—defeat racism and subtly one-up the black race at the same time: beat back that sacred black cool with a spastic, dare-to-do-it out-frontness that rendered coolness impotent and silly. How you gonna be cool in the face of Day-Glo freaking free love?

But here they were at the appointed time in the appointed place and things were not going according to plan—what was the plan again? Teri and her crew of stick-up women arrayed themselves in a hexagon around the out-of-towners, toting pipes, machetes, and chain saws like extras from a Naughty by Nature video.

"To say we're sorry?" the teacher squeaked, tucking his head between his shoulders like a turtle.

"You sure as fuck are," Teri agreed. "Now strip to your drawers. Macon Detornay ain't the only person who can rob white people. Put your wallets in the hat, jewelry in the gunnysack, cameras and electronics in the cardboard box. I want two piles of clothing: name-brand gear in one, generic-ass bullshit in the other. Hurry the fuck up before me and my girls get restless and give y'all chain saw lobotomies."

The vice-president of the chess club was in the midst of asking whether JCPenney counted as a name brand when the crack of a backfiring engine prompted Teri and her troops to hit the dust. A Ford pickup rounded the corner and two men with shotguns leapt from the still-moving vehicle, executing perfect military rolls and landing on one knee with their guns cocked and trained toward Teri.

"All right," said the one on the right, shoulder muscles bulging from beneath a barbecue-sauce-stained Confederate flag T-shirt, "y'all Negresses drop them home-maintenance tools and git yer hands behind yer heads."

"Y'all white folks put yer clothes back on an' jump on in the truck," said the one on the left, jerking his head at the mud-caked vehicle. He wore a ratty T-shirt adorned with Billie Holiday's portrait. The social studies class rerobed and headed shakily toward the Ford.

"What these men are doing isn't right, children," whispered their teacher, gathering his brood about him, "but say thank you, anyway."

"Now apologize to the white folks," demanded the first gunman, still squinting through his scope.

"Fuck you," said Teri. "I ain't gonna apologize for shit. Kill me, you cracker motherfucker." The ex-hippie cringed, plugged his ears, and waited for the blast, reflecting that black people were a foolish, prideful lot.

The vigilantes stared at her and then at one another. "We might need the ammo later, Raymond," offered the one in the Billie Holiday shirt. "We only brought one box of shells."

"Yeah," Raymond concurred, "I reckon we might." Slowly, the two of them backed away until they stood beside the Ford. Raymond pointed at Teri. "You're lucky, bitch." He and his buddy swung themselves into the cab and slammed the door.

"I tell myself that every day," Teri called after him as the truck rumbled away with the entire social studies class piled onto the flatbed like trophy bucks.

In the East Village, a white backpack rap crew known as the Power of Babble was scouring the record bins of You Ain't Hip Hop, a vinyl haven run by Brits whose categorical knowledge of the origins of every sample ever used manifested itself as unfettered disdain for any customer less proficient. The prices were stratospheric, but people tended to spend more than they'd planned just to impress the clerks.

"Yo, people need to listen to that nigga Macon, word up," said MC Tyrannorawness Sex, Power of Babble's frontman, as he pawed through a stack of pristine 45s. He had earned maximum respect in backpack rap circles by being one of the only whiteboys on the scene to grow legitimate-looking dreadlocks, thanks to the rigorous and ritualistic daily application of beeswax, honey, marzipan, and seven other secret ingredients to his domepiece. As a born-and-raised New Yorker, an MC, and a dread, he felt he had earned the right to say the word *nigga,* although he was careful to use it only as a non-racially specific term roughly equivalent to *dude*. He never said it in front of black people unless he was quoting a song. This, he did often. Not being able to lace his own lyrics with the word was, of course, a great handicap, and probably the reason he had yet to sign a record deal, but Tyrannorawness bore racism's burden with steadfast dignity.

"True dat," agreed his DJ, Prosthetic Ed. "That apology shit is the move. Course, he ain't talkin' 'bout us. We already down and shit, rye?"

"Oh, no doubt, son."

Their producer, Profettik, approached from across the store, a slab of vinyl in his raised hand. "Yo, I got the hot shit," he called. "This joint got the butter loop on it. We gon' go platinum offa this."

"Word," enthused Tyrannorawness. "That A&R nigga from Epicenter been dying to sign some white niggas ever since them Detroit niggas blew up. We 'bout to be in vogue, nigga." They exchanged pounds, chipped in a Jackson each to cop the record, and caught the 6 train to the Upper East Side to sneak into their prep school's state-of-the-art electronic music studio and launch their careers.

On their way to the iron horse, they passed a young Dominican man in a wheelchair, parked on the corner of Thirteenth and A with a takeout coffee cup in hand. His $150 Jordans were factory white, having never touched the ground, and their trim matched the red baseball cap twisted backward on his head. The silver-script name chain around his neck read *Edgar.* His coffee cup was empty, had been empty for five minutes. He glanced discreetly at his watch, soon to be late for his first appointment of the day.

He was too polite to roll away in the middle of a conversation, though, even a conversation with a stranger. Even a conversation as one-sided as this one had been from jump.

Edgar's interlocutor was a soft-spoken white man in his late fifties, with hair as fine and light as cornsilk. How they'd started talking, Edgar couldn't quite remember, but he had been expecting it. He'd looked forward to the Day of Apology with curiosity, and he took the man's approach in stride, feeling compassionate and well-equipped. Since the accident, Edgar's interaction with strangers had increased considerably. So, unexpectedly, had his opinion of humanity. People liked to help—if they could identify with you, anyway. No missing limbs, carefully dressed. It was funny; the Vietnam vets he'd met in physical therapy, who'd been through hell and looked it, who could barely get their chairs across the street, said they were generally ignored.

"No kidding," the man repeated, "my family goes back even before the *Mayflower,* to the Jamestown Colony. You ever heard of Jamestown?"

"Sure," said Edgar. "Virginia. 1610." He'd been a history major in college.

"That's right. That's when the first slaves came over. In the next few generations, my family got into the cotton business. By the end of the century, we were doing pretty well. Employed over one hundred slaves."

Employed, thought Edgar.

"I've been told," the man continued, "that we were the first Wilson family in the South, and that any African-Americans named Wilson are most likely our descendants. My family fought in the War of Independence, as a matter of fact. Had an ancestor named Samuel Wilson who was a real patriot, and he marched a whole battalion of his slaves up to Concord and Lexington to fight. He's mentioned in a bunch of accounts of the battle. I paid a genealogist to do a whole family history a few years back. Fascinating stuff. Samuel got elected to the state government after that, under the old Articles of the Confederacy. His son, or maybe his grandson, I forget which, was a politician, too. Had something to do with the drafting of the Fugitive Slave Act. You know what that is?"

"Sure," said Edgar. This guy seemed almost proud, he thought.

"Then, come the Civil War, we lost it all. The house, the land. Everything burned, ruined. We sharecropped for a while on a neighbor's land. Still had a few workers, freedmen, but we couldn't make a go of it. So the whole family relocated to South Carolina, bought some cheap acres and started over. Tobacco this time. My grandfather, he was incredibly bitter about the war, which I guess is understandable considering what it had cost him. He joined up with the White Knights of the Confederacy. Used to tell me fairy tales, when I was very young and he was very old, about a good dragon who had to defend his castle and his gold against a tribe of evil black elves. Raised my dad around that kind of stuff, and he became a sheriff. He didn't tell any stories at all, but the other kids told me plenty of stories about him."

The man paused to smooth his hair with the palm of his hand. "My high school was one of the first to be integrated," he said. "And in the true Southern spirit, they did it by changing the school district by one block, so one African-American family was in it. They had one kid. Clive Jackson was his name." He shook his head. "What a kid he was. I still think about tracking him down sometimes, and thanking him. He got out of there about one second after graduation, but he's the one who really changed the way I thought about things. Just watching the way he carried himself, with everything he had against him, was such a powerful experience. . . .

"I moved away myself, up to Chicago. Didn't speak to my father until he was on his deathbed. It's funny; I went back there and all his home nurses were black. The doctor, too. All local kids. And he had nothing but kind words for them. I don't know when he softened up. And considering what they must have known about him, I don't know why any of them were willing to care for the old bastard."

Edgar looked at his watch. He was ten minutes late, and five minutes away from where he was supposed to be. Oh well. "Thank you," said Wilson. "I feel like a million pounds just dropped off my shoulders." He plucked the coffee cup from Edgar's hand. "Here, let me throw that out for you. Oh. And, uh, sorry." He patted Edgar on the shoulder and walked off.

In the Bronx, Mr. Dudley James Johnson, aged ninety-three, was preparing to leave his house. He slipped into a powder blue polo shirt, matching powder blue slacks, and white buckskin shoes. He took his powder blue Kangol from the hat peg and kissed his wife good-bye. "Be careful, Toes," she said.

Lucia Johnson still called her husband by his ancient tap-dance nickname. In the thirties, Dudley had been one of the premier dancers in Harlem. He'd played on bills with the Count Basie and Duke Ellington orchestras and danced alongside Bojangles Bill Robinson. The Johnsons' modest Bronx home was filled with framed advertisement posters. Dudley had traveled throughout America back then, gotten standing ovations from people who wouldn't seat him in their restaurants or rent him a room in their hotels. He'd invested his money wisely and he and Lucia, an ex-choreographer, lived simply but comfortably in Co-op City. They'd never had children.

"I will, baby," he assured her. "I been waiting for this day my whole life." Dudley walked to the small park near their house, lowered himself onto a green wooden bench, and waited. It wouldn't take long, he thought. Who better to apologize to than a dignified, white-haired old man, stylish and stooped with age? Who could resist? In the screenplay of American race, he was as iconic as that wise old Native American Oliver Stone was always planting everywhere.

As silly as he felt, Dudley couldn't wait to hear the words. It would be a moment of uplift, like when Joe Louis beat Schmeling. Dudley had given up on seeing real justice in his lifetime long ago. But when it glinted for a moment, like gold in a prospector's pan, he still got giddy.

Not five minutes later, a white man and his young daughter strolled toward Dudley, the man walking with his hand around the girl's shoulders. They stopped in front of Dudley's bench, and the father stepped in front.

"Good morning, sir," the man said, nodding to Dudley.

"Good morning to you," replied Dudley, folding one powder blue leg atop the other. He smiled at the girl. She looked away, shy.

"Sir, you don't know me, but I want to say I'm sorry. I'm sure white people must have put you through a lot in your time. I remember how we used to drive into the black neighborhood and start trouble when I was a teenager . . ." He paused. "We didn't know much better, I suppose."

"Very few people did, son," Dudley said, a million dog-eared memories cakewalking through his mind.

The man looked down and poked a pebble with his toe.

"Well, I'm sorry now," he said.

"I don't give a rat's ass," said Dudley James Johnson pleasantly, still smiling. "Pardon me for saying so in front of young ears, but I don't give a good goddamn. I don't forgive you, and neither does anybody else. Being as old as I am makes you honest, son, and the truth is, there's not enough forgiveness in this world for white people. No, sir. Only God is that forgiving."

The man couldn't look at Dudley for long without dropping his eyes. His daughter played with a stick behind him. "I pray for God's forgiveness, too," he whispered, unable to find his voice.

"And I pray that He forgives you," said Dudley, extending his hand. The man clasped it between both his own, and Dudley had to pull back to reclaim it. "Good luck raising your daughter," Dudley said.

"Thank you," said the man. He gathered the girl to him, and Dudley watched them amble from the park.

Chapter Twelve

Macon, Dre, and Nique walked up Broadway to 125th Street, obeying the conditions of an unspoken pact that forbade them from discussing what they might find once they got there, or elucidating any of the myriad ways in which Macon's Day of Apology might send the city hurtling toward conflagration. Instead, Andre and Macon trudged silently, their paces synchronized. Nique strode counterpoint, listening to the news on a radio plugged into one ear and giving occasional updates.

"You wanna hear something crazy?" Macon said abruptly. Andre looked over and found his roommate fixing him with a grotesque stare, eyes jubilant with disgust.

"I guess so."

"It's about Cap," said Macon. "He's been on my mind today, you know?" He shoved his hands into his pockets. "That motherfucker grew up in straight Indian country, middle of Ohio. First ball team he ever played on was supposed to be all-Native. He had to pass for Indian." Macon looked up at the sky, then reconsidered and squatted on the pavement to address the dead. "You proud of me, fucko?" he shouted at the ground between his boots. "Family line's a fucking noose, huh, asshole? Hot enough for you down there?"

Andre stood and watched. Macon's hair was already thinning a little, the white of his scalp visible at the crown. He had never noticed that before. "Congratulations," Andre said, extending a hand.

Macon looked up at it and frowned. "On what?"

"Sidestepping the sins of the fathers," answered Andre.

Nique had walked on, and now he doubled back. "Fuck is the holdup?"

Macon rose at his rebuke, ignoring Andre's outstretched hand and pushing off the tarmac. "Just hollering at my redneck ancestors." He shrugged and brushed his hands clean.

"Well, maybe you can do that later." Nique pressed the headphone tighter against his ear and repeated the latest. "In Brownsville, cops just arrested three white men and six black women and seized rifles, machetes, and chain saws. . . . 'An aborted hate crime on what is already being called the most racially tense day in New York City history.' "

"Fuck," said Andre. "You know what happens if the pigs kill somebody, right?"

Nique continued: "Blacks in Harlem, Brooklyn, and the Bronx have already lashed out at the droves of white people visiting their communities with the intention of apologizing. Whites in Queens and Manhattan have also initiated violence. In Bensonhurst, a group of men with baseball bats was just detained by po-po after a black woman heard them chanting 'No apologies' as they walked past the house where she works. Honkies tried to say they were a softball team.

"Off-duty police officers have been asked to report in for the remainder of the day, to protect the legions of tourists wandering the city and ensure that no further violence erupts."

Macon spat on the ground and felt the saliva repool in his mouth. Once he started spitting, he could never stop. "Wonderful. Apologizers with police escorts."

Gingerly, he touched the butt of the gun stuck into the waistband of his jeans, making sure it was still there. Macon had convinced Nique to let him bring it along, just in case.

"Just in case what?" Nique had wanted to know.

"Just in case I want to kill somebody," Macon had answered matter-of-factly.

They turned onto 125th Street and walked east. Imported whites dotted the street, but it seemed like most of them had already learned to mind their business. Black people walked past them stone-faced, accelerating so as not to be addressed.

Not everyone had given up, though. Macon watched an obviously out-of-town white woman stop midblock and wait as a tall black man approached her. Her mouth popped open, but before she could speak he'd passed her by. She looked for all the world like a bum asking for spare change and being snubbed. "Excuse me," she managed to spit out to the next pedestrian, but the girl ignored her and continued on her way. The white woman was getting flustered. "I'm—" she blurted as another black man neared, then turned to watch him pass.

"Go home," he replied over his shoulder.

Macon approached her, said hello. "How do you feel?" he asked.

The woman didn't seem to recognize him. "Like shit. Like I'm less than human. Either they ignore me or they curse me out."

"Huh," mused Macon, wishing her well and walking on. "Maybe this is working better than we thought." They turned uptown on Frederick Douglass Boulevard and Nique continued with the updates.

"The Reverend Al Sharpton reaffirmed his support for Macon Detornay's Day of Apology today from his Harlem ministry, encouraging black people to view the gesture as 'long overdue and hopefully the beginning of a new era of responsibility.' Other black leaders simply called for calm. Jesse Jackson, speaking on National Public Radio this morning, encouraged black people to 'overlook what they might find offensive about the apology and take it in good faith.' "

On 127th and Frederick Douglass, several young black men

abandoned their posts against the wall of a corner bodega as Macon drew near. They formed a loose phalanx across the sidewalk, and Macon stopped before them. Nique and Andre flanked him, standing a step behind.

"Here to say you're sorry?" asked a cat in a Latrell Sprewell jersey-and-shorts set and suede work boots, a backpack slung over one shoulder.

"Just taking a walk," said Macon.

"You ain't gonna apologize, Macon?" piped a dude in blue linen, stepping forward and swinging his arms from the shoulders, like a boxer warming up.

"I didn't think you recognized me." Macon was pleased despite himself.

"Shit, we know all about you, big man. We your number one fans. And I quote: 'White people owe a debt, and we should be giving back before the people we owe start taking back.' "

"Brilliant," somebody said.

"Trenchant."

"Mufuckin' portentous."

"So what will you be giving back today?" asked Sprewell. He crossed his arms and dipped his eyes up and down Macon's frame. "Let's start with your wallet. I see you ain't wearing a necktie, thus frustrating my efforts at poetic justice." He turned to his boys and laughed—"That was slick, right, how he took them cats' neckties?"—then returned to Macon. "But I'll take those Tims, though. Just my size."

"I'm afraid I can't do that," said Macon calmly. "I don't have any money, anyway. All I can give back is my life."

"What the fuck I'ma do with your life?" Sprewell spat back. "You better run yo' shit. And what them two niggas witchu lookin' at? Word up, keep ice-grilling me and y'all'll get robbed, too." He circled to Macon's left and the crowd edged forward, obeying the street-fighting rules of conduct: Always pretend a scrap is going to be fair until the first punch is in the air, then rush the chump.

Macon lifted his shirt, and the sight of his gun backed everybody up. He felt like Ice Cube in *Boyz N the Hood:* had to restrain himself from licking shots at heaven and shouting a swaggering, *Now wassup, homey?*

"It's really a question of priorities," he said, coolly. The brothers stood stock-still, not scared enough to run but maintaining a respectful distance and silence. A captive audience, thought Nique, disgusted with his boy's display. He had to fight the urge to sucker-punch The Franchise in the side of the head himself.

"See," Macon explained, gun in his hand now and power flowing deliciously out from it, "if you beat me down, I'm out of the game at a pretty crucial moment. So while I may appear to be contradicting myself, it's all for the cause. Not everyone's a foot soldier. The extent to which a beat-down would expand my consciousness is insignificant, I can assure you."

The guy rocking the linen took a double step back. "I can see that," he said. Sprewell and two others nodded.

"I appreciate the thought, though. You gentlemen enjoy your day." As soon as the phrase left Macon's mouth, he realized it sounded like copspeak. Oh well. He spun on his heel and headed back the way they'd come. Nique stalked after him and Andre brought up the rear, throwing up his arms and shaking his head at the posse in an awkward what-can-you-do departure gesture.

Nique pushed Macon hard against a car as soon as they were out of earshot, back on the thoroughfare of 125th. "Are you fuckin' nuts? Don't you know any better than to go around flashing steel at motherfuckers? You don't show a nigga a gun unless you 'bout to use it, man. That's how cats get killed. Matter fact, gimme that." He snatched the heater from Macon's waistband and placed it in his own. "I don't know why I even let you bring it," he muttered. "What if those dudes had been packing, huh? You ever think of that? This ain't the only gun in New York City, you know."

As if to prove it, shots rang out and all three of them dropped to the ground, in time to hear bullets whiz inches above. Across the street, an obese, bearded white man screamed, "Nigger lover," and planted his feet like a marksman, both hands wrapped around the handle of a huge, antique revolver. Macon, Andre, and Nique scrambled behind the car for safety as the man squeezed off four more shots at them.

Macon grabbed the pistol from Nique's waist and pulled the trigger without aiming. At the sound of retaliatory gunfire, the assailant turned and ran, only to be tackled by a mob of Harlemites expressing their discomfort with his irresponsible use of the firearm and the term *nigger*.

The man's last five bullets had been stopped by the Volvo behind which Macon and company crouched, but the first ricocheted off a building and passed straight through the chest of a black statistician on his way to drop off his daughter at day care. He collapsed, and the bullet exited his back and bounced off a stop sign, a second building, and a third before coming to rest squarely in the head of the white woman Macon had approached. She was dead before she toppled to the ground.

Macon's bullet, meanwhile, arced high into the air and plummeted to earth eighty-three blocks south of where it had been fired. In front of the Army recruiting station in Times Square, a delegation of Black Hebrews stood on their customary milk-crate pedestals, preaching the gospel as they understood it to a swollen crowd comprising more skeptics and horrified tourists than believers.

"Read!" commanded the speaker, and his assistant reopened a dog-eared King James Bible. To all challenges concerning the logic of using this particular translation to prove their assertion that only the colored peoples of the world, the Twelve Lost Tribes of Israel, would be granted salvation, the group responded that King James I of England had been a black man. Their leader held up a worn picture of the monarch and said, "Looks like David Dinkins to me," whenever questioned, although the British ruler bore scant resemblance to the ex-mayor.

" 'Can the prey be taken from the mighty, or the captives of a tyrant be rescued?' " the reader bellowed.

" 'Can the prey be taken from the mighty?' " repeated the speaker. "Can the prey be taken from the mighty. What that means is—" He never finished the thought. Macon's bullet fell from the sky like manna and penetrated the top of his skull. He crumpled and dropped face first off his platform. A small trickle of blood leaked out onto the concrete and the crowd screamed and parted before it. To the untrained eye, it looked like an act of God.

The Black Hebrews knew better. They seized upon their fallen comrade, ascertained that he was dead, and turned their attention to the panicked crowd, assuming that one of them was the assassin. They attacked the mass indiscriminately, and soon the entire plaza was a gyrating clot of violence, spinning and spilling out into the busy street. A taxi skidded to a halt to keep from hitting three brawling men and was rear-ended by four other cars, one of which was due for factory recall and promptly exploded into flames. It threw fiery shrapnel fifteen feet, pulverizing the plate-glass window of a Gray's Papaya hot dog stand.

"They killed him!" came the shouts. "They killed Brother Ben-David!"

Prompted by clear visual, auditory, and olfactory cues—flames, tormented faces, blood, whirling fists, the shattering of glass, shrieks, car alarms, the smells of smoke and panic—the people of New York heaved a collective sigh of horror and relief that the day's mounting tension had finally broken, and commenced to get their riot on.

The nearest store windows were smashed with cinematic flair. Due to Times Square's nascent domination by megacorporations, these windows were owned by Disney, Warner Brothers, and Starbucks. Folks dizzy with confusion, rage, and giddiness were soon sprinting up the block toting such looted booty as huge stuffed Porky Pigs, Bugs Bunny wading pools, Little Mermaid lunch boxes, and gleaming stainless-steel cappuccino machines.

There was no joy in the air, though, no come-up-on-the-man get-me-some-free-shit carefree moment of release. This was Midtown Manhattan, not Any Ghetto U.S.A., and even as the fire spread, turning snubbed white apologist tourists, Black Hebrews, and indigenous pissed-off citizens from all sides of the racial divide into looters and pyromaniacs, everybody knew the mack hand of the law was coming down to diggum-smack some sense or at least some pain into the populace, piss on the flames with a huge flaccid Bull Connor fire-hose dick, and return the slightly singed $49.95 Foghorn Leghorn dolls to their proper top-shelf perches. The body of Brother Ben-David lay faceup in the dust, oblivious to the madness surging all around, as folks began trying in earnest to beat, rob, and flee one another.

Meanwhile, in Harlem, the first two officers on the crime scene were the 26th Precinct's own Dick Downing and Ray McGrath. They'd been on stroll patrol a few blocks south when the screams and gunshots echoed forth and brought them running, and they arrived to find two dead bodies sprawled on the ground, a huge crowd of black people exchanging hostile stares with a smaller group of whites from across the street, and a small knot of black folks kicking a fat white man to death. Downing and McGrath called for backup and an ambulance, and pounced immediately on the knot of blacks with Tasers and billy clubs. The crowd surged forward, screaming in protest. Downing stepped away from the fray and waved his gun at them. Wherever he pointed it, the people shrank away in fear.

"Stay back!" he shouted. "Stay back!" His partner had succeeded in subduing the knot of attackers; seven men and two women lay prostrate on the ground. McGrath walked from one to the next, treating anyone who moved to another electric shock.

"You are all under arrest," he screamed at their incognizant, twitching bodies. "Dick, this goddamn guy is dead. You fucking animals!"

"He had a gun!" shouted the crowd. "He killed them!" They pointed at the statistician and the tourist, now covered in African batik-print sheets from a nearby shop and guarded by multiracial circles of weeping strangers. Downing dropped to his knees beside the white woman, took her pulse, and stood back up. He walked over to the black body and poked it with his toe.

"Request immediate backup," he repeated into his walkie-talkie, clutching it so tightly that his knuckles turned the shade of glue. "Riot waiting to fucking happen up here, copy?"

He'd no sooner said it than the crowds surged forward and engulfed the street. McGrath and Downing went under in a human riptide, a miscegenation of frenzied bodies who knew only that they'd just witnessed three murders and that the color of their skin, the color of other people's skin, had brought or put them here, had caused this, was to blame. Their guilt, their anger, their attempts to do what they had thought was right—to teach, to be taught, to apologize, to forgive, to decline forgiveness, to remember, to forget—these things had smashed into one another and exploded, sent splinters flying. They had touched one another, invaded, been invaded, stepped foolishly outside themselves, and their daring had wrought death and madness.

They spun around now, understanding only color, and struck out. There was nowhere to go: Violence had toppled them against one another like dominoes and all they could do now was fall together, black on white on black on white, brick on glass and match on matchbook, torch on property. The block became a sea of chaos, a human tsunami throwing flames and people.

Cap Anson smirked at Macon and squirted a blast of tobacco juice right at the camera, grinning hands-on-hips as brown dripped sickly down the lens. He knew who always won these things as well as anybody.

More cops were there soon, trying to pull the plug, but it was too late. The police decided quickly that they didn't care; black people burning down their neighborhoods again was no big deal. White folks dumb enough to be up here apologizing, fuck it, they asked for it, leave 'em to the mercy of the niggers. The cops' orders were containment: Keep it in Harlem and get the tourists back on board their buses if possible. But before anything much could be done, the call came that Times Square was exploding, too, and most of the city's police forces were marshaled to defend Midtown, where the real estate was worth protecting.

At his campaign headquarters on Fifty-second Street, Marcell A. "Jackfruit" Preston was beginning to panic. He turned off the television set when the riot spread north of Fiftieth, and pressed his cheek to the window in fear. A mob of giant cartoon animals advanced up Broadway, smashing the windows of cheap electronics stores and grabbing display model telephones, radios, and microwave ovens—all of which had languished in those windows for years, baking, and none of which worked.

The congressional candidate was busy spray-painting the words BLACK OWNED over his plate-glass storefront when the mob bore down on him. In his haste, Preston forgot the *n* and scrawled BLACK OWED on his property.

"Damn right," a rioter agreed, slapping the graffiti writer on the back. "Black owed like a motherfucker." The man hurled a metal coffee grinder through the window and Preston's staff screamed and covered their faces as the glass collapsed, spraying tiny shards across the office floor. The mob poured in and helped themselves to the only goods the headquarters had to offer: a television set, two laptop computers, and three thousand straw derbies with the words *Jackfruit for Congress* printed on them.

"Nooo," moaned the candidate, realizing he was now the riot's official outfitter. In every news report, on every magazine cover, hooligans bearing his name on their heads would be documented ravaging the city.

"No justice, no peace!" chanted the mob, rifling through a stationery store and reemerging on the street with cards and envelopes enough for every conceivable occasion, from *Happy Anniversary to a Great Minister* to *Condolences on the Death of Your Pride.*

"Brother Ben-David dead! How many more?" shouted some as they ransacked a soup store and dumped tureens of New England clam chowder, garden vegetable, and other oppressive broths into the gutter.

"Who's dead?" asked others, attempting to pillage a bank and leaving with nothing more than armfuls of deposit slips and free desk calendars. "Is this part of the apology?"

Chapter Thirteen

Macon cocked his head. "What's that sound?"

Andre and Nique, walking with him through the detritus strewn in the wake of the rapidly advancing riot, knew exactly what it was.

"Choppers," Andre said. "Ghetto birds, we call 'em back home."

Burnt air stung their nostrils. A layer of invisible ash seemed to coat skin, words, the soles of shoes. The world was smudged and broken, heavy. Andre had the sense that if he lit a match, the emptiness in front of him would combust like a kitchen with the gas left on; violence lingered long after its perpetrators vanished. Nique treaded carefully over smoldering artifacts: charred shoe boxes, crushed CD cases, ripped and soiled clothing. He felt momentarily like an archaeologist on television, theorizing about the mysterious disappearance of some arcane, troubled civilization.

It had all happened so fast. Macon felt vaguely horrified, if such a thing were possible. He wanted to forget himself, pretend he was just an observer like anybody else. He tried to avoid looking at the small fires burning here and there in the wreckage of stores; it was too easy to imagine painted native urchins spying and whispering behind them, dashing from one hiding place to the next as if 125th Street were a Conradian river.

"This ain't L.A.," he said dumbly.

"It is now," said Andre. "It's Watts 1965, Detroit and Newark '67, and South Central '92." He shaded his eyes with the flat of his hand and squinted ahead. "Damn it," he said, scowling, "why do black people have such a fatalistic sense of direction? These fools could just as easily have gone south, toward Columbia, but no. They march east into Harlem, where there ain't shit but bootleg Tommy Hilfiger shit any damn way."

Nique followed the helicopters' paths. "National Guard," he said. "The radio stations don't even know about this yet. They're too busy covering the riot going on downtown."

"I hope Logan's okay," said Macon, glancing at Andre. The CEO's job for the day was to coordinate the setup for the rally. After the first skirmishes, however, which involved rogue members of NYU's College Republicans' Club heaving mangos stolen from a nearby Haitian fruit vendor's stand at the soundstage, Logan had panicked and struck a blow for justice. She pounced on the blue-blazer-and-khaki-attired ringleader with her bare hands, throttled him until he lay gasping on the ground, and fled back to her Lower East Side apartment. At the moment, she was watching the riot on TV, salving her guilt at deserting her post and her horror at what she had done with a bottle of Jack Daniel's and afraid to go outside for fear of what else she might do: whyle out, lay down her life for the cause, disembowel anybody who bore a passing resemblance to her boss. The rage, the power, the bloodlust she felt scared her. She gulped another drink, hoped Team Detornay would forgive her, and decided that as soon as she finished the bottle, she'd track down the guys, apologize, and finish seducing Dre.

Professor Andrea Jenson, arriving at the park prepared to speak, found the half-assembled soundstage being torn down by a frenzied bipartisan group of skate punks, College Republicans, and trust-fund anarchists, and decided to join them. She threw her speech, "From Guilt to Gestalt: Turning Your Pathetic Fears and Secret Fascinations into Revolution," to the ground and grabbed a passing Jamaican by the hand. "Rinehart," she said. "Rinehart, baby, it's me, Sybil. Let's rip this town apart."

The man looked at her quizzically. "My name's Clayton," he said. "Do I know you?"

Professor Jenson threw back her head and giggled with delight. "Clay," she purred. "How fantastic. Call me Lula, Clay, and pass me something flammable. This is going to be one hell of a rally."

"You're crazy, lady," said Clayton. "You wanna buy some smoke or not?"

"I want to buy some freedom—have you got any to spare? At what cost liberty, Clay? Oh Clay, Clay, do you know what Lula does to Clay? Do you?"

Clay broke free and walked away, out of the park and toward Fourth Street, where sanity still reigned. "No," he said over his shoulder, "and I don't care."

Professor Jenson shrugged and watched him go. "Yeah, me neither." She picked up a discarded mango, peeled away a strip of skin, and sunk her teeth in, letting the sweet juice drip down her chin.

Outside Yu's Electronics Supermart in East Harlem, the riot had mutated again, capitalist lightning striking the primordial anger soup and restructuring the mob's double helix into a dollar sign. The store had been looted with the quickness; aspiring DJs emerged from the gaping maws of the smashed windows holding Technics decks above their heads like tablets from God, then vanished down the block with glass crushed into their boot soles. Stereos, microwaves, and camcorders were ripped from their display mounts. Stragglers lingered outside the store, holding on to strobe lights and clock-radios like they were little sisters' hands.

Gradually, cats took note of the tourists caught up in the eastward gold rush. Outtatown white folks walked fast toward nowhere, clueless to the proper vector of escape. They strode a few purposeful blocks, then turned around when things didn't seem to be improving and doubled back the way they'd come, recalling with nostalgia that the black folks from whom they'd just fled hadn't actually done anything to them, whereas the ones on this new block looked downright dangerous.

Before long, the market dynamic of the riot was established. East 125th became a giant swap meet, with looters turning spontaneously into salesmen when they ran into a tourist. Fearing for their lives, the white folks nodded fast and bought whatever looted merchandise was offered, from TVs to turtles from the Jewish pet store, unsure whether they were being mugged or merely offered the bargain of a lifetime. Loaded down with booty and hoping their new possessions would somehow protect them, the outta-towners continued to follow in the riot's wake, like weary second-liners in a New Orleans funeral march.

Behind the last of them lingered the vultures, the repo men, scanning the herd for signs of lameness. They picked their marks with care and dove in fast, snatching just-boosted, just-bought items from the docile arms of their victims and meeting scant resistance. There was a festive mood to the pack; folks were too high-spirited for outright muggings, and instead the gentlemanly practice of appropriation and resale prevailed. Dudes sold plastic fishbowls and CB radios back to their quarries two and three times, enjoying the elongated torment they were foisting on their prey. The white folks, complying terrified with the repo men's bizarre spur-of-the-moment modus operandi, tried not to consider what would happen when their cash and valuables ran out. They trudged on, praying that oasis was near.

Upon unloading their merchandise, the looters sauntered up the block into a vacant, grassy lot next to the Paul Robeson Playhouse to soak up some free entertainment. The People's Cooperative Guerrilla Theatre, rally-bound on the downtown train platform when the riot broke out, had elected to stay in the hood instead and provide drama in the midst of drama. They were halfway through the first act of Aristotle's little-known play *How We Stole Math and Science from Them Egyptian Motherfuckers* and in fine form—resplendent in kente-cloth togas and enlivened by a swelling, nouveau-riche audience digging the show and making heavy contributions to the tips jar—when Officer Dick Downing staggered around the corner and collapsed in the weeds.

The audience rushed over to investigate. Downing's belt and gun were gone, his left eye swollen shut. He sprawled on his side, a razor tear splitting his shirt and a thin line of purpled blood across his exposed back matching the rip. A thespian bent down, rolled him over, and splashed a cup of water on his face. At the sight of six black men in togas fronting a dusky army, Downing's functioning eye bulged with fear. He clawed at his badge with a blood-caked hand, trying to tear it away.

An old man peered at him through thick spectacles, weight resting on a bamboo cane. "You thought putting on that badge would make you a man," he said, "and now you think taking it off will?"

"Hey, I know this motherfucker," came a deep, young voice from the middle of the throng. "Remember me, Officer? I'm home from Rikers now. Wasn't no criminal when I went in, but I sure learned."

"Show him what assault and battery looks like, G."

"I'm 'bout to show this pig sexual misconduct with a deadly weapon."

"Hold up." The lead actor strode over. "I've got a part for this sucker."

"Back up, man. We gonna *take* apart this sucker."

The actor faced the crowd and his cohorts massed behind him, thick arms crossed over their chests. "It's the part he was born to play," he said evenly. "Costume!" As the crowd watched, Costume rooted in a suitcase and tossed a white G-string at the cop's chest. Downing sat up slightly, wincing in pain.

"Get undressed, boy. You're the Emperor's eunuch."

Downing stared down at the G-string and then up into the happy, angry, cackling crowd.

"Strip, pig. Before we make you Method-act."

In the overgrown, trash-strewn middle of the lot, where cellular reception was better, Professor Umamu Shaheed Alam was making the most of the impromptu intermission. "Come on, come on," he muttered, fat fingers sweat-slippery as he re-dialed his agent's number. Finally, the call went through. "Marty!" he enthused. "Boyd. Listen: I just made another of my infamous discoveries. A theater troupe—wait till you see these guys. . . . I'm up in Harlem, man, with my people. What? Of course not; I drove the Range up. . . . No one's gonna steal it. Why do you think I shelled out so much dough for that red-black-and-green rear spoiler?"

A tap on the shoulder interrupted Alam's conversation. "Pardon me," said the young man from Rikers. "But did I hear you say something about a Range Rover?" His silver switchblade glinted in the mounting sunlight as he rubbed it gently against the professor's thigh.

Chapter Fourteen

"You've got to do something," Andre pled, as Nique rattled off the latest facts and figures of hysterical destruction between deep drags on his second-to-last cigarette.

"Me?" snapped Macon. "What the fuck can I do?"

"Get on TV. Call for calm. Tell motherfuckers to chill before they end up homeless and in jail with nothing to show for it but a ten-dollar size-XXL Jimmy Jazz T-shirt-and-shorts set." Andre's hand darted to his head and twisted the same dreadlock he'd been playing with all day. It was hanging from the root by a thread now.

"Fuck you mean, 'call for calm'? I ain't going out like King Junior."

The choppers hovered like gargantuan mosquitoes, browsing the riot. Nique glared up at them. "They're just making sure it stays in niggerville." He flicked his filter away and lit a new cigarette against a cardboard Radio Shack advertising cutout that stood burning in the middle of the street.

"You gotta say something," Andre pressed. "They're gonna blame this all on you."

"As well they should," said Macon, picking up a tennis shoe and heaving it listlessly through a hole in the window of a gutted sneaker shop. "If I hadn't had some faith in white people, just a little bit, this never would have happened. If I hadn't thought black people could handle their stupid asses . . . That's my problem, man. I overestimate folks." He made a fist and lifted it as if to punch himself in the forehead, then dropped and unclenched it, felt the blood drain away.

"Well, say that, then. Apologize. Do anything. Nique, gimme the phone." Andre snatched it, jabbed Memory One, and waited for Yolanda Prince to pick up.

"Yolanda? Hey, sugar, Andre Walker. Listen, I'm here with Macon on One Twenty-fifth and Lenox, and I need a live feed. I want him on that big-ass TV screen in Times Square. He's gonna talk to the people. Can you do it? Yeah, of course you're the first reporter I called. Five minutes? Word." He turned triumphantly to Macon. "She's just down the street, covering the show at the Apollo."

"Show?"

"Brothers broke in and they're making white people dance and giving them the gong. Sounds like a blast."

They made their way to a sizzling secondhand store and gazed at the grainy images playing on the only television left, a black-and-white Philco embedded in a wood cabinet, too heavy to be worth stealing.

"They came here and spat in our faces," a black man panted into the microphone as he ran past the camera, wheeling a giant *Star Trek* pinball machine behind him. Nique wondered if Lavar Burton ever felt like a sellout as the only brother on the *U.S. Enterprise,* and blind as a bluesman at that. Maybe he and Han Solo's Colt 45–drinking space-ho-macking running buddy, Lando Calrissian, could form a union and demand equitable treatment at the hands of the white gods of science fiction.

"We came here in good faith and they spat in our faces," said a white man, passing the camera with an armful of Marvin the Martian dolls. Questionable as a black alien, thought Nique, but he got mojo points for wanting to destroy Earth.

Nique looked over at Macon, found his face placid, and scowled at The Franchise. Blackness as a state of mind was bullshit. Him touting Macon to the media as *possessing rare insight* and *accepted by the brothers* was as ridiculous as Toni Morrison calling Bill Clinton the first black president in *The New Yorker,* or basketball heads geeked off Jason Williams's handle rhapsodizing over how black the skinny whiteboy's game was.

It was all semantic bullshit and everybody involved knew it and pimped it. If Clinton's the first black president, nobody has to feel bad that they didn't vote for Jesse. If we find traces of blackness in white folks, we can call that integration and kick the bona fide niggers to the curb like used-up batteries. It won't be long, thought Nique, before race quotas are filled by whiteboys acting black. And, he reflected, grinding his teeth, it'll be as much my fault as anybody's.

He walked over and bashed in the TV with his foot. The forty-year-old screen gave easily; the inner coils spasmed, twitched, and died and nobody reacted. Nique spun toward Macon, eyes flashing. "Why didn't you let those guys rob you?" he demanded. "You know why? It's like I told you. Like I knew from jump. You're full of shit."

He stood chest to chest with Macon and lifted his arms to crucifixion height. "Welcome to ground zero, Macon. The moment we find out how black you are. Whether you gon' give your life for the cause. How the song go? 'It's glorious to die for a cause / But you better find a cause soon, because you're going to die anyway / Just because you're black.' "

Nique was inches from his face, and talking hard. "Here we are, Moves. You know as well as I do that from here on in, it's black people that are gonna die today. National Guard, pigs, you know who they're gunning for. Dre told you to call for calm and you said no without even thinking about it. You know why? 'Cause you don't give a fuck about all the niggers that're gonna die and go to jail and get burned out behind this shit. You think it's a game. 'Not everybody's a foot soldier.' Please! You think Malcolm thought he wasn't? You think King or Huey or Frederick fuckin' Douglass or any of your supposed heroes ever thought they weren't? And you somehow got the fuckin' nerve to think you ain't?"

"Dominique, come on," said Andre, standing close behind him. "It's not Macon's fault."

"Oh, no?" Nique's eyes blazed. "Whose fault is it? Massa Lincoln? Cecil B. DeMille?"

Macon stood, thin and pale, arms dangling by his sides. "It's my fault," he said quietly. "I already said so. What more do you want?"

"See?" said Nique, jabbing the air in front of Macon with a finger. "See? Here he comes with that ol' 'If I take the blame, nobody can say shit else' shit. The best offense is to pretend to forfeit. What can black folks say to an apology? All they can do is feel fucking stupid because there's no way to respond. You can't be mad, can't be happy, can't accept it, can't reject it, can't say shit. It's the most brilliant mindfuck the white man has conceived of in a hot minute, that's for damn sure. And you know what else, Macon? If you knew what you were getting into, you never would have done shit to begin with. Say I'm wrong."

Macon was at a loss. "I didn't—" he began anyway, but the look on Nique's face stopped him.

"You know what I want from you, Moves? You know what would really mean something?" Nique started toward Macon, hands balled, and Andre stepped forward, locked his arms around Nique's shoulders from behind, and held him firm. Nique twisted backward, fixing Andre with a wild, scornful glare.

"You crazy? Get the fuck off me, nigga. I ain't gonna hit him." They both knew Andre was strong enough to restrain Nique; the only question was whether he would.

Andre's arms fell, and Nique jumped right back into Macon's face.

"Here's what you do, Moves. Grab that gun sitting next to your dick and apologize by blowing out your fucking brains. That's what I wanna see. That's a whiteboy who ain't going home when shit gets thick. That's John fuckin' Brown, baby. Take out the so-called blackest whiteboy in America, Macon. Kill off the latest, greatest new black leader. With his last ounce of strength, Macon Detornay gives up on white folks and eats lead. Dies by the gun just like a real authentic nigger. Word up. Ratings soar and millions mourn the martyr."

Macon pulled the gun and held it by his side. All three of them were still, and for the first time Macon noticed how hot it had become. The forecast had been wrong. It was eighty degrees, easy, and so humid he could hardly breathe. "If I give up on white people," he said, cocking the hammer back, "you're in more trouble than I am, Dominique. You're right smack in front of a pissed-off devil with a gun."

The two of them stood and stared, refusing to blink. Sweat danced on Nique's forehead, beaded on Macon's upper lip. Their hearts and the helicopter blades above seemed to beat at a common tempo: fast and steady, with the constant illusion of acceleration.

"Okay," said Andre finally, "enough with the Mexican standoff shit. Nobody's shooting anybody. Nique, shut the fuck up. Macon, put the gun away. Both of you, apologize. We've got a press conference in three minutes."

Without dropping his eyes, Macon slowly uncocked and resheathed the weapon.

"I'm gonna die black with or without you," Nique said. "You think I give a fuck?"

Yolanda Prince's voice cut through the tension. "Macon? Andre? Dominique? Where are you guys? We're all set up."

"In here," called Andre.

"Well, come on out," Yolanda shouted, exasperated. "I want to shoot Macon in front of what's left of Dream Weavers. We're going live, so if you curse, it's my ass, okay? You hear me, Macon?"

"I hear you," he said, walking toward the light. Andre followed, a pace behind, and Nique brought up the rear.

"You want makeup?" asked Yolanda, running frantic errands between the cameraman and the light guy, adjusting their positions and snaking her microphone cord over broken glass and garbage.

"Yeah," said Macon. He opened the case she handed him and gave himself two thick, black mascara streaks, one underneath each eye.

"Nice look," said Andre. "Outfielder of the apocalypse. Cap Anson would be proud." Macon shot him a vicious glare, but Andre had already turned away.

In Times Square, the planet's largest television screen came to life and boomed over the raging block. People stopped in mid-pillage to see what was going on, the basic American what's-on-TV impulse overriding everything else.

"Live in Harlem, this is Yolanda Prince." Her face filled the screen. "These streets are all but deserted now, but only minutes ago an angry mob burned and looted stores after two white tourists and a local black man were killed for reasons which remain unclear. The rioting has moved east now, further into Harlem, as the Day of Apology takes a drastic turn toward disaster. With me now is Day of Apology leader Macon Detornay. Macon, what do you want to tell the people?"

Macon glanced over at Andre and Nique. Nique scowled back with murder in his eyes, brought his forefinger to his head, and pulled the trigger. Andre lunged for Nique's hand and pushed it down to his side, and Nique turned and slapped the shit out of him. Andre grabbed him by the shirt and cocked back his arm as if to throw a punch, and Nique cocked his and they stood frozen for a moment in mutual, mirrored aggression.

Times Square held its collective breath. In the flickering glimmer of a dozen small infernos, rioters and heartsick protesters stopped beating one another up and turned their faces skyward, basking in the radioactive glow of Macon's face.

"I'm giving up," he told the world. "This whole thing was a mistake. White people, if you're listening, forget it and go home. I was wrong to think that you've got what it takes to change. Forget apologizing. It'll only make things worse. Power doesn't have the power to change, only to self-destruct. If you want to make a difference, kill yourself."

Macon shoved the barrel of the gun into his mouth and stared cross-eyed at the world beyond the hammer. He closed his eyes and tried to summon the courage to pull the trigger, feeling time stop and the city watch, but he knew immediately that he wasn't going to go through with it. He took the gun out of his mouth and dropped his hand.

"I can't do it," he said flatly. "I'm just as full of shit as all of you. I'm not gonna justify it like I did when I robbed those crackers and say I'd make a bigger difference alive than dead, or that I don't want to let you off the hook by dying for your sins. The truth is that I'm just not willing to die, for justice or for anything. Macon Detornay's a coward and a sellout, and maybe deep down I even knew this apology shit was gonna fuck up black folks worse than whites, paint them into a corner, get them killed. I'd apologize, but I wouldn't believe myself. So fuck it.

"I'm not gonna call for calm in the streets, either. I don't care. Tear this place apart. Kill each other. It won't change shit, and soon enough the cops will close it down and cart the black folks off to jail regardless, so you might as well get in a couple more hours of good, old-fashioned, honest race rioting before the spin control and white liberalism and pretending not to hate each other kicks back in. You might as well make somebody pay. I know I will. I'm out."

Macon pointed his gun at the cameraman. "Turn that shit off!" he yelled. The dude obeyed.

"All right," said Macon, "I'm getting the fuck out of here." He trained his weapon on the tubby, bearded *Action News* soundman. "Out of the van, homeboy. And what the hell: You might as well leave your wallet on the seat."

The soundman did as he was told, reached into his back pocket and deposited a billfold and emerged with his hands in the air. Macon waved the gun over everybody like a magic wand, and Andre, Nique, Yolanda, and her crew shuffled away from the van at his unspoken command. Macon slid into the driver's seat and held the burner out the window.

"You were right," he told Nique.

"I wish I hadn't been," said Nique, as sad as he was furious. "So where you going?"

"As far away as possible. I'm sure as hell not going to jail. Ten years of getting raped for what I don't really believe in when push comes to shove? I'll pass." He looked at Andre. "Sorry 'bout the bail money, dude."

"But not sorry enough," Andre replied stonily.

"Obviously not." Macon rolled up the window and peeled out, leaving them standing in the wreckage.

Nique raised his fist and thumped his heart. "Stay black and die," he whispered as the van disappeared around a corner.

BOOK III

RACE

I stood at home plate and watched the ball clear the outfield fence and let the bat drop from my hands. I stared back at the crowd, and for the briefest of instants I felt at one with all of them, with every person packed into the stands; we were united by the fact that neither I nor they knew what would happen next. The tacit script we'd all been following was gone; gravity had vanished and left us floating in midair.

For a preposterous instant, I felt that I had won, that it was over, that they would hush and shuffle home, too broken to hurt me. I stared down the Klansmen with no fear, no feeling even. I turned to look at Cap Anson and found that he, too, was expressionless, arms limp at his sides, mouth slack and bulging with tobacco. Red Donner and Buck Desota watched me from the second step of the dugout, ashen-faced but tensed to move. Everyone was poised for something; this was the moment when crowds turned to mobs, the moment when the bleachers emptied and a thousand frenzied white men killed me where I stood. To gawk and wait was worst of all, I decided, and so thinking I began to jog slowly toward first base, face lifted to the crowd. If I kept looking at them, I thought, perhaps the spell would last.

Halfway to first base the silence was unbroken. Every eye was on me, and soon I would have to pass Cap Anson and every eye would watch us both. As I approached, the fear swelled in my gut. Anson would do something. Stand in my way? Scream nigger *and regalvanize the crowd? Spit on my shoes again?*

Instead, as I neared the bag, Anson turned his back and walked away. Removed his hat and left the field, strolled straight into the dugout and was gone. The catcher followed, and the screaming started. The outfielders jogged in next, casually, as if the inning were over, and what I thought had been unbearable noise was nothing next to what came now. They roared at me, a tidal wave of focused, blaring hatred, so sharp I wanted to bring my hands to my ears in self-defense. Garbage flew out of the stands; detritus of all kinds rained onto the field and I kept my head tucked and forced myself to jog, to keep a steady home-run pace instead of sprinting for my life. I was practically alone now on the field; only the second baseman hadn't walked into the dugout. I glanced up as I rounded third and saw Buck gesturing frantically. The entire team was standing on the steps, screaming and beckoning. I took my time.

I reached the dugout and my teammates swarmed around me. "Let's get the hell out of here," said Buck, and the New York Giants hustled down into the guts of the building and through the tunnel to the locker room. We stuffed our street clothes and equipment in our duffel bags and made for the door.

The players' exit opened onto empty brambling countryside; a flat half-mile separated the stadium from the train tracks. "You'd better run, Fleet," said Buck. "They're gonna double back here quick and we won't be able to hold them off. You can hop a train before they catch you. Go." The hollers of the mob grew louder, and I could see them rounding the side of the stadium as I sprinted over the cracked tundra. There were hundreds of them, a human blanket rippling behind the leadership of Anson and the Klan. They moved with steady confidence, certain I was still inside. The sight of them turned me into a black blur and I ran with a swiftness born of total conviction: There was no question what would happen if they caught me. I prayed for a few more seconds of invisibility, knowing they would see me any moment, spot the dust my cleats kicked up. I prayed for a train, for speed; absurdly, I even prayed for justice. And suddenly, they saw me; I heard the cry of recognition and the heavy pounding of boots as they broke into chase.

Red Donner's stomach plunged as he watched the mob change direction from the doorway of the stadium. He knew I was fast, but what if there wasn't any train? What if I tripped and sprained my ankle, or leaped onto a passing car only to be ripped down from it like a piece of fruit? As I heard later from Buck Desota, Red removed his greasepaint from his satchel and scooped a heavy gob into his palm. He rubbed it all over his face, covered his hands in the bitter-smelling ointment, pulled his cap low, and turned to his teammates. "I'm blacker than Fleet Walker now," he said. "And those sons of bitches will have to choose which one of us to chase." Red passed the greasepaint to Joe Wagner and sprinted from the stadium, ninety degrees from the direction I had taken.

The mob saw him and split in confusion. Red's blackness was stark, unmistakable, unlike that of the hazy shape in the distance. Two of the front-runners switched directions to pursue him, and the mob followed. And then, like a Fourth of July celebration, a succession of black firecrackers exploded from the stadium doorway and shot out into the Georgia sun, streaking every which way with breakneck speed. The New York Giants had become a colored ball club.

I crossed the train tracks and kept running, and a minute later the ground rumbled. I doubled back and grabbed on to a cargo car, lifted myself and swung my frame inside, and when the train passed I was gone, nowhere to be found and never seen again in Georgia, to be sure.

Eventually, the mob rounded all the Giants up and figured out the truth, and no one had the stomach to kill a white man, even if it was for helping the nigger Fleet Walker escape. The Giants left town bruised and badly beaten but intact, on the next train that came along.

Except Red Donner. The mob caught him first of all and didn't check too hard to make sure he was the man they wanted, or maybe they just didn't care. Somebody had a knife, and plenty of others had their fists and work boots, and they stomped him to the ground and sliced him up and left him there to die, leaking blood and greasepaint into the parched Georgia soil.

Chapter One

All Macon needed, dipping from the city with lane-switching fervor, Jersey bound, *Action News* van lurching as he threaded it through traffic and hoped the TV emblems on the doors gave him carte blanche, was a plan: somewhere to go from here. Instead, his brain conjured nothing but hate mail, instant bullshit-motherfucker replays. As hard as he strained toward the future, the next half hour of his life, he couldn't wrench a tense-shift. *What is there to say? You either kill for the revolution or get killed for the revolution, and your punk double-crossing Jennifer Beals I-wanna-live-forever ass done blazed a middle coward's path, so you best run it till your lungs ready to pop, then dig yourself a hiding hole before you get what's coming to you from both splibs and jaspers, coons and honkies. Thought you was a hero but you chicken on a roll.*

It wasn't much of a plan, but when it came it hit him hard, and Macon hit the breaks and banged an exit-ramp right turn into the Newark Bus Terminal's parking lot: *France. Yes. Go to France. Punish myself with a smokescreen Los Angeles bus ride and then hop, skip, jump a plane to France.*

Why France?

It's far.

Come on, motherfucker, you can do better than that.

It's far and I don't speak French. Plus Baldwin, Hemingway, Wright, Dolphy, Dexter Gordon, Jack Johnson—

Oh, you mean all them storied stand-tall icons you just eye-conned, hustling the world by pulling off the mask to reveal the same mug beneath, twisted sinister now—underneath the blue-eyed devil lurks . . . a blue-eyed devil! Ha-ha, gotcha, yes I'm walking off the battlefield I plowed now, people—and the dupes scratch their decapitated heads, tucked under their arms like basketballs, and wonder, How did we not see that coming?

Macon bought a ticket to Los Angeles on the *Action News* man's Visa, swifted away from the ticket counter, and dropped the credit card into the nearest trash can. The bus was boarding. Macon found the terminal, climbed aboard the bus, and hunched against the window in a plush reclining seat. The coach's air-conditioned cool lifted the sweat from his body like a stain in a detergent ad, and Macon crossed his arms over his chest and shivered. He had next to no money, next to no plan, no passport. He didn't care. The gun was still on the floor of the abandoned van.

France. Yes. Fade into the ancient walls. Maybe toothpaste-squeeze my dome for any last kindness and look up Andre's moms and kick her some loot somehow—drop Grandma a note in the old-and-crazy home and tell her to send my college funds to Mrs. Walker, or—wait, wait, I'm slipping out of character. The new old real Macon Anson Detornay says fuck her fuck her fuck her. Shouldn't have trusted no race-trading whiteboy stranger, Andre, especially not one who tried to wax your great-grandpops. Let the bitch remortgage.

Hold up, hold up, he rebutted himself. *Just cause you ain' kill yourself at Nique's dumbass request don't make you White Devil.*

Maybe not, but fucking over black folk on a personal and epic scale and then skipping the country and consequences sure does.

You wouldn't say it like that if you didn't at least care.

I'm in transition. Give me a little time and I won't care at all.

Whatchu gon' do then, nigga? Join the Klan? The NAACP? What?

Just gonna accept who I am. Stop trying to be down. Learn not to give a fuck. Like all these other white folks out here. How hard could it be? I feel relieved already.

You can't unenlighten yourself.

Watch me.

Firm creases bracketed his mouth. The forces of good might have lost, Macon's grillpiece said, but at least the screaming had tapered off and it was quiet. He pictured himself posed with a pitchfork and some mousy bun-haired broad, *American Gothic* like a motherfucker, face sallow and eyes listless. *See?* he'd ask the missus, staring deadpan at the camera, *ain't life grand when you shoo justice from your mind?*

The bus pulled out, and Macon glanced over his shoulder and watched as a dude several rows back conducted a brisk, quiet business selling sedatives to fellow passengers. Macon performed some mental computations—a five-nine frame divided by two bus seats measuring four-six in total length, lumpy as hell and smelling faintly of disinfectant and tobacco, their undersides barnacled with chewing gum. He multiplied the results by three thousand miles and ambled back to cop some pills.

With the TV mascara smudged across his cheeks, Macon looked as if he had two shiners; the dealer and the rest of the seedy bus denizens avoided his eyes. His only luggage was an *Action News* tote bag he had found in the van and filled hastily with items that seemed potentially useful: a light green cardigan sweater, two dented microphones he figured might be worth something, a box of stale doughnuts that he'd devoured before the bus even pulled out, a blank spiral notebook, and a handful of cheap pens. Macon returned to his seat, swallowed a mysterious crimson pill dry, and picked up the notebook. He'd filled four pages when sleep lumbered up and body-slammed him: *in this corner, wearing red, from out of Ancient Greece, the undefeated weightless champion, Death's own cousin, Mr. Sandman himself, put your hands together please for Moooorpheus!* Macon passed out still clutching his pen.

He woke up hazy and disoriented, dreams and life still vying for primacy despite the sunlight beaming through the windows. Goddamn, Macon wondered, wiping mouth-corner spittle down into his palm and squinting ahead at the indifferent double-yellow highway ribbon as he swiped his hand clean on the seat beside him, what the fuck is in those pills? He felt sedated but not rested, worn out by his nocturnal emissaries.

The bus shouldered into a sun-baked lot, and Macon rubbed his eyes and squinted, trying to get his bearings. He'd slept clear through the night, it looked like. It appeared to be midmorning, and they were deep in the South: He knew it off the muscle though he'd never been down here before. Everything outside his window—people, buildings, cars—seemed coated with a honey glaze, a sheen of twang and drawl that slowed activity and thought down to a crawl. Evidence mingled with stereotype, and Macon infused every detail of every sight with quintessential Southernness. The bus shuddered to a standstill, and Macon's gaze rolled across the businesses squatting before him, haunch to haunch: a diner, a minimart, a Wendy's. The entire tableau struck him as almost unbearably down-homey.

He scooped the tote bag off the floor and rooted through it, taking stock of his possessions. A black Sharpie marker was the only thing that drew his attention, so Macon palmed it, flipping it through his fingers as he watched the other passengers file off the bus in pursuit of their grease-salt-sugar fixes. How many markers just like this had he worn out in his day? Macon's hand twitched and he took a discreet look around, popped off the marker's top, and hunched forward to catch a tag on the seat-back before him. He pressed the felt tip to the plastic, then stiffened. The quick, efficient softie letters he'd been perfecting for the last eight years would not come. It was a part of the identity he had disowned, left smoldering a thousand miles back. Macon squinted at his canvas for a moment, then wrote CAP in precise, curvaceous script, underlined the name with one bold meniscus-stroke, and slashed quotation marks around it all. He leaned back, pleased with his handiwork, and only then did it hit him. CAP. Ain't that a bitch. He'd just adopted the name of the most hated writer in graffiti history. CAP wasn't just Macon's progenitor, he was the Bronx renegade immortalized in the documentary flick *Style Wars,* the guy who'd pissed off every writer in the five boroughs by going over their masterpieces with his ugly-ass throw-ups. A total, classless prick. And to top it off, CAP was white.

Macon rose to his feet, disgusted with himself, and filed off the bus. A good three-quarters of the passengers had ignored the diner and beelined it to Wendy's, illustrating the principle on which Fast Food America was built: familiar-and-mediocre trumps unknown. The others milled about the parking lot, kicking up dust clouds that ended where their cigarette smoke began.

Only Macon, too broke not to shoplift his breakfast, headed for the minimart. He was halfway through the door, far enough inside to hear the doorbell clang, when the row of newspaper vending machines lining the store's outside wall caught his attention. He backtracked past the *Birmingham News*—aha!—to crouch before a copy of *USA Today* with elbows on his knees, palms sliding to a halt against his stubbled cheeks.

NAT'L GUARD WITHDRAWS FROM NYC, the banner headline read. Beneath twin aerial photographs of a hysterical Times Square and a decimated East Harlem ran the bold-print teaser for the related story: "APOLOGY" LEADER STILL MISSING. Macon rose, enduring momentary dizziness from the quick shift in altitude, and fished enough change from his jeans to cop a paper.

He snapped it open, rifling through the pages until he found a picture of himself standing open-mouthed before a barrage of microphones at his post-jail press conference, looking younger and stronger and unbearably cocksure. The article was essentially an interview with Nique, who was identified as the "newly appointed Chairman of Macon Detornay's beleaguered Race Traitor Project, and its de facto spokesman." Macon felt sorry for whatever reporter had been handed this assignment; even on the page, you could sense the incredible velocity of the bullshit shooting from Nique's mouth, the torque spinning his words shamelessly this way and that.

"Brother Macon has been suspended from the organization," Nique was quoted as saying, "until such a time as he is able to resolve certain personal issues and once again provide effective leadership."

Macon scanned each column, reading only what lay between quotation marks. "We have not heard from him, but we do hope he will reach out to us soon so that we can help him to help himself. . . ."

". . . I'll say again that the statements made during Macon's so-called breakdown were made under extreme duress and are in no way reflective of the Race Traitor Project's message, or even of Brother Macon's own true sentiments. And even so, as disturbing as they were, Brother Macon's words at that difficult juncture reflect the searing honesty—the prophetic honesty, I should say, by which I mean honesty regardless of consequence—that has always characterized his contribution to our struggle. . . ."

The conclusion carried over to a second page: ". . . I want to stress that the Race Traitor Project is not going anywhere. We are regrouping, we are forging important ties to other organizations and individuals, and we will continue to push the envelope in the most provocative of ways. With or without Macon Detornay, you haven't heard the last of us."

Macon quartered the paper, tucked it beneath his arm, and marched crisply across the lot. "I'd like to make a collect call, please," he said into the pay phone.

Andre picked up on the third ring. "Race Traitor Project. Please hold." A minute later, he came back and accepted the charges.

"Where the fuck are you?"

Macon squinted into the sunlight. "Parking lot," he said.

"Fuck you want?" demanded Andre. "I don't have a goddamn

thing to say to you." He wasn't as angry as he sounded, Macon thought.

"I owe you an apology."

"Fuck an apology. You owe me more than that."

"I know." Macon sighed. "I know I do. I'll figure something out. I swear."

Andre said nothing, but Macon could feel his roommate's anger draining; some of it, anyway. The promise of restitution, even if it came to nothing, had partially un-punked Andre in his own estimation.

"You better," he said finally. "You fuckin' better." Another pause, and then, "For real, where are you?"

"Someplace in Alabama, I think. Took a bus."

"Yeah, we know. The *Action News* guy called Visa. We kept it to ourselves."

"Oh. Thanks."

"Some things are happening," said Andre. "We've been hoping you would call."

"Why, so you could tell me I'm suspended from my own organization?"

"Take that up with Nique. It's his show now, in case you couldn't figure that out. He is the Race Traitor Project."

"More power to him," said Macon. "I want nothing to do with it. My new project is learning not to give a fuck. I'm gonna retrain myself to be white."

"It's not that easy, Moves." Nique had taken the phone. His voice was clear and strident, made Macon realize how softly Andre had been speaking. "I got a lotta shit popping off, dude, and you got a lotta debts to cover. Also a lotta folks who'd love to know where they could find you, starting with New York's Finest and the Feds. Not that I'd tell them anything, of course. Like I always said, Moves, you my nigga."

"Blackmail, Nique?"

"Whitemail, dog. Not even. I'm just trying to keep you appraised of your options, since I'm the motherfucker fielding your calls—not to mention the motherfucker you left standing here with his dick in his hand. The world doesn't stop turning because you leave town, you know."

Nique dropped his volume and his pitch. "Talk whatever shit you want," he said. "I know you still want to be forgiven, Macon. I'ma tell you what it takes."

"Not interested."

"Oh yeah? What would you say if I told you I'd been on the phone all night with a Dr. Conway Donner?"

"I'd say I hope he's an excellent shrink and that he helps you come to terms with your megalomania."

"He is a shrink, actually. He's also Red Donner's grandson. Also happens to be richer than God. Shall I go on?"

Macon's hand fluttered to the crown of his scalp and he scratched, violently. "Please."

"Con's got a business proposal for us, Macon. He's very eager to speak with you. All me and Andre ask is that you sit down with him. I'm not even gonna say anything else. As far as I'm concerned, you hear him out and me and you are good." Nique grace-note paused, then swooped in for the clincher. "Plus, you know, one could argue that you owe Dr. Donner that much. I mean, there is a certain historical . . . I don't want to call it a debt, exactly, but . . ."

Macon exhaled, and the telephone dissected his breath into static. He could feel Nique smirking on the other end of the line, satisfied that he had played his cards right.

"I'm two hundred miles east of nowhere, Nique," said Macon, eager to frustrate him. "I couldn't meet your boy if I wanted to."

"As luck would have it, dude, you're in Con's neck of the woods. He's got offices in Mobile, Chattanooga, ATL, Jacksonville . . . all over the South, basically. He said no matter where you are, he can come and scoop you within an hour. Two, tops."

Macon arched his eyebrows. "It's like that?"

"It's like that, Moves. So can I holler at him?"

"Tell me what this is all about first."

"I couldn't even do it justice. Con will break it down."

Perhaps, thought Macon, this was nothing more than a setup. He could imagine stranger scenarios than Donner simply wanting to do to an Anson what an Anson had done to a Donner. Nor was it so far-fetched to think that Nique and Andre might want to fuck him over the way he'd fucked them. Just because you're paranoid, he told himself, doesn't mean they're not conspiring against you.

"How is it," Macon asked, "that some old Southern cracker is your new ace homey?"

Nique chuckled. "You know my steez, dude. I'm trying to retire by twenty-five. All right, look, enough. You're running up the phone bill. Stay put and watch for Donner in an hour. Big Colonel Sanders–looking motherfucker. Can't miss him."

Nique hung up. Macon ambled clear across the lot before he realized that all he'd told them of his location was that he was in a parking lot somewhere in Alabama. Passengers were streaming back onto the bus now. The driver leaned against the hood, fingers scissored around a cigarette. He glanced up and jerked his thumb. "Better hop on, kid. We're on our way soon as I reach the filter."

Macon shook his head. "This is my stop. I wanna do some sight-seeing."

The driver raised his palms to his shoulders and shrugged. "Suit yourself. Next bus doesn't come through here for eight hours, though. And that one might be full." He looked around and grimaced. "You sure you got that many sights to see?"

"Yeah," said Macon, hoping that if he sounded confident enough, he'd fool himself. "I'll be fine. Thanks."

"Okay, then." The driver flicked his butt into the dust, spun on his heel, and climbed aboard. "Have fun," he said over his shoulder. The door creaked shut and the bus lumbered toward the exit.

Macon wiped his brow with the hem of his T-shirt, searched the lot in vain for a puddle of shade, and then decided, Fuck it: The six dollars in his pocket weren't going to get him much further, anyway. He walked into the empty diner, silent but for the delicious twin hums of fluorescence and air-conditioning, collapsed into a red vinyl booth, threw his legs up, and ordered a bacon cheeseburger.

Forty minutes later, a new rhythm imposed itself over the low pulse of the fan and the lights, the trochaic footsteps of the waitress. Macon looked up from his newspaper to see a helicopter easing its way to the ground, blades stirring up a storm of dust. A surge of panic catapulted him to his feet: The cops or the Feds or the National Guard had tracked him here, and any second now a SWAT team or a phalanx of sunglassed agents or, worst of all, the venerable officers McGrath and Downing would leap out and blitz the diner. Tackle Macon to the ground, cuff his arms behind his back, and carry him off like a battering ram, using his head to open every door from here to New York City.

Macon scanned the diner for a back exit, a bathroom, an extra waitress uniform, anything, but when he turned back to the window to gauge his assailants' progress, a willowy gray-haired gentleman was unfolding himself cautiously from the sedated chopper. A walking stick emerged first, like a scout, and then a pair of polished leather boots. The cane grazed the ground only in punctuation as the man made his way to the bottom of the diner's small staircase. There, he stopped and waved an overlarge hello, left arm tracing a huge semicircle above his head. Haltingly, Macon raised one hand chest high and wriggled his fingers in response.

The man grinned as he stepped through the door. "Macon, my boy." His teeth were small and orderly, the same cream color as his linen suit. He flung his arms wide in announcement. "I'm Dr. Conway Donner. Call me Con, or Don, or whatever the hell you like. You've eaten?" He cocked his chin at the waitress, who stood slack-jawed at the counter beside the equally stunned cook. "Give us a couple of chocolate milk shakes to go, would you, sweetie pie?" Donner reached into his pocket, produced a monogrammed gold money clip, and wrist-flicked two twenties onto the tabletop, watching Macon over his bushy eyebrows as he did so. "A meal's not a meal without ice cream in my book, Macon." A hearty laugh. "Well, breakfast maybe. Now. Anything else your heart desires for the road?"

Macon slid his hands into his pockets and rocked back on his heels. "Uh, no. I think I'm good."

"Well, good, then. Let's be on our way, shall we?" The waitress approached, her humid slouch replaced by a prim formality, and extended a folded brown bag. Conner accepted the package with a warm nod and dropped another twenty on the table. "Right this way," he beckoned, turning toward the door. "I'm parked outside."

Chapter Two

To Macon's surprise, he found the chopper empty when he climbed inside. Con himself settled behind the controls, removed the milk shakes from the bag, and handed one to Macon. "Welcome to the *Deus ex Machina,*" he said. "Ever flown in one of these?" He pulled on his straw with such vigor that his trim-bearded cheeks went concave.

"Naw," said Macon, watching as the old man flipped a switch and the propeller blades began to throb above them. A moment later, the *Deus ex Machina* was on the rise. Con navigated as casually as a cabdriver, ferrying the milk shake back and forth between his mouth and thigh every few seconds.

"Don't know why they can't design a cockpit with cup holders," he said, leaning back to smile at Macon. "I had to have the stereo custom-installed, too. Nothing but AM radio in these things, normally. Can you imagine?" He pressed a button on the crowded dashboard and an Al Green song issued forth from eight strategically placed speakers, flooding the small cabin with crisp digital sound. Donner tapped his pinky ring against the steering lever in time to the organ part. "There's a box of Cubans on the floor behind you," he said over the music. "Grab us a couple, if you like."

He stole another glance at Macon, and found his passenger staring intently at the ground below. They were perhaps three hundred feet in the air now, high enough to take in the colors of the land—the lush gamut of greens, the golden wheat, the broad pure-blue expanse of sky—but low enough to still appreciate the shifting textures, the intermingling of farm and forest, the narrow veins of streams, and the thick arteries of roads.

"Best way to see the land," Con said. "Your first time visiting this part of the country, isn't it?"

"That's right," said Macon absently. He was busy trying to prioritize the growing list of questions bottlenecking in his mind. What in the hell did Donner want? With what lies and truths and hopes and promises had Nique plied him? Why did it so palpably feel like this small whirring metal bird carried not just Macon and Conway, but the restless ghosts of Cap and Fleet and Red and the entire April 29, 1889, population of Robert E. Lee Stadium, from fans to batboys, peanut hawkers to ballplayers to Klansmen?

Macon decided to conserve his mental resources by letting his brain go limp. Only time would deliver the answers to such questions, and so Macon faked exhaustion and slumped against the wall, listening to first Al Green and then Sam Cooke compete with the blades. It didn't occur to him to wonder where he was being taken, so it barely surprised him when Donner brought the chopper down a half an hour later on the verdant front lawn of what looked for all intents and purposes like an enormous antebellum mansion. Macon extracted himself from the cockpit, blinked, and stretched beneath the blazing midday sun. Only the craft in which he'd arrived prevented him from feeling like he'd just stepped back in time.

"I can imagine what you must be thinking," Donner said as he led his guest across the vast, manicured expanse and toward the looming facade of the white-pillared house. "Place looks like there should be a few dozen slaves bailing cotton out back, doesn't it?"

Macon fixed him with a weak, sidelong stare. "Are there?"

Another hearty laugh from Donner. The guy was more nervous than he let on, Macon thought. That couldn't be a good thing.

"When I bought this place," said the doctor, lifting his cane to point at a second-floor terrace as they strolled, "it had been neglected for decades on end. Thought about remodeling, but in the end I had everything restored, right down to the trim. My feeling was, why hide from history? I'd rather stare it in the face, Macon, same as you. That's the reality of this land. Slaves worked it. Atrocities have been committed on it. Least I can do, if I'm going to live here—which I only do about five days a month, but still—is not forget that fact."

They walked into the building's shadow. Macon felt his wits sharpen the moment the shade engulfed him, felt color returning to his sun-bleached brain. "Personally," he said, "I'd knock the whole place the fuck down. Can't really see what playing slave master is helping you accomplish." He turned to face Donner. "Look, Doc, I don't know what you and Nique discussed, but no one's told me shit. I'd just as soon cut to the chase, huh?"

"Certainly." A flinty smile sprung to the doctor's lips. "The chase. As Cap Anson himself might have put it."

Macon's stomach bottomed out at the mention of his ancestor's name. "Oh Christ," he said, falling into a wicker chair and raking his hands back through his hair. "So that's the big idea?" He pictured Nique and Andre sitting before a row of telephones like auctioneers, fielding two and three calls at a time, selling the rights to Macon's life off to the highest and most poetically just bidder.

Donner seated himself in a matching chair and pursed his lips. "I'm afraid I don't follow."

"Let's hear it, then." Macon spoke without looking up. "What were you thinking, Doc, a role-reversal kind of thing? I run for my life like Red, you and your people chase me down, stomp me to death? Or maybe you've got a whole fuckin' replica stadium set up behind the house? Whatever it is, let's just get it over with, okay? I'd like to be in hell by dinnertime."

Donner threw his head to the sky and roared. It was a wholly different laugh than the one to which Macon had thus far been privy: It boomed easily from him, shook his entire frame, comforted Macon somehow. When his mirth subsided, Donner pitched forward, laying a heavy hand on his guest's shoulder. "Oh," he said, wiping away a tear nestled in the corner of his eye. "My God, Macon, the imagination on you. Come, son. We've got to get a drink in you posthaste. Come."

Macon followed him inside, through a succession of dark, cool, musty-smelling sitting rooms, and found himself seated at last on a low-backed leather armchair in a kind of office. Donner shut the door behind them, although no other human being was in evidence, and poured two glasses of something sap-colored from a crystal decanter sitting atop a sideboard. He handed one to Macon, took his place behind a stout mahogany desk, and pulled the chain on a green-shaded banker's lamp. Framed diplomas hung from the wall behind him, sandwiching Donner's head. Macon could make out only the embossed names of the schools. Emory and Harvard.

The booze, Macon assumed, was bourbon. Even without a point of reference, he could tell it was top-notch. He allowed himself a second nip, swished the liquor over his tongue, and swallowed as he placed the glass on the desk before him with a small clunk. Donner took the hint. He palmed his beard, leaned back in his chair, and got down to business.

"I don't suppose, Macon, that you've read *The Sneetches*?" Donner's eyes traced the upper shelves of the bookcases lining the walls as he spoke, as if he were searching the rows of hardbound psychiatric journals for the title in question.

"Of course," said Macon, surprised. "But not since I was five." He cracked a knuckle. "There's Sneetches with stars on their bellies and Sneetches without. The starless Sneetches are second-class citizens, until one day this guy shows up with a star-making machine. So all the Sneetches get stars, and nobody can tell who to hate anymore. Then the guy busts out with a star-removal machine, and a two-star machine, and all these other machines, and the Sneetches lose their fucking minds, trying to stay on top of the game."

"Exactly," said Donner, tapping his steepled hands together. "Remarkable memory. Do you remember the ending?"

Macon shrugged. "Not really. I mean, it's a kids' book, so I assume they all learned to get along somehow. But not specifically, no."

Donner smiled. "You don't remember the happy ending because the happy ending is bullshit," he said. "Everything up to that point is real."

"Hmm," said Macon, waiting.

"I have a lot of respect for you," the doctor intoned, leaning forward. "You've got passion. Integrity. And unless I'm very much mistaken, you see the absurdity in all this, too. You understand that race means whatever we make it mean. That it's just another commodity to be exploited. Something you can market, buy, sell, reinvent. Whatever you want."

"And what do you want, Doc?"

"I'm the guy with the star machine, Macon. I'm the person people come to when they decide they'd rather pimp race than be pimped by it."

Macon crossed his legs and frowned. "So what, you turn black people white?"

Donner shrugged. "Sometimes. I turn black people white, white people black, black people blacker, white people whiter. Last week I turned a Mexican kid Japanese. Whatever they want. Whatever angle they decide to play. It's like roulette, Macon: There are endless ways to win."

"Can I see the machine?"

The doctor laughed. "There's no machine. I don't actually alter appearances. No skin creams, no surgeries. That's nineteenth-century stuff. I'm a psychiatrist. I use a combination of hypnosis, therapy, psychodrama, various re-acculturation techniques, to alter an individual's self-image and the perception of him. It's a very complex program—or de-program, I like to say. Very involved. Not to be entered into lightly. I've been honing the process for more than forty years."

"Quietly, I'm guessing."

Donner nodded. "Very quietly. I could have been killed, you understand. Hell, some of my clients would have killed each other in the waiting room, if I'd had a waiting room. Initially, I worked mainly with white kids from down here, the children of old-money Southern aristocracies."

"Hard-core crackers, in other words."

"Precisely. These kids were going off to college and coming back home with ideas that scared their parents to death. This was the late fifties, early sixties. I'm sure you can imagine."

"Yeah," said Macon, remembering his drink and draining it. "I'm sure I can."

Donner reached across the desk, took Macon's glass, and rose to refill it. "These folks—who'd never dreamed of consulting a psychiatrist, mind you—were coming to me on bended knee. Offering to pay triple my fees if I could just get the radical notions out of their kids' heads. Scared to death of what their grandkids might look like if Debbie Sue kept on the way she was going." Donner raised one eyebrow as he leaned forward to hand Macon his bourbon.

"I took on a few cases, just to see what I could do. Thinking that if anything, I'd try to help the kids cope with their racist backgrounds." Donner eased back in his chair, his own drink cocked close to his lips. "But you know what? Some of them actually wished they'd never gone up North to school and learned the things they had. A few honestly and truly wanted to go back to the uncomplicated lives they'd led before—not worried about anybody else, totally unaware of injustice. Hell, Macon, they missed getting driven around by their Negro chauffeurs.

"That intrigued me. I started to wonder how you would go about reprogramming someone. All the literature, then and now, was focused on religious cults, so I started by adapting some of those techniques. How could I get these kids to act and think and feel white again?"

Donner sighed, slid lower in his seat, and gave Macon a rueful smile. "Course, I was young and idealistic myself then. Good liberal that I was, I couldn't justify what I was doing. So I expanded my program. Decided I could use the same techniques to help black people get ahead in the white world. Give them some confidence, some strategies." The doctor shook his head, staring into his glass as he tipped it to his mouth. "God, was I clumsy. . . . But times changed, Macon. The world got complicated, fast. I refined my programs, changed with it."

Donner opened his arms, hugging his domain. "As you can see, I've done well for myself. How we choose to construct race is going to go right on evolving, Macon, but the bottom line is that we'll never leave it behind. All hell would break loose if we did. Whole system would collapse. I'm not going to waste my time trying to fight the facts—and neither are you anymore, from what I gather. All I can do is give a few individuals who understand the rules a chance to get on top of the game. And as far as I'm concerned, that's plenty."

The desk chair rolled backward until it hit the wall, and Donner stood. "How about a tour?" he said, and beckoned Macon to his feet.

They left the office, freshened drinks in hand. Donner led the way up a wide, curved staircase, then paused before a locked door and typed a long series of numbers into a panel mounted on the wall. "This is our records department," he explained. Something inside the door clicked and Donner smiled, fisting the knob. "No one outside the organization has ever been in here before. Shall we?" The door swung wide, and Macon followed the doctor inside.

The room was a cavernous, spartan rectangle. Chest-high metal filing cabinets lined the perimeter; an antique conference table sat square in the middle. But what drew Macon's attention was the portrait gallery. Framed eight-by-ten photographs blanketed the far wall, floor to ceiling.

Donner hung back, pleased, as his guest ambled toward it. "A few of our satisfied customers. Go ahead and take a look. I've got a few files I need to go over; I'll be with you in a moment." He pulled open a drawer, removed a six-inch stack of thin manila folders, and sat down at the table.

Macon goggled at the collage of faces, eyes darting from one famous visage to the next. Colin Powell gazed stoically from the upper-left quadrant. Okay, thought Macon, fair enough. Must've needed some whitening up before he could fuck with Bush and them. Ditto Clarence Thomas, two rows below. Or maybe not; who knew? Maybe Thomas had been too white to begin with, and come to Donner for a little blackness refresher course. Vanilla Ice shared an eye-level row with Mariah Carey, Bill Bradley, Shelby Steele, Umamu Shaheed Alam, Michael Jackson, George Wallace, Quentin Tarantino, Mick Jagger, Kobe Bryant, and about fifty people Macon couldn't recognize. Decoding who had come for what reason was harder than he would have thought. Macon was about to ask whether Ja Rule, bottom row center, had wanted to sand down the rough edges of a thugged-out past or to invent just such a history when Donner strolled up behind him.

"Celebrities are the exception," said the doctor, "although we do get our share." He pointed up at Governor Wallace, then down at a portrait of Jesse Helms that Macon hadn't noticed. "Used to get a lot of Southern politicians looking to change their image one way or the other. If I told you one of these two came in to learn how to be a rock-ribbed racist and the other came in looking for black votes, would you be able to guess which was which?"

Macon shook his head. "No idea." He nodded at a glossy of a broad-shouldered black man flaring his nostrils at the camera from beneath a do-rag. "That guy looks familiar. Should I know who he is?"

"Not at all. His name is Calvin Braithwaite. Just a regular Joe, trying to climb out of the corporate mailroom and jump-start his life. Tired of white people being intimidated by him. Came here to learn to make them feel more comfortable. Said to me, 'Conway, I want to be a token.' His exact words. That was three years ago. He's married to a white woman now, making twice as much money as he did before. I think I have an updated picture of him around here somewhere. You'd hardly recognize the man."

"So you taught him to sell out."

"We taught him," Donner said indulgently, "the skills to achieve his goals. A term like *sellout* really has no place in this world, Macon. It's self-righteous. It denies the realities people are forced to live with. It implies that personal and racial identity are rigid, monolithic, which they certainly are not." He pointed at the wall. "Is Calvin more of a sellout than, say, his next-door neighbor there?" Macon followed Donner's finger and found himself looking at a photograph of Mark Wahlberg. "He came twice, matter of fact. Manager brought him both times. Once when he was a kid, doing his Marky Mark thing—they wanted to go all the way with that. And then again when he decided to switch to film and the old persona, which we'd been so successful in creating, had to go. Dismantling it was much more difficult than putting it together, I must say." Donner turned from the photographs. "I never judge my clients, Macon. The regular folks, especially. Most people just want to be happy, be accepted one way or another."

"So where," asked Macon, unable to tear his eyes from the wall, "do you get most of your business?"

Donner shrugged. "It's a mixed bag, nowadays. Lot of middle-class black families are starting to send their kids in. Telling me 'I don't want him to forget who he is, just to pull his damn pants up and speak proper English so he can get a job.' " Donner chuckled.

"More and more of my clients come from the entertainment world. Everybody there wants to be black—actors, musicians, comedians, you name it. Russell Simmons sends me a new white rapper every month."

Donner returned to the conference table, where twenty case files lay open. "Thanks to you, Macon, this country has got race on the brain. You've already brought me more business than O.J. Simpson, Willie Horton, and Rodney King combined. Just look at all these."

Macon darted his eyes at the scattered folders. "White people panicking about their kids?"

"Some. But just as many are white kids who want to be black. Or want to become 'race traitors,' as some of them put it."

"No shit?" Macon walked over to take a closer look.

"No shit. Which brings me to my proposal."

The doctor eased into a chair and pushed away the closest files. Macon took a seat beside him, crossed his legs, and cocked his head.

"The time has come," Donner declared, "to take this operation public. The world is ready for it. Hell, Macon, since you came along they've practically been begging for it."

"Seems like you're doing pretty good already," Macon said. "You fall behind on your helicopter payments or something?"

Donner waved his hand. "This is penny-ante stuff compared to what I've got in mind. I'm talking national marketing campaigns, Macon. TV, radio, billboards. Investors. Franchises. I'm talking, frankly, about getting the kind of acclaim for my work that I damn well deserve. But more than that, I'm talking about letting every single American know that my program is an option, and that my clients have been their friends, neighbors, coworkers, even their idols, for forty years. I'm talking about brokering a major change in the whole racial landscape, Macon. I'm talking the two of us on the cover of *Time* magazine."

"*Time* magazine, huh?" Macon interlaced his hands, leaned forward to rest them on the tabletop, and squinted over at his host. "And what am I doing there, exactly, Doc?"

Donner cleared his throat, composed himself, and dropped a hand on top of Macon's. "I want you," he said, brow knit above his gray, flecked eyes, "to be my official spokesman. The public face of the company. There's not a soul in the entire world I'd rather have. You're a human race card, Macon."

Macon's hands retreated to his lap. "I'm flattered," he began, "but—"

"I've been discussing the finances with Dominique," Donner broke in. "He explained how important it was for you to bring your own people along, and believe me, I wouldn't have it any other way. As far as I'm concerned, both Mr. Lavar and Mr. Walker have more than proved their mettle at the Race Traitor Project, and I'm happy to take them on as consultants and board members. Especially given the human-interest potential there—the Anson, Donner, and Walker families in business together after all these years. That's a dynamite angle in itself. Dominique and I also discussed in some detail the matter of stock op—"

"Whoa, whoa." Macon raised his hands. "Hold up a second, Doc. You're getting way ahead of yourself here."

Donner nodded into his lap, duly chagrined. "Quite right, Macon. Quite right. You have my apologies. First things first." He flashed a flushed grin, pushed off on the table, and rose creakily to his feet.

"Mr. Detornay," Donner said with a slight bow, his formal air compromised by the transparent confidence behind it, "will you do me the great honor of accepting the position of official spokesman, at a base salary of five hundred thousand dollars a year?"

Macon, who had risen with his host, nearly stumbled when he heard the figure.

"That's a lot of money," he heard himself say.

"You're a valuable asset. We have a deal, then?"

Macon stared down at the doctor's palm, jutting expectantly from his sleeve. "No," he said. "I'm sorry, Doc. We don't."

"Six hundred," Donner replied, unfazed. "And the chance to reinvent yourself. Believe me, Macon, the other offers you've gotten aren't anywhere near as attractive. They've come from law-enforcement agencies, mostly, and white militias. I can make all that disappear, son."

Macon traced the table's edge with a finger. "The only thing that's going to disappear is me," he said. "Nique probably neglected to tell you, Doc, but I'm retired. My passion for this shit got trapped in a tenement in Harlem. It burned up in the riot. Sorry."

Donner laughed. "Who's talking about passion? You think I want to work with a crusader? Hell no; I want a pitchman! You sold millions of completely indifferent people on the most outlandish scheme I've ever heard, Macon—actually got them off their asses, without them even understanding why. All I want is for you to do it again."

Macon was pacing the room now, tracing half-moons around the conference table as Donner spoke and trying not to look over his shoulder at the photo gallery for fear of who he might find leering back at him. "That's because I believed in what I was doing," he said. "This shit, I can't get behind at all. Why would I wanna convince white people to sign up for some kind of shortcut course in how to be me, or how not to be me? Fuck, Doc, I don't even wanna be me, or not me. I've spent my whole life trying to be down. Paying dues. Caring as deeply as I knew how. And the only part that was real, that meant something, was the journey, the experience. The exact part you're trying to do away with."

He stopped in mid-stride and fixed Donner with a pleading, hangdog stare. "I don't wanna be a pimp, Doc. I don't want to play both sides against the middle and get rich. If you can help some folks get over, well, more power to you. Personally, I just wanna go the fuck to sleep. Like those kids you taught to go back to their Negro chauffeurs, back in the day." Macon pulled a chair out and fell into it, suddenly spent.

Donner dropped his head, stroked down his whiskers with a thumb and forefinger, and sighed through his nose. "Well, I'm extremely disappointed, Macon. And more than a bit surprised. I was given the distinct impression that you would be quite receptive. That we'd be a perfect match."

"Nique doesn't know me as well as he thinks, Doc. I only came here out of respect for your grandfather, if you want to know the truth."

"I see. Well, in any case, I thank you, Macon." Donner extended his hand, and this time Macon took it. "I'm sorry we couldn't do business. Perhaps, given some time, you'll change your mind."

"Why don't you hire Dominique? I bet he'd be great."

"Smart kid, but useless by himself. People wouldn't recognize him if he wasn't standing next to you. Come." He threw an arm over Macon's shoulders and walked him toward the door. "I don't want to waste any more of your time, Macon. You've been generous enough in hearing me out. Least I can do is speed you on your way. Los Angeles, was it? Let me call the airport. We'll get you on the next flight."

Macon waved the favor off. "That's okay, Doc. I'd rather you just drop me back at the bus depot. The trip's kind of giving me some time to think, know what I mean?"

Donner forced a smile. "Fair enough." He pulled the door of the records department shut behind Macon, and the security panel gave a sharp chirp. The broad staircase sloped gently before them. "Fair enough," the doctor said again, and took the first step down in stride.

Chapter Three

Two hours later, Macon was alone in the parking lot again, as broke as before, growing hungrier by the minute, and with five hours to kill before the next bus arrived. Donner had taken him back from whence he came by land rather than air; the helicopter was low on fuel, so they'd peregrinated the back roads at a leisurely pace in a late-model silver Jaguar, once again letting Al Green and his organ do the talking for them.

Donner had shaken Macon's hand, told him, "Until we meet again," and pulled off, waving out the window until the car vanished down the far side of a gentle hill. As soon as it was gone, Macon spun away, cursing himself. Why the fuck hadn't he asked Donner for a couple of bucks, a little traveling money? Would that have been so hard? But no; the thought hadn't occurred to him until it was too late, until he stood facing the prospect of a ravenous future, a cross-country shoplifting spree—until he stood in the sweltering heat, dehydrating by the second, the only liquid in his system half a chocolate shake and three glasses of top-shelf country bourbon. Macon stalked across the lot and kicked a discarded Coke can as hard as he could, sent it rolling through the dust. Now what?

His head snapped up at the clang of the minimart's bell, in time to see an obese woman waddle out into the sun, plastic shopping bags swinging from each fist. She climbed into the driver's seat of a maroon SUV, and before Macon could properly contemplate jacking her for the stash of Twinkies, cigarettes, and Yoo-hoo she had no doubt just acquired, she gunned the mammoth engine and was off.

He traced her path back to the store and gave the door a cautious push, hoping to slip inside without setting off the bell. No dice: It rang, pinning the attention of the clerk on him, if only for an instant. The guy—bearded and baseball-capped, a pack of cigarettes rolled into the sleeve of his white T-shirt despite his fixed position in front of an entire wall of butts—looked up from the newspaper spread across the counter before him. Macon met his glance with a quick wave and swifted toward the snack department. The clerk responded with a two-fingered salute, unlit square in hand, then went back to his reading.

Macon exhaled a breath he didn't know he'd been holding, and ambled down the bright, well-stocked aisle, out of sight. A familiar surge of frightened bravado suffused him, and memories of his days as a spray-paint thief bounced through his mind. The weight of Macon's loneliness doubled, and he swallowed back a sudden sadness: What he wouldn't give to see Aura's face poke out from around the corner right now, smirking, giddy with the caper under way. Macon blinked. No time, no cause for that. Static was buzzing in his head now, the familiar vinyl-pops that herald the first notes of a favorite song. Any second, some rogue sunflower lyric was going to push itself up through the asphalt, toward the light—trick Macon into replaying the scene to the soundtrack, recalling some memory he should be trying to forget. He clenched his jaw, lifted the needle from his mental turntable, picked up the record, and smithereened it over his knee. Now. Where were the goddamn Fritos?

Burleigh the clerk closed his copy of the *Birmingham News* and passed it wordlessly to Johnnie, who was seated on an upturned milk crate to his left. They all took their lunch breaks at the Mart. It was in the middle, two miles from Johnnie's engine shop and two-point-two from the insurance place where Anton worked. Burleigh was stuck in there alone, bored as a broke-dicked dog, and besides, the place was air-conditioned. You could read whatever you wanted, even a porno mag, provided you didn't mess it up. And the diner next door made a damned good brisket sandwich.

Johnnie took the paper and swapped Burleigh the *USA Today* resting on the lap of his Pennzoil-stained jeans. "Wonder if my kid's football calendar's in here," he mused aloud, flipping to sports.

"Believe they printed the fall schedules yesterday," said Anton, next to him, through a mouthful of sandwich. He was curly-haired, darker than his friends and better dressed in a green tie and short-sleeved white dress shirt. "I still got it at my place. You're welcome to it."

Burleigh snapped open the *USA Today,* hairy forearms rippling with the slight exertion. He usually moved to sports and the advice columns pretty quick, but on principle Burleigh always looked at every page, from front to back. His daddy, during a regular half-hour breakfast before work, had been able to read every page of the *News.* "Quiz me," he'd say, scraping up his last grits and handing his son the paper as he stood to knot his tie. Burleigh would open up to any page and give the headline, and his daddy would relate the story, adding his own comments and epithets.

Burleigh had inherited his politics that way, headed off to school each morning able to repeat his daddy's take on things, declare a man a jackass or the best pitcher in baseball or nothing but an uppity colored boy. It was a simple fact of life that Burleigh wasn't as smart as his old man, but he still read the papers just as thoroughly, both local and national, which in his mind was one virtue he could claim over his daddy: Burleigh was a two-paper man. He hunkered down over the counter, scanning headlines and photographs, then straightened and peered at the top of his lone customer's head as it bobbed slowly along the fresh-mopped snack aisle. Burleigh frowned.

"Call me crazy," he said slowly, folding the paper in half and holding Macon's picture beside the video monitor that sat by Burleigh's elbow. Anton and Johnnie looked up just as Macon walked onto the screen.

Anton stared back and forth. "Well, I'll be damned."

The three of them watched for a second longer, transfixed, as Macon scanned a shelf. Then Burleigh bolted from behind the counter, slapping Johnnie's legs aside, high-stepping over Anton's. He walked to the front door with a swaggering seriousness of purpose and flipped the YES WE ARE OPEN sign around, then jerked his head at his buddies in a follow-me command and started down the snack aisle.

Macon turned from his contemplation of a box of Garden Herb Triscuits to find the three men arrayed before him, Burleigh front and center with his hands on his hips and the others flanking him, a pace behind, arms crossed over their chests. The overall effect suggested early-eighties rap choreography: The three of them were arrayed in a classic Run-DMC pose. He would have smiled, but the near-audible rush of their adrenaline froze Macon where he stood.

Burleigh lifted his hat, held it aloft while he swiped a hand through his long, greasy hair.

"You who I think you are?" The beard masked the flush of his cheeks, but Burleigh's nostrils flared.

Macon's stare ricocheted off each of them in turn. He jammed his free hand into a pants pocket crammed with two-for-a-dollar peanut sheaths, and shrugged his innocence.

"I doubt it," he said, trying to sound cavalier, and looked away, up at a shelf. As if ignoring them would make the bullies give up, drift away, go hassle some other infamous renegade-at-large a couple aisles down in Toiletries.

Burleigh narrowed his eyes, cracked his knuckles on the heel of his hand. Macon's eyes jumped to him. "And who do I think you are?" More frightening than the question was the cat-and-mouse lilt to his voice, the silence all around, the over-the-shoulder smirk he threw his boys as their prey fumbled for an answer.

"I don't know," said Macon finally, cracking his own knuckles in unconscious mimicry. The Fritos bag in his clutch crinkled noisily.

"Well then, how do you know that you ain't him?" Burleigh demanded, triumphant. Macon ventured a laugh, as if to say, *I get it, good one, see you later.* He was one step into his getaway stroll when Burleigh pulled a finger like a pistol and aimed it at Macon's chest.

"Don't move," he said. "Wait right here." The clerk whirled, stalked up the aisle, and disappeared. His cohorts leaned back to let him pass, but their feet stayed planted, their arms crossed.

A twitchy smile cracked Macon's lips. "C'mon, fellas," he implored, "isn't this the New South? What's with all the *Deliverance* shit, huh?"

"Just wait," said Johnnie patiently, palm patting down the air. Then Burleigh was back, his *USA Today* clenched in his hand. Macon saw it and his heart plunged to his bowels, ripping through his stomach during free fall. Burleigh stood before him and made a careful face-to-photograph comparison, his speckled green eyes flitting left-right-left. Macon stood motionless, unbreathing, as gray as the newspaper.

"Yup." Burleigh nodded at last. "We got a celebrity in our midst, boys."

"How about an autograph, Mason?" said Johnnie, leering at him.

"Macon, dumbass." Burleigh reached over and slapped his buddy in the chest with the folded paper. "Like the capital of Georgia."

"Helluva name for a nigger lover," chuckled Anton. "Boy, folks in Macon must be fixing to change the town name as we speak."

"Ex–nigger lover," said Macon.

"Beg pardon?" asked Burleigh lightly, turning to face him by gradual degrees. "Are you suggesting that *USA Today* has misrepresented you, Macon? Did you not say, and I quote, that white folks should waste a perfectly good Friday apologizing to the various and sundry niggers of New York?"

"I've had a change of heart since then," Macon answered, weak-voiced, eyes averted.

"Since Friday, Macon?" asked Burleigh knowingly, as if amused by the transparent fibbing of a favorite nephew. He stepped forward a pace, so he and Macon were nearly chest to chest, and smiled. "Or since you made my acquaintance and realized you were gonna be held accountable for your actions?"

"This ain't New York City, boy," piped Johnnie. "You're in America now."

Burleigh turned his head just far enough to wither his friend with a glare. "Johnnie, would you please shut the fuck up?" His eyes darted back to Macon. "Known him since we both was two," he said, quiet and confidential again. "He's been a retard since then, truth be told. Now, where were we?"

The clerk dropped his head, shook it as if to clear it, walked back a pace, then spun and looked Macon up and down. It was a sequence cribbed straight from some courtroom drama, Burleigh the prosecutor and Macon the hostile witness, Johnnie and Anton the jury to whom he played.

"Robbing white folks and giving the money to niggers." He lofted a chuckle at the ceiling. "Whoo, boy. Have to admit I laughed when I read that, Macon. Said to myself, 'This country's finally gone plumb batshit insane.' "

Burleigh plucked the bag of Fritos from Macon's limp hand, pulled it open, and popped a morsel in his mouth. "Maybe you came to town to educate us," Burleigh mused. He crunched loudly, then passed the chips to Anton, behind him. "Show us the error of our ways. If so, I'm game. I sure do love to learn. Is that it, boy?"

Macon gave a tight head shake, eyes following the Frito bag.

"Well then," continued Burleigh, "maybe you been sent here so we could educate you some. What do you think?"

Burleigh inhaled deeply through his nose, and Macon winced as he heard the phlegm pulling together at the back of the clerk's throat. A moment later, a rank wad was sliding down Macon's cheek, cool and hateful. His heart bucked with fear and fury, but he stood and took it, like a real civil rights pioneer. There was nothing else to do.

"I said," Burleigh thundered, "what do you think?" He reared back and his thick hand flew at Macon's cheek, the slap connecting with enough force to turn his head. Macon cringed and shielded himself with an arm, waiting for another blow. None came. The slap was no introductory remark, but a full statement in itself.

After a moment, Macon lowered his meager defenses and straightened, trying to disguise his fear and yet display a pointed lack of aggression. He touched his hand to the blooming redness and felt the sting, the smeared mucous. "Yes, sir," Macon eeked out, over the surge and churn of his insides.

Burleigh unfurled his shirtsleeve and produced a pack of Marlboros. "Gentlemen?" he offered with a flourish, knowing both Anton and Johnnie had quit, then lit up, shook out the match, and resumed pacing. "The thing is this, Macon," he began. "I ain't without certain sympathies for the—"

A tentative rap at the door cut Burleigh off. He twisted toward it, exhaled a plume of blue smoke through his nose, and strode manfully toward the front of the store, arms forming a wide horseshoe at his sides.

"Are you closed so early?" inquired the man standing on the threshold. He was a pleasant-looking older gent, his close-trimmed Afro rimmed with silver, his eyes dry and kind.

"No, sir," Burleigh responded gaily, plucking cigarette from lips. "Open for business. Damn kids musta flipped the sign. Come right on in." He ushered the man inside and relocked the door behind him.

The customer nodded his thanks and walked toward the refrigerators lining the back wall, his gait stiff with travel or with age. Anton and Johnnie turned wide-eyed to look at him, and as they parted the old man saw Macon standing between them, cheek red and raw from Burleigh's slap and distress blaring from his face.

The interloper gasped, and vivid fear raced down his spine. "Good Lord! What's going on here?"

Burleigh was right behind him. "That's a damn good question, mister," he said, jolly as all hell. He grabbed the man by the back of his neck and shook him at Macon like a rag doll.

"Look who dropped in, Macon. It's your ace boon coon from the ol' melon patch." He pulled the guy close, shoulder to shoulder, still squeezing his neck. "My name's Burleigh, stranger. What's yours?"

"L-Leo," he stammered.

"Well, all right then, Leonardo. I got a question for you. If I may." Leo's whole body was shaking. "You ever done anything for this man here?" He walked Leo toward Macon, tightening his grip on his captive's neck. "You saved his life, lent him some money, tap-danced for him?"

Leo shook his head ecstatically. "No, sir. I never even seen him before." His voice was older than he looked. Sixty, perhaps.

"Well, guess what, Leo?" Burleigh said, releasing his neck and rubbing Leo's shoulders with vigor. "This man here's a bona fide friend of your people. Likes 'em better than his own, matter of fact. Nothing he'd love more than to take all my hard-earned cash and give it to you, boy. Why, if you ask him nice, I bet he'll suck your big black ding-dong. How would you like that, my friend?" Burleigh shoved him from behind and Leo lurched forward, skidding to a halt near Macon. He was a small man, scarcely over five feet, and standing in front of Macon, he looked like a duckling seeking the protection of his mother's wing. He was so close that

Macon could feel the heat of his body; Leo's fear was in the air and it calmed Macon somehow.

"Whip it out, Grandpa," laughed Johnnie. "Show him old Mr. Peter." The old man was too terrified to move, but his eyes roved from face to face, frantic and immense, in search of something human.

"Aw, hell," said Anton, bored with all the talk and taunting. He found it unmanly somehow, and so he did what he knew how to: lifted his leg and kicked the nigger in the gut. Anton had been an all-county placekicker three times in high school. They'd made it to regionals his senior year, and in the months between Anton's league-championship-winning forty-five-yard field goal and graduation, he'd had more pussy than he knew what to do with. Not a day went by that Anton didn't recall that game, or raise his beer mug with practiced bashfulness when somebody toasted the famous kick.

He still had some leg left on him. The way Leo crumpled reminded Anton of the balloons at his daughter's last birthday party. Annabel had run up to him right after the cake and ice cream, with one flopping in each hand: "Daddy, Daddy, will you do Squeaky Bear for us?"

"Of course I will, Sugar." He took a blast of helium and had the kids practically wetting themselves. They didn't let him stop until he'd gone through three balloons and every Squeaky Bear routine he could muster, head aching like a sumbitch.

"Thing is, Macon," Burleigh was explaining as the four of them looked down at the writhing Leo, "somebody's gotta be the nigger. If it ain't Leo there, it's got to be you, or me. That's how this great nation of ours works, son."

He stepped forward and squeezed Macon's cheeks together with one hand, as if trying to force him to spit something out. "You're attempting to niggerize me, Macon," Burleigh said. He stepped back and turned sideways, lining up the angle. Macon watched, scared into a stupor. He didn't even register what was about to happen until the clerk's boot come into focus inches from his own stomach. Macon read the sole. Timberland. They sure did make a comfortable boot.

The kick connected and pain exploded inside him, burned and spread. The next thing Macon knew, he was gasping, flat on his back, clawing at the floor as if he might happen upon some secret pocket of oxygen. Leo was lying next to him. He tried to catch the older man's eye. But he couldn't.

"And," Burleigh resumed, "I resent it. Hell, I'm halfway niggerized already, working this shit job." He circled a few steps to the left, as if the two prostrate men were a campfire, and stroked his beard in assessment. The boys weren't hurt too bad, Burleigh decided, gratified. He enjoyed knowing they were capable of fighting back, but wouldn't. It felt like an admission of guilt.

A package of peanuts had fallen out of Macon's pocket. Burleigh stooped and snatched it up. "Stealing from me, too, huh, Make?" He snorted in derision. "S'pose that figures."

He stared at Macon as he spoke. "Got your truck, Anton?"

"Sure do."

"Well, be so kind as to bring it around back. I'd just as soon continue this conversation away from the surveillance cameras."

"Will do."

"I'd like to invite you boys to hang with us today." Burleigh crouched before them, patted Leo on the shoulder, then straightened. "You've got my word, Macon," he said, winking, "we'll treat the both of you as equals." He jogged away, and Macon heard keys jangling as Burleigh locked the register, ejected the videotape. Row after row of fluorescent ceiling tiles flickered off. The store grew quiet, the men's collective breathing loud.

Macon managed to fill his lungs. "Please," he wheezed, scissoring his legs and trying to push himself up into a sitting position. "This guy's got nothing to do with us. Just let him . . ." His air ran out and Macon coughed and fell back on his elbows.

"What did you say?" Johnnie bent at the waist and peered at

Macon like he might a writhing lizard, tail pinned underneath a rock. A note of wonder crept into his voice. He glanced toward the front of the store and worried his brow confidentially. "You'd best to start worrying about yourself, man."

"You thirsty, race traitor?" Burleigh was back. "Johnnie, grab a couple sixers for the road, huh? Put your wrists together, boys." Rough twine bound Macon's hands in a prayer position, so tight he felt them numbing. Anton honked his horn, and Burleigh pulled his guests to their feet and handed each one a six-pack of Miller High Life. The bottles banged against Macon's thighs as he stumbled toward the door.

"Gimme that," said Johnnie, aggravated. "You're shakin' 'em all up."

Leo's eyes glowed tumescent in the freezer case's footlights; Macon could hear the old man's labored breathing as Burleigh led him by the arm, calm as a bailiff. The four of them passed through the rear door and clambered up into the flatbed of Anton's pickup—Macon and Leo on the inside and Burleigh and Johnnie pressed against them, shoulder to shoulder. Anton fired up the engine and a scrim of dust kicked into the air, particles of mica glinting in the sun. He rambled his rig down the narrow, flat back road that trailed away from the little commercial lot.

The backs of the rest-stop buildings wizened, shrunk, and joined the past, and soon the road was surrounded by dense, intense greenery. Tangles of creeping wild vines formed a ground cover, and majestic, ancient-looking trees dotted the flat, endless land, casting wide nets of shade that provided the only relief from the yellow heat of the peaking sun. It was hard to know where the air's humidity ended and your own perspiration began. Drops trickled down Macon's forehead, into his eyes and ears. He blotted them as best he could, lifting his shirtsleeve to his face.

Johnnie opened beer after beer with his teeth, and passed them around. Macon gripped his bottle tightly, wondering what would happen if he turned and smashed it against Burleigh's head. The hunting rifle lying across Anton's passenger seat winked its one-eyed hypothesis.

"Much obliged," called Anton, lifting his brew in tribute. Johnnie responded in kind, and there was quiet as both men took long tugs at their already-sweating bottles.

"So what would you boys like to see?" asked Burleigh, suddenly avuncular. He swung an arm toward the uncultivated fields, serene in their wildness. "It isn't every day we get a visitor from up north." Silence. "We could take a ride into town, huh, Leo? Show Macon how your people live—all crowded together in their shacks, too lazy to work? We might get shot at, though." He lifted his hat, squinted appraisingly at the sun, and wiped his brow with the back of his bottle-hand. "More than a generation since the Honorable Dr. Martin Lucifer Coon got these niggers equal rights under the law, Macon, and you know what? They're doing worse now than they were when my daddy was coming up. I swear, they were better off as slaves. From my mouth to Holy Christ's ear, man. I seen 'em. Babies having babies, can't take care of 'em. What's the problem, you think, old-timer?"

Leo stared at him. "People like you," he said, voice low and uninflected. A bump in the road jostled them. Burleigh and Johnnie steadied themselves. Macon and Leo tipped briefly against their captors.

Burleigh was incredulous. "People like me! See, Macon, that's just what I mean. How is this man's problems my fault? I work honest hours, save my money, help my kids do homework. Earned what little I got. Meanwhile, niggers got affirmed-action jobs just waitin' for 'em, welfare food, fuckin' get-outta-jail-free cards. Hell, I'm broke as any one of 'em. But I got dignity. I came from something. Niggers got no self-respect, and hell, I wouldn't either if I was one of 'em. But it ain't my fault, old man. We done gave niggers a fish *and* taught 'em how to use a rod, and they're still starvin' to death!"

"So let them starve," said Macon. He gestured at Leo with his bottle. "This is not letting them starve."

"Well, no," Burleigh admitted. "This is something else." They rode in silence for a moment. Then Burleigh spoke again. "I can't just let 'em starve, Macon, because they're invading my home now." He swigged his beer. "Tell him what you was tellin' me about Bob Nathan, John."

Johnnie pitched forward and Indian-crossed his legs, talking to Macon like they were old buddies chatting during the lulls in a Little League game. "I came home from hunting last Saturday, Macon," he confided, tossing his empty bottle over his shoulder. The vegetation absorbed it soundlessly and Johnnie opened a new one. "And found my son Bob Nathan, eleven years old, with his hair all covered in gel and twisted up with rubber bands. Jumping up and down on my new couch and speaking in goddamn tongues, sounds like to me. His mother's baking in the kitchen just like nothing's wrong. I grab him by the arm and say, 'Son, what the hell's got into you?' He looks at me and he says, 'I'm a rapper, Paw, I'm Busta Rhymes.' He seen some fuckin' porch monkey monkeyin' around on cable TV and now Bob Nathan thinks bein' a nigger's just the cat's ass. I beat him till his butt was nigger-black, I tell you what. Put a quick stop to that foolishness."

"No, you didn't," Macon said. He felt like laughing despite everything, laughing in the face of whatever they had in store for him because Bob Nathan, some anonymous Alabama cracker child, had done the East Coast Stomp and tried to lock his hair: The struggle hobbles on. "You didn't put a stop to shit. That was how I started. Your son found something that moved him, and he's gonna keep on looking for it. And if you try to stop him, he'll just quit paying any attention to you at all." A stupid, untrue bluff, thought Macon—Obi-Wan Kenobi telling Darth Vader, "If you strike me down, I shall grow more powerful than you can possibly imagine," right before he bites the dust. And why did Macon want them to believe it, anyway? Stop trying to win, he told himself. You gave up on winning when you left New York. Try to survive instead.

"The legendary soulfulness of niggers." Burleigh smiled, tilting his cap to provide more shade as the road turned and the vegetation grew sparser. "Never did see what the fuss was, myself. I watch them videos and all I see is asses shaking and coons cooning. And hell, I'd admit it if I saw it. White race doesn't have to be the best across the board. If niggers could sing better, dance better, I'd say so. Hell, niggers can jump higher, stuff a basketball harder, probably run faster." Burleigh's eyes twinkled with mirth. "None of that wins ballgames, though." He tapped his forehead. "Game's ninety percent mental." Another pickup was approaching, flatbed loaded down with lumber: the first vehicle they'd seen. Anton and the other driver exchanged waves.

"Shoot," said Johnnie, glancing at Burleigh. "I'm a Michael Jordan fan. Nigger or not, that man was the best at what he did. I even bought my kid a Jordan video." He snuck another look at Burleigh, who leaned back and crossed his arms reflectively. "I don't hate niggers the way Burleigh here do," he told Leo. The old man, his face a death mask, refused to even look at him. Envy flickered across Macon's mind. Now that was dignity.

"I never said I hated niggers neither, Johnnie." Burleigh stared daggers at his buddy. "And don't you speak for me, you hear? Barely capable of speaking for yourself." He drained his bottle, tossed it, and beckoned for another. "Niggers stay invisible to me, I ain't gonna search 'em out and start no trouble. I don't want my kids around 'em, I don't trust 'em or like 'em, but I ain't no Ku Kluxer. Hell, I used to work with several niggers down at the brewery, remember? Never had no problem with 'em whatsoever. Boys knew their places and we got on fine. Hatin' niggers is like hatin' cattle. Waste of time.

"What I do hate," Burleigh continued, turning sideways to look at Macon, "is a man who doesn't know who he is. You, Macon Detornay, are a disgrace to the white race."

"So let Leo go," said Macon. "You just said yourself he doesn't matter."

Burleigh and Johnnie looked at each other, then at Macon in disgust. "You goddamn faggot," Burleigh said. He drew his knee back to his chest and kicked. His boot crunched sickeningly against Leo's face, and the man's head snapped back and then lolled to the side. Blood poured from his broken nose, seeping into his white cotton shirt.

"Hoo-whee!" whooped Johnnie, leaping up to examine him. With one hand on the cab for balance, he turned backward at the waist. "You knocked ol' Leonardo into the middle of next week, Burl." He thumped the roof with his fist. "Hey, Anton, looks like there's a new placekicker in town."

Burleigh raised his palms to his shoulders and shrugged, the reluctant disciplinarian, then let them fall into his lap and settle comfortably around his beer. "Now you can stop worrying," he told Macon. "He don't feel a thing. Far as him not mattering . . . well, Macon, he matters to me because he matters to you. You're my primary concern."

The land around them had opened up; parched yellowish grass stretched wide in all directions, three feet tall and buzzing with crickets. Strongholds of vines clumped here and there, huddling as if exhausted. The heat seemed to be too much for everything. Trees appeared infrequently now, and they were less imposing, more grandfatherly.

Burleigh squinted again at the relentless sun. "Quiet, huh? Not a soul for miles. Don't know how y'all can function in New York. Think I'd 'bout lose my mind in all that ruckus."

It wasn't long before road dust caked Leo's bleeding face like makeup. Johnnie slugged the dregs of his second beer and grinned. "He's sure lightenin' up some, ain't he?"

"White niggers and black whiteboys," said Burleigh. "Lions and tigers and zebras, oh my." He leaned over Macon and rapped on the window. "Hey, Ant," he shouted, "where we goin', brother?" Anton shrugged. "Well then, pull over," instructed Burleigh. "Next big tree you see."

The fear screeching through Macon's body jumped into a higher key. "Whatchu got in mind, Burleigh?" he asked. His voice was as sniveling, as utterly powerless, as he could make it. In tone, if not in words, Macon begged for mercy.

"I'm gonna give you one last chance to act like a white man, race traitor."

Macon clawed wildly at whatever hope might be embedded in the sentence. "Thank you," he whispered.

"Don't thank me." Burleigh jogged Leo with his foot. "Thank him." The old man didn't move, so Burleigh covered the top of his beer bottle with a thumb, shook it, and sprayed him with foaming brew. Leo twitched and blinked, the beer dissolving dust and blood. He lifted his elbows to shield his face and screamed when his arm touched his shattered nose. "Look alive, Grandpa," said Burleigh. "You passed out on us." Leo said nothing, merely clenched his teeth against the pain.

Anton rapped a knuckle on the glass divider. "What time is it?" he called.

Johnnie checked his watch. "Half past three."

"Fuck!" The horn bleated beneath Anton's fist. He leaned back to shout through the window. "I gotta pick up Annabel from school, y'all."

Burleigh heaved an exasperated belly-sigh. "Sweet Jesus, Anton. Now?"

"Ten minutes ago, brother." He slowed the truck and spun it in a vicious, fishtailing U-turn, flattening the grass with tire marks.

Burleigh clambered toward the window, bridging Macon's lap on hands and knees and sticking his head through the partition to bark some sense into his friend. "You're just gonna pull up at the elementary school with a flatbed full of bleeding, tied-up sons of bitches, Anton?"

The driver was resolute. "Got to pick my daughter up, Burl. Her mother'll kill me if I flake out again."

"All right," Burleigh sighed. Once Anton's mind was set—and his old lady did most of the setting—the boy was a goddamned boulder. "Drop us back off at the Mart and we'll take Johnnie's car instead."

Anton shook his head. "I ain't missing this, Burl. No way. Besides, somebody back there's liable to be looking for these boys."

"Well, what the hell do you suggest?" said Burleigh, fuming.

Anton glanced back through the mirror in assessment. "Macon doesn't look so bad," he said. "How 'bout if we clean him up and lock the nigger in the hold box?"

Johnnie reached across Leo and ran his hand appraisingly over the deep silver trunk that sat in the front of the flatbed. Anton stored his fishing gear in it.

Johnnie nodded. "He'll fit."

Chapter Four

"You promised," said Annabel, stamping her little foot so hard her blond curls bounced. Children scurried past her in the parking lot, chattering, finding their buses and carpools. Anton looked from her to Burleigh, still sitting in the flatbed, and Annabel followed his gaze. "Uncle Burleigh, he promised," she appealed. Her uncles always took her side. Annabel's eyebrows scrunched and she bit the inside of her cheek, swayed and pointed. "Who's that?"

"That's your uncle Macon," Anton said, extending a hand in his general direction. Macon waved. Burleigh had cut his wrists free with a hunting knife that remained pressed to Macon's side. "From New York City."

Annabel ran to the truck. "You live in New York?" she asked, breathless.

"Come on, honey." Anton said. "Hop in. I've got to get you home to Mommy."

She whirled on him, remembering her beef. "Mommy doesn't get home today until late," she reminded him. "That's why you promised we'd go fishing. Right, Uncle Burleigh?" She smiled at him, then at Macon.

"Right, sugar pie," Burleigh agreed. "I do recall your daddy saying something like that. And we got the poles lying right here."

Annabel surged with pleasure, knowing she had won. "Want to come fishing, Uncle Macon?"

He slurred his eyes at Burleigh. "Sure, Annabel," he said.

Annabel's small body could barely contain her exuberance. "And you'll tell me all about New York City?"

Anything you said to her was a promise, Macon realized. "Whatever you want to know," he agreed.

Annabel skipped over to the passenger door. "Hi, Uncle Johnnie," she singsonged over her shoulder as she climbed up and in. She stood on her knees to look through the cab's back window; Anton reached over and fastened her seat belt. "Bob Nathan got in trouble today," she informed his father.

"He did?" Johnnie feigned supreme dismay.

Annabel nodded. "Uh-huh. He felt on Joanna Kettewand's behind and Mrs. Meyers sent him to the principal's office."

"I thought you was in Mr. Gearing's class this year, Bel," Johnnie said.

"I am. But Megan Connolly told me at lunch. She said Bob Nathan was calling his self Bob Doggy Dog." She giggled. "Isn't that silly?"

Johnnie forced a gruff chuckle. "It sure is."

Anton exited the parking lot and made a left at the end of the block. In less than a minute, they were back on another empty road. The school, like the rest stop, was just a small patch of civilization in this sprawling wilderness.

"Do you live in a skyscraper?" asked Annabel.

"Sure do." Macon smiled.

"You must see a million people every day. I wish we lived in New York . . . Dad." She turned her head to accuse him.

"You couldn't go fishing if we lived in New York, sugar," he reminded her, glancing over with a playful smile and making a right turn. The vines were back, climbing the tree trunks.

"Oh yeah," she mused, putting a finger to her cheek and then curling it in a ringlet of hair. "Do you know how to fish?" she asked Macon. Pride rimmed the question.

"No, I don't," he admitted, lowering his head in humility. "Will you teach me?"

"I don't know," she said, solemn. "It's very hard. Maybe Daddy should teach you. One time he caught a catfish this big." She rubbed her belly. "Mmm. It was good. You know why fishing is the best sport in the world?" she asked, checking to make sure her father was listening. " 'Cause you can drink beer while you do it," she answered herself, satisfied.

The boys broke out laughing. "That's right, girl," said Johnnie, nodding deeply. "Did your daddy teach you that?"

"Uh-huh. He won't let me drink no beer, though. I asked him how'm I sposed to be a fisherman, then?"

Anton grinned. "And what did I tell you, Anna banana?"

Annabel glowed. "He said I'm a fisherlady," she reported. "What's the biggest one you ever caught, Uncle Burl?"

Burleigh smiled, and poked Macon invisibly with the knife. " 'Bout six feet long, I reckon."

Annabel cut her eyes at him. "Nuh-uh," she said, over Johnnie and Anton's guffaws.

"Uh-huh," Burleigh retorted.

"Did you eat the whole thing?" she asked.

"Yup. Fried it up for breakfast."

"Nuh-uh!"

"Uh-huh!"

Annabel leaned her elbows on the hold box—"Nuh-uh"—and came away with two small, sticky blotches of half-dried blood ringing them. Macon waited for her to notice.

Instead, she turned to him. "Don't you think I should get a kitten for my birthday?"

A Volvo approached and Macon stared at the driver, hoping stupidly for rescue. The car passed, and Anton made another right onto an even more remote road, practically a trail.

"Absolutely." Macon nodded, turning back to the expectant girl. "Don't you think so, Uncle Burleigh?" He had two chances, he figured. Get away somehow—which meant outrunning Anton's shotgun—or make friends. Which meant outrunning himself, becoming the New Macon with such ardor and velocity that they'd stop hating him, could not hate him because he was what he should be now, a redeemed sinner, a new fishing buddy who'd been crazy before, done some very wrong things and seen the error of his ways, taken the beating he deserved and been reborn, and hell, you couldn't fault a man for yesterday if he stood changed and repentant today. He would be Uncle Macon, the best damn Uncle Macon he could be, the citified and backward-thinking but fast-learning, lovable, spineless, chameleon-changing, credit-to-his-race, great-with-the-kids, helpless, have-mercy-on-poor Uncle Macon. *He sure do take to fishing, Uncle Macon. Aw hell, let Uncle Macon go. I couldn't look my little girl in the eye if we hurt him; I can already hear her askin' when her uncle Macon's coming back to visit.*

"Hey, Annabel," said Uncle Macon, "how can you tell if there's an elephant hiding in your bed?"

She giggled. The corner of Johnnie's mouth lifted. "How?"

"By the peanut shells on the floor." Annabel threw back her head and covered her laughing mouth with both her tiny hands.

"Tell me another," she pleaded.

"Why do elephants stand on top of marshmallows?" Annabel raised her shoulders in exaggerated pantomime. "So they don't fall into the hot cocoa." Macon could tell she didn't like it as much as the first one, but it didn't matter. Annabel was in the mood to laugh now, and she cackled as loud and long as she thought plausible, even slapping her knee for effect.

"Another."

Macon furled his lip. "That's all I know. Maybe Uncle Burleigh can tell one." Macon smiled over at him. Trees on either side of the road leaned together over them, creating a shady tunnel. Soft, mottled sunlight bled through, painting kaleidoscopic patterns on the truck.

"Okay." Burleigh leaned forward slightly. "It's kind of dumb. Why do firemen wear red suspenders?"

"Why?" asked Annabel, suspicious. She reached forward and snatched a leaf that had fluttered down onto the hold box.

"To keep their pants up." She stared at him. "Told you it was dumb." Annabel crinkled her nose.

Something was spreading through Macon, sliding through his veins. He felt like a high-speed reverse film clip of decay: Instead of ants, microbes, time itself stripping a dead horse of flesh and fat and muscle, picking it dry and leaving the skeleton to rot and disappear, Macon was being rebuilt, stitched together. Strength rushed to his brain for one last panicked, manic rant, all the conviction of his will to live infusing him with a final gobletful of that rugged breakbeat-science, pimp-or-die, tongue-twisting, slick-wristed elixir. Uncle Macon was gonna flip so much motherfucking shit, his shadow'd still be rapping at them while he hobo-hopped the getaway train with the Fleetness. *Let them hang my ghost: I bang the most plus slang the toast. I ain't the best? Dang close; peep how my slang floats. . . .* Fuck Audre Lorde. He would use what hip hop had taught him to destroy what hip hop had made him.

"Hey, Uncle Burl, pass me another beer, wouldja, good buddy?" He slammed it open against the side of the truck and checked the inside cap. "I won!" Burleigh and Johnnie nearly butted heads to look and Macon closed his fist around it. "Just kidding." He winked at Annabel—"I got them, huh, sugar?"—threw back his head and laughed. "I been tricking them like that for years, dollface, your daddy, too. We have a good old time. I trick them and they tease me 'bout being a city slicker who don't know nothin' practical, like how to fix a truck or catch a fish. 'Macon,' your daddy says to me, 'you wouldn't last a week out here in Alabama. Why, you couldn't catch a fish if I threw one right at you.' "

Burleigh stared at him with a mismatched expression: brow furrowed, mouth upturned and parted in bemusement. Light and shadows crossed his face with sinister artistry. Macon eye-checked him and rapped on, bobbing slightly as the truck crawled over the rugged road. "So I says, 'We'll see about that, my chicken-fried-steak-eatin' friend. I'm gonna come down there and catch me the biggest fish you ever saw in your whole everlovin' life.' What do you think of that, sweetheart?" He tipped his beer to the sky and drank. The bottle caught a sunlight refraction, drenched his face in swirling light. Annabel giggled, half-delighted, half-embarrassed. She knew she was being flirted with, performed for.

Macon killed half his beer and popped the bottle off his lips and kept on talking as if he hadn't paused. He reached out and tapped Johnnie on the chest with the back of his hand. "Your uncle Johnnie here says to me, 'Macon, if you catch anything at all, well, I'll be so surprised I'll give that fish the biggest kiss you've ever seen, smack on the lips.' "

Johnnie rubbed at a mosquito bite on his biceps and snorted. "What the hell's he talkin' 'bout?" he asked Burleigh.

"Ah, you see that, Annabel?" Macon pointed at him and winked at her. "You see that, Uncle Burleigh? Looks like Uncle Johnnie's scared he might have to pucker up and smooch that catfish, huh?"

Anton could never watch his daughter laugh without cracking a smile, too. "What's so funny back there, Anna lama ding-dong?"

She grinned and blew her cheeks full for a moment, finger and thumb clamping her lips shut. It was what she did when she was sore from laughing. "Uncle Macon's silly."

"Boy, I'm glad to be out here," Macon blazed on in the meantime. "New York was driving me crazy. Mix a fella up so bad that he forgets just who he is, just like you said, Burl. I can't thank y'all enough for letting me come down here and get my head straight. Say, here's one for you. Thiz a New York joke: If a nigger, a Mexican, and a Puerto Rican are in a car together, who's driving? The cops." He'd heard it in high school, "black guy" in place of "nigger," from some jackass in somebody's parents' basement, hazy with weed smoke. He'd let it slide—he'd usually let it slide, he reminded himself. This New Macon wasn't such a stretch. He'd never given a fuck, really. Not in his heart of hearts of hearts, a place to which he seldom even granted himself access. Johnnie laughed a little. Burleigh's face did not change.

Macon clocked the clerk through low-slung, ground-zero eyes. "No bullshit, man," he stage-whispered, snatching an over-the-shoulder look at the girl. "That bus was gonna take me to L.A. and I was gonna catch the first plane outta this country and never be heard from again, I was so fucking sick of my old self. But you know what? I'll stay right here if that's what I've got to do to show you who I really am." He released a long shudder-sigh. "You don't understand, man."

The truck reached the top of a hill and suddenly Macon's voice was a whip cracking—"You listening to me?"—and Burleigh flinched before it like a classroom daydreamer called to attention. He nodded and Macon dipped his head a bit and caught Burl's eyes: held them and flared his own, the flecks of color pulsing briefly like the shards of an exploding firecracker. "When that shit in New York blew up in my face, it was like I came back to my senses," he said, glancing to his left and then hunching down, intimate. "I feel like I'm back from a war in some savage country, man. Like I got so used to the conditions in some fucked-up village that for a minute I forgot what civilization was like. Burleigh . . ." He paused for effect. "I been living with niggers, talking to more niggers than white folks for years. Can you imagine what that's been like?"

The truck eased down the slope. Burleigh shook his head soberly. "No, Macon," he said. "I sure as shit can't."

"Well, man, on Friday I saw. I saw what I'd tried to pretend I didn't know all these years, and I couldn't pretend anymore." He halved the distance between them yet again. "They'll turn on you, Burleigh. On each other. They're animals. You can't help them."

"We're here," Annabel exclaimed, and Macon looked up to

find that the forest-flanked dirt road had ended in a little clearing. Beyond the trees and scrub-grass that encircled the hollow, down the hill from the incline at which the road culminated, there burbled a wide, well-hidden creek, rushing clear and cold over a bed of polished rocks. Pretty. Macon thought of racing down the hill and jumping in, letting the current sweep him who-knew-where, holding his breath as shotgun pellets punctured the water around him and the girl screamed.

Burleigh jumped out and pulled Macon after him, clutching his captive just above the elbow. The bruises Macon had sustained in the store reasserted themselves as he stood. *What did I do,* his mind crooned in a wry, Armstrongian octave, *to be so black and blue?* Johnnie double-checked the lock on the trunk, then reconsidered and opened it, lifting the lid and peeping inside like a kid with a field mouse in a shoe box.

"Sleeping like a baby," he muttered, relocking it and jumping off the truck.

"I only got three rods," Anton apologized, coming around to unhinge the flatbed. Annabel took her small fishing pole from her father and awarded Macon the extra. "I want to see Uncle Johnnie kiss a fish," she giggled. They all walked down to the water, then hiked up a small grassy hill that lay a bit back from the bank and, at its summit, jutted out over the creek. "We been fishin' here since we was her age," Anton told Macon, tousling his daughter's hair.

"Maybe soon we'll catch something," said Burleigh. Anton and Johnnie rewarded the timeworn quip with slight chuckles.

"Shh," Annabel scolded. "You'll scare the fishes."

Burleigh sat on the ground, one leg hugged to his chest and the other straight before him. He slapped at a mosquito. "There used to be a saying in this town," he told Macon softly. " 'No one comes here by accident.' " Macon stared out at the water, tracing his fishing line to the vanishing point, and tightened his slack two-handed grip.

"You'd have to intend on coming here," Burleigh elaborated,

"or you'd never have any reason to so much as get off the bus." The water nibbled at his words. The rest of the fishing party sat pensive, father and daughter shoulder to shoulder a few yards away, holding their rods, and Johnnie leaning back, ankles crossed, behind them all. The woods rustled softly with life. Burleigh let the quiet build, then reached for his pack of smokes, selected one, and tamped it on the box to pack it. He spoke into his chest. "I think you wanted to get caught," he said. "People might not know it, but they like discipline. Makes them feel like there's still right and wrong left in the world. My kids taught me that."

"Maybe so," said Macon. He felt like asking for a cigarette, just so Burleigh would have to be generous with him. "You musta had kids pretty young. All of you."

Burleigh nodded. "The two of them right out of high school, me a year later. My boy Randy'll be ten next month, and I got a kindergartener and a two-year-old baby girl at home."

"Seems like people settle down here quicker than up North."

"Wouldn't know." Burleigh ashed into the bottle cap of his beer. He grinned over at Macon, baring two perfect rows of faintly yellowed teeth. "I can do whatever I want with you," he said. Simply voicing it seemed to give Burleigh great pleasure. "You might think you know what that feels like, but you don't. It ain't like you felt giving those big speeches with the whole country watching. A million strangers who might take what you say to heart is not the same as one person right next to you, close enough to touch." He patted Macon's cheek, the cigarette between his fingers. "Who lives or dies at just your word."

Macon's skin crawled, and the smoke stung his eyes. "You're a sick fuck, Uncle Burleigh."

"You and me both, Uncle Macon. You and me both." They fished in silence, the sun warming their backs. Not a bite. Macon glanced over his shoulder at the truck, certain he heard Leo pounding. Burleigh followed Macon's eyes. "Wonder how much oxygen's in there," he mused idly. Then: *bang*. Macon was sure he heard it this time. The man was trying to get free.

Annabel started. "What was that?"

"Nothing, sweetheart." Her daddy put an arm around her thin shoulders. "Prob'ly just a coupla chipmunks goofin' around." *Bang*. Macon thought he saw the trunk's lock quiver. Anton's eyes tore a path to Burleigh: *My daughter can't see this.*

"Hey, Annabel," said Macon brightly, "how do you get an elephant on top of an oak tree?"

She turned to him, concern playing on her face. "How?"

"You stand it on an acorn and wait fifty years." She gave him a distracted smile, sorry for Macon if he thought that was funny.

"Guess what, darling," her father said abruptly, scooping Annabel to her feet. "I plumb forgot, we've got to pick up Donna at her mom's house."

Annabel's face brightened. Things today were getting better and better. "We do?"

"Yes, ma'am. I told her I'd watch the both of you while she ran errands."

"Can she come fishing with us?"

"Sure can."

Annabel spun and faced Macon, ecstatic. "Me and Donna are best friends forever," she explained. "You wanna come and meet her?" The entire trunk was rattling now; Macon could picture Leo thrashing inside it, desperate to escape the tiny darkness. Burleigh and Johnnie were on their feet, inching toward the noise. The second there was nothing to occupy her, Annabel was sure to notice.

"Uncle Macon has to stay here and keep Uncle Johnnie and Uncle Burleigh company, sweetheart. But I'll tell you what: Before we go, how 'bout if you show him where the possum lives?"

"Okay!" She grabbed Macon's hand and led him farther along the bank, darting between trees. Make a break for it, he thought, feeling her rough, boyish fingers. Jump in the water. Throw her in and vanish while they save her. Pick her up and scream you'll break her neck unless they toss you the car keys. Just fucking run.

Now he was crouched, hands resting on his knees, watching Annabel peer scientifically at a knotty hole in the trunk of a tree. "I guess she's out looking for food," the girl concluded, disappointed. When Macon straightened, Anton was right next to him.

"Time to go, Anna. Say bye to Uncle Macon, for now."

She hugged him. Macon put one hand on her shoulder and one on the back of her chest-high head. Her hair was clean and glossy, odorless. "Bye, Uncle Macon. Will you come over for dinner tonight? Can he, Daddy?"

Anton smiled. "We'll see, hon, we'll see. Come on." He hung a fraternal arm on Macon's neck and shepherded his daughter with the other, fingers light against the small of her back. When they reached the truck, Burleigh was standing beside it, hand heel resting atop the barrel of the hunting rifle as if it were a walking stick. Johnnie was not to be seen. The hold box was open. Empty.

"Don't forget about us out here," Burleigh joked. "Bye, Annabel."

"Bye, Uncle Burleigh." She and her father hopped into the pickup and rumbled off down the hill.

"That's what I mean about kids," Burleigh said, gesturing at the road. "They always gotta come first, no matter what plans you might have." He smiled. "Big responsibility."

Johnnie stepped into the clearing, dragging Leo behind him by the belt, and pulled him to within a few paces of Macon. The old man's hands were still tied; his legs wobbled, but his eyes burned. Two more minutes, Macon thought, and he'd have busted that lock open and run.

"All right, Uncle Macon," said Burleigh, taking up position between his two captives. "Anton or no Anton, it's time to show and prove." The rifle bisected the triangle Burleigh's legs formed with the ground and lent him a balanced, ceremonial air.

"Nothing very difficult," he assured Macon. "Just ball that

meat hook of yours up into a fist and hit the nigger good and hard for us. Real simple."

Macon stood and stared: right into Leo's eyes, then down at the man's trussed hands—rubbed raw and bleeding at the wrists from his attempts to struggle free—then back up at his face. He took too long. Less than five seconds into Macon's brain-scrambled deliberations, just as he was darting his eyes once again down Leo's body to his hands and thinking that those hands were everything, those shackled hands dripping with the impossible, self-annihilating effort to break out of bondage, just as Macon was blinking back the sunspots suddenly obscuring his vision, just then Burleigh rammed the butt of his rifle into Leo's stomach and folded him in pain. Leo clutched his gut, breathless. Then his eyes closed, and he pitched forward to the ground.

And then the rifle came at Macon, hard and fast, and the hurt shot upward from his testicles into his stomach and he collapsed onto the ground and writhed and jerked his legs as if to run and squeezed himself all over, looking for a point of origin so he could tie the pain off. But the pain was loose and everywhere.

"Equal treatment under the law," Burleigh crowed. He motioned for Johnnie to stand Leo up, then grabbed Macon by the armpits and hefted him easily to his feet. "You better lose that hesitation, boy. This is as serious as your life." He shook his head in gleeful consternation. "Thought a college man like you would be a little quicker on the uptake. Shame, ain't it, Johnnie?"

"Shame," Johnnie affirmed.

"Let's try that again." He hefted the rifle, trained it at Macon, cocked it back, and squinted through it. "Macon, hit this nigger or I'll kill you right now."

Leo's eyes bulged huge with naked terror. Only Johnnie's hands on his rib cage kept him upright.

"I'm sorry," whispered Macon. "I'm sorry." He lurched forward, feeling at every moment like his body would never be able to carry him there, that the burning in his shoulders and his guts and heart and loins would freeze him somewhere between here and Leo, that even if his legs could carry him those few piddling feet, something else would intervene: The universe or God or his own soul would pull a hidden rip cord, unleash some magic, and shatter this scene before Macon's four fingers closed and his thumb locked them together and his elbow stiffened and the blow gathered direction and speed, became a death blow, Leo's or his own, he knew not which. But someone, something—perhaps a part of himself—would die if Macon did what he knew he had to do.

Leo's face was soft and pulpy. Macon's fist sunk in. Johnnie let go of the old man and stepped back just before the punch landed, and when it did, Leo fell straight backward, with no way to brace himself. His entire body hit the moist ground at the same time, with a horrible, flat thump. Macon's head rang; he cupped his hands to his temples to press away the spangles of light, the deafening hum, which seemed now to engulf him.

When he let his fingers slide down off his sweating face and blinked the world back into focus, Macon heard the cheers and hollers.

"Way to go, Make!" Burleigh came at him and Macon flinched and lunged away. But Burleigh only wanted to slap him on the back.

"Felt good, didn't it?" from Johnnie.

Burleigh nodded like a proud father. "I knew he had it in him." He walked over to Leo, bent at the waist, and rooted in the man's pockets until he found a wadded dollar bill.

"Here you go, Macon." He thrust it into the front pocket of Macon's jeans, his thick fingers burning against Macon's thigh as Burleigh shoved the money deep.

Kill me. The words pulsed in Macon's clotted, clodding brain. But he couldn't make himself say it. He clenched his mind against it, then his jaw, and then his fists.

"You done robbed your first nigger, boy," said Burleigh. "So far, so good. Now take this." He thrust the rifle to Macon's chest. Macon raised his arms, reflexively, to hug it.

"It's ready to go, Make." Burleigh was an inch from his face now, all stubble and excited breath and horny eyes. His voice was throaty, motivational. "Put him out of his misery and all this is over, Macon. All this is over and you're forgiven. You're walking over there a worthless nigger-lovin' faggot, but you're gonna walk back here a bona fide white man as good as me or any. Go." He slapped Macon on the ass and pushed him in Leo's direction. Macon stumbled, clubfooted, toward his victim, clutching the rifle to his chest. Leo's left arm twitched, but that was all. Macon stopped and spread his legs and brought the rifle to his shoulder and found Leo's chest between the crosshairs.

"Go 'head, boy. Be a man," he heard behind him. Macon whirled, off-balance, the rifle still on his shoulder, and faced Burleigh. He steadied himself and squinted until he saw that motherfucker's torso in the gun's sights.

"What the hell you doing?" yelled Burleigh. Macon clenched his jaw and felt his body come abruptly into focus, tingle and stiffen and belong to him again. He lined the shot up, best he could.

"I said what the hell you doing, nigger?" Out of the corner of his eye, Macon saw Johnnie approaching on his flank. He swung the rifle toward him, and Johnnie fell back. Macon retrained the gun on Burleigh and expelled all breath from his lungs, preparing.

I don't fucking know, he thought.

"What I have to," Macon rasped, and squeezed the trigger.

A hollow pop. Nothing. Burleigh stood laughing at him, bellowing, belly in his hands. The rifle slipped from Macon's grip and thudded to the ground.

"Too little too late, you stupid son of a bitch," Burleigh cackled. "Come to your senses, hell. Couldn't even shoot a half-dead nigger with an empty rifle." He reached behind him and pulled a snubnosed pistol from the small of his back.

Macon's legs went numb and he fell forward to his knees, not in supplication, but defeat. His heart was throbbing in his ears now, growing louder by the second, blocking all external sound; Macon had to fight the urge to close his eyes and succumb to it, let the rhythm lull him to sleep. Burleigh roared something; Macon saw his mouth contort, but he heard nothing. He shaped a syllable between his own lips, pushed it forth with a feeble gust of breath: *Puh*.

It was all Macon could manage; the sound died before it reached even his own brain. And yet it seemed to have had an effect; Macon blinked through the spangles of red dancing in his field of vision and saw Burleigh's gun-hand fall, degree by gradual degree, until it hung limp by his side. He and Johnnie lifted their heads and stared slack-jawed at the sky, as if God had chosen this moment to put an end to countless millennia of deadbeat fatherhood and was cleaving the heavens with a staff of lightning, hellbent on setting shit correct.

Macon followed their gazes and realized with a jolt that the sound pounding in his eardrums was not the last-dance palpitation of his sin-singed heart. The *Deus ex Machina* hovered in the air, blades unblurring as it eased onto the ground. Macon splayed his fingertips, pushed off against the soil, and regained his feet just as the engine cut off and the chopper doors flew open.

Conway Donner and Dominique Lavar stepped from the craft, sporting identical white Panama hats, and sauntered down the hill.

Macon goggled at them. Donner grinned and waved. "Whaddup, Moves?" Nique hollered, jubilant, breaking into a half-jog. "Told you my man Con was a bad motherfucker, right? Now you see for yourself."

Donner doffed his brim and cupped it to his chest. "My deepest apologies for the subterfuge, Macon. But the only way to really appreciate the effectiveness of the program is to experience it firsthand." His gesture took in Leo, Burleigh, Johnnie, the entire scene. "The psychodrama element is crucial, you see, in breaking down the client's self-perception. Prepares the canvas, so to speak." He tapped the headphones clamped around his neck and turned to look at Nique. "From what we've heard, this has been a rather extreme encounter. For a rather extreme client." He smiled. "Well played by all. A wonderful Plan B, Dominique."

Macon narrowed his eyes, cleared his throat, and hocked a gob of blood and spit. "Thanks, Nique."

"Think nothing of it, dude. Just glad you've come around."

"Fuck you."

"Come on, Moves. You know you can't front on this. Stop trying."

"Boss?" said Johnnie.

Donner silenced him with a raised palm. "Hold on. Now, Macon, I'm prepared to substantially increase my offer—"

"Boss, he needs help." Johnnie was pulling Leo to his feet, draping the old man's arm over his shoulders and holding him around the waist. "We ought to get him to a doctor."

Leo's face was bloodied and misshapen, almost unrecognizable. He half-lifted a rubbery arm and winced with the effort of speaking. "He broke my nose," the old man managed, in a blood-garbled whisper. "He didn't pull a single punch. He—"

"It's true," vouched Johnnie. He shifted under Leo's weight, rebalanced him, and glanced over at Burleigh with nervous eyes. "He knocked him unconscious, Doc, and hit him with the rifle, too." Burleigh squared his shoulders, face set hard. The pistol dangled from his finger.

Nique fisted his hands on his hips, looked the clerk up and down, and turned to Donner, scowling. "This how you treat the brothers, Con?" he demanded. "What kind of hillbilly assholes you got working for you, man?" He pointed a long, sharp finger at Leo. "What type of acting you call that?"

"I'll deal with this later!" Donner roared. "I'm trying to negotiate, here!"

"You'll deal with this now," said Burleigh placidly. The woods went quiet, and suddenly Macon was staring straight into the small black barrel of the pistol. "As for acting, well, I guess you could say I been playing myself these past few months, Dr. Donner. Could've kept at it a while longer, but sometimes life presents you with certain opportunities, and you gotta take advantage of 'em while you can. Letting this son of a bitch live would be a goddamn crime against humanity."

Acting, thought Macon numbly. His limbs felt heavy, alien, his body no longer his own. Acting. That's all any of us does. The idea struck him suddenly and from a great distance, like the whistle of an approaching train.

"Motherfucker!" Nique charged forward, only to stop cold when the gun lined up with his chest.

"Easy there, boy." Burleigh shooed him with the pistol and Nique retreated, palms raised to his chest. "This ain't about you. Not unless you make it. Same goes for you, Doc. Far as I'm concerned, you've done some good in your time, so you best to just walk away and let me and Macon finish up our business man to man."

Burleigh trained the gun. Macon blinked at him, then closed his eyes and clenched his teeth, waiting with a calm beyond horror for help or hell. This is how a martyr dies, he thought, pulse sounding in his ears. At the hands of some redneck, some meaningless fucking stranger he's never seen before. And yet there was something intensely familiar about Burleigh: a gruesome glee that Macon recognized despite his desire not to.

"Burleigh, no!" Johnnie scrambled to the clerk's side, anguished. "Please, Burl," he pleaded. "I know you don't wanna kill a white man."

Burleigh squinted at his target. "He ain't been white for a long time."

"You saw the way he hit the nigger, Burl. That's gotta count for something."

Burleigh cocked the gun. His voice was low and even.

"He's gonna die for his cause."

Macon heard the words and opened his eyes. The world poured in. He squeezed them shut and shook his head.

"No."

Burleigh pulled the trigger, and Macon joined his ancestors.

Acknowledgments

Thanks to Kat Aaron, Richard Abate, Jon Caramanica, Jeff Chang, Eugene Cho, Dave Cohen, T Cooper, Ricardo Cortes, Michael Cunningham, Gerald Cyrus, Ann Douglas, Michael Eric Dyson, Percival Everett, William Fisher, Stik Figya, DJ Frane, Josie Freedman, Keith Gessen, Lauren Grodstein, Victoria Häggblom, Mike Heppner, Danny Hoch, Christen Holzman, Brian Horton, Chris Jackson, Jim Kaplan, James Kass, KEO, KET, The Apple Juice Kid, Binnie Kirshenbaum, Adam Bhala Lough, Charles Mansbach, David Mansbach, Nancy Mansbach, Douglas McGowan, Mariann Nogrady, Robert G. O'Meally, PHASE 2, Scott Poulson-Bryant, Jonathan Powell, Tricia Rose, Ameen Saleem, Gil Scott-Heron, Kelvin Sholar, Mercer Sparks, Terry Southern, Johnny Temple, Brian Tester, Brandee Tidwell, Touré, Clyde Valentin, Oliver Wang, Andre C. Willis, Vernon Wilson, William Upski Wimsatt, Mario Yedidia, and David W. Zang, whose book *Fleet Walker's Divided Heart: The Life of Baseball's First Black Major Leaguer* was a valuable source of information.

About the Author

Matthew L. Kaplan

Adam Mansbach's previous books are the novel *Shackling Water* and the poetry collection *genius b-boy cynics getting weeded in the garden of delights*. He is the former editor of the award winning hip hop journal *Elementary,* and his writing has appeared in the *Boston Globe,* the *New York Times,* the *San Francisco Chronicle, JazzTimes, Slate, Wax Poetics, The Best Music Writing 2004, Brooklyn Noir*, and elsewhere. He lives in Berkeley, California, and is at work on a third novel.

For more information, visit www.adammansbach.com